ISABELLA

AND THE

TALE OF THE UNANSWERED QUESTION

A NOVEL

LINDA WHITTAKER

To my son, Michael, who inspires me to be the best that I can be
To John, Linda, Cece and Stephanie – gifted guides
To all the brave souls who have embarked upon their own quest

PROLOGUE

The siren screamed demanding passage through the clogged streets. Inside the ambulance the team worked feverishly to staunch the damage done to the woman.

"No pulse," the medic said. "Hurry, we're losing her."

"Paddles charged," barked his partner. "Clear!"

✦

PRIORITIES

"It has begun" cawed the raven.

"You're certain?"

The raven dipped his head nodding and said, "I am." He was a huge bird with shiny black feathers tipped in midnight blue. A single white star twinkled brightly on his forehead. Perched on the wings of the dragon throne, the cross-eyed bird cocked his head from side to side, golden eyes studying the man standing before him.

"You must hurry then, Nightwalker. There is very little time."

The raven hesitated, the tips of his feathers fading from blue to black, the star on his forehead dimmed, his lacquered bill dull. "Highness, she will need more than I can provide. This journey will be difficult, and she may not survive."

The king smiled gently. "Once she begins, the Queen and I will make certain she receives all the help she needs. You just have to help her begin." The raven bowed his head in assent, spread his great wings and soared through doors that opened onto a vast garden of manicured hedgerows, arcing fountains, and brilliant flowers. Far into the distance an ancient forest of pines stood tall and silent guarding the outer walls of the castle grounds.

The king watched until the raven disappeared into the trees. He walked to the throne of his ancestors – twin dragons, one black, one white entwined together for all time. As he seated himself, he reached for a leather bound manuscript lying on a small marble table. Before he could turn back the cover, there was pounding on the chamber door and a short muscular man crossed the threshold. The man's woolen cloak, leggings and boots were caked with mud; his leather helmet and face guard coated with dust, the only feature of his face distinguishable from his headdress a pair of striking blue eyes. The air crackled.

"Darius," said the king, frowning as he returned the manuscript to the table, "Why have you returned?"

The Commander of the Elite Guard removed his helmet and faced the king. His close cropped beard and hair were streaked with white and his face bore numerous scars of past battles. "May I speak freely, Sire?" the warrior growled. The king nodded. The legionnaire shook his head and said gruffly, "The situation in the North is beyond anything you and I could have imagined. Horses are being made ready for you to return with me as soon as you can equip yourself."

The king leaned back into the throne as he considered the commander's words. After several moments of silence he replied softly, "I received word she has begun her journey and with any luck will arrive soon. Once I speak with her I will do as you ask."

The soldier scowled. "I fear for any delay. We must leave now."

The king's expression tightened such that two scars running the length of his face paled in anger. "You forget yourself, Darius. I suggest you rest and collect your thoughts; we will review the situation in the Northern Province at evening meal."

The officer frowned, bowed stiffly and turned to leave the room. When he reached the threshold he paused briefly. Turning back, his posture softened and he said, "Stefan, she will only bring trouble to the kingdom. I implore you one last time, join me now. This is the graver danger."

When the king did not respond, the commander straightened and strode briskly out of the throne room. As his clipped footsteps faded into silence, the king rose and walked to the open garden doors. A soft breeze scented with lavender and mint blew into the room carrying voices from all over the kingdom. "She's coming home," the voices whispered. "She's coming home."

"Yes," smiled the king with a sigh of relief, "she is coming home."

✦
LONGING

Long ago in a forgotten land and forgotten time lived a little girl in a forgotten village. She was smaller and more slender than most children her age. In fact, few people would have guessed she had just celebrated her eleventh birthday. Her black hair was pulled back into a thick braid that hung to the middle of her back. Much to her dismay strands of hair often escaped and fluttered about her face giving her an untidy look. She had large brown eyes with long lashes and though her eyes were quite beautiful no one noticed for she rarely looked up. Most people did not notice her at all for she was a quiet child who rarely spoke.

It would have surprised the villagers to know she had a secret, one she carried from the beginning of her memory. Her secret was a longing in her heart so profound she ached at times. Yet the child was confused for she could not name what she longed for and this troubled her deeply. She wondered if others had such heart ache but knew not to ask; people in her village did not speak of such things. Not knowing what to do to ease the pain, she could only wait and hope clarity would come.

Thus the days of her life passed filled with work and chores. In the summer the girl would rise at dawn with her mother. As her mother prepared a breakfast of cold pottage made from barley flavored with onion, garlic and a bit of salted pork, the girl swept the dirt floor and spread fresh rushes to keep down the dust. After breakfast her father went to the fields, and she and her mother began the day's laundry first soaking their clothes and linen in lye, then beating and scrubbing away any remaining soil, finally hanging them all to dry. Her mother would then prepare a lunch for the girl's father while the child pulled weeds and watered the vegetable garden behind their cottage.

At noon the girl would go to their fields with her father's lunch. Though the spring planting of barley, oats and beans was long complete, he was clearing land for the fall seeding of winter wheat. Silently they would eat freshly baked rye bread spread with ground berries and cheese. Her father washed his meal down with a jug of ale; she had water sweetened with honey. After their meal the girl walked in front of the ox plow pointing out stones in the rocky soil. Time and again the animal would stop as she and her father pried the stones from the earth and carried them to the edge of the field. As dusk approached they trudged silently back to their cottage.

When they arrived home, both went straight to the barn. While her father raked out the animal pens, the girl fed their livestock – oxen, cow, pigs and chickens. Only when the animals were cared for did they enter into the cottage for a meal of cabbage stew with bits of rabbit, cheese and blueberries gathered from the woods. After dinner, her mother would spin or weave by the light of the hearth fire; her father would repair his tools or worn furniture; the child would mend the family's clothing. It was only until all were overcome with fatigue did they allow themselves to sleep. They rose the next day to the same tasks and challenges, and the next day, and the next and the next. Such was the drudgery of their lives – grinding work from dawn to dark.

As dictated by church doctrine, Sundays were deemed a time of penitence. The village priest commanded young and old to ponder their sins lest they fall into the eternal abyss. The moment the church doors opened, the child escaped to the woods surrounding her house. Deep in the forest she would lie on the ground, look up into the leaves of the trees, and watch the sunlight and wind create dazzling patterns of gold and green. The ever changing chorus of birds and wind filled her head with music and the smell of earth was the sweetest perfume in the world. The river that feed the land gurgled and murmured stories of faraway lands and adventures. She was happy in her magical woods.

When fall came, she attended the village school as required by the church. Each day after morning chores she plodded through the forest to the one room school house. Rows of benches faced the front of the room where the tall grim headmaster stood teaching letters and numbers. Each child was given a bone stylus and wooden tablet coated with green wax upon which to do their lessons.

At lunch she and the other children were allowed to eat and play outside. The girl was very shy and did not talk or play with the other children. Through lowered eyes she watched the other students laughing and screaming, chasing one another playing prisoner's base or blind man's bluff. No one ever asked her to join them. In the afternoon she and the other students were dismissed to help their parents with fall harvesting.

One day while walking home from school, she heard strange music coming from the forest. Curious, she followed the sound. Through the trees, she saw a small caravan of wagons scattered about a clearing. *Gypsies* she thought, a shiver running down her back.

She had been taught to fear strangers, especially gypsies. "They will hurt you," her mother had warned her as a small child. "If you ever see them in the woods, run! Get home as quickly as you can for they will steal you, and we will never find you." Though the girl was afraid, the music was unlike anything she had heard before. *I will go just a little closer and only watch for a minute* she thought. *I am tiny and quiet. They will never notice me, and I will work extra hard at home tonight for disobeying Mother.* The child crept forward and crouched behind a large oak tree so she could observe the group unnoticed.

A man and woman her parents' age were seated in the center of the clearing playing a fiddle and mandolin. They were surrounded by dancers. The men wore shirts of red satin, purple velvet and green silk. The women twirled about, their wildly patterned skirts fluttering about their legs, their bold earrings jingling as they tossed their heads, their bracelets sparkling as they lifted their arms to the afternoon sun. On the far side of the camp, a dozen children laughed as they played tag and chased dogs that happily joined in the games of their humans. A group of elders smoked ornate pipes and played a game of dice occasionally glancing at the children to make sure all was well.

Closest to the girl's hiding place sat a young man and woman. They were holding hands and smiling at one another as they spoke. The young woman said something, and the man took his sweetheart's hand and gently raised it to his lips. The young woman smiled shyly. Feeling she was doing something improper by watching the young couple, the little girl looked away.

Her attention was finally drawn to several women cooking over an open fire. The aroma of beef stew, cumin and hickory chips filled the air along with the chatter of their easy conversation. Everyone in the caravan seemed happy and carefree. They certainly did not look dangerous to the girl.

A deep rumble filled the forest. *Thunder* she thought. *Odd it did not smell of rain today.* She noticed a flash of lightning streak across the tree tops. The gypsies stopped their activity and scanned the sky. Quickly men, women and children began to gather belongings and run for the shelter of their wagons. A second crash of thunder was so close it startled the horses who strained against their tethers, their eyes wide with fear.

The child looked about her and wondered if she should run towards home or beg for safe harbor with the gypsies. As she was about to step into the clearing, a bolt of lightning zigzagged through the sky and struck the ancient oak tree which sheltered the girl. Suddenly, the child was flying through the air, her arms and legs aflame, the stench of burning flesh filling her nose. She opened her mouth to scream but all went black.

✦
AGAIN

"Hospital ETA?" the senior medic barked.

"Two minutes," yelled the driver of the ambulance.

"Make it one. The shock didn't work; I don't have a heart beat or pulse. I'm bumping the joules to two fifty. Paddles charged. Clear!"

The woman's body jerked and shuddered as the ambulance roared into the emergency bay.

✦
BROKEN HEARTED

The little girl woke gasping for breath, frantically beating her body to smother the flames. She sat up; her mind foggy with fear as she desperately scanned her arms and legs. *How could there be no burns? I was on fire!* Her eyes darted around her surroundings, and she realized she was on her sleeping pallet in front of the cottage hearth. Across the room, her parents were asleep in their bed, and the light of dawn was just beginning to creep through the cottage windows. *How did I get to my bed? I was in the clearing after school with the gypsies. There was a storm and lightening hit me; I felt it.*

She dressed quickly and moved quietly through the cottage so not to wake her parents. Once outside the door, she ran towards the gypsy camp. *Why isn't the forest wet from the storm?* When she reached the clearing, all she found was a smoldering campfire. She walked over to the fire and crouched down on the ground. *Were they here or did I just dream them?* She picked up a stick and began poking the dying embers.

The morning quiet was broken by the cawing of a crow. Startled, she looked up into the branches of the oaks and saw not a crow but a huge shiny black raven. The bird cocked its head from side to side, its golden eyes watching her. *I did not know there were ravens in these woods* she thought absently. Turning away from the bird, she threw down the stick. She sighed as she stood and brushed the dirt from her hands. *I must have dreamed it all.*

As she trudged back to her home, the child thought *I don't understand what is happening, but I know I saw the gypsy caravan, and Mother is wrong. The gypsies were nice and happy. I am sure they would have taken me in from the storm.* So deep in thought was the little girl, she did not notice the raven following her, flying from one tree to the next not allowing her out of his sight. As she approached her cottage clearing she thought *I would not have minded them stealing me.* She sighed. *I suppose I will have to confess that on Sunday.*

Two days passed and the child did not confess her thoughts to the old parish priest. After church she went to the barn to feed the animals. It was a warm day and the outbuilding was filled with the musky smell of cow and hay. The child heard her cat meowing in one of the dark corners of the barn and went to find her.

"Hello, sweet girl," she cooed, "come here and let me pet you." As she sat on the hay and stroked the little black cat, the animal stretched out and began to purr. Soon the cat closed her eyes and was fast asleep. The child relaxed and fell into her own deep sleep.

As she began to dream, the little girl sensed something terribly wrong. A heavy weight pressed on her chest; she could not move or breathe. Though no one was present, she heard a man snarl, "So you wanted to go with the gypsies? You think you deserve something more than you have? I'll show you what you deserve."

Fear flooded the child as she felt hands squeeze her throat until she could no longer breathe. Suddenly a raven, a star blazing on its forehead, darted through the dark dream. She was so startled by the raven's appearance she woke gasping for air. Her hands went to her neck as she took in great gulps of air. *What a terrible nightmare!* Shaken, the girl jumped up and rushed out of the barn brushing hay from her dress. *I was selfish to nap; I need to see if Mother needs help* she thought seeking to calm her wildly beating heart.

Indeed her mother had much work for the child to do; all afternoon the girl hauled and stacked wood to feed the insatiable fire that warmed and fed them. As the sun began to dip in the sky, the girl walked to the river to collect water for the evening meal. Exhausted, she fell back and watched fluffy clouds sail through the sky, barely aware of the birds twittering in the trees or the soft lapping of the water among the reeds. *Whoever he is, he is right* she thought woodenly. *I was a fool to think there could be something different for me.* She closed her eyes and began to weep.

✦ WOUNDS

The doctor scanned the chart one last time and slowly closed the folder as he glanced at the clock. The woman's family was waiting for him in the consultation room down the hall.

What is the truth for them? he wondered. Massive blunt force trauma to the head, a shattered pelvis, cardiac arrest; he did not believe she could survive her wounds. He sighed as he rose from his desk. Slowly he walked to the door and the family waiting down the hall.

$\Leftrightarrow$

THE JOURNEY BEGINS

Dusk deepened. Evening dragonflies darted among the jewelweeds lining the riverbank, and a kaleidoscope of butterflies flitted among the orange and yellow flowers sipping their nectar. All the while fireflies winked at the frogs serenading the willows lining the river's banks. The child knew her mother would be angry waiting for the evening water but she could not rise. She thought *what shall I do for I cannot bear to go on?*

"Isabella, open your eyes," a kind voice called to the girl. Startled, she bolted upright, hastily wiping her face with the back of her hands not wanting her sadness to be known. She looked around. No one was there. "Are you ready to leave?" the voice asked.

Bewildered, the girl followed the sound of the question and tilted her head upward. There in a willow tree sat a golden eyed raven. He was the largest raven she had ever seen. The bird's iridescent black feathers were tipped in midnight blue and a single white spot twinkled on his forehead. His long bill was lacquered black and thick shaggy feathers draped his throat. The raven's eyes were crossed, so he cocked his head from side to side as he studied her. The great bird opened his wings and glided to her side on the riverbank, the beat of his feathers the sound of rustling silk. The trees shivered with anticipation. Magic was afoot.

Who is he? she wondered. *He seems very familiar though we do not have ravens in these woods.* His wing gently lifted her chin, and as he gazed into her beautiful eyes he asked again, "Are you ready to leave?"

Confused, the girl said, "How do you know me?"

"We birds of the forest know all who live among our trees," the raven replied.

"Who are you?" the child asked.

"I am Nightwalker. I have come to help you begin your journey," smiled the raven.

The child stared at the bird, wide eyed. "Where am I supposed to be going?" she asked bewildered.

"Does it matter?" the raven replied as the star on his forehead sparkled.

Of course it matters! I must be dreaming again. As she was about to speak, the girl heard the strains of a gypsy mandolin and fiddle ballad float through the air. The jangle of bracelets and the laughter of children mingled with the songs of the forest birds. The raven cocked his head back and forth listening. "Lovely, isn't it?" he said.

A sudden movement caught the girl's attention. She turned her eyes away from the bird to the river. Wispy images of dancing gypsies, laughing children, and whispering sweethearts floated on the water's surface for just a moment before the mist dissolved and vanished. She stared at the empty water for several minutes. *There must be more for me than the life I have* she thought.

"There is, Isabella, so much more. You just have to say yes."

How did he know what I was thinking? she wondered. The girl looked into the ravens eyes. They were kind and honest. *I want to leave but I am afraid.* Birch and aspen trees along the bank shivered with anticipation. "She struggles. What shall she decide?" they murmured to one another, their silvery leaves aflutter. "Look, she turns to him..."

The girl stared once more into the eyes of the raven and then nodded her head ever so slightly. "Yes," she whispered so softly a tiny white butterfly had to carry the word to the raven. As soon as yes was spoken, the trees applauded, the birds cheered, the river laughed and Nightwalker turned a somersault. Out of the corner of her eye, the girl saw the bow of a boat peek around the bend on the river and move slowly toward the bank. In seconds, it touched the shore. The wooden vessel was of a good size, sturdily built and appeared to have all sorts of supplies packed neatly under the bow. The girl sat dumbfounded, staring first at the boat and then at the raven next to her.

"Ready?" smiled the bird.

When the child did not speak, the raven flew from her side and settled onto the bow of the boat. The craft rocked gently under his weight. "Let me help you in, Isabella," he said as he raised his wing to her.

Looking down into her lap, she muttered, "I was foolish to say yes. I take it back."

"You are afraid," said the raven solemnly.

The child nodded staring into the lap of her dress. When the girl did not continue, the great bird said, "What do you fear will happen if you enter the boat?"

The child sighed. "I have never been on the river before," she said as she closed her eyes ashamed. "I do not know what to expect."

"I see. Yes, I see," the raven said kindly as the river gently lapped against the sides of the boat. "Is there anything else you fear?"

The girl hesitated. Still unable to raise her eyes to face the raven, she said, "I am afraid to be alone; I am afraid I will be not able to handle trouble if it should come."

"Ah," said the bird nodding his head deeply. "Would it help to know you will not be traveling alone?"

The girl sat silent considering the words spoken by the raven. She lifted her head slightly so she could peek at the bird. "I am not sure," she said.

The raven hopped off the boat and returned to the girl's side. "Isabella," he said kindly, the tip of his wing caressing her face. "I am just extending an invitation. You need not accept, if you are not ready."

"Thank you," she said relaxing just a bit. She raised her face to a sudden a gust of wind inhaling the fragrance of beef stew, cumin and hickory chips swirling through the air. "It smells heavenly, doesn't it, Isabella?" asked the raven.

"Yes, it does," she replied pensively. *More, more, there must be more for me.*

The woods went perfectly still and silent as the raven and child sat side by side. *I will die if I do not go* she suddenly thought. Trembling she took a deep breath, stood up, waded into the river, and climbed into the boat. The trees along the river bank shook their leaves in wild approval and song from all manner of bird and animal filled the air.

"Now all things become possible," cawed the raven bobbing his head and clapping his wings. The wind from Nightwalker's great flapping wings nudged the boat away from the shore into the river's current. The water was smooth, and for a moment, the girl felt she was in a fairy tale being carried along by friendly spirits. *I will find my gypsies after all* she thought happily.

When the boat reached the middle of the wide river, she noticed the water was becoming choppy, and the temperature was dropping. Suddenly the sky darkened, and she heard thunder in the distance. She looked about frantically to see if she could get back to shore, but all she succeeded in doing was dangerously rocking the boat. A stabbing pain tore at her stomach. A snarling voice filled her mind. "I will not allow this journey."

The nightmare voice! The girl closed her eyes and pressed her hands against her ears. "Stop now! Stop! Stop!" she shouted. A weight hit the bow of the craft and Isabella screamed. Nightwalker brushed her hands from her ears and commanded, "Look at me, Isabella!" The moment the girl opened her eyes and met the raven's fierce gaze the water calmed, the dark clouds drifted away and the nightmare voice was gone.

"What happened? Why did everything change so quickly?" Isabella cried.

Nightwalker realized the dark man was at work. He was moving far more quickly than Nightwalker had anticipated. "Child, time is of the essence," he said urgently. "Listen carefully as I give you instructions for the days ahead."

Trembling Isabella folded her hands in her lap and meekly nodded yes.

"You will be gone for quite some time though I am not sure how long," Nightwalker said choosing his words carefully not wanting to frighten the child even more. "There will be many people and places ahead, Isabella. Some people will be pleasant; some will be difficult, at least at first." He smiled as he spoke these last words. He paused and said, "Every situation, every person you meet will offer you a gift. You need only accept it." The squirrels on the riverbank nodded yes as did the frogs in the reeds and the doves in the trees.

Isabella stared at him unable to make sense of his words. Finally she stammered, "Nightwalker, sir, I am so sorry to have wasted your time but…"

The raven gently raised his wing to silence the child. "You said yes, Isabella. There is no going back." A gray cloud passed over the vestige of the setting sun and the air filled with the nervous chatter of birds. The great raven frowned. The shine of his feathers faded to dull black. The star on his forehead darkened and his golden eyes became murky. "Isabella, I know this will not please you, but I must leave. You are protected and everything you need is present, Isabella – everything."

Before the child could utter a word of protest, the great bird hopped to the edge of the boat, opened his great wings and took to the air. Almost instantly he was swallowed by the forest.

✦ THE PREDATOR

It had been difficult leaving the child alone on the river, so profound was her fear, but Nightwalker had not expected the dark man to move so quickly. He had no choice but to leave Isabella and confront the growing danger.

The raven traveled far to reach the sulfur waters pushing deep into the swampy darkness. The great bird alighted upon a blackened branch of a tree long dead. Below him a man stood behind a bloodied table hacking away at the carcass of a swamp pig. Tall and muscular, the man's blond hair, matted and greasy, fell loose to his shoulders. A beard of many days growth covered his face and neck. His frayed tunic and sagging leggings might have been brown but were so crusted with dirt and entrails, one could not rightly discern their color. Muscles and bulging veins rippled up and down his arms as he repeatedly slashed the bloodied remains. His hands and nails were black with dirt and dried blood.

"I know you are there," the man snarled. "I smell you."

"Let the child be," squawked Nightwalker, twisting his head from side to side as he watched the man. "This quest is hers to take. She must be given the chance to decide how it will go."

The man lowered the knife gripping the handle with knuckled fury. He turned toward the branch where Nightwalker perched, his face contorted and his blue eyes slits of hate. His full lips pulled back in an ugly sneer as he growled, "It will end badly for her whether she travels deeper into the kingdom or not. If she is allowed to continue she will only cause pointless pain and damage to us all. I will protect us from that." He turned back to the carcass, viciously hacking the stinking meat in preparation for his meal.

"You are wrong," thundered Nightwalker. "The outcome is undecided. There are many ways it can go."

"It will end in death," the man roared, flinging pig guts at Nightwalker.

Nightwalker screeched as the waste hit his body. "We will oppose you," he said, his feathers bristling with rage.

The man laughed. "Do you think I am afraid?" he mocked. "Others have tried to contain me and failed; so will you. Be gone before I make you my next meal."

Undaunted, the bird flew from the branch to the edge of the scarred table. The man's scent of rusty iron and sickly sweet decay was overpowering. As the raven opened his mouth to speak, the man reached out and nicked the bird's chest with his knife. A thin line of blood stained the black feathers. "There will be no other warning, Nightwalker. Next time we meet this knife will find your heart."

"You are a fool," screeched the raven as he disappeared into the darkness.

$\bigstar$

THE RIVER

Stunned, Isabella watched Nightwalker vanish into a thick stand of aspen and pine. Once the raven was lost from sight, all sound in the forest ceased. Gone was the chatter of the birds, the scampering of small animals, and the whispering of the trees. Color drained away from the trees, the sky, even the river leaving them all leaden gray. The clammy air made the girl's skin crawl. *How could he leave me?*

Just then the little girl heard a wee gentle voice sing, "Isabella, sweet Isabella, you have a lovely name – the name of an explorer. It is a name just right for adventures and discoveries. Please let us take you to them. Please." The gray swells swirling around the boat softened to a robin's egg blue.

Isabella scanned the sky and tree tops looking for the source of the voice. Not a leaf stirred, not an animal moved, the landscape was lifeless. Trembling she eased herself to the bottom of the boat and curled into a tight ball. *This is too much…too much* she thought.

"Isabella, you need not be afraid. You are safe in our arms," cooed the voice.

The girl uncurled her body and slowly lifted her head to see above the rim of the craft. Her eyes widened when she saw the river was now a beautiful sky blue. She gingerly pulled herself to the side of the boat and peered cautiously into the moving water. "Are you talking to me?" Isabella asked hesitantly, as she scanned the surface searching for the source of the voice.

"Yes," the river replied tenderly.

"I did not know you could speak." Isabella said wide eyed, pulling back into the boat ever so slightly.

"Oh yes, we have spoken forever and a day," the river hummed happily, the water deepening to azure blue. "Come closer, Isabella," the river urged. "We long to speak with you."

Isabella edged back to the vessel's rim and said, "I have not heard you before."

"You were listening with different ears," replied the river, her voice as soft as silk.

"Why can I understand you now?" Isabella asked, a confused frown wrinkling her forehead.

"Once you sent your desire for a different life into the Great Mystery, everything was set into motion," the river murmured with delight. "Now that we carry you, you will see things differently, hear things differently, and know things differently," the river cooed, her currents sparkling ribbons of sapphire.

"No, river, you are mistaken," Isabella protested, shaking her head. "I am the same ordinary girl I have always been. Nothing has changed."

"Oh, Isabella, dear, everything has changed." The river sighed with deep contentment. "You will see. You will see. Once a quest has begun, things are never the same." The river's gentle waves shimmered sky blue, azure and sapphire

"This is too much for me, river," said Isabella as she sat back into the bottom of the boat. Her eyes began to well with tears.

"Did you not long for more? Did you not ponder if there could be laughter and joy – even love for you?" asked the river quizzically, small purple capped waves curling about the vessel.

"How did you know?" asked the little girl.

"Child, you came to us each day. We heard the longings in your heart," the river said softly. "The answers you seek are in this journey, sweet Isabella. The answers are in this journey." Content truth had been spoken, the river sighed with pleasure, indigo ripples spreading out across the river.

Isabella sat silently, pondering the river's words. She rose to her knees and watched the ripples of the river spread wider and wider and wider until they gently reached the riverbank – indigo meeting leaden gray. Gathering her courage, the girl leaned over the side and whispered, "Is there more for me, river?" The river was silent as it carried the boat gently along.

SEEKING ANSWERS

The woman's husband sat staring at the computer screen. He had searched all the conditions listed by the doctors. Tears streamed down his face as he now read:

SUBDURAL HEMATOMA

DEFINITION: *A subdural hematoma is a collection of blood on the surface of the brain. It lies beneath the outer covering of the brain and the brain's surface.*

CAUSES, INCIDENCE, RISK FACTORS: *Subdural hematomas are most frequently the result of a head injury. The inciting event often is a focused blow to the head, such as that produced by a hammer or baseball bat. Traumatic subdural hematomas are among the most lethal of all head injuries with a mortality rate of greater than 50%.*

TREATMENT: *A subdural hematoma is an emergency condition. Treatment goals include implementation of lifesaving measures, control of symptoms, and minimizing or preventing permanent brain damage. Lifesaving measures may include support of breathing and/or circulation.*

PROGNOSIS: *Acute subdural hematomas present the most significant challenge with high rates of coma, death and injury. Sub-acute and chronic subdural hematomas have better outcomes in many cases, with symptoms going away after drainage of the blood collection. There is a high frequency of seizures following subdural hematoma; however, these seizures can be controlled with medication.*

The man stared numbly at the screen unable to move, to think, to feel – just like his wife.

PREMONITION

Dusk fell on the river as the small craft drifted with the current. Isabella crawled to the bow of the boat and threw back a tarp. To her relief she found several woolen blankets to warm her against the clammy evening air. Creating a soft nest in the bottom of the boat, she lay down and thought *Nightwalker will be back in the morning. He will help me.* Staring into the deepening nighttime sky, Isabella watched the stars and moon dance their way onto their stage. Lulled by the starry night and the motion of the boat, the exhausted child drifted off to sleep and began to dream.

One moment she was closing her eyes and in the next Isabella was standing in her village cemetery. All around her graves were covered with stones to thwart forest scavengers from digging for the dead. Isabella looked down and saw she stood at the lip of an open grave. "Mother!" she wailed.

As is the way of dreams, she was transported from the cemetery to the stoop of her cottage. She could hear sobbing within. From the doorway, she saw her mother crying – her head on the table. Isabella's father stood stiffly, staring into a coffin which was laid across benches in the middle of the room. Candles surrounded the narrow box. Their flames flickered as Isabella entered though neither parent looked up as she walked slowly to the coffin. When she looked down, Isabella looked into a face like her own. Covered with a sheer cloth, the girl's features were bloated, and her skin was mottled black and green. A terrible odor filled the room. Horrified, Isabella stumbled outside the house and vomited. Wiping her mouth with the back of her hand, she ran towards the edge of the forest and plunged blindly into the woods.

Her mind was flooded with the sight of the girl in the coffin, the stench of the room, and her parents' pain. On and on she ran, hot tears of sorrow burning her cheeks. Finally, she began to tire and slowed her pace. As she did so, Isabella noticed something was wrong. When she entered the forest, the day had been hot and clear. Now it was cold, and a strong wind tossed the trees branches back and forth. Isabella did not recognize where she was; in fact, everything seemed unfamiliar. As she tripped on roots and thorny branches in the wild underbrush she thought frantically *These are not my woods. Where am I?*

Suddenly it began to rain. Within seconds the temperature dropped, and the rain turned to snow. Confused she stopped and stood perfectly still in the swirling snow, thick flakes falling faster and faster sticking to her arms and face, trees and ground. Paralyzed with fear, Isabella dropped to her knees. The snow continued its mad dash to blanket the forest and the unprotected child. *Mother and Father are too sad to look for me* Isabella thought woodenly. *But why should they? That was me in the coffin. I am already dead.*

Isabella gasped and bolted upright. She drew in huge gulps of air and looked about trying to take in her surroundings. The sky was a pale gray – dawn was breaking – but it seemed to melt into an indigo blanket. *Where am I?* Then she remembered the boat. *I was dreaming.* Isabella reached over the side of the craft and splashed water onto her face and neck, the water cooling her burning body. "It was just a stupid dream," she mumbled to the trees and the river. Raising her voice she yelled, "Nightwalker, it was just a stupid dream. Do you hear me? Come back; I must talk with you!"

As the sun continued its climb into the leaden sky, Isabella muttered, "Well, I am sure he will be back soon. I think I will check the supplies while I wait for him. The time will pass more quickly if I am busy. Besides I am hungry. There must be something to eat in this boat. I will just stay busy until Nightwalker comes back. I will stay very busy."

Isabella carefully moved to the front of the boat and released the tarp a second time. "Let me see what is here." The little girl was soon absorbed in her task. Within minutes, Isabella was surrounded by carefully wrapped loaves of bread, jars of honey and jam, packets of

31

dried meat and fish, a cloak and fresh dress, soap, towels, even a looking glass. She thought she had pulled everything out when she noticed a tiny package wedged into the very tip of the boat. "What is this?" she said to the air.

"Oh my," she gasped when she unwrapped the brown paper. Lying on the paper was a tiny yarn doll the size of her hand. The doll's body was made of twisted brown threads covered with a bit of blue cloth for a dress. Her hair was a mass of wild strands of black yarn. She had wooden buttons for eyes but no mouth. "Maya," the little girl said dumbly. "How can this be?"

Isabella remembered the day she lost Maya. The peddler had come to the village, and her mother was excited to go into town to buy a new pot and some cloth. Isabella was about five years old and begged her mother for a new toy all the way to the village. "You are tired of that old doll of yours, eh?" teased her mother.

Isabella was horrified. The yarn doll had been a present to Isabella the day she was born. Not a day or night passed that Maya was not safely tucked under Isabella's arm or in her the pocket of her dress. Maya knew all of Isabella's secrets, played all of Isabella's favorite games, and comforted Isabella when she was sad or afraid. In short, she was the best friend a child could have.

"Oh, Mother, I could never tire of Maya," Isabella said earnestly as put her hand into her pocket and patted her beloved doll. "I just would like a new toy that Maya and I can play with together."

"I wish it were otherwise, Isabella, but we do not have the money to buy you another toy. You will have to make do with what you have," sighed her mother.

Though disappointed, once they reached town Isabella was caught up in the excitement of the peddler's visit: seeing his wares, hearing the news from other towns, listening to the women gossip about the affairs of the village. Like Isabella's mother, many of the women had their children with them. A group of boys and girls several years older than Isabella were running about laughing and screaming. Her mother was deep in discussion with the peddler about a bit of cloth so Isabella ran over and asked if she could play.

"You have to give us something, if you want to play," said one boy wearing a red cap. Though he smiled at Isabella, something in his eyes made her uneasy.

"I don't have anything," said Isabella looking down at her feet.

"Well, you can't play with us then," snickered a girl wearing a beautiful blue coat trimmed with white fur. "Besides you look too poor to play with us." She stuck out her tongue at Isabella.

Her face burning red, Isabella jammed her hands into her pocket and felt Maya. "Wait, I have a doll I can show you. Maybe we can play with her," she said hopefully. The children crowded around Isabella as she pulled Maya out of her pocket.

"Oh, she's an ugly doll," sneered the boy with the red cap, "but we can use her as a ball." Before Isabella could say no, he plucked Maya out of her hands and dashed off throwing the doll to the girl in the fur trimmed coat. All the other children joined in the game of catch running and throwing Maya from one to another.

Isabella ran after the children trying to rescue her doll, but she was too little and too slow. "Stop that! Stop! Give her back," she cried. "She will get hurt. I don't want to play with you."

Alerted by Isabella's cries, several mothers stopped their chatter and turned to see what was amiss. Noticing their unwanted attention, the red cap boy sneered, "What a whiny baby you are. We don't want to play with you or this ugly doll anyway. In fact, this doll is just too ugly for anyone to play with." He ran to the peddler's cook fire and threw the doll into the flames.

Isabella ran to the fire and was about to reach in for Maya when someone jerked her back. "Child, what are you doing? You will burn yourself!" yelled her mother as she shook Isabella's arm.

Isabella started to cry harder. "Mama, they threw Maya into the fire! Please get her out!" Her mother turned to see the flames licking Maya's arms, legs and head. "The doll is burned up, child," her mother said brusquely as she pulled Isabella away from the fire.

Isabella's sobs turned to wails. "Please, get her out for me!"

"Silence," her mother said sternly, pinching Isabella's arm. "You are making a spectacle of yourself. I will not have the neighbors thinking you ill behaved." Her mother looked about to see if anyone was watching them. "The doll is gone," she said curtly. On the long walk home Isabella's mother continued to scold her "That is what you get for trying to play with children above your station. I told you to stay with me. Now Maya is gone because you did not listen to me. It is entirely your fault and a lesson you will not soon forget!"

"Why are you being so mean, Mother?" whimpered the little girl.

"It is my job to teach you the ways of the world. Trust no outsiders, Isabella." Her mother pulled her shawl tight around her shoulders. "Now stop sniveling. There is no point to it." Mother and child did not speak the rest of the way home. Isabella swallowed her sorrow until she found her way to bed that night. She cried for Maya that night and many nights thereafter. Finally, she exiled the memory of her beloved doll to a distant corner of her mind.

Now her tattered friend lay in her lap. "Oh, Maya, I am so sorry I let those mean children take you. Forgive me," whispered Isabella. When she picked the little doll up, the fragile strands loosened, and Maya unraveled into a pile of worn threads. "No, no, no," muttered Isabella. "Go back together." As the child fumbled about trying to pat the doll back into shape, the threads began to fray and dissolve. Within seconds Maya was a pile of dust. "Maya…," moaned Isabella.

"Oh Isabella," whispered the river sadly, the wake behind the boat coal black, "you miss her so, do you not?"

"Yes, river, I do," whimpered the child. The child sat silently for several minutes staring at the pile of dust in her lap. Isabella carefully wrapped Maya's remains with string and tucked the small package into the bodice of her dress next to her heart. Then she curled into a ball on the bottom of the boat and wept. "I cannot bear what I feel, river. Everything hurts…I do not know what ails me. Please make it stop."

Though the river did not answer, Isabella was not alone as she cried through the night. The fish of the river formed a protective circle around her boat; the animals of the forest stood witness on the banks of the river as she moved past and a beautiful woman with skin the color of ebony, walked along the riverbank ensuring no harm would come to the broken girl that night.

INNOCENCE

The man walked into the kitchen to find his two children bent over the kitchen table coloring furiously. As he looked over the shoulder of his six year old son, he read the card the child was writing to his mother. In big letters the boy wrote:

> Hi Mom. I rley love you
> Your th best mommy
> I love you
> Mom
> I mis you alot
> I love you
>   your son
> xoxoxoxoxoxoxoxoxo

Lopsided hearts filled the empty spaces around his words. The man kissed the boy's head as his eyes filled with tears.

"Look, Daddy, look," smiled his four year old daughter as she held up her picture – a family of four stick people, a big smile on each face. "Mommy will love this, won't she?" she asked, her head bouncing with each word. He nodded silently, the lump in his throat making it impossible for him to speak.

✦
SIR ALFRED

Isabella stirred in the bright morning sun. She twisted this way and that trying to block the glare only to bump into jars and packages of all sorts. She kicked them away, threw her arm over her face and fell back to sleep. She awoke at dusk, and after eating a hard biscuit and drinking water from the river decided to move the supplies under the bow so she would have more room to sleep.

The task of moving provisions exhausted her. Once finished Isabella reached into her bodice and pulled out the package containing Maya. Loosening the string, the little girl shook the contents into the river. The dust quickly disappeared into the coal black water.

"Sad, Isabella…sad, Isabella," the river sighed, the water as thick as tar.

The child laid down in the bottom of the boat and drifted in and out of sleep – waking, crying, and sleeping again. Thoughts of home, school and the village all began to slip away. She did not know where she was, where she was going, and soon she did not care.

The third morning after releasing Maya, a warm breeze scented with lavender and mint woke her. As she stretched her body her stomach grumbled, and she was surprised to feel hungry. She sat up and moved stiffly about the boat until she found grapes, cheese and blueberry muffins. Fresh water from the river quenched her thirst. She thought to sleep again but found she felt neither tired nor tearful. In fact, she felt nothing.

Wrapped tightly in a gray blanket, the child sat numbly in the bottom of the craft staring over the rim of the boat. She realized the flat gray beaches of river rocks and heavy stands of black pines of the past several days had been replaced with white sandy dunes, lush ferns, and a thick forest of maple trees that stretched as far as her eyes could see. At mid-morning, the boat turned against the current and headed toward the shore. When the boat scraped the beach, the girl had no energy or reason to move.

A flicker of movement caught the child's attention. She turned her head to see a man coming down the beach. As the visitor got closer, Isabella saw he was an older man – tall, thin and formally dressed in black. He wore a black surcoat over a tunic of white silk. His black wool trousers were tucked into high black boots. The man's thin white hair was tied back in keeping with the fashion of the day and his face had no facial hair except for a thin mustache. When the visitor stood before her, Isabella noticed three rows of official looking medals and ribbons pinned to his jacket.

"Miss Isabella, you are right on time!" Though the man's words and inflection were crisp and precise, his tone was cordial. "I believe introductions are in order here. I am Sir Alfred Gielgud, Esteemed Advisor to His Royal Highness King Stefan." Sir Alfred bowed deeply to Isabella. Isabella had no energy to stand but as she had been taught to do when greeting adults, she silently nodded her head with eyes downcast.

"Well, we must be on our way. We have a schedule to keep," stated Sir Alfred crisply, as he stepped into the boat. "May I help you onto your seat, Miss Isabella? It may be more comfortable for you than the bottom of the boat." Sir Alfred offered his hand to the girl.

Isabella sat in silence considering the old man's outstretched hand. Her training to obey ran deeper than her profound fatigue and desire to ignore, so she rose stiffly. She did not take the man's outstretched hand for she was far beneath his station. Instead she slowly climbed over the seat opposite Sir Alfred sitting with her back to the Royal Advisor, the gray blanket wrapped tightly around her thin shoulders. One precisely arched eyebrow went up as the Royal Advisor observed Isabella's actions, but the old gentleman did not comment. With both hands, he straightened his jacket, adjusted his medals and smoothed his trousers. A lavender mint breeze moved the boat into the brilliant turquoise current. Isabella sat silently, her back stiff.

FLOODING

"BP 70/45," the recovery room nurse said, "pulse running 120."

The doctor nodded, "Abdomen is extended, muscles rigid to touch. Skin is cold and clammy, no color; she's bleeding out. Call OR and tell them we're coming back; got a probable Class IV Hemorrhage. Get all available A Positive units stat! Jesus, something else blew."

✧
ONE MILLION QUESTIONS

"Miss Isabella, get down!" shouted Sir Alfred above the roar of the water. "Hold on to the seat! No matter what, do not let go! Do you hear me, do not let go!" Isabella dropped to the bottom of the wooden craft wrapping her arms around her seat as the first wave of blood water hit them nearly capsizing the boat. A second wave lifted the vessel pitching them into a narrow canyon. Torrents of raging water churned through the canyon slamming against the chasm walls towering above the travelers. Debris and rocks the size of boulders showered down upon the river. Caught in the violent backlash of the waves, Isabella and Sir Alfred clung to their craft as it was tossed about like a twig.

"Rocks! Rocks ahead! Hold on, child! I fear we cannot avoid them," bellowed Sir Alfred above the roar of the churning water. No sooner were the words out of his mouth than the boat crashed into a boulder the size of a house. The boards shattered as onrushing water pummeled the boat against the rock. Isabella and Sir Alfred were thrown into the roiling red river. Isabella struggled to keep her head above the churning water but wave after wave pushed her down. Each time she opened her mouth for air, bloody water filled her lungs. The last thing she saw before her body struck the razor rocks was Sir Alfred struggling to reach her.

Only a short time before, the water had been calm and the landscape kind. "You are a quiet child, aren't you?" Sir Alfred had commented an hour into their journey. Sitting stiff with her back to the man, Isabella had not spoken a word since leaving the beach.

The girl flinched at his words. "I know my place, sir," Isabella mumbled stiffly gripping her woolen blanket tightly around her thin shoulders.

"That is interesting. Since I value precision, where is that place exactly?" asked the Esteemed Advisor furrowing his eyebrows as he spoke to Isabella's back. Her shoulders tensed further. The statesman had the same formal speech as her headmaster. *Have I offended him?* she wondered trembling, her eyes filling with tears as she stared at the turquoise water ahead.

"Miss Isabella, you most certainly have not offended me. I ask questions because I am curious," the Royal Advisor said matter-of-factly. Isabella inhaled sharply. One of Sir Alfred's esteemed eyebrows shot up. "Nightwalker did tell you we, of this kingdom, have the ability to know the thoughts of others, did he not?"

"We were together a very short time," Isabella mumbled.

Sir Alfred nodded and then said, "Might you be willing to turn in your seat so we may face one another? I do so like to look at the person I am conversing with."

Fearing the consequences if she did not comply, Isabella reluctantly gathered her skirt and slowly put one leg over the seat and then the other until she sat facing Sir Alfred. She continued to clutch the blanket about her shoulders as protection and she dared not meet his gaze.

"Thank you so much," the Advisor said with a nod and a smile.

"You can read my thoughts, sir?" Isabella said warily, her eyes averted.

"Yes," replied Sir Alfred, "we all can." Isabella fell silent again. The stately gentleman searched Isabella's face. "Miss Isabella, are you not curious why I am here?"

"I assume you will tell me when you are ready." Isabella stared at the puddles in the bottom of the boat as she braced herself for the reprimand that was sure to come.

"Child, look at me," Sir Alfred said kindly. Yet it was not the gentle request of the Royal Advisor that Isabella heard but the harsh words of the headmaster at the village school. She was six years old again and very afraid.

"Good morning, class," the headmaster barked as he strode briskly into the room. All the students jumped to their feet and bowed to the teacher, a tall thin man with a dour expression. "You may all sit down with the exception of you, Isabella. Come to the board," he snapped as he began to scribble numbers on the slab of black slate that hung behind his desk.

Isabella disliked math and dreaded being called upon to answer number questions. Her legs were shaking as she walked to the black board. "Solve this problem," ordered the headmaster impatiently tapping the board with a long pointed rod.

Isabella stared at the board. She had never seen such a complicated equation in all her life. She stood frozen looking at the numbers – then at the headmaster – then back to the numbers. One of the boys in the class whispered loud enough for the others to hear, "She's a simpleton." Several of the other children snickered.

"I do not know the answer, sir," Isabella said miserably.

"What? How can you not know the answer?" the headmaster demanded. "We covered this material yesterday. Are you so thick you cannot retain information one day?!" The headmaster shook his head in disgust. "Go back to your seat." He glared at Isabella as she turned to go to her chair.

"You did not cover this material yesterday," muttered Isabella under her breath as she walked to her seat.

"What did you say?" bellowed the headmaster.

"Nothing," mumbled Isabella sitting down.

The headmaster strode to her seat. As he towered above her, he pinched her cheek with his forefinger and thumb and said coldly, "Don't lie to me, girl. What did you say?"

Isabella drew back in pain and blurted, "You did not teach us this yesterday. I would have remembered." Isabella's body jerked forward as the headmaster brought the rod down across her back. "Don't you ever challenge me," he said, his face flaming red and voice cold as ice. "I will not have some girl-child contradict me." He turned to the class and demanded, "Did I teach this yesterday?" The children bobbed their heads up and down in agreement despite the fact that the headmaster had not taught math at all the previous day. "Leave my class," he roared, "and do not return until you are ready to show me the respect I deserve. In fact, I will have to reflect on whether I want you in my class at all!"

Stunned, Isabella fled the school. When she got home she sobbed as she related the story to her mother. Isabella's mother listened silently, her lips pressed into a thin line, a red flush creeping up her cheeks. When Isabella finished, her mother snapped, "You have shamed me, daughter. All in the village will be talking about my failure. To have a child with such poor manners is a disgrace."

"But, Mama..." Isabella began to wail.

The woman slapped Isabella hard across the face. "Do not interrupt me. I do not want to hear your excuses. You will apologize to the headmaster in front of the class for your impudence and lie. If he allows you to return to school, I do not ever want you to show disrespect to the man again. You must learn your place. Do you understand?"

Isabella's face was blazing with pain and shame. She hung her head and said, "Yes, Mama, I understand." In one week's time Isabella returned to school and did as her mother ordered. For the rest of the year, Isabella rarely spoke in class though the headmaster took every opportunity to ridicule and diminish her. She learned the lesson of humiliation and betrayal that year.

Isabella was startled from her thoughts when she realized Sir Alfred had placed his hand gently on her arm. "Come back, Isabella. That time is past and I am not that man," he said kindly.

"I don't know what you are talking about," Isabella said, embarrassed the old man had been privy to her shame. Sir Alfred opened his mouth to speak and then closed it. He sat with his hands on his knees looking at the child thoughtfully. He straightened his jacket and smoothed his pants. Then he said, "I would like to tell you where we are going. I think it is good for people to have as much information as possible. It prevents all kinds of misunderstandings and helps everyone feel safer. Wouldn't you agree?"

"I do not know anything about that, sir."

"Well, I am here to escort you to the court of our king. He would like to meet you."

Did I hear him correctly? "A king wants to meet me? How does a king even know I exist?" she blurted out raising her eyes and looking straight into Sir Alfred's face.

"Three questions, good, good, very good!" the Esteemed Advisor said, slapping his skinny knees in delight. "I love questions. I really do, and do you know why, Miss Isabella? Because one can learn such interesting things by asking a question; wouldn't you agree?" Sir Alfred was almost beaming.

"I do not know about that," Isabella repeated, her mind whirling with the news of a king.

"Well, yes, forgive me, I digress; now back to the king. Yes, yes, he wishes to have dinner with you this very night," said Sir Alfred recovering his official composure, all traces of a smile wiped from his face.

As was her habit in times of stress, Isabella reached behind her ear for a loose strand of hair, twined it around her finger and began to twirl the curl. Instead of calming her, her thoughts became more jumbled. *I do not want to meet the king, but how do I refuse Sir Alfred? Sir Alfred is so imposing, and he must be important to be an Esteemed Advisor. How does one talk to an Esteemed Advisor? How does one act around an Esteemed Advisor? What is an Esteemed Advisor?*

Sir Alfred chuckled softly, "I have that effect on people. I seem to make them curious about all sorts of things."

Isabella stammered, "I am so sorry, sir. It is not my place to think such things. How do I stop my thoughts?"

Sir Alfred raised his thin hand ever so slightly and said, "You need not apologize for being curious, Miss Isabella. You cannot learn if you do not ask questions."

The girl became still averting her eyes again. "In my village it is not proper to question an adult. A child must only obey." She continued as if reciting the law, "If you do not, you will be punished. If you say what is on your mind, you will be punished. If you tell the truth, you will be punished. If you disagree, you will be punished. It is why I so rarely speak."

Sir Alfred was silent for a very long time; the only sound the lapping of azure waves against the bow of the boat as they moved through the water. When Isabella had the courage to look up, she saw sadness in the old man's eyes. "Miss Isabella," he said gently, "those rules do not apply in this kingdom." The statesman sat looking at Isabella for a long time.

Finally he said, "As Esteemed Advisor to King Stefan, I have many responsibilities and duties. My favorite is asking one million questions a year. By gathering answers, I am better able to advise King Stefan."

Sir Alfred then pointed one long finger to a jeweled pendant pinned to his coat amidst his other medals and ribbons. It was shaped like a question mark. The pendant was set with dozens of rubies and hung from a golden twig; a sparkling diamond dangled from the end of the question mark. "This is the Curiosa. It gives me the right and authority to ask anyone and everyone whatever I wish."

With great formality, Sir Alfred removed the Curiosa from his jacket and leaned close to Isabella fastening the pendant to the shoulder of her dress. "Miss Isabella, you now have the full protection of the king and this kingdom to ask one million questions. No one will ever stop you or harm you in any way for asking a question – no one." He bowed his head to the child.

The girl sat stunned by Sir Alfred's gesture. It took her a long moment before she could stammer, "I cannot take this, sir. Such grand things are not for me."

"Child, such grand things are indeed for you. I insist and I am the Esteemed Advisor, am I not?" said the old gentlemen trying to hide his smile as he straightened his tie. "Besides, rubies look lovely on you."

"I have never seen such a beautiful thing, Sir Alfred. I do not know what to say," said Isabella as one finger softly touched the pin.

The Advisor nodded graciously. "You may begin at any time, Miss Isabella," he said. "You now officially have one million questions to ask."

Suddenly the wind rustled through the trees on the banks of the river and the songs of doves and nightingales drifted through the air. The scent of lavender and mint swirled about the boat. *What dare I ask first?* she wondered.

Finally she said, "Sir Alfred, how do you do that – read thoughts?" Instead of waiting for Sir Alfred to respond, Isabella immediately went on to ask, "Isn't it confusing? What if you have bad thoughts? What if you don't want the other person to know what you are thinking? Why do you even bother having conversations?" She couldn't seem to stop herself or wait for his answer. In fact, she asked four more questions before she took a breath and said, "Oh my, I feel so strange." She was tingling all over, the hairs on her arms and legs standing straight up.

Sir Alfred leaned towards the girl and awkwardly patted her on the knee. "There, there, nothing to be alarmed about. The Curiosa has a power of its own, and it takes the wearer a bit of time to become accustomed to it. It has some special properties: whoever wears it seems to become quite curious and they can't but help ask questions. You will learn to manage the impulse and find a rhythm that suits you. You may also notice warmth that emanates from the pendant; actually it is quite pleasing and comforting and it reminds the wearer the pin is there."

"Thank you for explaining that," the little girl said gratefully. She paused to sort through the questions tumbling through her head like squirrels scampering about a field of fallen acorns and walnuts.

Taking advantage of the pause, Sir Alfred said, "I do want to address one of your questions, though. It is a wonderful question actually: why bother having conversations? A voice must be used to speak truth clearly, Miss Isabella. There is power in speaking and naming things, ideas, especially truth; wouldn't you agree?" asked the Royal Advisor as he searched the little girl's face.

"I do not know, Sir Alfred. That is not the way in my village," said the little girl.

"That is most unfortunate, child," said the statesman with a sigh. "I am grateful our ways are different here. Now are you ready with your next question?"

Isabella stared out at the water behind Sir Alfred. She began to frown and said, "Sir Alfred, why is the water turning red?"

THE UNSPOKEN QUESTION

Isabella sat up, her head pounding and body aching. *What happened to us? How did I get to shore?* Vaguely she remembered Sir Alfred swimming towards her before a wave pushed her underwater and then blackness. As she looked about she realized she was alone on a rocky beach. Shrieks pierced the air. Frightened, Isabella forced herself to her feet and slowly stumbled along the edge of the now calm waterway, moving downstream away from the howls.

Sir Alfred must have come ashore somewhere. I have to find him. She was so dazed she did not notice the shadow shapes following her. Suddenly the beach ended in a wall of red splashed granite and Isabella could proceed no further. As she leaned her head against the canyon wall, she heard vicious barks behind her. Turning she saw four black and brown humpbacked hyenas creep out of the shadows, hideous grins contorting their faces. The largest of the group moved steadily toward the child.

"Little missy, you seem lost," growled the animal, its pink tongue licking mottled lips. "Think we could help you?" the hyena cackled.

"I do not need any help," Isabella mumbled, pressing her back into the rock wall. "I am meeting a friend of mine." Her voice cracked. The ugly beasts broke into howling laughter.

"Can't we be your friends?" hissed the leader, slinking ever closer. The hyena grinned again, showing sharp, yellowed teeth flecked with the blood and skin of a previous kill. The beast tensed: the hairs on his ruff bristling, then he lunged toward the child. With a sickening thud the hyena knocked Isabella unconscious to the ground and climbed onto her chest. The rest of the pack closed around the girl. As the leader bent for Isabella's throat, a fiery arrow buried itself deep into its back. A second and third shaft of fire followed. The creature screamed; its body aflame. Another fiery burst struck a second brute, a third and fourth projectile pierced the remaining predators. In pain and confusion, the pack turned and ran upstream plunging into the river; their bodies ablaze; their shrieks filling the air.

Two men ran from the shadows and knelt beside the unconscious child. "Sir, we must hurry," said the first. "The beasts smell death and will follow once they regroup. Shelter is over the ridge. I shall carry the child on my back but I need your help to secure her." Sir Alfred Gielgud, Esteemed Royal Advisor, nodded. Taking the man's rope Sir Alfred quickly bound Isabella to the archer's back. The two men moved hastily across a narrow channel in the river and began to scale a rocky bank. The rocks gave way to a network of massive gnarled roots. Soon the men stood at the base of an ancient redwood tree, so tall that its branches were hidden in the evening clouds. A hemp ladder hung against the trunk of the tree.

The woodsman put his foot onto the first rung. He turned to Sir Alfred who nodded he would follow. Up and up and up they climbed. Finally they reached a narrow wooden catwalk high above the clouds. "We are almost there," said the archer. The man carried the limp child into a tree house built into the massive branches of the redwood. A single torch lit the quarters which were clean though sparsely fitted. A table and two benches, several wooden chairs and sleeping mats were the only furnishings. Sacks of food stuffs and barrels of cider were stacked against the walls. Warm pine scented air floated in through un-shuttered windows which ran the circumference of the tree house.

As the woodsman laid Isabella onto a sleeping mat, the night air was filled with low-pitched hoots, screeches, and hisses of forest owls calling one another to the ancient redwood. In seconds a tiny Elfen Owl perched on an open sill, its tufted ears turning this way and that listening for its approaching brethren. Moments later a Snowy White glided silently onto the next window ledge. It was followed by a Long-Eared Owl, a heart faced Saw-Whet, and a massive Barred Owl. Dozens of nightjars floated noiselessly onto the ledges – their great unblinking eyes staring into the room, then turning their heads three quarters this way and that to view the land below.

"Can you manage from here?" the man asked Sir Alfred. "I must withdraw the ladder to ensure we are secure for the night though I feel our night watchers will keep us safe," said the woodsman bowing to the owls.

"I can," nodded the Royal Advisor as he settled on the floor next to Isabella. "Aden, the kingdom is in your debt."

"I am here to protect, sir." The man melted into the shadows.

Just then the little girl moaned and slowly opened her eyes. Relief filled her body as she looked up into the concerned face of the old gentleman. "Sir Alfred," she murmured, "I was so very worried you were drowned…the beasts…their teeth…"

The old man smiled gently. "You are safe, child," he said leaning towards Isabella and patting her hand. With his help, the child slowly sat upright. The room was spinning and her head throbbed. Sir Alfred asked, "Can you move to the bench? There is cider on the table. It might help refresh you."

"No cider," she said as her stomach began to churn and bile filled her throat, "but I would like to sit at the table." Sir Alfred took her arm and gently helped her to the seat. "What happened to us on the river?" Isabella whispered.

"I am not certain but I shall be forever grateful Aden found us as quickly as he did. These are strange times and there is much danger afoot." As Sir Alfred spoke, the woodsman returned. Isabella watched the man as he hung his bow and quiver on a peg and removed his cloak. His hair was white and fell past his shoulders; his face was the color of newly fallen snow. Though she first thought him young, Isabella could not actually tell his age. Quickly, the woodsman set about lighting more torches. "Do you have any ideas what is amiss with the White River, Aden?" Sir Alfred asked turning to look at the man.

"I do not, sir. Normally the White River is one of the most serene waterways in the kingdom though as of late the channel has turned red and hostile without any seeming reason. I was dispatched to this area to analyze the situation and warn travelers of unusual conditions. Unfortunately, I was not quick enough to keep you and the child out of harm's way." When Aden finished lighting the torches that lined the walls of the room, he said, "If you will both excuse me, I have water and sediment samples to study while they are fresh."

"Of course," Sir Alfred nodded his head courteously to the man.

"Who is he?" asked Isabella wide eyed after the man withdrew.

"A member of the Royal Rangers – he and his peers watch over the forests, rivers and deserts. They also protect those who travel unpopulated areas."

At that moment the Elfen Owl began a low-pitched hooting which was joined in by the other watchers. In moments the room vibrated with a thrumming that grew louder and louder until Isabella's head began to pound. The child's mind was flooded with images of the boat breaking up on the jagged rocks, Sir Alfred struggling in the water, and the viscous hyenas stalking her. She tried to push the terrible memories away, but they were too strong. Her mind skittered back farther to each difficult moment on the river even unto the gypsies in the clearing. Suddenly the Curiosa's power surged with such force Isabella felt her skull would explode. Questions tumbled around and about and around until only one remained - the one unspoken question she had feared most to ask these many days past. The owls' thrumming stopped.

In the infinite silence, Isabella whispered, "Sir Alfred, please, where am I?"

"We are in one of the outposts the Rangers maintain to survey the kingdom," Sir Alfred said calmly as he reached for a glass of cider. He knew this was not the answer Isabella sought but he feared he could not respond honestly until the pressure in her mind ebbed.

"No, I mean *where* am I? I know I am not at home anymore, but I do not know where I am." Isabella's heart was pounding so hard she could barely breathe.

As one, the owls turned to stare unblinking at the old man. Though he did not look at them, the Advisor paused, nodded imperceptively and said very gently to the child, "You are in the kingdom of the Lower World."

"The Lower World!" she exclaimed. The girl's head throbbed as her parents' admonishments flooded her mind. It all made sense now; all the terrible events of the past few days, the terrible dreams; how could she not have realized this before? Tears spilled from her eyes as she cried, "My parents, the priest, the headmaster all told me if I was bad this would happen." The room was a watery blur. "I tried hard to be good, Sir Alfred." She reached for the old gentleman's hand across the table. "Truly, I tried so hard every day to be what they wanted, but I could not please them and now my punishment is the inferno."

TWENTY FOUR HOURS

Three heavy hearts yearning for hope faced three heavy hearts holding little.

"We stopped the bleeding in the abdominal cavity – that's the good news," said the surgeon, "but the swelling and pressure in her brain increased significantly." He looked at his colleague to continue.

"We were forced to induce a coma," the neurologist said slowly, looking at the three facing him. "This will slow the blood flow to her brain giving it a chance to rest and the swelling to decrease."

"We have to be honest with you," the internist said finally. "There is nothing more we can do for the next twenty four hours. If the swelling doesn't go down, she will die. It if does, she is still not out of the woods. Induced coma is a tricky procedure so there may be permanent brain damage after we bring her out."

The three beating hearts across the table broke under the weight of the doctors' words. "Surely there is something more that can be done than wait," said the old woman.

"Pray," said the neurologist.

✛
THE LOWER WORLD

The child was trembling with such force Sir Alfred rose from his seat and moved to her side. Stiffly, the statesman patted her back and said, "Oh Miss Isabella, this is not the place your adults threatened you with." He stopped, pressing his fingertips on the table as he searched for an explanation the child could understand. "Think about it this way," he said gently. "Sometimes one must go deep to find something precious. For example, in your village doesn't your sweetest water come from your deepest wells?"

"Yes," whimpered Isabella, tears staining her cheeks.

"And aren't trees anchored by roots that run deep in the earth, sometimes more than twice the height of the tree itself?" Sir Alfred asked one thin arm reaching toward the sky and the other grazing the floor. "Can you imagine the depth of roots of this magnificent tree?"

Isabella's tears began to slow. "I once saw a tree that had been toppled by a terrible storm," she said wiping her face with the back of her hand and the nose on her sleeve. "The roots were very long indeed. I was very surprised."

"And so it is with us," Sir Alfred continued as he sat straight and tall in his seat, his hands now flat on the table. "The kingdom is quite unique, Miss Isabella," he said with a gentle smile. "Not to boast but the Lower World has many varied regions and an infinite number of interesting subjects. You cannot even imagine their variety."

The torches in the walls flickered as a breeze moved through the open windows of the tree house, ruffling all manner of owl feathers as the night eagles followed the conversation of the old man and young child. The Elfen Owl took silent flight and landed on Sir Alfred's shoulder. "Oh my," said the girl as she glanced at the window from which it came. "Who are they?" she asked staring at dozens of owls perched on the windows lining the perimeter of the tree house.

"Friends," smiled Sir Alfred, "wise friends. They will let us know if anything foul approaches tonight." The tiny owl swiveled its head hissing and hooting into Sir Alfred's ear. The old gentleman listened and nodded. Satisfied its message had been received, the owl flew back to its perch, the circle of protection complete once again.

"Our friend reminded me to share one more interesting facet of the Lower World," Sir Alfred said. He paused, the light of the torches casting shadows across his regal face, as he chose his next words carefully. "The kingdom holds knowledge, Miss Isabella – knowledge of what is truest in the hearts of its subjects. In some cases she knows more about an individual's inner life than that person knows about herself or himself. Now that you are here, she holds that knowledge for you." The owls collectively beat their wings in silent agreement.

Shaking her head, Isabella said, "Sir Alfred, please stop. None of this makes sense and my head feels like it is going to explode."

The torches flickered in the tree house as the wind rustled through the room creating mysterious patterns on the walls and floor. Night hawks deep in the forest called to one another as they hunted for food. Mice could be heard scurrying along the walls of the tree house scavenging crumbs. The scent of pine and rich earth wafted through the windows. Ancient branches scraped against the roof of the tree house.

Just then Aden returned with coverlets and cushions. "I apologize for the austere accommodations," he said, "but I am not accustomed to royal guests. I hope these will soften the sleeping pallets." He proceeded to lay the bedding upon the mats on the wooden floor. As he stood, he said, "I suggest you retire soon. My craft is moored on the river, and if conditions on the river are stable in the morning, you may have the boat to continue on to the castle."

"Thank you, Aden. I think sleep is a fine suggestion. It has been a stressful day, has it not, Miss Isabella?" said the Royal Advisor kindly. Isabella nodded woodenly as Aden bowed and left for his sleeping quarters on the other side of the tree house.

"You will stay next to me the whole night, won't you, Sir Alfred? I do not want to be alone," she said miserably. The old gentleman nodded as the little girl went to her pallet and laid down. As Sir Alfred covered her with a red velvet quilt, Isabella asked quietly, "Am I far from home?"

Tucking the edge of the quilt under Isabella's chin, Sir Alfred replied, "Not far in distance but far in the sense that we do and see things very differently here." A wolf howled in the night letting its pack know it was on its way home.

"I fear I will never return home," she said sadly. A single tear ran down her check and dropped onto the coverlet. She closed her eyes and in seconds she was asleep. The owls watched through the night. They departed at dawn but not before each left a feather beside the head of the sleeping child.

When the two men and child rose the next morning, the land and water were shrouded in a heavy gray fog. After a cold breakfast of hardboiled eggs, salt pork and bread, all walked to the river in silence. When they reached the rocky riverbank Aden said, "I was out earlier this morning. Though the fog is thick, the water is smooth. I believe it is safe to proceed."

"Thank you, Aden; you have been of great service to us." Sir Alfred bowed deeply to the woodsman. Aden helped Isabella into the vessel: it was long, sleek, and low in the water – a craft made for speed. He nodded to the travelers as the boat moved into the river; the water muddy brown, thick and slow moving. "Safe journey," he called out as Isabella and Sir Alfred were swallowed up by the fog.

SURRENDER

"Good! We are on our way," Sir Alfred said briskly, straightening his tie and smoothing his jacket. "We are actually not too far behind schedule." Though Isabella sat only inches from the statesman, she could not see him so thick was the fog. The two floated in silence for quite some time, each lost deep in their own thoughts. The girl had spoken little since rising but finally called out, "Sir Alfred?" her voice small and muffled by the fog, her hand clutching the owl feathers.

"Yes, Miss Isabella?" he answered.

"My head feels better this morning."

"I am so glad to hear that, child."

"I have been trying to remember what you told me last night. You said so many things I did not understand. Did you really say the answers to what I long for are to be found in the Lower World?"

"I did," came his hushed response through the fog.

"Is that really true?" she asked timidly.

"It is," returned the statesman.

"I will not find the answers in my village? she whispered

"No," said Sir Alfred somberly. "That is why you have come to us."

"Everything is so dark and gloomy here. How can there be anything good in such a place?" she said sadly, her shoulder slumped forward, her hands clasping the owl feather tightly.

"Child, there are treasures and delights here you cannot imagine. You simply have not seen them yet," reassured the old gentleman.

Isabella thought about this for a while. *Can I believe him?* she wondered. You are certain?" she pressed again.

"I am most certain. Miss Isabella. I will never lie to you, I promise."

Isabella sighed and sat quietly as the boat drifted in the thick fog and sluggish river current. *Can I trust him?* Many more minutes passed in silence. *There is nothing for me in my village. I will take a chance and trust him.* She whispered, "I want to stay and find my answers, Sir Alfred."

The fog quivered with relief and royal blue ripples spread through the river. Though Isabella could not see him, the Royal Advisor smiled. "I am glad, Miss Isabella," he said.

Another minute passed and Isabella said, "I have more questions, Sir Alfred. May I ask them?" The fog was so thick Isabella did not hear Sir Alfred chuckle. He composed himself and then replied with great seriousness, "By my calculations, you have approximately 999,958 more to ask."

"Thank you." Isabella said. She placed one hand over the Curiosa and felt it warm her fingers. The other clutched the owl feathers. "Sir Alfred, can you tell me how the king knows I am here, and why he wants to meet me? I am not anyone important." Isabella could not see the Royal Advisor and feared if he fell from the craft, she would not hear the splash.

To her relief she heard him say, "All of us know when a visitor comes to the Lower World. The king feels it is his responsibility to personally welcome each guest and, Miss Isabella, in this kingdom, you are *very* important." Isabella wanted to ask more but stopped when she felt the boat turn sharply. As they rounded a river bend, she thought she heard the beating of drums. The slow deep throbs grew louder and louder reverberating through the air. Within seconds the fog dissolved. Directly ahead of them was the castle.

"Oh my," Isabella gasped, her hands going to her face, the owl feathers released to the wind.

THE CASTLE

The castle, a pentagon three stories high, was built on a huge hill. Massive watchtowers anchored the five corners of the building so no one could approach without being seen. The outer walls of the castle were white marble. Dark red tiles covered the steeply peaked roofs. Black, red and white banners bearing the royal insignia of twin dragons – one white, one black – fluttered atop the towers. Groves of white flowering trees surrounded the castle. The sweet smell of apple blossoms floated through the air.

A wide lake circled the base of the hill. Black and white swans glided along the shore. Neither friend nor foe could enter the castle grounds unless an enormous drawbridge was lowered. Since Sir Alfred and Isabella were expected, the bridge was down and two dozen guardsmen, in black, red and white uniforms, lined the bridge beating their drums to announce the arrival of the two travelers.

The boat floated to the riverbank where an open-air carriage drawn by two white and two black horses waited for the child and old man. Sir Alfred helped Isabella out of the boat and led her to the coach, a carriage of black lacquered wood with seats of red silk. The driver placed a tiny red stool before Isabella so she could easily step into the coach. When Sir Alfred was seated, the driver blew a trumpet announcing their approach to the castle manor. In no time at all they traveled over the drawbridge and were inside the castle's defensive walls.

When the carriage came to a stop, the coachman opened the door and Sir Alfred said, "Come with me, Miss Isabella. King Stefan is waiting for us in the garden." The Royal Advisor straightened his tie and tugged down on his jacket as he stepped out of the carriage. He ran his hands over his hair and across his thin mustache. Then he reached up to the girl and offered Isabella his hand so she could exit the carriage.

Once on the ground, the girl hesitated. "Do I look presentable?" she asked anxiously looking down at her rumpled smock.

"Yes, yes. You look lovely. Let us proceed; we must not keep the king waiting," Sir Alfred said crisply, very much a Royal Advisor.

"Sir Alfred, stop, please. I feel afraid again. I am all dirty and I do not know how to meet a king or speak to a king. Help me," she said reaching for his hand.

The old gentleman looked into the little girl's eyes. "My apologies, dear; of course this is a bit overwhelming." He smiled and squeezed the child's thin hand. "Let me assure you, Miss Isabella, you do look lovely and our king is a very nice man. All will be well. You let me know when you are ready to proceed."

I will trust him she thought *I will trust him.* As her heart slowed, she said, "I am ready." Holding his hand, Isabella and Sir Alfred walked toward a second lake which encircled an island on which sat the castle settlement. "Now do as I do, Miss Isabella. All is well," Sir Alfred instructed as he walked to the water's edge and released her hand. As he was about to step into the water, a great stone rose to meet his foot. With his next step, a second stone arose, and then a third, a fourth, and on and on, a walkway rising out of the lake all the way to the castle keep. "Isabella, please come," the Royal Advisor said smiling as he turned to see the child staring open mouthed at his progress.

Staring into the lake Isabella saw the stones were not stones at all but ancient sea turtles, their massive shells forming a path. When she gingerly stepped on the first shell, she heard a soft wheezing sound. The old turtle poked his head out of his shell and rasped, "Welcome, child. We are glad you are finally here. Hurry along, the king waits for you." He pulled his head back into the shell. Isabella looked up and saw Sir Alfred at the wall of the keep. He was motioning for her to continue, so she jumped from shell to shell as quickly as she could. When she reached the old gentleman, he pulled a huge key out of his pocket and unlocked a small door hidden in the wall. As Isabella stepped through the doorway, she glanced back and saw the turtles silently sink beneath the surface of the lake. In seconds the water was as smooth as a piece of glass.

The child and old man walked quickly along a long narrow passageway ablaze with twinkling lights. The floor, ceiling and walls were solid stone - slabs of black and white granite. Isabella could not see a single flower but the passageway was filled with the fragrance of lilacs, lilies of the valley, and ginger blossom. "Sir Alfred, what…?" Isabella started to ask.

"Quiet, Miss Isabella," Sir Alfred whispered so softly the girl could barely hear the old man. "The fireflies are dreaming. We do not want to startle them or they will awake, and we will lose our light." Isabella nodded and followed Sir Alfred silently as the passage way turned left, then right, then left again. *Dreaming fireflies! Amazing.*

"We are here," Sir Alfred announced as they came to a closed door. As he spoke the passageway was plunged into darkness. "See," he said wryly, "I woke them up."

Sir Alfred slowly pulled the heavy door open for Isabella and said, "You may go through, Miss Isabella." Isabella stepped into a garden. Jeweled flowers blazing red, pink, yellow and orange bloomed everywhere, their sweet scents filling the air. Bursts of water arced back and forth along a lane of jumping fountains. Plumed birds trilled joyfully from their nests and perches. Green, blue and purple ribbons tied to branches fluttered in the wind. Isabella was enchanted.

Sir Alfred quickly led Isabella into a hedge maze where they were swallowed up in a channel of green. The hedge was far taller than Sir Alfred so all Isabella could see was the blue of the sky, the green walls of the hedge and the pink stones of the path. The girl and Royal Advisor made a rhythmic swooshing sound as they walked through the maze. "What is that noise, Sir Alfred?"

"We are walking on sea shells. The sea is far away so when we traverse this path, it reminds us of the sound of the ocean waves." *What a wondrous place* marveled the child.

When they reached the end of the hedge maze the girl saw a man sitting on a red blanket under a huge oak tree; he was reading a book. He was a handsome young man in his twenties, strong and muscular with wavy black hair that fell loose to his shoulders. Isabella thought he

59

would probably be tall when he stood. He was dressed in a simple navy tunic and leggings and had an air of confidence and authority about him. As they got closer, Isabella saw two long scars running side by side down the right half of his face. Sir Alfred stopped several feet from the man, bowed low and said, "Highness."

✛
INTRODUCTIONS

The king looked up, smiled and put his book aside. "Welcome back, Alfred. I see you and our guest have arrived safely." A family of five playful squirrels picnicking on fallen acorns close to the blanket stopped their play when the king spoke. They looked from the child to the king and back again.

"I will take my leave, Sire. I have duties to attend to." Sir Alfred gave Isabella a quick smile and withdrew into the maze. The king motioned for Isabella to come forward. So too did the squirrels inch closer curious to see what would happen next.

"Welcome, Isabella," the king said graciously. "I have been looking forward to our meeting. I trust Sir Alfred was a good traveling companion." The king's voice was deep and strong. Isabella's heart was pounding so hard in her chest, she could barely breathe; the lump in her throat was so large, she could not utter a word. She stood frozen, her head lowered and eyes glued to her feet.

"You must be tired from traveling. Why don't you sit with me and rest a bit? I could send for some food if you are hungry. Would you like that?" the young king asked kindly.

Isabella walked very slowly to the farthest edge of the blanket and knelt on a corner not wanting to take up any space that rightly belonged to the king. Still looking down, Isabella stammered. "No thank you, Highness. I do not want to be any trouble. I am not hungry." Just then Isabella's stomach rumbled and growled. The king smiled but said nothing. The squirrels wrapped their bushy tails over their eyes and mouths least a giggle escape and embarrass the child. Shamed by her body's betrayal, Isabella wanted to say anything to cover the unseemly noise but her mind was blank. Then she felt a warm glow through her smock – the Curiosa. Looking down at the blanket, she blurted out, "Sir Alfred was wonderful to me. He gave me the Curiosa so that I would feel safe asking questions. I hope you don't mind. I will be happy to give it back. I know I was wrong to take it."

"Isabella, I don't mind at all. In fact, I think it is a wonderful idea. Sir Alfred is very wise." The king paused and then said gently, "Isabella, I think we might have a better conversation if we look at one another. What do you think?" Five squirrel heads bobbed in agreement.

"Oh, Highness," she said dropping her head even lower, "that would be disrespectful of me. You are the king and I am a girl-child."

"And that means what?" he asked curiously.

Isabella was so surprised by his response she looked up for just a moment before dropping her gaze again. "Well, Highness, in my village, children know their place, especially girls. We move quietly, stay in the background and say as little as possible – particularly around important people."

"I see," said the king. "Well, in this kingdom, all children are valued and encouraged to speak; their insights are often amazing." Three baby squirrels beamed in delight as their proud parents nodded in agreement.

He is not what I expected Isabella thought. The two sat quietly under the tree. The cooing of mourning doves nested in the branches above comforted the tree and all its guests. As Isabella listened to their song, she could feel the warmth from the Curiosa spreading to her neck and throat as questions swirled about in her head. She took a deep breath and glancing at the king said in the tiniest voice possible, "Highness, may I ask you something?"

"Of course," the king replied, "anything."

"Highness, why you are sitting in a garden alone reading a book?" her voice so earnest the king could not help but smile.

"What were you expecting, Isabella?" he inquired.

"To see you in court listening to debates among your advisors, or hunting, or getting ready to go into battle but certainly not reading a book," she stammered. "You are not even wearing a crown!"

This time, Stefan, King of the Lower World, laughed so loud the birds in the tree paused singing for just a moment to peer at the king and little girl. When they saw all was well, they resumed their own conversations. "Well, Isabella, I am sorry if I disappoint you," the king said pleasantly. "The simple answer is I love books. They are filled with new ideas and new places. In fact, I trust that whenever I have a question, the right book will find its way into my hands. The Queen Mother is the same way. I know this will surprise you, but I also like to cook." This was just too much for Isabella. She raised her head and looked directly at the king. She asked seriously, "Are you really a king or are you and Sir Alfred playing a trick on me?"

"I am a king," said Stefan, green eyes twinkling. "I do those other things you mentioned – I just don't do them all the time. That would be quite boring, don't you think?"

"I am not sure. It is beyond my experience." Isabella dropped her gaze again. Suddenly a dark cloud blocked the warmth of the summer sun and a cold breeze passed over the two. The squirrels tipped their noses upward. With a nod from the parents all five scampered up the mighty oak and into their nest tucked deep in the branches of the tree. Isabella shivered. *Why did the weather change so quickly?* she wondered uneasily.

The king looked about and frowned. He stood and said, "Isabella, a storm is coming. I think we need to retire to the castle manor before the weather becomes more threatening. Though his voice was kind, all playfulness was gone from his manner.

"If that is what you wish, Highness," Isabella said rising obediently.

"I will point out some things along the way that you might find interesting," he said as they passed through a series of outbuildings that made up a small village. "Much work is done here to ensure the smooth functioning of the castle," explained the king as they passed through carpentry shops, blacksmith stalls, laundries, tailor shops, butcher shops, kitchens, employee's quarters, stables and kennels. Everywhere they went the king greeted people warmly by name. It was apparent to Isabella both king and subjects held one another in high regard.

"Now to the interior of the castle," said the king. He showed Isabella a ballroom three times the size of her cottage; it was entirely ornamented in white. They toured music rooms, a pottery barn, a dance studio, even a theater. Isabella had never seen such wealth and beauty.

"Now we are in my favorite wing," said the king as he showed her the castle's observatory, an alchemy laboratory and the medical clinic. When they walked through the library, King Stefan said, "I wish I could spend more time here; there is so much to learn. I hope you will make use of the library while you are here." The king grew silent as they continued down a long corridor until they stood before a great red door. The young king paused, drew in a deep breath and said, "I think you will find this room very interesting."

✧
HOPE

At 2:30 AM, the man's phone beeped once indicating the arrival of a new text message. He read:

> *MRI results back. Swelling has started to go down. We are watching for CSF buildup around the brain. Meet me in ICU at 10:00AM.   DL*

$$\downarrow$$

THE PAINTINGS

Upon entering the room Isabella saw dozens of canvas paintings covering the walls. Many more were stacked in piles scattered about the chamber, and several were on easels covered with sheets. A number of tables were cluttered with paint tubes, jars, brushes and rags. The scent of oils and cleaning fluid filled the air, but Isabella detected another odor – something sickly sweet and cloying. "What do you think of the images?" asked the king quietly.

"Oh my, Highness," muttered Isabella as she stared at the canvasses. Before them hung a huge portrait of a great raging river, flowing blood red. The swirling waters rushed wildly down a deep canyon over giant boulders and broken trees, splashing blood on the steep walls of the canyon. Blood seeped from the canvas staining the legs of the easel and forming a puddle of red on the floor. *Sir Alfred and I were on that river!*

A second painting was of a mighty redwood forest – or rather the remains of an ancient forest. It was as though a massive fist had smashed the enormous trees into kindling. Where giants once stood, shattered and crushed tree bones littered the landscape. The next was what was remained of lush farmland. Charred land radiated from a gaping crater in the middle of the field. The smell of rotting meat emanated from the canvas. Isabella could not continue. She put her hand over her eyes. "Highness, the pictures frighten me. I cannot look at them. What do they mean?" she whispered.

"The kingdom is in great pain," said the king as he stared at the paintings. His voice was so sad that Isabella dropped her hands and looked up at the young man. "I don't understand, Highness," she said.

Without taking his eyes off the paintings, the king replied, "Several weeks ago the paintings began to appear. Each day they were more and more disturbing. The kingdom is telling me something is terribly wrong."

"Sire, what do you mean the kingdom is telling you something?" Isabella asked confused. *He sounds like Sir Alfred talking about the kingdom like a person.*

"It is one of the ways the kingdom communicates with me – through paintings," Stefan said as he walked among the easels. Isabella's heart began to race and she reached for a strand of hair below her ear, twining it tightly about her finger. "You know I can read your thoughts, Isabella," King Stefan said without looking at her. "You are afraid. Why?"

"You speak of the kingdom as a person. That is not possible."

The king turned and looked down at the girl. He said, "In the Lower World, the kingdom is a living entity. Everything in the kingdom is alive and connected – a body of sorts. There is a communication with all who live here, not speech as you and I share but a way of communicating. Sometimes it is the weather, sometimes pictures such as these; sometimes it is just a feeling that floods the land." The king moved to one of the covered easels. "Several days ago this one appeared."

He tugged at the sheet covering the painting. As the sheet fell to the floor, Isabella saw a painting of what appeared to be a library. Hundreds of books had been pulled from the shelves and were scattered on the floor - save one. High on the top of an otherwise empty shelf was a tiny book with an intricately carved cover.

"Given my love of books, I assumed she was telling me something important was in this particular book. So I went in search of it. I have gone through every book in the castle but have found nothing of use. I was about to broaden the search in the kingdom when the next painting appeared. Follow me, please."

King Stefan and Isabella walked to an easel at the far end of the room. It, too, was covered with a large canvas sheet. When he pulled the sheet to the floor, Isabella stared at the image stunned. "It is me," she whispered. Isabella was walking through a deep forest. The top right hand corner of the canvas appeared to be unfinished. When

Isabella stepped closer she saw a faint image of a book sketched onto the corner.

"I believe *you* are to find the book, Isabella," said the king quietly.

Isabella felt a sickening pain begin in her stomach and move up through her chest and into her head. "Respectfully Sire, you must be mistaken," Isabella cried as she turned to the king. "Surely you are mistaken about the meaning of the painting?"

"No, Isabella, I do not think I am," he said as he looked down at the little girl. "I admit I was surprised, but I trust the wisdom of the kingdom. I believe you are to seek the book."

Isabella felt an invisible weight press down on her shoulders and back. She dropped to the floor and bent so low her forehead touched the floor. *Impossible* she thought *impossible*. The king knelt and placed his hand gently on Isabella's hair. "Look up, child." When she did, Isabella saw the king's green eyes were soft and kind. "The people of your village are wrong, you know. You are very capable. After all, you have come this far by yourself which is quite an accomplishment, one to be proud of, don't you think?" The king sat on the floor, legs crossed, facing the girl. "I know this is much to absorb. Though I believe you are to pursue the book, you do have the right to say no. That choice is yours."

"Children do not have choices, Highness. We obey or we are punished," she said bitterly.

"In the Lower World, everyone chooses for themselves, especially children."

"Will I be punished if I say no?" asked Isabella, looking down into her lap.

"You will not be punished, but I cannot say there will be no consequences to the kingdom. What they would be, I do not know," the king said seriously.

Isabella sat silently thinking. Tilting her head up to look at the king, she said, "If I say yes, you will come with me to find this book, won't you?"

The king looked sad and did not answer immediately. He sighed and said, "At first I thought of course I would accompany you. That made the most sense to me. Yet I am being called away to attend a crisis in a far province – one that cannot wait. I do not know when I will return, so I believe you are to do this without me."

Isabella clasped her arms around her chest and began to rock back and forth. "Then my answer is no, Highness. I cannot do this," she said in a small voice. "You are asking me to do more than I am able."

The king was silent for some time. When he finally spoke he said, "I will honor your decision, Isabella, though I ask a favor of you. Please take a bit of time to reflect on all you have seen and heard. If you should change your mind all the resources of the kingdom will be made available to you." The king rose from the floor and extended his hand to Isabella. "Your journey has been long, and you must be exhausted. I shall take you to Cook and have her prepare a light snack for you. Then Sir Alfred shall show you to your chambers so you may rest. Later tonight I would like you to join me for dinner. If it would please you, I will even wear my crown," he said trying to ease the child's burden. Isabella nodded miserably as she rose to her feet and followed the king out of the room.

✦
REFLECTIONS

As the child ate in Cook's kitchen, Sir Alfred, Nightwalker and the king convened in the king's private quarters.

"Thoughts?" asked the king.

Sir Alfred sat straight in his chair with his fingertips resting lightly on the table edge. "I am not surprised she refused. She is fragile, Sire. There were any number of times I did not think she would reach the castle, and yet, there is a determination beneath her fear. She fought to survive on the river."

"I agree she is more than she first appears," said Nightwalker from his perch on the back of a second chair. The raven cocked his head from side to side so as to see the reactions of both men. "There is something sweet in her manner, isn't there?" he mused. "I must confess I feel protective of her which I had not expected. I am also saddened she is angry with me for leaving her on the river."

"You did what you needed to do, Nightwalker," the king replied. "Things could have gone very badly had you not left for the swamp." The great raven nodded gravely.

"I, too, feel protective stirrings," smiled Sir Alfred slightly, "but I think our goal is more than protection. We must help her feel safe enough to take the next step alone. What do you suggest, Highness?"

"I think for now she needs to continue spending time with our Esteemed Advisor. You have served her and us well, Alfred – she trusts you," said the king. "Nightwalker, you have another to track and I advise you leave soon. He grows stronger and that is very worrisome to me. No doubt there will come another time for you to be with the child." The raven nodded.

"We have left one question unasked, Sire," Sir Alfred said thoughtfully as all made way to leave.

"Will she change her mind and do what I ask of her?" replied the king. "Who could say? That question does not yet have an answer."

PILLOW TALK

Sir Alfred found Isabella in the kitchen finishing her meal. "If you are done, I would be pleased to take you to your quarters now," the stately gentleman said. Isabella nodded. She thanked Cook for her kindness and rose to follow Sir Alfred. The Royal Advisor led the child through a series of hallways to her chamber. Standing before a great wooden door carved with butterflies, Sir Alfred said, "I hope you will be comfortable, Miss Isabella. Please let me know if you need anything. I will return to escort you to dinner this evening."

The child stood frozen before the door. Seeing her hesitation, Sir Alfred asked, "Would you like me to come in with you – perhaps show you around your quarters? They are quite nice."

"Yes, thank you. I would appreciate that," said Isabella with relief.

Pushing the door open slowly, Isabella's eyes grew wide. A floor tapestry embroidered with black and gold dragonflies covered the black wooden floor of the sitting room. White silk chairs and a damask couch faced a black marble fireplace. A fire was burning and the smell of hickory filled the air. Black, gold and red pillows were scattered about the room for comfort.

One wall of the room was lined with bookshelves; whimsical paintings adorned the others. Isabella especially liked a portrait of two regal cats seated side by side on an ornate throne of gold. Crystal vases filled with yellow wildflowers graced the tables, and tall windowed doors opened to a private garden and fountain.

"Your bedchamber is this way," Sir Alfred said as he crossed the room and opened a second door carved with butterflies. He waited outside while Isabella entered. A huge four-poster bed dominated the room; damselflies embellished the wrought iron headboard and balusters. Yards and yards of white gauze draped over the spindles creating a magical tent. Off the bedroom was a private dressing room. Isabella walked over to a table of sculpted silver. Ivory combs, jeweled brushes, perfumes and lotions covered the dressing table. Above it hung an oval mirror, framed in diamonds. Sunlight from the garden windows hit the jeweled frame splashing dancing rainbows onto the walls. This was a room designed for a princess.

"Do your quarters please you, Miss Isabella?" asked Sir Alfred when Isabella returned to the sitting room.

"Oh, yes, Sir Alfred. Everything is beautiful," smiled Isabella.

"Good," Sir Alfred said with a nod. "Then I will leave you to settle in. I will return later to gather you for dinner." He bowed, turned and left the room.

As the door closed, Isabella heard a soft tapping behind her. She turned to see two cats sauntering towards her, their claws clicking on the wooden floors. *They must have been in the garden* she thought. *Oh my, they are the cats in the sitting room painting!* "My, you two must be very special to have your own portrait!" said Isabella to the visitors with a shy smile.

"We certainly are special," answered an elegant black cat, her tail flicking lazily back and forth. Isabella's eyes widened. Then she thought *if ravens, rivers and hyenas speak, why not cats?* Dropping into a curtsey she said, "I am very pleased to meet you. My name is Isabella."

"She has lovely manners, doesn't she, sister?" purred the black cat. Without waiting for a response she continued, "My name is Lady Jillian, and this is my sister, Lady Joanna. It is a pleasure to meet you." As she wound herself through Isabella's legs, she asked, "What do you think of our rooms?"

Isabella took a quick breath and said, "These are your rooms? My apologies; I will ask Sir Alfred to move me at once."

"It wouldn't matter," said Lady Jillian haughtily, her yellow eyes ablaze, "all the rooms in the castle belong to us. I do approve of your respectful demeanor, though. You may stay, and I think we shall visit awhile." With that, the cat yawned and plopped onto her side stretching her body into a curve of a crescent moon. She began to groom herself.

Her sister, Lady Joanna, was sitting upright in a puddle of sunlight studying Isabella.

"How do you like our castle, Isabella?" asked Lady Joanna tilting her head ever so slightly. Her voice was deeper and softer than her sister's. Larger and rounder than Lady Jillian, Lady Joanna had a beautiful face, large green eyes and a swirling coat of gray, brown and black. She wore a black collar set with diamonds and a tiny silver bell.

Relieved the royal sisters were not offended Isabella sat on the floor to speak with them more easily and said, "I have only just arrived. The king showed me about." Looking at the two cats, Isabella suddenly felt a wave of sadness flood her.

"What is it, child?" asked Lady Joanna noticing the child's eyes filling with tears.

"I have a cat at home and meeting you both has reminded me of her. In fact, she looks a bit like Lady Jillian. Right now she is probably sleeping in our barn."

Lady Jillian stopped her grooming to stare at Isabella. "A barn you say? How terrible! Did you hear that, sister? Her cat sleeps in a barn. How can you be so cruel?" howled the black cat.

"Now, now, Jillian, they have different customs in the Village World. I am sure Isabella adores her familiar, isn't that so, Isabella?" asked Lady Joanna.

"Oh yes, she is great company." The little girl sighed. A tear fell from her eye. A second tear fell followed by a third tear. Lady Jillian and Lady Joanna looked at one another. After a moment of silent communication, they jumped onto Isabella's lap and stretched, gently licking the tears that dropped from each eye.

"You are a sweet child," purred Lady Joanna rubbing her head against Isabella's face. "What is your friend's name?"

"Kitty," said the little girl, wiping her face with the sleeve of her smock.

"Not very original, is it?" sniffed Lady Jillian. One look from her sister silenced the black cat.

"Whenever I feel sad, I go to the barn and find Kitty," said Isabella as she smoothed tendrils of hair from her face, tucking loose ends behind her ears. "We would often nap together." Isabella paused for a moment and shyly asked, "May I invite you to nap with me? I am very tired and need to rest before I have dinner with the king tonight."

"Actually that is a lovely idea," yawned Lady Jillian. "Both of us have a favorite spot on the bed." The trio walked into the bedroom; with a single leap, both cats were on the bed and disappeared into the gauze tent. *How do I get up there?* Isabella noticed a dainty glass step stool by the side of the bed. She placed her foot gingerly on the first step and then the second. With a tiny hop, she too was on the bed and crawled into the gauze tent. The royal cats playfully pounced on her licking her face with delight. Isabella began to feel better.

"Thank you so much," the child said gratefully. "I appreciate your company. I know I am being bold, but might you stay with me while I am visiting the castle?

"It is hard to say," said Lady Jillian as she burrowed into the coverlets, "for we rarely think beyond the moment."

"I would find it a great comfort if you would honor me with your presence. You remind me of home." Isabella persisted, saying, "Please stay with me."

"It is a lovely invitation, but we do not know what tomorrow will bring; what new adventure might catch our fancy," Lady Jillian replied casually, her black tail flicking from side to side. "Our nature is such that we come and go, isn't that so, sister?" Lady Joanna was already fast asleep, curled in a little ball, tail wrapped around her body, snuggled at the foot of the bed. Seeing her sister such, Lady Jillian took one last look at Isabella and said, "I am sure you understand, don't you?" Without waiting for an answer Lady Jillian closed her eyes and in seconds was twitching, lost in cat dreams.

✦
AN UNWANTED VISITOR

I do not understand! Isabella tossed and turned in the canopied bed.
Unable to sleep she decided to rise and sit in the garden. Perhaps the
late afternoon sun would soothe her hurt feelings. As she walked
through the door into the garden she thought *I do not understand why the
Royal Ladies won't stay with me. They are selfish.*

"They're selfish? I think it is you who is selfish!"

"Who is there?" asked Isabella startled by the voice. Anxiously she
looked around the garden. From behind a bush stepped a very odd-
looking little man. Though he was Isabella's height, he was much older.
The man had wild black hair flying out in all directions. His demeanor
was even stranger than his looks. He couldn't seem to stand still.
Jumping back and forth, up and down, he was in constant motion and
something appeared to be buzzing about his head. "I am Critiques – at
your service, girlie."

Isabella felt annoyed simply being in the man's presence. "This is
my garden. What are you doing here?" she said a bit too quickly.

"Snippy miss, aren't you? When did this become your garden? I
come and go whenever and wherever I please. So there," said Critiques
mockingly as he pranced around Isabella.

"I don't want you here. Please, leave now!" Isabella was startled by
the sharpness of her words, but she couldn't seem to help herself. She
seemed to be growing more annoyed by the moment. She also felt dizzy
turning this way and that trying to face the little man as he continued his
wild dance.

"Well, that's too bad, isn't it? I don't feel like leaving, and you can't
make me go. I plan on staying for quite some time," gloated the ugly
little man.

"I will simply ignore you. I have no desire to visit with someone so unpleasant," retorted Isabella. *What in the world is happening to me? I am as unpleasant as he is* she thought miserably.

"Oh, I am hard to ignore. I am at my best talking, talking, talking; I love to talk. All I need are ears that listen. People always try to put their hands over their ears to block me out, but that doesn't work. Ha-ha!"

"You are so ill-mannered!" Isabella stopped turning about trying to follow the little man's antics and stomped over to a small fountain by the garden wall. *Perhaps if I sit close to the falling water and do not look at the man, I can block him out.* Critiques followed her.

"So you are thinking pretty well of yourself right now, aren't you – talking with ravens and royalty? I've been watching you taking in their compliments, accepting their gifts, enjoying all this luxury, and now you're mad at the ladies? Uppity girl, that will come back to haunt you, I assure you. And all that complaining about your village, the grownups and the way things are done. The people back home aren't going to like that. Wait and see what happens to you once you get back." Critiques's voice was an angry buzz. Isabella did not want to hear more, so she put her hands over her ears.

"I told you that won't help! And you think you can help the king? How could anyone like you do anything for someone as important as a king?" he fairly screamed. "You are too stupid to be of service. When you fail, the king will be disappointed and the whole court will mock you." With each word, the buzzing noise around the little man increased. Finally, unable to ignore him, Isabella looked at him. Buzzing insects were flying about his head. *I have to get away from him* she thought desperately.

"I heard that! Remember we hear everything," the little man shouted in the child's face. Then he snickered wickedly, "I want to take you down memory lane, Iizzy, lest you think you are a grand lady who can do grand things. Remember the Coming Home Festival? For the life of me, I don't know why they ever picked you to say that poem, but your performance was memorable wasn't it?" He started to laugh hysterically.

"Please stop. You are being so mean. I did the best I could." Isabella stammered her face flushed red.

"I did the best I could," he said in a sing song voice mocking the child. "It was quite pathetic, wasn't it?"

Isabella was flooded with the memory of the Coming Home Festival. Everyone in her village wanted to be part of the event. The mayor's son was returning from war a decorated hero, and the village was planning a huge celebration. For some reason the mayor selected Isabella to open the festivities with a poem he had written in honor of his son. Isabella had been surprised and thrilled to be selected since the headmaster was so critical of her abilities. She worked for days to learn all the words – most of which she did not understand. The mayor insisted she not read the parchment the poem was written on, so she practiced reciting the poem in the barn, over and over and over again until she had memorized the entire piece by heart.

The day of the celebration she was both excited and nervous. Wearing her nicest dress, she went up to the stage and looked over the crowd. Everyone in the village was there: the mayor and his wife, their son, her mother and father, all the children in the village, all the grownups.

Isabella began. The words came easily at first but distracted by the noise in the large crowd, she lost her place in her recitation. She stopped, took a breath and started over from the beginning only to stumble in the same place. Isabella looked over to the mayor hoping he would give her the next words to jog her memory. He stared at her with a terrible frown on his face. Isabella looked for her mother who was staring down at the ground. Out of the corner of her eye, Isabella saw her father walk away.

The child started one last time but could not remember one word of the poem beyond the first line. She stood mute on the stage until all in the audience stopped talking and were staring at her. Someone hissed. Someone laughed. The master of ceremony snapped his fingers and angrily motioned for Isabella to leave the stage. As she walked off the platform and into the crowd no one looked at her or said a word of comfort. Later that night at home her father said, "Girl, you made a fool of yourself. Don't try to be more than you are."

Critiques was pleased with his work. "That was a great memory, eh?"

"Why are you doing this?" asked Isabella her face burning.

"Actually I am helping you, Isabella. I want to protect you from ever making a fool of yourself again. Do you ever want to be that humiliated again? I don't ever want you to forget you can't succeed in big things, so forget about helping the king. Finding that book is a million times bigger than reciting that stupid poem." Critiques was circling around Isabella getting closer and closer to her. When he was inches from her face, he leaned to her ear and whispered, "And you know what happened the next day…"

"Stop! Stop!" the child screamed, her hands over her ears. "My head hurts, please stop!"

✦

CARING BRIDGE

The woman's husband re-read his entry on the Caring Bridge website:

Thank you so much for your continued support. I don't know what we would do without it. Here is where we are as of 10:00 PM tonight. As per a previous post, we were relieved when the swelling of the brain eased. Her neurologist warned us we were not out of the woods fearing there might be a buildup of CSF (cerebrospinal fluid) in the space around the brain which often happens after a serious head injury.

A cranial ultrasound this morning confirmed significant fluid buildup which left untreated could lead to infection and permanent brain damage. She went back into surgery at 1:00 PM. A shunt was inserted into the ventricular system of the brain re-routing the excess CSF to the abdominal cavity where it can be absorbed into the bloodstream. Now we wait hoping the part of the brain that produces CSF will return to normal functioning. Please continue to send her love and prayers.

He hit send, closed the computer, and went to kiss his children goodnight.

QUEEN OF THE DREAMTIME

Critiques giggled maliciously as Isabella continued to scream, "Please stop. You are hurting me!" Undeterred, the ugly little man opened his mouth to spew more poison into the air when Sir Alfred burst into the garden.

"Critiques, stop," Sir Alfred commanded, his tone firm and calm. "You are to come with me at once."

"I will not!" Critiques retorted angrily.

"I order you to stop."

"No, I am my own man!" Critiques screamed raising his fist in response. "No one can make me to do anything I don't want to do!"

"Then you force me to take action." Dignified, logical, calm Sir Alfred marched over to Critiques, picked the little man up, tucked him under his arm and strode out of the garden.

Awakened by the commotion, the royal cats scampered into the garden. "Isabella, are you all right? Dear, did he hurt you?" the sisters asked with great concern as they rubbed back and forth against the child's legs.

"No, I am not all right," Isabella moaned as she leaned against the garden wall. "That little man was so rude and spiteful. He said very mean things to me, and I was mean to him too. My head hurts terribly, and I feel so dizzy and queasy."

Lady Joanna jumped up onto the ledge of the garden wall and snuggled close to the child's head. "Critiques has that effect on people," she said sadly, "I am so sorry he hurt you, child."

Just then, Sir Alfred returned. "Miss Isabella, how are you?" he asked a frown puckered between his brows.

"I am sorry for being so much trouble. I always seem to create trouble," whispered the little girl miserably. Sir Alfred and the cats looked at each other. Critiques' harsh words had found their mark.

"Miss Isabella, would it help if we sit with you for a while?" asked Sir Alfred.

"Thank you very much. I do not want to be alone should Critiques sneak back." The child was trembling from head to toe.

The Esteemed Advisor took Isabella's arm and led her to the couch in the sitting room. "Perhaps you might like to put your legs up," he said as he pulled his chair close to her side. The Royal Ladies jumped onto the couch and curled up by Isabella's feet.

"I feel sick, Sir Alfred. My stomach hurts and my neck feels stiff. I hurt all over."

Sir Alfred nodded sympathetically. "Take big deep breaths and blow out, Miss Isabella. Breathe in slowly – slowly – slowly. Good. Breathe out slowly – slowly – slowly. Breathe in again…. Ladies, could one of you cuddle next to Miss Isabella's stomach and the other snuggle her back? I have found that comforting when I am upset."

"I cannot imagine you upset, Sir Alfred," said Isabella in a small voice.

"Oh, yes, child, even me." The cats settled in close to Isabella and began to purr. Soothed by their whirring and warmth and Sir Alfred's presence, Isabella began to relax and slowly closed her eyes. A tear rolled down her face as she murmured, "I could have finished the poem if the mayor had just given me the next word."

"No doubt you could have, child," said Sir Alfred as he awkwardly patted her head.

Isabella began to breathe deeply as she fell asleep. The room, Sir Alfred and the ladies faded away as she began to dream. In her dream, Isabella found herself standing on a moonlit bridge. The girl had no difficulty seeing her surroundings for the moon was full and hung so low in the sky she felt she could touch it. The forest was awash in sound: the wind whispering through the leaves, small animals snuffling in the underbrush, the stream gurgling as it rushed over rocks and sticks. Then Isabella heard something that did not belong to the forest. *Are those bells?* She listened intently and indeed there was a faint jingle.

Glancing about she saw a light flicker between the trees. It disappeared, then appeared, then disappeared again. *A traveler's lantern* she thought. *He must have bells tied to his staff.* A wolf howled in the distance. It was soon joined in chorus by other wolves, their calls much closer to Isabella. *I am not safe alone. I must catch the traveler.*

Though the sound of the bells was becoming fainter, Isabella spied a wink of light and ran down the bridge and through the woods. "Please, whoever you are, wait for me," she shouted. The bells stopped and she saw the light from the lantern hold steady for moment and then start to move again. A path opened for Isabella as she ran through the trees and brush. The light was becoming brighter and the bells louder, so she knew it would be just seconds before she saw the traveler. She stumbled as she scrambled up a hill, the light disappearing as the traveler descended the other side.

When Isabella crested the hill, she drew in a breath. A staff and lantern were moving through the forest. Not powered by human hand, the staff moved on its own – step by step by step. *I cannot lose the light* she thought *or the wolves will attack. But how is the light moving?*

As the child followed the jingling lantern, the trees began to thin then became no more. When Isabella walked out of the woods, the staff stopped and faded into nothingness. She saw she was yards from the river that had taken her away from home. She also saw she was not alone. At the river's edge stood a woman holding a white basket. The woman was flanked by two great panthers – black as coal they stood tall to her waist, long claws extended from massive feet, their tails hypnotically swaying back and forth keeping any from approaching the woman from behind. Over and over the woman reached into the basket and tossed handfuls of shimmering white seeds into the river. When the basket was empty, she placed it on the ground and turned towards Isabella.

"Welcome, Isabella, I am glad you found your way," the woman said, her voice deep and strong. "Join me, please." The girl was speechless. The woman's skin was black as ebony. Her head was bald, crowned by a simple strand of stars. She was dressed in a long tunic of black silk cut to her thigh and cinched with a silver belt. Silver chains draped her neck and wide silver cuffs were fastened to her wrists and upper arm. Her feet were bare though silver bracelets adorned her ankles. The woman was as tall as a man, lean and muscular. Her demeanor was serene, but when Isabella looked into the woman's green eyes they were fierce. *She is a warrior queen* thought Isabella.

As Isabella walked the last few steps to the river's edge, one of the panthers moved in front of the woman baring long yellow fangs. The woman gently patted his head and the massive cat moved aside so that Isabella could approach. "Warrior Queen. I like that, Isabella," said the woman chuckling. "Actually my name is Setine."

"I am honored to meet you." Isabella stammered, embarrassed she had forgotten once again that everyone in the kingdom could read her thoughts. Setine took Isabella's hand and led her along the riverbank. The girl immediately felt calmed by the woman's touch. As they walked along the grassy waterfront Isabella looked out onto the water to see thousands of glowing seeds floating on the river's surface. "What were you doing?" asked the girl staring at the shimmering water.

"I was seeding dreams," replied the woman.

"Why?"

"I am the Queen of the Dreamtime."

"Oh Majesty, pardon my poor manners," Isabella said, releasing the woman's hand, lowering her eyes and dropping into a deep curtsy. "I should have known you were of a royal station," she stuttered.

"Not to worry, child," the queen said smiling, "I am not fussy about such things. Come. There is a lovely spot on the river just a few steps from here where we can sit and talk."

"I am honored," Isabella said. She followed Setine along the river's edge and saw a chair-back swing suspended between two giant oak trees. Long hemp ropes secured the swing to thick branches high overhead. Garlands of white roses twined the ropes filling the air with perfume of rose and jasmine. Upon their approach, the trees bent low for their queen. As Setine and Isabella settled into the chair, an orange fox cub hopped into the queen's lap. The two great panthers settled into the grass, their eyes surveying the area making sure of their queen's safety.

When Isabella, the queen and the cub were comfortably arranged, the swing began to sway out over the river back and forth, back and forth. In the comfortable silence, Isabella began to feel the glow of the

Curiosa through her smock. She was surprised to feel soothed by its warmth rather than frightened. When the glow reached her throat, Isabella said in a tiny voice, "Majesty, I am confused. I was just with Sir Alfred and Lady Jillian and Lady Joanna."

"I know. Sir Alfred is a very good man and the Royal Ladies are – well – royal," laughed Setine as she stroked the fox cub's silken fur, her bracelets tinkling. The cub looked at the queen, nibbled her fingers in affection and curled into a little ball deep in her lap.

"Where am I then?" asked Isabella perplexed.

"You are in the Dreamtime, my kingdom," said Setine serenely.

"I thought I was in the Lower World," Isabella said confused.

"You are. The Dreamtime is but one region of the Lower World. Your nap brought you here."

Isabella's eyes widened. "I did not realize I had fallen asleep. I do not feel asleep." The stars in Setine's crown twinkled in the moonlight.

"I assure you, you are," said the queen with a smile. "That is how you traveled here."

Isabella could feel the heat of the Curiosa moving through her entire body. It was strangely reassuring. Sir Alfred had been right; she was growing accustomed to its warmth. "Why am I here, Majesty?"

The queen smiled. "All humans come here when they dream. You do remember your dreams, don't you?" asked the queen as she gently surrendered the cub to the ground where its mother sat waiting patiently with her other children.

"Never, though the last weeks have been so different. I have been having terrible nightmares." As Isabella spoke, a flash of lightening streaked across the sky. It lit up the night air charging it with electricity. A second later, a clap of thunder shook the ground. The swing stopped rocking for just a moment and then began its gentle swaying again.

"If you wish, I will help you understand the ways of the Dreamtime so you need not be frightened here," said the queen as the swing rose high over the river, its waters shimmering with thousands of seeds of light.

Isabella thought for a moment and said, "Yes, I do want to understand."

"I am pleased," Setine replied. One of the panthers raised its head and grunted in approval. The queen continued, "Humans become so busy in the Village World they often forget who they really are. When they sleep, they remember."

"Majesty, how could anyone forget who they are?" asked Isabella incredulously. "My mother knows she is a mother. My father knows he is a father, and I know I am their daughter."

Setine laughed softly, her voice like velvet. She ran a jeweled finger gently down the child's face, her bracelets falling gracefully down her arm. "People are more than a role, Isabella; each human has many parts." As Setine spoke, animals began to gather at the river's edge to drink. Slowly, deer and elk, badger and beaver, boar and mole approached the water. After their thirst was satisfied, each of the forest creatures drew near and nestled in the grass. The queen smiled and nodded as they joined her court.

Puzzling over the queen's words, Isabella thought of her mother. The little girl remembered her mother cooking, cleaning, mending and marketing. If she was not working, she was worrying or angry with her father or fretting over some village slight. Setine said tenderly, "Ah Isabella, your mother is more than that. Did you know she longs to paint? You found one of her tiny watercolors hidden in the corner by her pots, didn't you?"

Isabella nodded. She couldn't understand why something so pretty was hidden away, but she had been too afraid to ask her mother about the painting. Often when she was alone in the cottage she would pull the little canvas out and admire it. It made her happy to look at it.

"Your mother painted that field of flowers when she was your age. She dreamed of becoming a famous artist. Though it pains her to see that little picture, she has never been able to throw it away. She paints in her dreams."

"Why didn't she become an artist?" Isabella asked frowning, a tiny pain stabbing her stomach.

"Her parents and teachers told her no. She was not strong enough to be who she was meant to be."

"Why didn't she ignore them?" Isabella knew the answer to that question even as she asked it. Still she felt a lump in her throat thinking of the beautiful little painting hidden among the blackened pots. Thunder echoed through the forest and huge drops of rain began to fall. The massive oak trees locked their branches creating a thick green canopy to shelter Isabella and the queen. The staccato of rain on the leaves momentarily silenced them both.

Setine said gently, "Your mother's journey is not yet over."

The girl nodded. She hesitated a moment and then said, "Setine, what does this have to do with me?"

"Your dreams of late are, in a sense, waking you up – showing you who you really are."

"Well I must be a very bad person then. My dreams are terrible," cried Isabella. She began smoothing the wrinkles in her dress to avoid looking at the queen. "If what you say is true then I don't want to know who I am."

"Actually I think you do," the queen said kindly. The animals in the royal court bobbed their heads in agreement. The swing came to a stop and the queen rose from her seat reaching for Isabella's hand. "The storm has passed. Come with me, Isabella; I have something to show you."

CAVE OF MIRRORS

Escorted by the panthers, Setine and Isabella walked from the river's edge back into the dark forest. In minutes the woman and child were in a small grotto awash in moonlight. Isabella gazed upon hundreds and hundreds of white roses spilling down stony walls. "How beautiful!" she murmured.

"This is a special place," Setine said as she moved among the flowers, bending low to inhale their fragrance of rose and jasmine. "Actually it is the key to my kingdom."

"I do not understand," the child replied looking around.

"Look closely. We stand before the entrance to a cave." As the queen spoke, the white roses parted to reveal a narrow crack in the rock wall. "I wish for you to enter the cave," Setine continued. "Once you understand what you see within, you will have access to all the secrets of the Dreamtime."

"You will come with me won't you?" Isabella asked as she stepped closer to the queen reaching for her hand.

"I will be with you in a sense," Setine replied as she untied her belt. With a gentle shake the chain became a silver rope. "Take one end and tie it about your waist. I will hold the other," she said. "We will be connected as you explore."

"Majesty, please, come with me," Isabella pleaded.

"No," the queen said firmly, stepping back from Isabella. "I will be waiting here." By the tone in her voice, Isabella knew if she chose to enter the cave, it would be alone. Slowly, the girl wrapped one end of the silver rope around her waist and tied several knots. She took two deep breaths, looked at the queen who nodded her approval and squeezed through the crevice in the stony wall.

When her eyes adjusted to the shadows in the cave, Isabella saw she was in a space the size of a small room. The girl shivered for a moment for it was much cooler in the cave than in the forest. She took a deep breath and was comforted by the fragrance of roses and jasmine. After looking about for a few seconds, Isabella saw a narrow hole in the wall to her left. Getting down on her hands and knees the child squeezed through the gap, crawled through a short tunnel and entered a second cavern.

As she stood, Isabella gasped; the cavern was larger than anything she had ever seen before. Torches the size of giant oaks lit the cave revealing thousands and thousands and thousands of mirrors of differing shapes and sizes covering the walls. The girl was dazzled. As she approached the first mirror, she fully expected to see herself. To her surprise, she saw Setine. Moving to the next mirror, she saw her father and mother. In the next mirror, she saw a dancer; in the next a newborn baby; in the next a short little man with wild black hair his back turned to her.

Isabella moved from mirror to mirror. Some mirrors reflected places in nature or weather. Other mirrors reflected houses. The most common reflections were people. There were so many different people: some were old, some young, some kind and some horrible and mean. The people were every color, every size and held every station in life. The strangest mirrors reflected swirling mists of colors. When Isabella looked deeply into each color, she was overwhelmed with a specific feeling. Some mists evoked sadness, others disgust, others irritation, others fun.

Isabella was puzzled because some of the reflections felt familiar to her but she wasn't sure why. One bothered her in particular. It was a dark, shadowy figure she could not make out well. She moved away quickly for she felt great danger emanating from the reflection. On and on she walked, the mirrors never ending. The more she saw, the more curious she was about the next reflection. After some time, Isabella felt a tiny tug at her waist, the silver rope singing, "Isabella, it is time to return." *I want to see a few more* she thought. *I will go back shortly.* A few more minutes passed and the silver twine became taut. This time the rope commanded, "Return now, child. You can become lost in this world if you are not prepared. You have other tasks to attend to first."

Disappointed, Isabella obediently retraced her steps looping the silver cord around her arm. Once she returned to the entrance of the mirrored cavern, she glanced about one last time, fell to her hands and knees and crawled through the tunnel to the entry space. She sat for a moment not wanting to release what she had just seen.

When she came through the crevice of roses, Isabella saw Setine sitting on the ground, holding the end of the silver rope, waiting for her as she had promised. A sleeping panther lay on each side of the woman. "Setine, please do not be cross with me for wanting to stay longer. It was amazing!" Isabella exclaimed as she threw herself down on the ground next to the queen. "I have never seen such a sight!"

"It is quite wonderful, isn't it? I am pleased by your reaction." Setine gently reached out and untied the cord from the child's waist. Once released it became a belt which the queen returned to her waist.

"Majesty, I must confess, I am not sure what I saw," Isabella said breathlessly.

"Well, what does a mirror do, Isabella?" the queen asked as she stretched and leaned back against one of the great cats, the bracelets on her arms and ankles sparkling in the moonlight.

"It shows you what you look like," replied the child.

The queen nodded. "What does that tell you about my Cave of Mirrors?"

"I don't know," the girl said thoughtfully. "I did not see myself in the mirrors even once. I saw many other things but not myself."

The Queen of the Dreamtime leaned toward Isabella and touched her cheek. "In fact, each of the mirrors was a reflection of you," she said. "Each person, place or thing you saw or felt is actually a reflection of some part of you."

"How can that be? I saw you in the very first mirror and I certainly don't have a part of me that is like you!" Isabella said astounded by the queen's words.

Isabella looked so surprised Setine laughed a deep, beautiful laugh. "Dear Isabella, you most certainly have a part of yourself that is like me. You may not recognize that yet, but it does not make it untrue." One of the panthers chose that moment to rub his head against Isabella's arm, almost knocking her over. Isabella was even more surprised when the big cat licked her arm from finger to elbow.

"He likes you." Setine gently pulled the panther back to herself and said, "Just remember the Dreamtime is an infinite book of clues. It can tell you what frightens you; what makes you happy; what makes you sad. It can show you what actions to take or what actions not to take. Each element of a dream is you, be it a tornado or mouse, a mother or little man with wild black hair."

Isabella frowned. "I think one would have to be very smart to figure all this out. I am not that smart." Her face flushed red as the headmaster's face flashed through her mind.

"You underestimate yourself, child," said Setine seriously. One of the panthers rose and stretched. He looked at the queen who nodded slightly. The great cat moved away from the woman and settled next to Isabella. When he laid his head on the child's lap, Isabella froze, her eyes wide. "He is just a bigger version of Kitty," laughed Setine, "and like her, he likes to be scratched behind the ears." Isabella tentatively reached out and grazed the panther's head with her fingertips. He began to purr. The child relaxed and gently placed her hand on the great cat's head. Watching the two, Setine said, "You must agree the Cave of Mirrors makes for great mystery does it not? You like mysteries don't you?"

"I suppose I do," said Isabella as she carefully scratched behind the panther's ears. "I do like listening to the old men tell wild tales of werewolves and vampires and missing people. Mother says I have a hidden dark streak." Isabella smiled at the memory of her mother trying to get Isabella away from the campfires only to settle in herself to listen to the old men's stories.

The moon drifted behind the clouds. The forest became darker and there was a slight chill in the air. Both panthers stood up; they looked at the queen and then sauntered away into the trees.

✛
TWINS

Setine and Isabella rose from the ground and followed the great cats. As they walked silently through the night forest, the wind rustled through the leaves carrying the notes of night birds and the whispers of small animals dreaming. Twigs snapped here and there as wood rats rushed to hide from hungry owls. The moon rose above the clouds and painted the trees silver. Breaking the silence, Isabella said shyly, "If the Dreamtime is part of the Lower World, you must know King Stefan."

Setine shimmered in the moonlight, the stars of her crown sparkling, her bracelets and necklaces glistening. She looked down at Isabella and smiled. "I know him very well. He is my twin brother."

"Your brother!" exclaimed Isabella as she stopped dead away to stare at the young queen. A shaft of moonlight broke through the branches and bathed the woman and girl in pale light.

"Yes, dear one, my baby brother by several minutes. I rule the night dreams; he rules the daydreams. We have a friendly competition as to which is more valuable, though in truth, our worlds are more alike than not." The queen resumed her walk as Isabella stared at her open-mouthed. One of the great panthers circled back and gently nudged Isabella forward.

The child barely noticed for the Curiosa was scorching, its rubies blazing fire red. "Do you live in the castle with him?" she asked as she caught up to Setine.

"No, I have my own palace."

Isabella tripped over a root. As the queen reached to steady her, Isabella noticed entwined dragons etched onto the silver cuffs adorning the queen's arms. Barely pausing to take a breath, Isabella continued, "Where is your palace then?"

"The Curiosa is working well," the queen laughed. "My home lies at the center of a spiral labyrinth on the far side of the Lower World".

"Do you only see the king when he dreams?" asked Isabella as she was already formulating her next question.

"That is one way. Stefan and I are able to meet in either realm at dusk and dawn when the veil between our kingdoms overlap." Before Isabella could ask more, Setine changed the direction of their conversation. "Isabella, I am taking you to meet someone."

Isabella's happy mood disappeared immediately. "Majesty, I thought we were going back to the castle. I am tired, and I do not think I could bear to meet anyone else tonight." Isabella's anxious thoughts went back to Critiques in the garden.

The queen seemed not to hear Isabella's objections. "The Curiosa is lovely, isn't it?" said Setine as she continued walking. Her fingers lovingly brushed the pendant on the child's smock; the jewels glittering in the moonlight.

"Yes, I have never worn anything so beautiful," Isabella said as she placed her hand over the broach.

"I believe she will help you in this meeting."

Isabella sighed, "If we must go, Highness, please make it a short visit."

"I will not be joining you for I have other dreams to visit," said the queen with a gentle smile. When Isabella inhaled sharply, Setine said, "Of course, you may decline my request. Remember everything in the kingdom is a choice."

Isabella frowned and said, "Everyone says that." The little girl suddenly felt very tired and slowed her pace. She fell so far behind the queen one of the panthers again circled behind her giving her a gentle bump. When the child slowed even more, the great cat pushed Isabella forward.

When she reached the young queen, Setine said, "The person I want you to meet is only a short walk from here. What have you decided?"

Isabella muttered, "Because you ask this of me, I will try."

With a nod, the queen broke off the main trail following a faint fork through the forest. Immediately, Isabella noticed a change in the terrain. Trees gave way to thorny bushes; the soft forest floor was now littered with sharp rocks and burned branches and the night sky was empty of stars. Just ahead was the flickering light of a campfire. "I will leave you now," said the queen, gently brushing tendrils of hair away from Isabella's face. "Make your way to the fire. Remember questions open the way to all understanding." Setine was gone.

Isabella hesitated not sure what was ahead. *It must be safe* she thought *the queen would not put me in danger.* Isabella took three deep breaths and started walking. When she reached the fire, she gasped. *How could the queen ask me to talk to him?* Isabella was furious. She was about to turn away when Critiques glanced up at her. The little man was trembling all over and the buzzing noise around him seemed louder than before. "Leave me alone, troublemaker," he yelled raising a fist. "Sir Alfred is angry with me, and it's your fault!"

Isabella was shocked. "All my fault...? Ha! How dare you say that!" she said as she stomped her foot. "You were the one who came into my garden! You were the one who said horrible things to me! You deserved to get into trouble and I am glad you did!" The wood in the fire cracked and popped, angrily throwing sparks into the darkness. *What can I possibly talk about with this unpleasant man?* The Curiosa was radiating warmth, but Isabella did not feel soothed. In fact she was so irritated she was tempted to take the pendant off. *I don't want to ask this horrible man anything. Setine said I had a choice!* She turned and started marching back up the trail when she saw two yellow eyes glowing in the dark. Startled, the child stopped and let her eyes adjust to the darkness. It was one of Setine's panthers.

"Our queen has requested you reconsider, little girl," the panther purred. The great cat looked calmly into Isabella's eyes and flicked its tail back and forth, back and forth.

"Will you eat me, if I refuse?" pouted the child.

"I think you would be very sour," the panther returned. "Besides, I grow fond of you. Please go back to the fire and ask one question. If you are still unhappy, I will take you back to our queen."

"One question is all I am willing to do," Isabella said curtly. She turned and stomped back to the fire. Critiques did not even bother to look up. After staring at him for a minute, she said in tight voice, "What are those things flying around your head? They bother me just looking at them. How can you tolerate them?" Two questions; the panther smiled and settled down for a nap.

✦
REMORSE

The old woman sat straight backed in her chair. Impeccably dressed, not a hair out of place, she had been scheduled to chair her committee meeting at the Museum of Modern Art that afternoon. Instead she sat alone with her daughter. Earlier in the day the medical team had informed them excess fluid continued to flood her daughter's brain. Thus they could not remove the shunt, nor attempt to bring her daughter out of the coma. It was too dangerous they said. The brain is very delicate they said. There is so much we do not know they said. It was up to her now they said.

The old woman rose stony-faced and stepped to the woman's bed side as she knew a good mother should. Dutifully she reached out and touched her daughter's bandaged head with a long manicured nail. She pulled a handkerchief from the pocket of her tailored jacket and wiped her hands.

As she turned to go back to her seat, her eyes fell onto her child's fingers so bruised and swollen, nails jagged and torn. She stared at them unable to look away. A shudder went through her frame as she felt for the first time the violence done to her daughter's body. She stood rigid as her eyes traveled down the woman's form. A tear spilled from her eye and then a second and then countless more. The old woman reached out and stroked her daughter's fingers.

"I remember the first time I kissed your fingers when they brought you to me," the old woman whispered, her voice cracking. "I kissed each one. I just couldn't believe how tiny they were. How perfect they were."

Awkwardly the old woman lowered the bed rail. She leaned over her daughter and brushed her lips against her child's torn face as a mother would kiss her beloved newborn.

"I know I was not the mother you needed or deserved," the old woman cried softly. "Can you forgive me? Come back," she wept, "so I can try to show you how much I do love you. Please."

DEMONS

Critiques glared at Isabella as she stood before the fire, hands on her hips and a frown on her face. "What are you talking about? There is nothing flying around my head," the little man snapped as he threw branches onto the fire.

"Yes, there is. How can you not see them or hear them?" Isabella insisted sharply, stomping her foot again.

"You are a simpleton. Go away." Critiques screeched his voice an octave higher than normal.

"I am not a simpleton! I will show you, you mean little man!" Isabella marshaled all her courage, marched over to Critiques and clapped both hands around one of the buzzing insects. "Come close and look, now!"

Perhaps startled by Isabella's boldness, Critiques did as he was told. Barely opening her fingers, Isabella and Critiques stared at a tiny creature. Isabella was not holding an angry pest but a tiny demon. The demon was black and gray in color. A huge horned head sat directly on top of clawed feet. Its eyes were slits and its twisted mouth was filled with sharp pointed teeth. Two razor sharp wings were attached to the back of its head.

"That was flying around my head?" asked Critiques shocked.

"Oh my...! I thought they were bees or something. Yes, this was flying around your head, and there are many more," said Isabella unable to take her eyes off the ugly creature.

"I never noticed," he said dazed. "What are they?"

Isabella leaned forward and asked the creature, "Who are you?"

The demon screeched, "My family name is Fear and Judgment. Release me immediately. I will chew off your fingers if you do not release me." Isabella's head jerked back. The demon's threatening voice was that of a full grown man, not a tiny insect. She was about to open her hands when a burst of heat from the Curiosa shot through body. *Not yet* she thought as she tried to hold her trembling fingers steady.

"I am sorry, but I cannot release you just yet," she said in a shaky voice. "We need to know more about you." Isabella turned to Critiques desperate for help.

"Why are you flying around me?" Critiques demanded.

"What a dullard," hissed the demon. "How can you even ask such a stupid question? We have been with you since you were a child of five."

"You have been flying around my head since I was five?" stammered Critiques in disbelief, staring at the creature through the bars of Isabella's fingers.

"You really are stupid, aren't you? That is what I just said," screamed the demon. "We came to you after your mother died and have been with you since. More of my relatives have joined since then. Let's say you were open to the company," the demon said sarcastically. "You don't remember what happened, do you fool?"

Critiques stared at the ugly demon unable to speak. The creature continued, "After your mother died, you were sent away to relatives because your father didn't want such a troublesome miserable boy. He didn't bring you home after he remarried though he brought your brother home. Your own father did not want you. No one wanted you." The demon started laughing, "Pathetic coward, you ran away. You were all alone, except for us. We kept you company and this is how you repay us, by not even knowing we are here. Idiot! Now enough of this talk of the past. I must return to my family. Release me!" the demon commanded his tone as sharp as his taunts.

Isabella was stunned by the cruelty of the demon's words. When she looked at Critiques, his face was ashen. "No," she said.

The creature screamed in rage, "How dare you challenge me, ignorant girl? Your own demons will make you suffer for this. I demand you obey me!"

"I don't have demons flying around my head," Isabella exclaimed.

"You are as thick as he is," the creature sneered. "Oh, you have demons; I can smell them," he said inhaling deeply. "Oh yes, they are there. You can't see them, but they are there – inside of you." He pressed against Isabella's fingers; his mouth pulled back into a grimace; its fang-like teeth shining in the firelight. "They are from the family of Doubt and Worry, a noble family," he said. "Now I order you to let me go! I am the leader of my clan and must return to them!"

Isabella was horrified by the thought of demons inside of her. She was about to release the terrible creature when Critiques yelled, "No, Isabella, don't let him go. I want to kill him."

Isabella started to tremble. She knew the creature could do harm to them both, but she did not want to be party to murder. She closed her hands tightly around the demon so that Critiques could not grab it. "Critiques, there must be another way," she implored the little man. "Please, we must think of another way out of this."

"What other way can there be? I must protect myself," said the little man, panic written on his face. "I must kill it to rid myself of it." As they stood there staring at each other, Isabella realized the demon's buzzing had stopped. She opened her fingers slightly.

"You will pay dearly for this, Critiques," said the demon. "Release me. I tire of this conversation." Though the demon's words were strong his voice had weakened.

Together, Isabella and Critiques said, "No."

"I must return to my brothers and sisters. We are not made to be apart from the tribe. We draw strength from one another." Neither Isabella nor Critiques replied though Isabella opened her hands ever more slightly. Then as the two watched, the demon's form began to change. The claws, horns, sharp teeth, and wings were sucked inward. Slowly, the demon was losing its shape. In seconds it was transformed into a stone the size of a walnut. Pressed into the stone was a face with hollow eyes and a gaping hole for a mouth. It was no longer an angry face but a fearful face. The demon moaned, "Please, I cannot be powerful alone. I cannot be fierce alone. Something terrible is happening to me."

Isabella and Critiques remained silent looking at the creature in Isabella's open hands. Its mouth became larger and the demon began to howl. "I feel sadness; I cannot hold back the sadness. Please return me to my brothers and sisters for I am strong in their company. If you do not, I shall die of sorrow." The demon moaned several more times and then dissolved into a pool of tears in the girl's cupped hands. The tears sighed deeply and vanished. She and Critiques looked at one another.

"What happened?" Critiques asked.

"I am not sure." The two stood there, not knowing what next to say or do.

Then Isabella looked at Critiques, "The buzzing about your head has slowed down. Should we try to catch the others?"

"I don't know," said Critiques woodenly. "This is all so very confusing." He walked over to a log in front of the fire and sat down heavily.

Isabella followed him. Without looking at him, she said, "Are all those things he said about you and your family true?"

"I haven't thought about those things for years. It happened a long time ago." Critiques' shoulders hunched forward as though a heavy weight lay across his back. He looked very old and tired. Isabella's heart softened toward the little man. "You must have been very sad," she said slowly.

"I don't remember. Perhaps I was." He got up and walked away from the fire and the girl. He stood staring into the dark trees. Isabella could hear the remaining demons start to buzz again. As Isabella watched him walk away, she was struck by something familiar. *I think I saw his reflection in the Cave of Mirrors* she thought *I only saw his back, but I am sure it was him. Oh my, if what Setine says is true, I have a part of me that is like him. How can I be like him? My life is so different than his.*

As Isabella got up from the log and walked over to Critiques, she thought she heard the tinkle of bells. Looking about she saw a flash of light among the trees. "Questions, Isabella, remember questions," whispered Setine's staff.

Hesitantly she said, "Critiques, I do not want to intrude, but I would like to hear about your mother and that time in your life. Might we sit together and talk?" Isabella fully expected him to refuse.

"Why would you want to hear anything about me?" he said dully, his arms hanging limp at his sides. "You said I was a mean little man, remember?"

"I'm sorry. I think I just felt bad because I believed some of those things you said about me when we were in the garden, and I wanted to get back at you."

Not moving his eyes from the trees, Critiques said, "No one has ever asked me to talk about my mother or my family. I am not sure what to say," he said as he turned and looked at Isabella. His face was worn and wrinkled, and his eyes were dark with sadness. "I am afraid to think about that time." Tears started rolling down his pockmarked face. "I do not think a kind word has been spoken to me since my mother died. Perhaps that is why I cannot be kind to others."

The girl tentatively laid her hand on his arm and said, "Let's go back to the fire. I will put some wood on so we will be warm."

"It's funny," said the little man, shaking his head. "I never noticed them flying about my body, and now I feel the air moving as they beat their wings, and I hear that terrible buzzing. How could I not have been aware?"

"Maybe we can catch some of the others like we did the first and ask them questions. Who knows, maybe they will turn into tears too and be gone from you," said Isabella trying to be helpful. "Do you think we should do that?"

"I am not sure. I really am not, but it feels right to be sitting here at the fire," said the little man.

"Well, good – then we will simply sit. We need not speak. Is that all right with you?"

"It is," he nodded.

And so, the little girl and wild haired man sat silently before the fire. They sat in such a way for a very long time before the little girl asked a question and the man haltingly answered. More time passed and she asked a second question and again he answered. Silence followed until the wild haired man turned to the child and posed a question to her. She took her time responding. The man nodded as she spoke. In such a way the two began to talk – an awkward and tentative talk – but one that lasted through the night, witnessed by a great panther with glowing yellow eyes.

BREAKFAST WITH THE KING

The first thing Isabella saw when she awoke was Sir Alfred dozing in the chair next to the couch. His mouth was open and he was snoring softly. So as not to embarrass him, the child stretched loudly to let him know she was awake. Immediately the stately gentleman straightened himself in the chair, adjusted his tie and tugged neatly on his jacket.

"So you are finally awake," he said, smoothing his eyebrows and mustache. "You must have been tired for you slept through the afternoon and night."

"I did?" asked Isabella. She sat up in a panic. "Oh no, I missed dinner with the king. Why didn't you wake me? He will think ill of me."

"Do not be concerned, Miss Isabella. He left instructions for you not to be disturbed. I have scheduled the two of you for breakfast this morning."

Isabella sighed with relief. "Thank you, Sir Alfred. You certainly are organized."

"It comes naturally," he said with a smile. "Now, how are you feeling?"

"Better. Actually, I am feeling quite a bit better, lighter. Where are Lady Jillian and Lady Joanna?"

"They knew you were safe, so they went off to chase birds," he said rising from his chair. "Well, I will leave you for I need to attend to my responsibilities and duties of the day. I had Cook lay out a dress for you on the bed. I hope it pleases you. Do not dawdle, Miss, the king is waiting." He bowed and made his way to the door.

Isabella smiled. Though he was not one to display his emotions, Sir Alfred was very kind. As he disappeared through the door, she called out, "Thank you for staying with me." She didn't see him smile as he hurried down the hall.

Isabella got up and walked into the bedroom. After splashing water on her face she loosened her braid and ran a brush through her hair. *What a strange evening it was* she thought. *I wonder what Critiques is doing now.* With a sigh Isabella tried to redo her hair but her efforts resulted in a lopsided braid. *Why is this so hard?* she wondered as she gave up and tied her hair back with a ribbon. For an instant she remembered gentle hands doing her braid, and then the memory faded. A wave of sadness flowed through her. *Where did that come from?* she wondered. Thoughtfully, she turned and walked to the bed to find the dress left by Cook.

"Oh my," Isabella murmured as she ran her fingers over the beautiful fabrics. She removed her smock and folded it neatly, placing it at the foot of the bed. She reached for a narrow sheath of copper satin, pulled it over her head and let it fall straight to the floor. The fabric felt smooth against her thin arms and legs. Next she pulled on an overcoat of sheer purple silk which matched the length of the slip. She fastened the amethyst buttons that ran down the front of the coat. Finally she stepped into a pair of copper slippers placed next to the bed. Everything fit perfectly.

Ready for breakfast, she ran out of her rooms into the hallway, but something did not feel right. *I forgot the Curiosa.* She went back to her smock, removed the Curiosa and pinned it onto her gown. Immediately her chest filled with a warm glow. When she returned to the hallway, two mourning doves were waiting on the marble bench outside her door. Perched side by side, they were rubbing necks and cooing in delight of one another. "We would love to take you to our king," the pair murmured when they noticed the little girl.

"Thank you," said Isabella, "I was wondering how I would find him."

"Just follow us, please." The birds flew through the winding passages of the castle leading her to a private dining room. Upon entering, Isabella saw the young king seated at his desk surrounded by maps and stacks of reports. Unlike yesterday, he was dressed in a black and red military uniform with the royal insignia of the twin dragons embroidered above his heart. His face was serious as he studied several maps.

When he heard Isabella and the doves enter the room, the king looked up and smiled. As he rose from the desk he said, "Thank you, my friends for being such kind escorts." The pair cooed, bobbed their heads respectfully and disappeared through the window. "Good morning," he said as he crossed the room and took the child's hand. "You look lovely, Isabella."

"Thank you, Highness. I have never worn anything so pretty," Isabella said shyly as they moved to a small round table covered with crisp white linen, settings of china plates, goblets of gold and sterling cutlery. The table was laden with stacks of hot cakes, fresh cream, ripe strawberries, sausages, bacon and piping hot biscuits slathered with butter and honey.

"I trust you are rested?" he asked as he pulled a chair out for her.

"Yes, Highness, I am." Then, forgetting her shyness, Isabella blurted out, "Sire, I met Queen Setine in my dream. We had an amazing visit!"

"My sister is an impressive woman. I assume you visited the Cave of Mirrors, yes?" the king said as he seated himself across from her, shaking out his napkin.

"Oh, yes!" said Isabella nodding her head and smiling broadly. "I have never seen anything like it. I do not understand its meaning as well as I would like, but I will continue to think about it."

"I think that is very wise," King Stefan replied, encouraged to see Isabella had taken the visit so well. After sipping from a goblet filled with orange nectar, he said, "I hope the breakfast pleases you."

"I was so excited thinking about Setine, I did not even notice what Cook prepared. It is wonderful, all my favorite foods. Thank you, Sire," said Isabella as she hungrily filled her plate. After taking a few bites, Isabella said, "I also spent some time with Critiques in the Dreamtime last night."

"Yes, I heard about your encounter with him in the garden. He is a most challenging household member. I could contain him, if you so wish."

"No, I think not," Isabella said shaking her head. She took a sip of milk from a huge golden goblet studded with emeralds. "He does not scare me as much as he did when we met in my little garden." As the child poured cream over the strawberries, she asked shyly, "Do you think if a person holds great sadness inside them, it can become something hurtful or ugly?"

"What do you think?"

Isabella returned the crystal pitcher of cream to the table. "I think that is what happened to Critiques when he was a little boy," she said staring at the king. "I am wondering if it might be good to cry when one is very sad; perhaps it would help the sadness go away. What do you think?"

"Well my mother would agree with that," said the king, not wanting to share his own confusion about the very question Isabella posed. "She taught both Setine and me to name our feelings. She laughs that sad, mad, and happy were our first words."

"She sounds nice. Will the Queen be joining us for breakfast?"

"Not today," said the king smiling. "She likes to spend time outside the castle. In fact, she loves the outdoors far more than the indoors. She is quite an interesting woman. I am sure you will agree when you meet her." The two ate in silence. The king carefully put his fork and knife down and looked at Isabella. He said, "Isabella, we must talk about the book."

The food in Isabella's mouth suddenly turned to dust. "I don't want to, Sire. I was so enjoying our conversation I had hoped you had forgotten about it."

"No, I have not. The situation in our Northern Province worsens, and I must leave this morning, so this will be our only opportunity to speak." Isabella began pushing the food around on her plate not wanting to look at the king. The king sighed and placed his napkin on the table. "Another canvas appeared last night."

"What did it show?" Isabella asked as she laid her fork down and looked at the king.

"The forest is gone. Now there are only whirling clouds of darkness. You are in the middle of the darkness trying to catch the book which is spinning away just beyond your grasp. I think the message remains the same. You are to seek the book, only now there seems to be more urgency."

Isabella looked at the king with shame in her eyes and said, "I do not believe I can succeed, Highness. I think the painting points that out – the book is beyond my reach – and even if I agreed, I would not know how to begin." Isabella placed her hands in her lap and looked down at her plate. She could not bear to see judgment in the king's eyes.

"I have been thinking about that and would like to propose an idea," the king said, thoughtfully. He laid both his hands flat on the table. Isabella saw he wore an insignia ring bearing the twin dragons. "If I were to begin searching now for something priceless, a one-of-a-kind object, I would go to the town of Kronos." The king watched Isabella intently.

"Why that town?" asked Isabella, a bit curious in spite of herself. *It must be the Curiosa!*

"In a sense, Kronos is the information center of the kingdom. The people of that town are highly valued for their abilities to manage tasks and work situations. They are sought after by many in the kingdom. In fact, many of the workers in the castle are from Kronos. More important, because of their travels, they are well versed in the goings on of the realm. If anyone would know of the book, I think they would."

"I see," said Isabella, the Curiosa's interest competing with her fear. "And what is your idea?" she asked, barely getting the words out of her mouth.

"In a few days after you are well rested, two of my guides will take you to the Mayor of Kronos. Roget is his name; he is a very knowledgeable man. You can speak with him."

Isabella waited for the king to continue. When he did not, she asked, "And then?"

"Well, that would depend on what information Roget has," answered the king, taking a sip from his goblet.

"That is your idea, Sire?" Isabella clenched her hands into balled fists, her nails digging into her palms. Suddenly the cream in the pitcher curdled, the hotcakes turned to stone and the cutlery trembled. "Highness, no," she said.

Without a glance at the distress of the table, Stefan said, "It is a first step. Isabella, you always have the option of not continuing after Kronos – of returning to the castle. I thought having a first step might help you decide as to whether or not you might proceed."

"Please don't make me do this. I just cannot." The king watched the little girl's shoulders begin to tremble. The strawberries spilled from their diamond studded bowl onto the table staining the crisp white linen dark red. The blemish spread across the width of the table and dripped to the floor in an ever widening puddle of blood red stain.

The king rose slowly and walked to the girl's chair. "I will press you no further, Isabella," he said quietly. "Let me walk you back to your chambers before I leave."

"I do not want to keep you from your responsibilities. I am sure I can find my way back," the child said stiffly.

"I have no doubt that you can," replied the king gently. "I do this out of pleasure."

"Thank you." The table and accessories were still once again returned to their original form.

✦

SCARS

The king and little girl walked through the castle halls without speaking. As they approached her rooms, they passed through a long corridor lined with portraits of stiff backed men in full military regalia. Their faces were stern, their lips pressed into thin angry lines and their eyes cold and dark. The portraits' eyes followed the progress of the man and child with obvious distaste. King Stefan waved a hand and said, "My relatives. As you see, I come from a long line of warriors. To be quite honest though, this hallway depresses me." *What an odd thing to say* Isabella thought. *I wonder if he got his scars in battle.*

"So you are curious about the scars, are you?" asked the king, turning his head slightly to look at the child. Isabella was mortified he had read her thoughts again. "If you wish I will tell you how I came to have these scars."

"Only if you think it is important for me to know," stammered Isabella. Some of the warriors turned their backs to the pair, not wanting the king's tale to be told.

"Several years ago, a rich trade route between the Lower World and Upper World, our sister realm, became a point of conflict. Merchants from my kingdom claimed bandits from the Upper World were attacking them. The merchants demanded I claim the trade route as part of my kingdom and place it under military protection."

"Does that mean the trade route did not belong to the Lower World?" asked Isabella relieved the attention was off her and the quest for the book.

"Actually, the ownership of that land had passed back and forth between the worlds so many times, no one knew who it really belonged to. We had an informal arrangement that allowed everyone to use it. That changed when the raids started."

"What did you do?"

"I had just been crowned king and decided this was the perfect opportunity to make my mark as a fierce leader – remember I am from a line of warriors." As they reached the end of the hallway, the men in the final portraits stood taller with heads held high, their eyes bright with power and pride, their weapons gleaming. As the young king and the girl turned down another passageway leaving the old men behind, Stefan said, "At the time, my military advisor was General Tarek, the bravest warrior this kingdom has ever known. He was also a very wise man and urged me to negotiate with the Empress of the Upper World. The General knew the Empress well and was absolutely certain a fair agreement could be worked out. She was as unhappy with the activity of the bandits as we were."

The king and Isabella reached the marble bench outside her chamber. Stefan motioned for her to sit down. He remained standing and began to pace. He continued, "I would not consider negotiating. I thought it would make me appear weak, so I ordered my armies to the trade posts. The Empress considered the troop movement an act of aggression and immediately dispatched her troops. It was quite a show of force, on both our parts."

The king stood silent, lost in memory. "What happened?" Isabella finally asked.

The king sighed and sat next to the child. "Tension among the troops was incredibly high as they awaited their orders. A rumor broke out among my soldiers that I had been wounded in an assassination attempt. A squad broke rank and attacked the Empress's troops. Of course, they fought back. Once the line was broken, I felt I had no choice but to order a full assault. For two days we fought like crazed men. On the second day, two spikes from a flail grazed the side of my face. I barely noticed because the fighting was so intense."

"Did you win?" asked Isabella breathlessly.

"Indeed we did win, and word of the victory went out to all the citizens of both realms. I was filled with pride and satisfaction; people were calling me the young Warrior King." Faint cheers and clapping could be heard from the hall of warriors. Stefan shook his head. "Warrior King, how pathetic," he said. The cheers faded into silence.

"But why do you say such a thing? You won, you were a hero," asked Isabella, shocked by the despair in the king's voice.

"The morning after the fighting ended, General Tarek asked me to join him on the battlefield," the king said. "I thought he was going to congratulate me and compliment my bravery, my leadership." He stood and began to pace again. In the silence of moments he seemed to age before Isabella's eyes. "What I saw horrified me. Thousands of men were wounded or dead, men from my kingdom, men from the Empress's armies, innocent citizens who had somehow gotten caught in the crossfire."

The king's face was ashen, and suddenly the corridor reeked with the odor of sulfur and the decay of corpses. Isabella fought the urge to gag. When the stench faded Stefan continued, "The General told me that a caravan of children traveling to a summer retreat had been caught in the fighting. All were killed – one hundred children killed. The General, the bravest warrior in the kingdom, with tears flowing down his battle hardened face said, 'Highness, negotiations might have prevented this. If the talks had failed, at least the effort would have been made. Was your victory worth this?'"

Isabella sat silent. King Stefan continued as though speaking to himself. "I realized my pride drove me to fight. It would have been nobler to have opened talks with the Empress, but I thought fighting would make me appear stronger. Looking at the wounded and dead – knowing one hundred innocent children on holiday had been murdered – I realized the cost of my arrogance."

He stood up and looked down into the girl's face. "Every day I am grateful the scars on my face did not heal. They remind me of the thousands that were sacrificed to satisfy my ego. Indeed I have not been in battle since. Not very kingly, is it?" he said bitterly.

"It is not for me to say, Sire. I am but a child," Isabella said looking down into her lap.

King Stefan smiled sadly and said, "I understand fear, Isabella, and I respect your decision not to seek the book. You are free to stay in the castle as long as you wish. Sir Alfred will look after you. I have my own demons to face." The young king bowed deeply and walked down the hall.

✦
THE QUEEN MOTHER

She knelt in the garden pulling weeds. Out of the corner of her eye she saw the king approach. She leaned back on her heels and brushed the dirt from her hands. "I thought I would find you here, Mother," he said.

The Queen Mother took her son's hand and stood. She embraced him warmly. "I do love my flowers, but not as much as I love you," she said smiling happily, kissing him on both cheeks.

Stefan stood face to face with the Queen. "Mother, I failed. Isabella will not seek the book."

"Why do you look so sad?" she asked linking her arm through his and leading him to a bench surrounded by black and white roses.

"It was my responsibility to persuade her to pursue the book."

"You provided her with information, Stefan. The choice to use it or not is hers. You know that," the Queen Mother said gently.

"But what will we do?"

"Wait. Patience is what is needed now, son," she said. The Queen Mother stopped and broke off a perfect white rose, handing it to her beloved child. "You have an adventure of your own to attend to."

"I feel like a hypocrite," he sighed. "I am disappointed Isabella's fear holds her back and yet I do not know how I will deal with my own fears in the Northern Province."

"It is as you told the child, go there and see what presents itself. I have great faith in you, Stefan," said the Queen Mother smiling at her boy. The king kissed her hand and left his mother surrounded by her beautiful roses.

PRECAUTIONS

"Is this really necessary?" the man asked.

The detective responded, "It's precautionary. The case has received a lot of media attention and now there is the reward money for information. The tip line received several calls that some political fringe crazies might be involved. The callers referenced your wife's work in Europe so we want to check it out. We'll post a uniform outside her door for the next couple of days just to be on the safe side."

✦
COURT IS NOW IN SESSION

"Court is now in session," declared Sir Alfred as he brought the gavel down with a bang. "To those present in my courtroom, today I will be assisted by Miss Isabella, Explorer. I see the only case on the docket is *Rose vs. Rose vs. Rose.* Are the parties present?"

Three men stood. They looked remarkably similar in appearance with the exception of their turbans. The first Mr. Rose wore a turban of red silk, the second Mr. Rose wore a black velvet turban, and the third Mr. Rose wore a turban of white satin.

"Please approach the bench, gentlemen," Sir Alfred instructed in a very solemn voice. "I see you are petitioning the court for dissolution of a family business and to name one individual as general manager; a claim each of you has made. This is a very grave matter, one I am loathe to see. Are you certain this is the course of action you wish to take?"

"It is, your honor," Mr. Rose with the black turban said sternly. "I wish to have it done immediately. I cannot stand to be with these two anymore. They are totally incompetent and are running the business into the ground. I can do far better operating the business alone, my way."

"Incompetent!" exclaimed Mr. Rose with the red turban. "You are arrogant and overbearing. As soon as something doesn't go your way, you start ordering us around, demanding we do this or that. You're the one chasing our customers away with your coldness and rudeness. You act like a pompous king, begging your pardon, Sir Alfred," the man stammered turning as red as his turban. Turning back to his brother he shouted, "*I* can most effectively manage the business. You are the one who needs to go!"

Mr. Rose with the white turban looked miserable wringing his hands, sweat flowing down his face. "Your honor, I am so tired of these two fighting all the time. They are constantly bickering and so very unpleasant with everyone. After they become crazy with each other, they start to harass me when I have done nothing to earn their wrath. All I want to do is run away and hide from these two. It is so upsetting, so upsetting."

"What a sniveling whiner you are. A weakling! Helpless!" yelled Mr. Rose with the red turban. "You are pathetic! We only brought you into the business because we knew you couldn't make it on your own! We were trying to protect you, take care of you, and all the thanks we get are insults!"

Sir Alfred slammed the gavel down. "Enough of this, gentlemen; it is clear to me we are going nowhere at the moment. Therefore, I will hear the facts of this case only after you have answered a series of questions I have prepared for you. I would like you to retire to one of the tables in the back of the courtroom and *together* fashion the responses. Miss Isabella, please distribute the court questions."

Isabella had been sitting next to Sir Alfred observing the proceedings with great interest. She felt very important taking the court documents from Sir Alfred, walking around the judge's table and presenting the questions to each of the Roses.

After glancing at the single sheet of paper, Mr. Rose with the black turban sneered, "You cannot be serious. The first question asks: What is already working? Are you mad? Nothing is working that is why we are here!"

"And look at the next one: What makes it work? Preposterous!" sputtered Mr. Rose with the red turban.

"I can tell you the answer to the next one right now," moaned Mr. Rose with the white turban. "What do we want to accomplish'? Well, *I* want to get away from these two mean men as quickly as I can. They are so nasty to me and everyone else. It is unbearable." Mr. Rose looked like he was about to burst into tears.

"More whining. Be still before I silence you!" Mr. Rose with the red turban thundered. "Sir Alfred, these questions are ludicrous! The last two make no sense: What are the benefits of working together, and what can we do even better to move closer to our objective? Our objective is to end this miserable relationship. We can't be any clearer than that!" Mr. Rose with the red turban was so angry, Isabella thought he would explode.

"Gentlemen, you are in my court and will follow my instructions," said Sir Alfred calmly. "Now please, take your seats at one of the tables and begin your work. There are writing utensils and additional paper if you should need them. I will not proceed with this case until the assignment is complete."

The three Roses stood before Sir Alfred: Mr. Rose with the red turban, red in the face sputtering and muttering, Mr. Rose with the black turban arms crossed tightly against his chest drumming his fingers on his arms, and Mr. Rose with the white turban shaking from head to toe. None were willing to move from the front of the courtroom.

"Gentlemen, I will not proceed on any ruling in this case until the questions are complete. Of course you may choose not to answer them and then I will ask you to leave my courtroom. The choice is yours," Sir Alfred said with a calm professional air.

The Roses stood there silently, glaring at Sir Alfred. Then Mr. Rose with the black turban muttered, "Let's just do this quickly and be done with each other." Each man turned and took a different route to the round table closest to the courtroom door. They sat down. No one spoke. Each stared down at the table.

"Now, Miss Isabella, let us watch what happens next. This could be very interesting," said Sir Alfred with a confident smile.

"Nothing is going to happen, Sir Alfred. I wager they sit there for one minute before one of them leaves," said Isabella. She did not know one man in her village who would ever answer any of those questions.

"Maybe – maybe not," Sir Alfred replied. "Shall we wager an ice cream cone?"

Isabella laughed at the thought of the proper Sir Alfred licking an ice cream cone. "Why, Sir Alfred, I would not have thought you liked ice cream. It is so messy," giggled Isabella. "And yes, I would like to wager. My favorite flavor is chocolate."

"Mine is pecan sandy. There is a wonderful stall in the market place that has the most delicious ice cream. I used to take the king there when he was a small boy. It has been a good while since I was there."

"Well, let us get ready to go. They should be leaving momentarily," laughed the girl happily.

"Well, you watch them. I have some papers to look over. Let me know when you notice anything." Sir Alfred was soon engrossed in official court documents.

Isabella watched the three Roses who looked this way and that way and this way and that way. They sighed, they huffed; they puffed and sighed again. Still no one left the table. After an hour passed, Isabella's eyes grew wide. "Sir Alfred, look!" she exclaimed.

"Now isn't that interesting? I thought it might take more time than this," said Sir Alfred putting down his document and looking at the back of the court room.

Mr. Rose with the black turban was actually talking. He spoke less than fifteen seconds, but the other two Roses looked at him. There was a very long pause, and he said something else. This time Mr. Rose with the white turban gave a very, very slight nod. Isabella almost did not notice it.

"I wish I could hear what they were saying," said Isabella curiously. "I cannot believe they are actually talking instead of yelling or fidgeting."

"Well, to be precise, one of them is talking and the other two appear to be listening."

The three men sat in silence. Mr. Rose with the red turban began tapping his fingers on the table – harder and harder, faster and faster. Isabella was sure he would jump up from the table and dash out the door any second. Then he looked at Mr. Rose with the white turban and spoke directly to him. Mr. Rose with the white turban turned a bright red.

"Well, he has insulted him again. It's over now," said Isabella.

"Child, assumptions can be dangerous and are often wrong. Let us watch," Sir Alfred advised.

Mr. Rose with the white turban seemed to regain his composure. He sat there for a full minute and then reached out to gently touch the other man's arm for just a second. Mr. Rose with the red turban pulled back startled.

"Oh my," breathed Isabella amazed.

Silence again. The three men appeared to be struggling with what to do next. Then Mr. Rose with the black turban spoke again and the other two nodded. Each took paper and charcoal and began to write. After thinking and writing and thinking and writing for some time, the three placed their writing implements down. No one spoke. Finally, Mr. Rose with the white turban took a deep breath, looked at Mr. Rose with the red turban, and read something from his sheet. Mr. Rose with the black turban nodded. Then Mr. Rose with the black turban read something from his papers. Soon each of the men was taking a turn reading from their papers.

Isabella noticed the pauses between comments were shorter and the comments themselves seemed longer. Soon the three men were involved in a halting conversation. The longer Isabella watched them, the more animated they became. At one point Mr. Rose in the white turban said something and the other two laughed.

"What in the world is happening?" asked Isabella in amazement.

Sir Alfred replied, "They are answering the questions. As soon as Mr. Rose in the black turban gave his first answer to 'What is already working?' his focus changed from what's wrong to what's right. Mr. Rose with the white turban was hooked with the second comment. You saw him nod. Mr. Rose with the red turban shifted when he found something positive to say to Mr. Rose with the white turban."

"I still do not understand, Sir Alfred. All they did was answer one question."

"It is a very powerful question, Isabella. People tend to focus only on the negative and forget all that is positive. I have found there is always something of value in every relationship or situation. Of course, you may have to look very, very, very, hard to find it, but my experience has been there is always something of value there. However small it may be, once you find the first thing that is working, others seem to follow."

Just then Mr. Rose with the white turban reached out to hug Mr. Rose with the red turban. Isabella put her hand to her chest. "Oh my," she said. The men began writing again this time with even more energy. After three more rounds of discussion, the men put down their instruments, stood and shook hands with one another, and approached the judge's table.

"May we speak, Sir Alfred?" asked Mr. Rose with the black turban.

"Of course, gentlemen," replied Sir Alfred with a courtroom nod.

"Sir, we wish to withdraw our petition," announced Mr. Rose with the red turban. "After going through each of the questions, we have discovered there are many things that are working quite well in our business. We simply lost sight of them."

"I agree, Sir Alfred," piped in Mr. Rose with the white turban. "We really do all want the same thing – to take care of our customers, each other and ourselves. We have worked out a plan that builds on the strengths each of us brings to the business and how together we can be more successful." Mr. Rose with the white turban was smiling.

"We want to thank you for insisting we answer your questions, Sir Alfred. Who would have thought such simple questions could bring us to this point. We are amazed, Sir. You are truly a wise man," said Mr. Rose with the black turban. He bowed as did the other two men.

"Case dismissed, gentlemen. This court is adjourned," said Sir Alfred slamming the gavel to the table with a bang.

As the three Roses left the courtroom talking away, Isabella said, "Sir Alfred, I think you were lucky this time. I suspect most people would have chosen to leave rather than answer those questions."

"Well, child, I use those questions in every case that comes before me whether a husband and wife wish to end their union, a child wishes to have new parents, businesses want to declare insolvency or neighbors argue over property lines. Most of the time people chose to answer the questions as the Roses did, and most of the time they discover a positive way to work out their disagreements." With a shake of his head, Sir Alfred said, "I confess – in the beginning when I was experimenting with this approach – I was surprised at how well the questions worked. Now I know they just do." Sir Alfred stood and offered his arm to the girl. "Shall we go get that ice cream cone?" he asked.

"Yes, sir," Isabella said smiling as she took his arm.

SIR ALFRED'S ENGLIGHTENED QUESTIONS

The courtroom was empty. The papers left behind by the Roses lay quietly on the table. Though the air was still, the papers began to rustle, then they began to quiver and then to shake until the Rose's responses fell from the page. The parchments sighed with satisfaction knowing they had done well yet another day.

All that was left behind were Sir Alfred's five enlightened questions:

What is already working?
What, specifically, causes it to work?
What is our objective/goal/vision?
What would be the benefits to all concerned in reaching our goals?
What might we do better?

Through the courtroom window, three squirrels entered to finish their afternoon chores. They quickly rolled each parchment into a tidy scroll, tied each with a black and white ribbon and brushed the table clean of words. Satisfied with their work, they deposited the scrolls unto Sir Alfred's desk to be used another day and with a wink were out the window onto an afternoon game of hide and seek.

PLAYING HOOKY

The next day Sir Alfred and Isabella returned to the royal offices and were busy from morning through dusk. In the first meeting of the day, Sir Alfred received trade emissaries from the Western Province who wished to establish business with the Eastern Province. Late morning the Royal Advisor reviewed billing correspondence from vendors who supplied the castle. In the afternoon Sir Alfred mediated several cases brought before the court by the citizens of the kingdom.

As Isabella followed Sir Alfred about she discovered the Royal Advisor addressed a myriad of tasks each day – some mighty, some mundane. She also observed that Sir Alfred brought dignity, intense curiosity and logic to each task at hand. He was also respectful of every individual he met without regard to status, age or temperament.

On the last morning of the week, Sir Alfred met with key spiritual leaders to discuss religious tolerance within the kingdom. After the meeting ended Sir Alfred began clearing his desk and said, "Miss Isabella, it has been a long week. What would you say if we played hooky for the rest of the day and went to my favorite spot on the lake? It is filled with fish."

"Why, Sir Alfred, I would never have imagined you liked to fish!" said Isabella in surprise.

"Is that so?" said the Esteemed Advisor as he dusted his desk and put out a clean pad of paper and new writing tools. "I wonder why that is?" he said with a wink.

"I would love to go," giggled Isabella.

"Come along then," he said. In no time they were armed with fishing poles, a large blanket and a basket of food. They left the interior of the castle and came to the lake of ancient turtles. As Sir Alfred stepped into the water, a turtle rose to meet his footstep. "We are off to the willows," the Advisor announced as he sat down on the massive shell.

"Ah, yessss," hissed the turtle as it began paddling away from the castle with Sir Alfred on his back.

"Come along, Miss Isabella," Sir Alfred called back to the girl.

As Isabella was about to step into the water, another giant shell floated to the surface. "It is an honor to escort you, young mistressss," wheezed the second turtle. In seconds the girl and old man were riding the turtles side by side, the castle becoming a distant spot on the horizon. They soon came to a beautiful stretch of lakeshore. Dozens of weeping willow trees lined the banks, their long branches swaying rhythmically in the wind. Dragonflies skittered along the surface of the water, and yellow and white butterflies fluttered in the leaves of the willows. All was peaceful and calm.

"Thank you, gentlemen," Sir Alfred said to their escorts. "Please come fetch us at dusk." The turtles sank beneath the water with barely a ripple.

As they approached the trees, Isabella heard, "Welcome, beloved son. It has been a long time since your last visit."

"It has been. I am delighted to be in your presence, Mother."

"Come and rest in my shade, dear boy. Please bring your young friend too."

Isabella was speechless. Sir Alfred was talking to a tree. It was the biggest, most beautiful weeping willow she had ever seen, but it was a tree. The willow graciously opened her low hanging branches wide to reveal a broad bed of soft green grass that ran to the water's edge.

"Thank you, Mother," said Sir Alfred as he spread his blanket out next to the water. Matter-of-factly he said, "Miss Isabella, I believe you would be more comfortable if you joined me on the blanket, but of course if you would rather stand there gaping, go ahead." Isabella scurried to join Sir Alfred under the branches. "Mother, I would like to introduce you to Miss Isabella. She is visiting for a time. Miss Isabella, this is Mother Willow," Sir Alfred said smiling.

"Welcome, child. I am so pleased my boy has brought a friend to visit," sang Mother Willow as she brushed her branches against the Royal Advisor and child.

"I am delighted to meet you, Madame," stammered Isabella.

"Well, you two play nicely. I will just enjoy having you here with me," said the old tree sighing with contentment. Sir Alfred patted the tree trunk and readied himself to fish. First he took off his coat, folded it carefully, and placed it on the blanket. Then he removed his boots and placed them neatly next to his coat. Finally, he sat down and removed his socks, rolled each into a neat little ball and tucked one into each boot.

"Almost ready," he said as he precisely rolled his pant cuffs up to his knees. "Now I am ready," he said as he picked up his pole, baited it with a piece of honey bread and expertly flicked the line out onto the water. "I brought lots of food. Please feel free to use anything in the basket. The fish love it all."

Isabella reached into the hamper and pulled out a slice of apple, put it on her hook and dropped her line into the water. The Curiosa was blazing hot, and Isabella had a million questions she wanted to ask. They remained unspoken for they were of a personal nature. As open as Sir Alfred had been in their week together about his work, the Esteemed Advisor had not shared anything of his private life.

"I understand the king would like you to visit the town of Kronos in search of a special book," Sir Alfred said as he watched the line in the water.

"I told him I would not go," said Isabella, her body suddenly rigid. "He said I did not have to. He said I could stay in the castle as long as I wanted to and that you would take care of me." She started to jerk her pole from side to side.

"I think you would be better served by letting the line drift," the old man advised, not taking his eyes from the water. "Yes, Stefan did say that," said Sir Alfred. His pole bent and then went slack. When he pulled it in, the bread was gone. He calmly baited the line again, this time with a strawberry. "That was fast. It seems the fish are hungry today."

Isabella barely heard his words. "Sir Alfred, I don't have to go, do I? I mean, I have not been a bother to you, have I?" she asked anxiously.

"You have been no bother at all. I have enjoyed your presence tremendously. One would say you are very good company."

Isabella breathed a sigh of relief. "I am so glad. I thought you were going to send me away." She raised her pole and saw the apple was gone. She reached into the hamper and pulled out a grape. As she baited her line, she said shyly, "I feel safe with you. Actually, it is the safest I have felt in a very, very long time even before I came to the Lower World."

"Why thank you, child," he said and then closed his eyes as he leaned against the trunk of the willow tree. When he opened them, he said, "I grew up in Kronos. Did the king tell you that?"

"No, he did not!" said Isabella surprised. "Is it a nice town?" she asked.

"An interesting town, I would say. I loved going to school there. It was where I found my calling."

"What do you mean?" asked Isabella turning to look at the old man. He looked very peaceful and relaxed holding his pole – the line drifting ever so gently in the lapping water.

"My parents died when I was very young. I had no other relatives and was sent to an orphanage in Kronos." Sir Alfred pulled his line in, baited it with pumpkin and cast it back out. "There were so many children in the home, so many. Because I was such a quiet child and nondescript, I was overlooked. One day a teacher commented that she liked a little story I had composed. I rather enjoyed the attention and wrote another story. She liked that one too and read it to the class. Everyone clapped when she finished. It felt wonderful. Then she announced there was going to be a story contest. The winner would get a medal. Well, I wanted that medal, so I worked on my story very, very, very hard."

"Did you win?" asked Isabella, irritated because there was a tug on her line. She could care less about the fish. Sir Alfred was the one who held her interest.

"Yes, I did. The other children and teachers were most impressed, but more important to me than the medal, was the fact that I hit upon the formula for being noticed – doing well in school. I put all my energies into my studies from that time on and was rewarded nicely for my efforts."

A voice could be heard whispering, "Alfred found out he was smart…very smart."

"Did you hear that, Sir Alfred?" asked Isabella looking around. "Who said that?"

"They did, I imagine," Sir Alfred said, one long thin finger pointing into the water. Isabella leaned over to peer into the lake and saw a huge school of fish swimming right along the edge of the bank. Red fish, blue fish, orange fish, pink fish. Dozens of fish were swimming in one direction, and then, as if on cue, all turned and swam back in the opposite direction.

"You mean *they* said that?"

"We did. We did," gurgled the fish, their scales flashing like brilliant jewels.

Isabella sat back startled. "Who are they, and how do they know you were smart?" she asked.

Sir Alfred chuckled. "Miss Isabella, I would like you to meet my cousins. I read those early stories to them. I showed them my medal. I told them about my marks in school and the awards I received," Sir Alfred replied. "They said I was very good company for them."

"Sir Alfred, why are we trying to catch your cousins?" asked Isabella horrified.

"What on earth gave you the idea we were trying to catch them?" he said both eyebrows going up.

"Fishing poles, bait? It seems quite logical to me."

"Dear one, I brought the fish treats. They love all sorts of food. Usually we play our version of Snapping Dragon to see who has the quickest reflexes – them or me."

"Funny Al! Funny Al! laughed the fish swirling around and around in a rainbow circle.

"As I was saying before they interrupted me," said Sir Alfred trying to look stern but scooping up a great handful of garlic toasted bread crumbs and throwing them into the water, "from that point on I excelled in school."

"Thank you, cousin. Thank you, cousin," chorused the fish as they swam bumping and bouncing into one another as they gobbled up their treats.

"Did that help you find a new family, Sir Alfred? Excelling in school?" Isabella could not imagine living in an orphanage nor having fish as cousins.

"Actually, by then I was a bit old; most people wanted a baby." A shadow of sadness passed over Sir Alfred's face. "But I had a family of sorts. In time I was the oldest child in the orphanage and took it upon myself to watch over the younger children. It became very satisfying to me, and I thought it was very important work. So between my studies and caring for the children, I was very busy."

The fish chanted, "So busy! So busy!" Sir Alfred nodded tossing bits of chocolate covered cherries into the water.

"When did you leave?"

"That was quite interesting actually. I was there for so long and did so well with the children that the staff came to depend on me more and more. When the headmaster of the orphanage retired, I simply assumed his position. It was quite natural."

"How did you come to be the king's advisor then?" asked Isabella all interest in fishing and feeding gone.

Sir Alfred smiled, "The Curiosa suits you, Isabella. I love your questions." Isabella blushed; Sir Alfred patted her hand and continued, "The King and Queen, Stefan and Setine's parents, were touring the provinces and decided to visit the orphanage. They said the orphanage had quite a wonderful reputation for efficiency and order, and they wanted to see it for themselves. The King was very impressed and asked if I would like to assist him in managing the kingdom."

"And here you are."

"Actually, I said no," replied Sir Alfred. The old gentleman reached into the basket and drew out a flagon of lemonade. Opening the flask he asked, "Would you care for a drink, Miss Isabella?" When the girl shook her head no Sir Alfred nodded, tipped the flagon back and drank deeply. After returning the lemonade to the hamper, he said, "I felt very, very responsible for the children of the orphanage. I just did not believe anyone could care for them as I did. So, I declined."

"He was so responsible. So responsible," sighed the fish settling heavily on the lake bottom.

"But you are here."

"Well, after they left, the Queen and I began a correspondence. The Queen is a unique woman. Her letters often left me baffled and confused, and I was not accustomed to that."

"Poor Alfred was confused. Confused," mumbled the fish, still moored to the lake bottom – all color now drained from their scales.

"What did she write?"

Sir Alfred smiled shaking his head as he said, "Well, she asked me many questions and they were generally about feelings. It was quite perplexing to me because I had no regard for things emotional. I lived in a world of facts, analysis, logic, order. Had she not been the Queen, I simply would not have responded to her. Frankly, I thought the letters were very inappropriate."

"No feelings. No feelings," whispered the fish hidden in lake water suddenly brown and murky.

Sir Alfred stroked his chin thoughtfully. After some moments with only the sound of the wind rustling through the willow leaves, Sir Alfred continued. "The Queen was quite wise, actually. I very much needed to reflect on those 'inappropriate topics' though I did not realize that until much later. But I was very intrigued by one question in particular. She asked if I could do something different than take care of the children, what might that be? Well, I realized I was a bit bored and wanted to take care of something bigger than an orphanage; I wanted to take care of a kingdom! I was good at organizing things and I wanted the challenge and the recognition. I was quite ambitious without even knowing it."

"And so you came to court."

"Yes. I found someone very capable to run the orphanage and came to court."

"And were loved and respected and held in high esteem by all," Isabella said happily clapping her hands.

Sir Alfred started laughing. Mother Willow started laughing. The fish started laughing so hard little waves splashed onto the picnickers. "That was hardly the case, Miss Isabella! I think I was described by those at court as controlling, a know-it-all, overbearing and bossy, and those were the nice descriptors!" Sir Alfred actually snorted he was laughing so hard.

"You were a bossy boy! Bossy boy! Bossy, bossy, bossy boy," the fish retorted suddenly energized zigzagging back and forth and back and forth along the shoreline.

"Oh, Sir Alfred, I simply cannot imagine that," said Isabella. "Are you teasing me?"

"Not in the least. Those words described me quite accurately," he said wiping a laugh tear from his eye.

"Well, you certainly don't seem that way now," said Isabella. "I don't like to think of you as controlling. Controlling people scare me."

"Well, people can change, Miss Isabella. I certainly do understand you not liking those who are controlling. Many in the kingdom bristled under my authority and to be honest, in time, I didn't like myself very much, but I did not know any other way to be."

"No like. No like. No like," lamented the fish, their scales coal black.

"Thank you, cousins," Sir Albert said to the fish. "I think we get the point."

"What did the King say about all this?"

"He was gone to war a great deal of the time and one day did not return," sighed Sir Alfred. "I believe that is why I felt so responsible in caring for the kingdom."

"What about the Queen? What did she say?"

"The Queen was unusual in that her family came first. She had young babies to care for and chose to be fully occupied with them. When Stefan and Setine were a bit older, she looked about the kingdom and was quite shocked by the coldness she discovered. I was running things well but everything was just so cold."

"Then he came to me," Mother Willow said as she lovingly swept her branches across Sir Alfred's shoulders and face. "You were such a tired man, so unhappy, so empty. You didn't know why or what to do to make it better."

"So true, Mother, so very, very true," Sir Alfred said softly.

"The Queen sent him to me, to us." Mother's branches rustled in the wind pointing to the other willow trees that edged the river bank. "We welcomed him every day. It took a long time before the noise in his mind quieted so he could hear us, but each day his hearing became better."

"Well, in my logical world, trees had nothing to offer me," said Sir Alfred as he raised his face to receive the soft caresses of the willow. "How mistaken I was."

"We loved to give him shelter from the sun and the rain. We loved to tickle his tired body with our leaves. We loved to sing to him and tell him ancient stories, mysterious stories, fantastic stories of a time when the trees ruled the land. We just loved our boy."

Sir Alfred smiled sweetly. "I loved the stories and simply resting with the trees. I love my intellect and sense of order, Miss Isabella, but the trees taught me there was more than just intellect and order. I did nothing for them – no organizing, no fixing, no mediating, no discovering, no analyzing, nothing – and they loved me."

"My sweet son," sighed the willow as her branches embraced Sir Alfred.

Sir Alfred smiled. "Now I come here to rest when the world is too much with me or when I think I have all the answers or try to control things I have no control over."

"But Sir Alfred, you never seem to control. You ask more questions than anyone I know!"

"I had to learn to ask questions. Do you know who gave me the Curiosa?" Isabella shook her head no. "The Queen; it has been in her family for generations. She thought it would be helpful to me and indeed it has been."

"Oh, Sir Alfred, how could you have given it to me then? I am not worthy of such a gift," exclaimed Isabella. "Please let me return it to you."

"No, Isabella. No, Isabella. No, no, no!" the fish exclaimed, their scales bright red.

"I agree with them, dear. It was mine only temporarily, and I have learned its lessons well. It is now yours; it is back in the line of queens."

"It is yours! Yours! Yours!" cheered the fish, returning to their blazing shades of pink, red, blue, yellow, green and orange, as they darted back and forth along the shoreline.

Sir Alfred smiled at his cousins as he tossed crumbled blueberry muffins into the water. After brushing his hands off, Sir Alfred turned to the girl and said, "Miss Isabella, I want to speak of Kronos again. I know it may not seem logical for you to go there but sometimes one must step out in faith and do what does not seem logical. I would like for you to reconsider."

Sitting there in the safety of the willow's embrace, soothed by Sir Alfred's presence and the charm of the fish, Isabella felt the tiniest, tiniest, tiniest longing in her heart for adventure. "One step, Isabella," Mother Willow whispered. "Just take one step."

Though her heart was beating wildly, Isabella asked, "If I go to Kronos and then change my mind, may I come back to you, Sir Alfred?"

"Of course, you can, child."

Staring at the old man Isabella thought *I am so tired of being frightened all the time, so very tired. Could something good come from going to Kronos? Sir Alfred thinks so. I will trust him. I will trust him. He promised he would never lie to me.* She looked at the willow lovingly sheltering them both; she watched the fish gracefully swimming back and forth, a moving rainbow in the water, and said, "I will go to Kronos."

CURIOSITY

The shift charge-nurse came in carrying a saline bag. She swapped out the empty pouch hanging high above the woman's bed for the full one. After attaching the bag to the line running into the woman's arm, she watched the droplets drip slowly making sure the line was clear. She moved on to check the other lines running in and out of the woman's body – lines carrying morphine for pain, antibiotics for infection, and platelets to build up her white blood count. Next she turned her attention to the machines buzzing, whirring, clicking and beeping and charted heart rate, CSF levels, temperature, brain wave activity, blood pressure, oxygen levels, and urine output. When her checks and notations were complete, the nurse stood beside the woman's side and simply looked at her.

"I pray for you when I leave here. I really want you to make it – for your sake and for your family," the nurse said kindly as she gently held the woman's hand. "But I also want to ask you where you go. I wonder if you're here and can feel what your body is going through – if you know what we do each day to help you. Or does your spirit go away to the Divine, and if it does what do you see? Or do you travel to see your children and friends? Forgive me if I am nosey, but I love to think of such things." She patted the woman's hand and said kindly, "So you need to come back to tell me."

✦
THE KRONOS MANAGERS

As morning dawned, the haunting songs of the doves woke Isabella. *I don't want to get up* she thought lying in bed listening to the birds. *Why did I agree to go to Kronos?* She pulled her covers over her head. Shortly thereafter, Sir Alfred came to fetch her. "Time to get ready, Miss Isabella. Your guides are waiting," he said.

"I have changed my mind, Sir Alfred," mumbled Isabella under the covers. "I had very bad dreams last night. They scared me. I don't want to go."

"I see," the old gentleman said solemnly.

Isabella peeked over the cover and sighed, "I felt very brave yesterday. I do not feel brave today."

The stately gentleman nodded. "I understand." He stood staring into her eyes.

"Please give me a moment, Sir Alfred. I need to think," the little girl sighed.

"Take all the time you need, Miss Isabella. I will await you in the hall."

Isabella rose slowly and changed into her woolen smock and village slippers. After she fastened the Curiosa to her gown, she sat back on her bed. *Sir Alfred looked so sad. I want him to be proud of me. I will go and come back and he will be proud of me.* Isabella sighed, slipped off the bed and opened the door to find Sir Alfred waiting patiently.

"What have you decided, Miss Isabella?"

"I will at least go to Kronos," said Isabella quietly.

Sir Alfred nodded. "That is all we ask. I will lead you to your guides." Isabella did not look at the Royal Advisor nor speak to him as they made their way through the castle to the outer walls and across the

133

drawbridge for fear she'd change her mind. When Sir Alfred handed her a satchel of clothing and food, he said, "Good luck, Miss Isabella. I will miss you." He bowed, took Isabella's hand into his own and kissed it. "I look forward to your return, dear child."

Moved by Sir Alfred's tenderness, Isabella raised her eyes to his. "Thank you for allowing me to spend these days with you," she said softly, "I will miss you too." She straightened her thin shoulders with forced resolve and said, "What am I to do now?"

"Just follow your guides," replied Sir Alfred.

"Where are they?" Isabella asked looking about.

Sir Alfred smiled and said, "They have been singing to you all morning. There they are." The Advisor pointed to the tree closest to them. There in the lower branches were the two mourning doves that had escorted Isabella to the king's dining room when she first arrived in the castle. She had no doubt they were the same ones who had awoken her earlier that morning. "They are eager to go," Sir Alfred said.

With that, the doves flew off. Isabella hesitated for just a moment then ran after the birds. She turned back once to wave to Sir Alfred then dashed down the road. In minutes, the girl was standing in the middle of a beautiful meadow. The field was filled with brilliant red poppies, yellow lilies, blue daisies and pink and white wisterias stretching as far as the child could see. Each time the wind blew, the colors rearranged themselves into different patterns. Isabella was in a flower kaleidoscope.

Then the wind, scented with lavender and mint, gently drew her face upward. Isabella had never seen a sky so big, so blue and so clear; it took her breath away. Though she felt dwarfed by the vast openness of land and sky, in that moment she was not afraid. In fact the openness soothed her anxious heart. The faint cooing of the doves broke her reverie. She looked about and spotted them headed for a lone tree in the distance. "Please wait for me. I am not as fast as you," she cried, breaking into a run. The flowers opened a path nodding and bobbing in encouragement as she sped through the field.

Isabella was relieved when she saw the birds settle onto the tree, but as soon as she reached them they opened their wings, caught a puff of wind, and sailed away on the breeze. Isabella ran through the meadow keeping them in her sights. So it went for the next three days, a game of tag: the doves flying some distance until they found a perch to rest, Isabella scampering to catch them, the doves flying on to their next roost and Isabella following. When it came time to eat, Isabella unpacked the provisions Cook had prepared for her. When evening fell, the doves lead Isabella to thick stands of pine that sheltered her from the wind and provided a soft carpet upon which to sleep. When morning came, the game of tag resumed.

On the third day, the doves flew over a road and on into the woods. Unlike the dirt roads in Isabella's village, this one was covered with gravel. *This must go somewhere important* she thought. Distracted by the paving, she had taken her eyes off her guides. Now she looked about to see which way they had flown, but the doves had disappeared.

She waited a few seconds for their return. *Where are they? Why are they taking so long to come back?* A wave of panic swept over her as she stood alone on the road. *They have left me.* Isabella then took a slow deep breath and then another and then another as Sir Alfred had taught her. *They all said help would be available. I just need to pay attention. They would not lie to me.* She closed her eyes and took three more deep breaths. When she opened her eyes she felt better and looked around. At that moment she noticed a small sign set back a bit from the road with an arrow pointing the way. The sign was marked **Kronos**. Isabella sighed with relief and began to walk. Soon the gravel road gave way to cobblestones which gave way to a grand road of large granite slabs. The girl smiled. *I am on the right path.*

Within the hour, Isabella was in the middle of a bustling town. Unlike her village where market was held once a week in the square, the streets of Kronos were lined with permanent stalls and shops bursting with goods ranging from cloth and housewares to lumber and tools. As she walked it appeared the streets were laid in a grid pattern around the central market place. One street was filled with market stands overflowing with vegetables, fruits, meats and breads. The next accommodated the guilds – their banners identifying skilled millers, smiths, carpenters, weavers, masons, barbers and shoemakers. The third was filled with storefronts overflowing with wares from distant lands: fine woolens, silks, carpets woven with threads of silver and gold, pearls and perfumes, and pungent spices. Wherever Isabella walked she observed workers busy sweeping the streets, repairing carts, brushing down horses; assisting customers.

Though the streets were full, it was surprisingly quiet. No one was yelling or laughing as was common in Isabella's village. Most people appeared to be dressed in their best clothes wearing official expressions and everyone appeared to be in a great hurry. She noticed that occasionally people would stop for just a moment, look at their wrists then scurry on.

So many grownups she thought *where are all the children?* Instantly she saw an orderly parade of school children marching down the street toward her. They looked like a gaggle of geese; the tallest students leading the way followed by the younger children with the tiniest bringing up the rear. Except for their size, the students looked identical – identical brown tunics, belts, leggings for the boys; brown ankle length kirtles for the girls; identical caps, identical satchels, and identical frowns. Something distracted the two smallest students at the end of the line, a boy and girl of four. They started to giggle and began to push each other out of line. As the children marched past a worker busy polishing the wagon wheels of a laundry cart, the man tapped the two little ones on the shoulder and shook his head no. They immediately fell into the orderly line with the same frown as the older students. The man nodded his head in approval.

"Oh my," muttered Isabella.

As she continued to walk the streets, the girl was struck by the fact that all the whitewashed houses were identical in size and shape, capped with the same neatly thatched roofs. The spotless cottages were spaced evenly from one another; all had the same gardens, the same flowers and the same trees. The only difference from one cottage to the next was the color of the door and matching shutters – be they blue, green, red or yellow – and the homeowner's name plate. Isabella noticed the names were in alphabetical order.

Now that she reached the town, Isabella did not know how to find the Mayor. She wandered up and down the streets until she found herself in front of a tall brick tower dominating that section of the town. At the top of the tower was an extremely large clock which at that moment struck four. Everyone stopped for just a second and checked their wrists.

"Ah, Isabella, I have been keeping an eye out for you. I expected you *yesterday*. Welcome to Kronos," said a clipped voice behind her. Isabella turned around quickly and saw a very short thin man formally dressed and wearing a huge gold medallion around his neck. "I am Mayor Roget," he said clicking his heels together.

Isabella curtsied. "I am pleased to meet you, sir," she said, "But why were you expecting me yesterday? How did you even know I was coming?"

"We have an excellent communication network that links us to other parts of the kingdom. Sir Alfred notified us of your departure and we know it is precisely a two day walk from the castle. Where have you been?" he asked curtly.

"I apologize for being late, sir. I did not know I was expected, so I took my time enjoying the walk. I lost track of time actually," Isabella murmured feeling she had committed a terrible transgression by being tardy.

"Hmmm, walking for enjoyment, that is not a very productive activity," said the Mayor drumming his fingers on his crossed arms. "Your delay caused me to have to rearrange my schedule, quite an inconvenience, quite an inconvenience, most inconsiderate." The Mayor glanced down at his wrist. "Let us go to my office. We have work to do."

Walking quickly to keep pace with the tiny city official, Isabella said, "Sir, I am curious. Why do people keep looking at their wrists?"

"Why, they are checking their timepieces to make sure they are on time. What an odd question," said the Mayor looking at Isabella strangely. He glanced at Isabella's arm. "Where is your timepiece, girl?"

Isabella felt her cheeks getting hot. "I don't have a timepiece, sir. I have never seen one on a wrist before. I do not believe anyone in my village has seen such a thing," she stuttered. The Mayor came to a quick stop and looked at Isabella dumbfounded. "But how do you manage to complete your work on time?"

"I don't know, sir," said Isabella haltingly.

"How irresponsible!" snapped the Mayor. "How slovenly! Now I understand your disrespectful attitude towards the schedules of others."

"Mr. Mayor, I am sorry. Truly I am," said Isabella anxiously.

"I am not interested in excuses, Isabella. There is no more critical task than to manage time and work well. Time is a limited commodity. You should know that!" The Mayor was obviously agitated and spoke more quickly with each word. "It is imperative to get to our appointed meetings on time. It is vital that we finish our tasks on time so we can move to the next activity quickly." Now he was waving his hands in the air and people were beginning to stare at them. "How can you function without a timepiece? Without monitoring your time, how do you manage your efficiency and effectiveness? How do you maximize your productivity? How do you manage all your important responsibilities? How do you accomplish all that needs to be done! Your life must be chaos!" By this time the little official was so agitated he was shouting.

Isabella was mortified. As luck would have it, the clock tower chimed four times again followed by a single lower tone. The Mayor immediately dropped his arms to look at his timepiece. "Four fifteen on the dot. The Tower of Time has been precise to the second for more than a hundred years. We citizens of Kronos are very proud of that." The Mayor seemed to be soothed by the chiming of the clock.

"That is quite impressive," Isabella agreed bobbing her head up and down vigorously, grateful for the distraction. "Very impressive," she said again, happy to deflect attention off her own deficiencies.

"Well, here is my office. Please follow me." With crisp short steps, Mayor Roget marched into a wood paneled room and went directly to a massive desk that filled the room. As he settled in his chair, he motioned for Isabella to sit on a tiny stool in front of his desk. When she sat down, she could barely see the Mayor. The little man folded his hands on the enormous desk top and said, "I only scheduled thirty minutes for our meeting. It is almost up, so I must speak quickly. I have other important work to do." Isabella was miserable. It was obvious the Mayor disapproved of her.

Mayor Roget continued on quickly, "I understand you are pursuing a book for the king. A very nasty fellow came through our town several weeks ago. He told Timex, one of our citizens, he had a priceless book in his possession – in fact, a royal book. He said he had come upon hard times and was willing to sell it for a great sum of money. Timex went to see the book in hopes of negotiating its purchase."

"Was he successful?" asked Isabella hopefully.

"No, he was not. The fellow was so unsavory Timex broke off discussions with him. In fact, he filed a complaint with our constable stating that when he asked to hold the book and examine its pages, the fellow refused. When Timex insisted he had to examine the manuscript, the man became belligerent and threatened him physically. Naturally Timex left immediately. The constable went to confront the man, but the fellow had disappeared."

"Oh, dear," murmured Isabella. She was so taken aback by his last remarks she didn't know what next to say. Then the Curiosa started to warm her shoulder. *I need to ask a question, I need to ask a question* thought Isabella. *What question?* "Mayor, do you have any idea where the man went?" popped out of Isabella's mouth though she sincerely hoped he did not have the answer.

"Actually, I do not," the Mayor said as Isabella heard a bell ring outside his door. The Mayor looked at his timepiece. "We are done," he said. "My next appointment is here. By the way, on your way out, look at the award the king gave us last year. It is posted next to the front door. We are very proud of it."

Isabella rose from the tiny stool, startled to be dismissed so abruptly with so little information. As she walked through the office doorway, the Curiosa became very hot. Summoning all her courage, Isabella turned and asked, "Mayor, where can I find Timex? I would like to speak with him about the book. Any information would be helpful in my search."

Surprised by the girl's question, the Mayor paused for a second looking at her. "I can appreciate the need for more information," he said thoughtfully. "Having the right information can cut down on the time it takes to do a task correctly. Good thinking, Isabella," the Mayor said tapping his finger against his temple. "Timex works down the street in the Treasury Building. He is the king's money manager in this province. His counsel is much sought after so he is often in meetings

139

from morning to night. I do not know how successful you will be in making an appointment to see him."

"Thank you for your time, Mayor," Isabella said as she left his office. The heat from the pendant was now a warm throb. As she was about to leave the building, Isabella paused to read a plaque posted by the door. It said:

CONGRATULATIONS CITIZENS OF KRONOS
FOR WORK WELL DONE!
YOU ARE AWARDED THE ROYAL TITLE:

MIGHTIEST MANAGERS IN THE LOWER WORLD

✦

TIMEX

Once on the street, Isabella stood startled and perplexed by her abrupt dismissal by the Mayor. *The king is sorely mistaken if he thinks the citizens of Kronos are very helpful* she thought forlornly. She stood with her back against the wall of the mayor's building and watched busy men and women walk up and down the street entering and leaving the huge stone buildings that lined the boulevard. No one looked approachable. After watching the flow of people for some moments, Isabella took a deep breath and stepped into the moving throng asking a woman walking past her for directions to the Treasury Building. "I am on my way to a meeting," the woman replied crisply, barely slowing her walk. "Come, I don't have time to stop to talk, but I will be passing the Treasury Building and can point it out. You will have to keep up with me for I do not have time to dawdle."

"Thank you, Madame. I walk fast," Isabella said as she ran to keep pace with the woman. Several minutes later, the woman pointed to the Treasury Building and quickly continued down the street without saying goodbye.

When Isabella entered the Treasury Building no one seemed to notice her. People were busy moving from desk to desk and room to room. Many people were clustered in groups deep in discussion. Others were writing furiously in leather bound books. It seemed to Isabella important work was being carried out in this building. The girl approached a man and asked where she might find Timex. The man pointed to a hallway and said, "At the end, in the corner office." Before Isabella could ask how to schedule a meeting with Timex, the man was talking with someone else.

"Did I hear someone mention my name?" a booming voice asked.

Isabella turned around and saw a tall man break away from a group that had been poring over papers on a desk. The man was elegantly dressed in a black silk suit and sparkling white shirt. His silver hair was combed back and tied neatly with a leather cord. Timex had an unmistakable air of confidence and power.

Isabella automatically curtsied, "Yes, sir, I did. My name is Isabella, sir. I am so sorry to bother you but Mayor Roget suggested I see you."

"The Mayor you say? Well, if the Mayor sent you, it must be important. Give me a few seconds to conclude my work here," he said in a booming voice. Timex went back to the group, issued a series of quick instructions and returned to Isabella. "Follow me to where we can speak more privately," he said. Isabella followed Timex into his office. It was twice the size of the Mayor's office with windows on two sides. Shelves from floor to ceiling covered the other two walls. His desk was even bigger than the Mayor's. Once again, Isabella was motioned to sit on a small stool in front of the desk.

"You are in luck," Timex said smiling broadly. "I have ten minutes before I leave for the castle. I am presenting the monthly tax accounts to the king. The province has done very well this month, very well indeed," he said proudly.

"I see," said Isabella. She knew she didn't have much time, so she did not tell Timex the king was not in the castle. *I guess they don't know everything that happens in the kingdom after all* she thought wickedly.

She took a deep breath and said, "The king asked me to find a certain book for him. Mayor Roget mentioned a special book came through the town several weeks ago, and you were interested in it. Could you tell me about it?"

"The king you say? Of course if the king is involved – yes, I remember that book," he said. "I heard of a very rare, one-of-a-kind volume being offered to the highest bidder. I met with the seller thinking the book could be an excellent investment."

He sat back in his seat and started to smile as he said, "Actually, I have a keen interest in collecting rare objects. They appreciate in value so quickly. I spend whatever free time I have seeking them out though I seem to have so little free time these days. Just last night my wife was telling me I do not spend enough time with her and the children, but it is my job, after all, to provide well for them and they enjoy many fine things. In fact, the children just love the new pony, and now they need a new saddle, and perhaps new riding clothes."

Isabella's head was spinning and aching as she tried to follow his conversation. Truth be told, she was no longer sure what they were talking about when she heard him say, "Well the ten minutes are up. It has been lovely speaking with you, and I must prepare to leave for the castle."

The castle, the king, the book skittered through Isabella's mind. The Curiosa was starting to get hot, but she had a horrendous headache and did not want to ask any more questions. "Sir, wait please, just a few more minutes." Isabella stammered as the Curiosa began to blaze. "Remember, I am here at the king's request, and I must report back to him. What can you tell me about your meeting with the seller of the book?"

"Oh yes, the king's request, you did say that. You need to report back to him. Yes, yes. Well, there is not much more to report. I met with the man but after a few minutes I decided not to pursue the transaction," Timex said frowning.

"Why, sir?" asked Isabella.

Timex thought for a second and said simply, "I didn't like him." He sat looking at her silently.

"I see," said Isabella. The pendant was blazing, so she pressed on. "Sir, why did you not like him?"

"There was something very disturbing about him," Timex said frowning even more but offering no further explanation.

Isabella felt a shiver go down her spine. "What do you mean?" she persisted.

"He was cold, vacant." Timex pushed his chair away from the desk, stood up and began shoving papers into his satchel. "I lost all interest in discussing the manuscript when he refused to let me examine its contents or condition. In fact he threatened me when I insisted we could not negotiate a price if I did not know more about the book."

Timex closed his satchel and began moving to the door. Isabella desperate for clues asked, "Can you tell me anything about the book? What is its size – color - anything?"

Timex stopped with his hand on the door latch, "I only glimpsed the volume for a second; he pulled it out of a satchel, waved it in the air and shoved it back in his sack. It happened so quickly I cannot give you a description." Opening the door he said tersely, "Did you not hear me? The man is dangerous. Now I have important work to do and cannot waste one more second on this subject. Our meeting is over."

"Sir, please, I need more information," begged Isabella. "I have nowhere else to go."

Timex's voice became harsh. "I suggest you give up this search and put your efforts into something more productive. A girl your age needs to be in school preparing for her career, her future, instead of chasing phantom tomes. In fact, I will tell the king we met, and that I recommended this course of action to you. Chasing books is foolish. Chasing this man is dangerous. Good day." With a curt nod of his head, Isabella was dismissed.

WARNING SIGNS

"How is she?" the surgeon asked.

"In this moment stable, but we had a scare an hour ago. Heartbeat jumped to 210; blood pressure 200/90," said the neurologist. "Then it dropped back down to 100 and 130/60. We don't know what caused it so we're setting up more tests. I am worried about seizures and stroke."

LATISHA'S FEAST

Isabella walked out into the street not sure what next to do. "The Mayor and Timex were no help," she muttered to herself. "Well, maybe they were. Now I know a bad man has the book. The king could not possibly want me to continue. I just have to figure out how to get back to Sir Alfred, and he will take care of this with the king." She did not notice people staring at her as she walked down the street mumbling to herself.

"Child, are you not well?" someone asked tapping her on the arm.

"What?" asked Isabella startled out of her thoughts.

A slight woman of sixty with snowy white hair and dark brown eyes was walking beside her. "You seem to be having quite a conversation, though with whom I am not sure. I wanted to make sure nothing was amiss."

Isabella's cheeks grew warm. "I didn't realize I was thinking out loud. How embarrassing!"

"I do that myself sometimes," smiled the woman, "and often the conversations are quite satisfying." Isabella laughed. The woman seemed nice. "Where are you going?" the woman asked.

"At the moment I am not sure, but I need to find my way back to King Stefan's castle. Would you know how to get there?" asked Isabella hopefully.

"Isn't that where Al is these days?"

"Al?" Isabella laughed out loud in spite of herself. She could not imagine anyone calling Sir Alfred, Al – except the willows and the fish.

"Yes, Al. That amuses you?" the old woman asked, smiling herself.

"I am accustomed to hearing him addressed as Sir Alfred," Isabella said. "It is hard for me to think of him as Al."

146

"Oh, yes, he is someone important these days, isn't he? Well, Al and I went to school together, and I just remember him to be somewhat self-important. He liked to boss all of us around and impress us with his intellect. He was not a bad fellow, just a little too sterile for my taste. Very thin too, didn't eat much."

"He is very nice now. Very nice!" said Isabella earnestly. "That is why I would like to return to his care."

"Why do you want to be under his care?" asked the woman with genuine interest. Her voice was kind and open. Isabella felt comforted by her presence.

"It is a long story," sighed the girl.

"By that sigh, it seems to be a rather unhappy long story."

"I guess it is," Isabella said sighing again.

"Hmm," said the old woman. "I don't like to see little girls so unhappy. I live right down the street. Would you like to join me for a cup of tea and perhaps something to eat? I bet that would make you feel better." After the abrupt dismissals by the Mayor and Timex, the woman's kindness was like a warm blanket on a cold night. "Oh thank you so much. Tea sounds wonderful. Are you sure it would not be a bother?" asked Isabella shyly.

"No bother at all, a delight in fact," said the woman. "I am Latisha, and you are?"

"Isabella," replied the girl with a quick curtsy.

"I'm happy to meet you, Isabella. Here we are," Latisha said as they turned onto a walk that led to a house that was identical to every other house on the street with the exception of its red door and red shutters. Even before the door opened, Isabella's mouth started to water. The aroma of sautéing garlic and onions, and roasting meat wafted through the windows. "What is that wonderful smell?" she asked turning to the little woman.

"Oh, I always have a little something cooking," Latisha said smiling as she walked into her home. "Now sit, sit, and I will get us some tea and bring you a snack."

"Are you sure I am not inconveniencing you?" Isabella asked

"Heavens, no inconvenience at all – none at all," the woman said with a broad smile. "I will just be a minute." She fairly ran into the kitchen humming a little tune. Isabella took a seat at an enormous table situated in the center of the front room. The table was set for twenty covered with fine pewter dishes, silver cutlery and crystal goblets. *She must be getting ready for a party and did not want to tell me. How kind of her. I shan't stay long. A bit of tea, a bite to eat and maybe the name of someone who can direct me to the castle, then I will be off* she thought. Latisha came bustling in with a teapot, cream and sugar. "Help yourself while I lay out the table," she said, her eyes bright with pleasure.

"Thank you, again. I see you are having guests, are you sure I am not a bother to you?" asked Isabella anxiously.

"Oh, I'm not having guests. What gave you that idea?" asked Latisha surprised.

"The table...? The cooking...?"

"Oh, it's always this way. Habit, I guess. I was the chief cook for the royal family and their court for twenty-five years. I retired a few years ago and just cannot give up my love of cooking for assemblages. I will be right back." By the time Isabella poured herself a cup of tea, Latisha returned with a rack of lamb baked in a crust of garlic and herbs, garnished with sprigs of mint, and surrounded by mashed yellow turnips swimming in butter. She placed the platter in front of Isabella.

"Oh my goodness," said Isabella wide-eyed. She had seen such a dish only once when the bishop of their church visited the village on a holy day. The women of the hamlet had cooked for days, and everyone was filled with anticipation. Isabella could still remember the smell of garlic and butter as the platters of lamb were placed on the trestles in the church hall. The meat had been cooked to perfection, the skin a crispy brown on the outside, the inside pink and juicy. As glorious as the holy feast had been, Latisha's creation was even more magnificent.

"I have a few more things you might enjoy," said Latisha with a wink.

Out came a suckling pig and stuffed pheasant. Next were platters piled high with mashed potatoes, sweet potatoes, and baked potatoes. This was followed by wild rice, grains and vegetables of every kind, sauces, creams, and fruit molds. Latisha shuttled back and forth from the kitchen to the table serving an endless stream of food. "Eat, child;

begin or the food will get cold. I just can't stand cold food, can you?" asked Latisha her face flushed red.

"Oh, I could not begin without you joining me. Please, sit. Latisha, there is enough food here to feed my entire village," said Isabella. She thought she heard the table groan under the weight of all the food.

"No, no, you go right ahead and eat. I'm not hungry. I had lemon cake for breakfast this morning. Besides I want to make sure I keep these plates filled for you."

Isabella did not know where to begin. She took a bit from each serving dish until her plate was full. She took her first bite and then the next and then the next, sighing with delight as she swallowed. The food was heavenly; the food was divine; the food was unlike anything she had tasted before.

"Here is one more thing to try," said Latisha as she put a plate of flaming cheese in front of Isabella. "In fact I will sit for just a minute and try this myself for it is a recipe my sister gave me yesterday. Everyone in my family cooks and we are always sharing recipes. My sister claims this is the best cheese dish she has ever made." The two ate in comfortable silence lost in the smells and sensations of the food. It was a feast unlike any Isabella had known.

"This is the best meal I have ever had. Thank you so much. I can't remember when I was this full!" Isabella said smiling happily as she wiped her lips with her napkin. "I will be pleased to help you clean up."

"Oh, girl, you have hardly eaten. Here help yourself to some more."

"No, thank you, I –," Isabella had not even finished her sentence when Latisha scooped a huge spoon of mashed potatoes from the serving dish and plopped it right on Isabella's plate. "Here's a little bit of meat and gravy to go with it," said Latisha as she filled Isabella's plate. "You really didn't have much of this. Now eat, eat!"

To be polite, and because the food was so tasty, Isabella said thank you and started to eat once again. When her plate was empty, Isabella said, "That was wonderful and I just cannot eat another bite. I am very full."

"No you are not," said Latisha brightly. "You have hardly eaten anything at all. Besides a skinny thing like you needs to put some weight on her bones. Hasn't Al been feeding you properly? Now eat up, think of all the starving children in the kingdom."

"But what has that to do with me?" asked Isabella confused as she looked at the slices of pork and wild rice that Latisha was piling onto her plate.

"I feel so happy feeding people," Latisha said almost swooning with delight, ignoring Isabella's question. "Doesn't that make you feel good to know you are pleasing an old woman? Now eat, eat, eat. Clean your plate like a good girl." To please the old woman, Isabella ate and ate and ate some more. Each time her plate was empty, Latisha filled it again. Finally, Isabella had to stop for fear she would explode. The warmth of the house, the comforting smells of the food, and the fullness in her stomach made Isabella very sleepy. Latisha noticed Isabella's heavy eyes and said, "Why don't you nap a bit, child? After you wake up, we can have some dessert."

"And talk about how I can get back to the castle?" asked Isabella drowsily.

"Oh Isabella, we won't worry about that right now. Why don't you put that out of your mind? Do you not enjoy my company and the food?" the old woman asked dreamily.

"Of course, Latisha, of course I do. I feel so very comforted by you," Isabella said with a huge yawn. "It's just…"

"Well then," Latisha said interrupting Isabella, "just forget about the castle for now. Let me get you settled in a chair. Put your feet up and rest. After I clear the table we can have some sweets. I know you will just adore them. I have made all the family favorites."

Isabella staggered from the table to a small chair by the fireplace. She napped for several hours and awoke feeling refreshed. When she got up, the table was set with dozens of pies and cakes and tarts and puddings. Latisha clapped her hands in excitement when she saw Isabella and said, "Good, good, you are up. Come let us enjoy dessert!"

The old woman looked so happy Isabella did not have the heart to say no. One bite and the girl almost swooned with delight. The desserts were the most heavenly sweets she had ever tasted. This time Latisha did not have to refill her plate. Isabella ate well after the sun had set and everything on the table was gone. "That was wonderful," she sighed.

"Do you want me to help you clean up?" This time she hoped Latisha would say no because she was so full she could not move.

"Oh, don't worry about cleaning up. It is late. I believe you will feel so much better after a good night's sleep by the fire," said Latisha patting Isabella's arm. "Let me get your bed ready." The old woman hobbled over to an ornately carved chest in the corner of the room. Opening the heavy lid, Latisha pulled out velvet coverlets, mink throws, a fat goose down pallet, and two satin pillows. "You will sleep like a princess tonight," Latisha smiled arranging the bed linens for the sleepy child. As Isabella laid down and pulled a coverlet close under her chin, she heard Latisha say, "I have already planned our breakfast menu. I think you will be pleased."

"Wonderful," mumbled the girl as she drifted off to sleep.

Isabella and Latisha ate their way through the next three days. Rather Latisha cooked, and Isabella ate and slept. At the end of the third day Isabella could not remember how she had come to Latisha's house or why she was there. There seemed to be something the woman was going to help her with but Isabella could not quite remember what and each time she came close to remembering, Latisha offered her another tasty morsel.

The morning of the fifth day of her visit, there was a knock on the door. "Don't bother answering that," Latisha called out from the kitchen. "I am not expecting anyone. Besides I am right in the middle of this soufflé and if the door slams the soufflé will fall."

"Of course, I understand," said Isabella from the chair by the fire, her stomach the size of a watermelon. "I can hardly wait to try your soufflé. I have never had a soufflé before. Is it good?"

"Divine, one of my masterpieces," was the old woman's happy reply.

The pounding got louder. Fearing the noise would cause the soufflé to fall Isabella got up slowly and waddled to the entrance. When she opened the door perched on the top step of the stoop was Nightwalker. She was so surprised she did not know what to say. "May I come in?" the great raven asked politely, the star on his forehead twinkling brightly. Without waiting for an answer, he hopped into the front room and onto the table. Eying the empty dishes, platters and goblets littering the table, he said, "My, I see you have had quite a feast." Isabella sat down at the table without answering.

"It's done, and it's wonderful," sang Latisha waltzing into the room with a magnificent soufflé in hand. When she saw Nightwalker, she stopped abruptly and said, "Oh!"

"Hello, Latisha. I see you have been busy."

"Have you come to spoil my fun, you bothersome bird?" said Latisha pushing dirty dishes aside with her elbows to find a spot for her soufflé.

"You call me a bothersome bird? My lovely Latisha, have you forgotten I was your most prized taste tester," said Nightwalker cocking his head from side to side. "Whenever you invented a lovely new dish for court, who did you have taste it and give you a review? Who helped you refine the recipe on those rare occasions the dish needed just a bit more of this or that to make it truly unforgettable?"

"Yes, yes, I know you were helpful, but I also remember it was you who disrupted my retirement party – my greatest achievement," she snapped, straightening up placing both hands on her bony hips.

"How so?" asked Nightwalker innocently, as he pecked a lonely piece of pork left behind on a platter. "This is very good! You have not lost your touch."

"You cannot change the subject with your flattery – though of course I have not lost my touch. The party – you scared everyone off," she barked.

"As I remember your party, it was magnificent. The Queen Mother and I complimented you such in the kitchen as we were leaving. I remember we three had a lovely leave-taking chat," Nightwalker said sweetly. "If you don't mind, I will just have a taste of this leftover mutton. It is calling to me."

"Well, all I know is by the time we were done chatting in the kitchen, everyone was done eating and gone," said Latisha stamping her foot.

"Dear, that is what happens at the end of a fifty course meal. People are still talking about it," laughed the bird. "And I'll have a piece of this venison, if that is all right."

"Well, they should be talking about it. I worked very hard to provide all that comfort! Humph! Now what are you doing here?" she said arms crossed against her chest, brown eyes blazing.

"Your food would be reason enough to visit," said the bird, wiping his mouth daintily with the tip of his wing, "but I have come to fetch Isabella. I have not visited with her in quite a while and thought she and I might spend a bit of time together."

"No, not fair, I found her when she was sad and now she is happy, aren't you happy?" said Latisha, her voice getting louder and more shrill.

Isabella had barely been following the conversation so satiated with food was she. In fact, she had been trying to figure out how to rise from the chair to reach the bed and take a nap. "Isabella," yelled Latisha, "tell this bird you are happy!"

"I am happy. I think I am happy. I think I am happy when I am eating your food..." Isabella said, losing her train of thought.

"See, she is happy," said Latisha adamantly, staring hard at the bird, her eyes narrowing into slits. "I know what you are thinking, Nightwalker. You want her to go after that book again. I met with the townspeople while she slept, and we have decided the task before her is too dangerous. Let her be. Let her stay with me. She has forgotten all about that silly book anyway."

Isabella heard silly book and brightened a bit. "That's it! That is what I was trying to remember – the book, Timex, the Mayor. They were quite unkind to me, the Mayor and Timex. Latisha, you were going to help me get back to Sir Alfred."

"Don't think about that, child. It distresses you, you said as much. Now here, we cannot let this soufflé go to waste. Come have some," said Latisha as she began to serve the dish.

Sir Alfred. That is what I have been trying to remember. If I eat I may forget him again, but I have never eaten a soufflé. Maybe one bite she thought wistfully. Nightwalker suddenly cleared his throat bringing Isabella back to the moment. Trying to sit a bit taller in her chair, Isabella said, "I think I will pass, Latisha, thank you." The dish smelled delicious and Isabella's mouth began to water. Latisha placed the steaming soufflé right in front of the girl. "Remember the starving children," said Latisha.

Isabella felt her will weakening, and said, "I think I will go outside and get some air. It might help clear my head." Isabella stumbled out the front door, Nightwalker hopping after her.

"Oh fiddlesticks!" muttered Latisha sitting down to the soufflé alone.

When they got outside Isabella's stomach began to churn. "I don't feel so well," she moaned. "I think I have to sit down," she said dropping onto the stoop.

"I'm sorry to hear that."

"I ate too much," said the girl. Nightwalker nodded. "I don't think I will ever eat again," Isabella said mournfully, holding her stomach, rocking back and forth. When the bird did not answer she said, staring straight ahead, "I did not think I would ever see you again either."

"I know, child. It pained me deeply to leave you so quickly. I had no choice," Nightwalker said quietly.

"Pained you deeply? Had no choice? You told me everyone in this kingdom has choices," muttered Isabella, her throat burning with the pain of these unspoken words. "You chose to abandon me on the river. You left me all alone. I could have died and you did not care about that – you cared only for yourself."

"I left you in Sir Alfred's capable hands," said the bird quietly.

"You left me in his hands?" the child snapped as she clutched her churning stomach. "No, Nightwalker, he came to find me. Sir Alfred came, not you. I want to go back to him. Sir Alfred is the only one I feel safe with."

"I know," replied the bird. "I have come to take you back to the castle." Isabella looked at Nightwalker suspiciously. "We can leave immediately." Only then did the child stop rocking.

STRANGERS

"I have her mail," the volunteer said softly as she handed the old man a bundle of letters and cards. "My, she has so many friends."

The old man nodded silently as the woman pushed her cart to the next room. He looked around for a place to lay the stack. There were cards on the table and nightstands, on the window sills, taped to the walls. He did not know where to put this newest batch of love letters, so he sat down heavily with the bundle in his lap.

He stared at the tubes running in and out of his daughter's body, the monitors beeping and blinking, the machines wheezing and pumping – all working so hard to keep her broken body alive. "Every day these letters come in," he said to her, his voice gruff with emotion. "I never knew you had so many friends." His eyes dropped to the treasure in his lap. "I never knew you touched so many lives."

The only response was the beep of the monitors. His heart was filled with sorrow. "I am so sorry," he said shaking his head. "All I ever cared about was my work and my life; I never took the time to notice yours." The old man gazed at his daughter and said mournfully, "We need to change that...no, I need to change that. I want to know you as they do. Please give me that chance."

$\star$

NOTHING SPECIAL

The pine trees stood shoulder to shoulder lining the road for as far as Isabella could see – sentinels guarding the only way in or out of Kronos. She was glad to leave the town. "I don't think I will ever be hungry again," she moaned as she and Nightwalker trudged down the road. Though it was very early in the morning, Isabella was surprised they were the only two travelers on the thoroughfare. Frankly, she was pleased, not wanting to bump into Mayor Roget or any of the town's important residents.

"Well, Latisha obviously doesn't agree based on the size of the basket she packed us," said Nightwalker dryly as he hopped along the path beside Isabella. Though he much preferred to fly, he thought it best to stay close to the girl.

"She is a wonderful cook, isn't she?" sighed Isabella as she struggled with the enormous basket. She could smell the cookies the old woman baked just for their journey.

"Indeed she is; she just doesn't know when to stop," said the bird shaking his head.

"Well, she has a way about her that makes it hard to refuse her food. She's so comforting." Isabella sighed again as she put down the basket, stretched one arm and then the other. Nightwalker jumped onto the hamper and said, "Isabella, if I may suggest something; let's take a few things and leave the rest. It will make your travel easier."

"I think you are right. This food is such a burden," sighed the girl yet again. She pulled out a few apples, a small wheel of cheese, and a loaf of bread tucking them into a satchel Latisha had packed into the hamper. Leaving the basket by the road side, the girl and raven proceeded on their way. Though her load was lighter, Isabella continued to drag her feet moving slower and slower by the moment. "What is amiss, girl?" asked the raven, turning to look up at Isabella. In the morning light he saw Isabella's dress was rumpled and her hair hung limply around her face and neck. There were dark circles under her eyes.

"I feel terrible, Nightwalker. I did not sleep well with Latisha…all that eating. I am so embarrassed to say I did not feel like bathing or changing my clothes. All I did was eat and forget," Isabella confessed sadly.

"Let us rest, at least for a moment," said the bird. He looked about and spotted a log lying a dozen yards back from the main road. Light spilled through the forest canopy splashing the forest floor and bathing the log in sunshine. "I think I see a spot that will do us nicely," he said as he flew off. Isabella trudged through a sea of ferns to join him and slumped onto the log. She looked quite forlorn with her elbows perched on her knees and her chin in her hands. After staring at the ground for a few seconds, she plucked a frond from the fern sea and started picking it apart, leaf by leaf. When the last bits of leaf fluttered to the ground, she plucked another and started again.

"What are you doing?" Nightwalker asked curiously as he nestled down on a sun warmed spot of bark.

"Thinking about Kronos," replied Isabella glumly. "It wasn't what I expected. I thought the people would be like Sir Alfred. Nicer and more helpful. They were just so busy being important." She meticulously tore every bit of leaf from the stem she was holding. After twirling the stalk in her fingers a few seconds, she threw it on the ground.

"That troubles you?" inquired the bird politely.

"When people act like they are better than everyone else, yes that bothers me." Isabella looked about for her next victim pulling several plants out of the ground.

"Did they do that? Act like they were better than everyone else?" asked Nightwalker surprised.

"Well not directly, but all their talk about time and productivity and work and this person being important and that person being important, scheduling meetings – all of it bothered me, and how they dressed and their homes, that bothered me." Isabella was now ripping the leaves off in chunks, one quickly after the other.

"I see," said the bird as he looked at the girl and the growing mountain of leaf remains.

Isabella stopped her assault and looked at Nightwalker. "Nightwalker, do you have a profession?"

The raven nodded. "Officially, I am the Royal Messenger, but mostly I play."

"Royal Messenger – that sounds very important. I am impressed," said Isabella nodding her head thoughtfully before she tore the next frond in two.

"I did say mostly I played, didn't I?" asked Nightwalker the star on his forehead twinkling.

"Mayor Roget would say playing was not a good use of time," the girl said in an exaggerated tone. "Did you know Timex said I should be in school preparing for my career, my future?" Nightwalker laughed so hard he almost fell off the log.

"It is not funny, Nightwalker," said Isabella frowning. "I got a stomach ache in Kronos even before I met Latisha." She rubbed her hands together brushing off the remains of her most recent casualty. "I guess everyone intimidated me a little, a lot actually." Isabella reached down and picked up two fronds twirling them by their stems. Around and around and around they went.

Nightwalker watched the twirling for a bit and said, "The people of Kronos have great value and skills as managers, Isabella, and those skills are needed and necessary to run the kingdom. They have always been efficient and productive, but I think they may have become a bit extreme since they received that award."

Isabella stopped twirling the leaves and became still. "I could tell they didn't think well of me," she said quietly.

"Whatever would make you say that?" asked Nightwalker.

"I am nothing special," she said sighing deeply. Isabella remembered when she discovered that. The women of her village had decided to sew a new cloth for the town hall meeting table. Every afternoon they would meet in the public room to sew and gossip. Isabella was about nine and loved to accompany her mother whenever she went to the hall. She would read in the corner as she listened to their conversations. One afternoon the talk turned to their children.

"Oh my Tanya, she is a wonderful singer. Just the other day, the choir master said her voice was better than the bishop's cathedral soloist. He feels she will be famous one day," gushed the butcher's wife.

"How wonderful," said the school master's wife her needle paused mid-air. "My Joshua is a brilliant student. My husband has already spoken to the friars at the monastery, and they are eager to take him as a student even though he is still quite young. They feel his aptitude for reading and writing will make him a leader among scribes." She smiled a smile of great pride.

"All so lovely," nodded the magistrate's wife as she knotted off a final stitch. "My twins have a wonderful aptitude for numbers. They help my husband calculate taxes and already make suggestions as to how to increase the wealth of the village. I have no doubt they will have great financial means and will provide well not only for themselves but for my husband and me." All the women murmured how very fortunate she was to have children with such skill and potential.

"Ah, and my Alicia, what a beauty she is," beamed the mason's wife. "Each day she grows more beautiful; her hair is so thick, her skin so white, and her eyes so blue. I love to dress her well to show off her beauty. I have no doubt she will marry well." She stitched away happily and said, "I can see myself the mother of a duchess or countess. Can you imagine my daughter with a title? How wonderful she is."

"We are so fortunate to have such special children," said the magistrate's wife. "How good to know they will go on to be important and respected and rich!"

Isabella was listening to the conversation with great interest. She waited eagerly for her mother to join in praise of her, but she waited in vain. Her mother was the only woman who remained silent. When they left the hall, Isabella said, "Why did you not speak of me?" Her mother replied, "There was nothing to say." Isabella never accompanied her mother to the sewing circle again.

The girl dropped the final leaf and did not seek another. She looked at Nightwalker sadly. "I should not be mad at the Kronos managers. They are not the problem. I am. I simply am of no value."

"Oh, child," said Nightwalker softly. He moved closer to the girl and brushed her face with the feathers of his iridescent wing. She closed her eyes under Nightwalker's feathery stroke. "When the king showed me the paintings and said I was the one to find the book and help the kingdom, I was terrified." She opened her eyes and looked at the raven. "I am still terrified, Nightwalker, but a part of me is pleased. It makes me feel special, important that I am to find the book – not the king – me. If I find it, perhaps my mother will see I am special after all."

Nightwalker pondered how best to respond to the child. He could see her beautiful brown eyes brimming with tears. Putting both wings around her, he said, "Child, do you know what I think? I think we need to have some fun right now."

THE GUARDIAN OF MAGIC

"Fun…? How in the world can you speak of fun?" wailed Isabella, tears streaming down her face as she pushed Nightwalker away. As the little girl sobbed, Nightwalker began to sparkle; his body grew broader, his bill longer and lacquered purple, his feathers shimmered black, blue, purple and silver in the sunlight, and his eyes became robin egg blue. The sound of rustling silk and the scent of lavender and mint filled the air around them. Isabella's tears stopped as she looked at the great bird.

Nightwalker said, "Isabella, earlier you asked me my profession. I said I was the Royal Messenger and I am, but I also have another title. I am the Guardian of Magic."

"What is that?" asked Isabella wiping the tears from her face startled by the change in Nightwalker's appearance.

"I will try to explain this simply and then I will show you. Is that acceptable to you?" Isabella nodded and Nightwalker continued, "In the Lower World, we believe each of us can give shape to our future by how we think about it. We can think, 'What if I…?' and 'Wouldn't it be nice if…?' and 'I think it would be possible to…' We believe a clear dream takes shape and draws form to itself – makes the dream so. My job is to take each person's dream into the Great Mystery. If it is true and for a higher good, I bring the magic out and the dream comes true."

Isabella shook her head. "I do not understand at all."

"Perhaps a little demonstration will help." Nightwalker spread his wings wide and said, "If you could wave a magic wand and wish for fun, what would it look like?"

"Please do not ask me such things," Isabella cried. "I have no knowledge of fun, only work."

The star on Nightwalker's forehead blazed a light so bright Isabella could barely look upon him. "I ask you to dream for just a moment, child."

I must say something if only to stop this. "I would ride a horse," she blurted. Isabella blinked twice, surprised not only by the answer but that there was an answer.

"Very good," Nightwalker cawed, silver sparkles shooting through his feathers. "What kind of horse?"

Isabella blurted again, "I just loved a little black mare I saw in the royal stables." *I don't understand where these ideas are coming from.* At that exact moment, a small black mare trotted out of a thicket of trees. On her back was a blazing red saddle just Isabella's size. Bells attached to the bridle jingled as the horse trotted over to Isabella and Nightwalker. "That's the mare! Nightwalker, how did she get here?" Isabella gasped as she rose from the log and walked over to the mare. The horse rubbed her head up and down Isabella's arm.

"Magic...! Get on, and let's go!" The bird flew from the fern sea to a tree by the road and waited for Isabella to mount the mare and follow him. Isabella looked at Nightwalker and then at the horse. "This is some trick. What are you doing?" she demanded. Flying back to the log, Nightwalker said, "This doesn't please you? All right, answer again, quickly – if you could do something fun, entirely different than riding a horse, what would it be?" He seemed to grow bigger and brighter with each word.

I will show him he cannot trick me. Putting her hands on her hips Isabella retorted, "I want to catch fireflies." Though it was still morning, dusk fell like a blanket, and the evening air was filled with thousands of flashing fireflies. They twinkled throughout the forest as far as Isabella could see. Little diamonds flickering in the darkness. "How are you doing this?" Isabella asked wide-eyed.

"Let us try once more; dream big, Isabella. If you could do anything in the world, anything, what would you do?"

"I would fly," shouted Isabella.

Nightwalker clapped his wings. "My, my, what is that up there?" he asked mischievously. Isabella glanced up and could not believe her eyes. A huge hot-air balloon floated over their heads. "Come, Isabella. Let's see where it lands," squawked the raven. Isabella raced after the bird through the woods. Though the firefly dusk was deepening, she glimpsed the sailing ship through the canopy of trees. Its panels were thins strips of lemon and black leather, and lines of thickly braided hemp attached the billowing cloud to a passenger basket of skillfully woven rushes. Isabella ran on until she came to a huge clearing. The ship's basket was just touching the ground and appeared to be empty.

"Well, you wanted to fly. What are you waiting for?" asked Nightwalker as he landed on the rim of the balloon's basket, his talons holding him steady. "Get in!"

"Is it alright?" asked Isabella staring at the balloon in disbelief. Just then the sailing ship started to lift off. "Wait, wait for me!" shouted Isabella as she dashed to the balloon, climbed into the basket and tumbled to the floor. In seconds they were airborne. "Oh my, I am flying, Nightwalker! I am actually flying!" Isabella said clapping her hands as they rose higher and higher into the sky. "Nightwalker, how is this happening?" asked Isabella peering over the edge of the basket.

"Imagination," smiled Nightwalker. "If one can imagine something, one can begin to create it. You and I created this."

"Oh you did this; I did not," said the girl her eyes glued to the sights below her.

"Oh yes, you can do this and much more, Isabella. You just need a little practice and a teacher," smiled the bird, "and I am the best teacher in the kingdom!"

Evening had fallen and the sky was filled with a brilliant full moon which illuminated the scene below. As Isabella looked down she could make out the rough outlines of neat fields and villages, vast tracts of forests, the river, and roads that looked like ribbons. Far off in the distance Isabella thought she saw the outline of turrets. "Oh look, there is the castle."

"I told you I was taking you back to Sir Alfred," said the raven gently.

"Thank you, Nightwalker. You are being kind to me. I am sorry I was so sharp with you at Latisha's."

"You had every right to be, Isabella."

"And now we are flying together. I simply cannot believe I am flying," said Isabella shaking her head.

As the turrets of the castle came closer, Nightwalker said, "Isabella, I would like to propose something. We can return to the castle straight away – in fact we will be there within the hour – or we can explore for a bit, perhaps a few days. You might enjoy seeing more of the Lower World from this vantage point. It is a lovely kingdom."

Isabella turned to look at Nightwalker. Part of her wanted to be in the comfort and safety of Sir Alfred's courtroom and yet, another part of her did feel magic was afoot. She paused for a moment feeling the gentle tug of opposing wants and then there was agreement. "I think I would like to explore, Nightwalker, just for a few days. I am sure Sir Alfred will not mind."

A comet shot through the night sky followed by a second and third. "Wonderful! Why don't we let the wind take us where it will and see where we end up? That is a real adventure," smiled the raven delighted to see a spark of wonder in the little girl's eyes. As the land below disappeared into darkness, Nightwalker said, "It is a beautiful night for stargazing, don't you think?" The child nodded. "Now I have another game in mind – just right for nighttime. It is one of my favorites and this one might help you with your career dilemma."

"And what game is that?" Isabella asked as a shooting star brightened the sky.

"The game is Imaginary Lives, and we play with the stars," Nightwalker said spreading his wings to take in the vast night sky. "Each star represents an imaginary life you would find exciting to live. We take turns and see who can name the most."

"Nightwalker, you come up with the strangest games," said Isabella. "I could never name that many lives. I do not know if I can even come up with one imaginary life."

"You might surprise yourself," said the bird. "Pick something you find interesting. I will begin so you can see how easy it is." He gazed at the star closest to the moon and said dreamily, "I have always wanted to be a puppeteer!" Isabella giggled. She could just imagine Nightwalker manipulating puppet strings with his beak and talons and getting knotted up in the many lines. "Now you," said Nightwalker looking at Isabella expectantly.

"I don't know yet," she said gazing at the stars. "I'm still thinking. You go again."

"All right, but this is the last one," said Nightwalker waggling a wing at Isabella. He looked into the night sky again and said, "Hmmm. I imagine myself to be a world class chess master!"

"Really?" said Isabella her eyebrows going up. "That's interesting. I would not have thought that of interest to you."

"I love strategy. I love thinking about moves and countermoves. I love trying to get into the thinking of the player on the other side of the chess board. I love the beauty of the carved pieces. I love the silence that envelopes the players." The bird smiled, "When two play this game, see what you can learn about the other? Now it's your turn."

Isabella stared hard into the sky. She took a deep breath. "I have always loved sparkly things, so I would like to be a jewelry maker," she said shyly. "I loved Setine's jewels. I think it would be so much fun to make such beautiful things."

"That's wonderful, Isabella," smiled Nightwalker nodding his head in approval. "That is just wonderful. Now name another life so we will be even."

"Let me see," said the girl, looking up just as another star streaked across the sky. "Ah, that one is mine because I like how it took center stage." She thought a moment more then looked at Nightwalker bashfully. She said almost in a whisper, "My next imaginary life would be that of a writer of plays. I love writing stories, just like Sir Alfred when he was a little boy. I never told anyone that," the child said blushing deep red.

Nightwalker clapped his wings and said, "Fabulous choice! See, it's not so hard."

Isabella giggled. She ran her hand down Nightwalker's wing and said, "I think I like this game, Nightwalker. Thank you." Nightwalker smiled. And so they continued, the raven and the child, until they had named an imaginary life for each star in the nighttime sky.

✦

AMONG FRIENDS

Isabella and Nightwalker sailed the skies for weeks. Whenever they were hungry, Nightwalker imagined a meal into being. When they were bored, Nightwalker suggested a new game. More often than not, the girl and the raven passed the time in comfortable silence gazing down upon the terrain of the Lower World or up in the evening sky.

They soared over rugged mountains, whose peaks were hidden under snow and clouds. They drifted over desolate deserts. They floated over seemingly endless expanses of water. The water so still one minute and wild the next. One morning Isabella awoke early and peered over the side of the basket to see miles and miles of a green so vivid it hurt her eyes. "What are we looking at?" she asked Nightwalker who had awakened when he heard Isabella gasp.

"The forest of rain," replied the bird softly. They glided transfixed over miles and miles of wild rain forest broken only by a meandering river that occasionally spilled down a thundering fall only to find its balance and wind through more green jungle. Then Isabella noticed a break in the greenery. As they got closer the girl realized she was looking at an immense circle. Within the circle a spiral pathway of pure white stone curled this way and that bending back on itself though it also moved forward. Finally the path opened onto the center of the circle. In that immense center was a magnificent palace of moonstone surrounded by gardens of jungle flowers and steaming hot baths. "Setine's palace," Nightwalker said. Isabella nodded with a smile as the wind took the sailing ship past the Kingdom of the Dreamtime.

While much of their time was spent alone, Isabella and Nightwalker were visited by birds that stopped to chat and share news of the kingdom. Isabella always asked if there was word of the king's book or

166

the stranger who claimed to have possession of a valuable manuscript. The answer was always the same. No one had information about the book, but all knew of the stranger and feared him. The birds warned Isabella to stay away from the man and advised her to give up her search. More than one said, "He hurts everyone he meets. He is a bad man."

"Where would I find him?" Isabella once asked a flock of starlings who paused to visit.

"He travels the circuit of cockfights and bull-baiting," was the response of one.

"In the forest," said another

"In the swamp," replied a third.

"Stay away from him," the trio said in unison and they flew away.

After the trio disappeared from sight, Nightwalker asked, "Am I correct to assume from your queries you have chosen to seek the book?"

"Oh my no!" exclaimed Isabella. "I plan on telling Sir Alfred what the birds said so he will know I tried to be helpful. I also want him to know why I can go no further in seeking the book. You heard all the birds; this man is bad. This is a search for the king and his soldiers."

"I see," nodded the raven. Silence enveloped the two travelers as the warm wind carried the balloon through the azure blue sky.

One day a coven of thirteen young ravens approached the sailors of the sky. "Teacher, how pleased we are to have found you," said a young raven flying circles around the balloon. He was a beautiful bird, coal black with a single white feather running down the length of his left wing.

"I am pleased as well, Sky," said Nightwalker flapping his wings in greeting. "Come here and let me give you a proper greeting!" Nightwalker hopped to the edge of the basket and motioned for his student to approach. When both were settled on the basket's rim, Nightwalker moved closer to Sky and laid his beak on the back of the young bird's neck. Slowly he began to preen his student's feathers, cleaning each one gently. Sky sighed in contentment.

"So my young friend, what brings you so far from home?" asked Nightwalker when he finished cleaning the last feather.

"We have a letter for Miss Isabella from Sir Alfred."

"How wonderful," Isabella said as she eagerly reached for an envelope Sky plucked from beneath his wing.

"Well, child, if you don't mind, I will go play with my young friends while you read," said Nightwalker. "It is time I stretched these old wings of mine."

"Oh please do, Nightwalker," said Isabella as she tore open Sir Alfred's note. "Have fun."

With a great flapping of wings Nightwalker soared into the sky, high above Sky and all the other ravens. When it seemed he could go no higher, Nightwalker abruptly flipped into a nose dive and folded his wings to his body. Plummeting towards the ground, the raven began spinning like a whirling top making 360-degree spins in rapid succession.

Startled by the calls of the young ravens, Isabella looked up from her letter to see Nightwalker twirling downward. Down and down he went until Isabella feared he would hit the ground. Seemingly at the last possible moment, Nightwalker slowly extended his wings, banked to his right and gracefully descended to the top of a large boulder. The air was filled with the excited caws of his students applauding his acrobatics.

Nightwalker's show seemed to energize the young ravens. Suddenly the air was filled with birds flying half loops, full loops and double loops – often in breathtaking combinations. Isabella set Sir Alfred's letter aside to watch the youngsters play. She found herself clapping as each show of skill became more daring and complex.

Then she noticed Nightwalker and Sky. Master and student climbed upward until they were high above the balloon. They abruptly flew away from each other only to turn back on a collision course. When a head on collision seemed unavoidable, Sky flew upward just a fraction of an inch while Nightwalker rolled onto his back. As they passed over and under each other, they hooked talons and began spiraling down through the air. Around and around and around they went. Down, down, down. *If they don't release their hold on each other soon, they won't be able to pull out of that spin. As fast as they are falling, it will kill them* Isabella thought gripping the edge of the basket as she watched them fall.

Then barely five feet above the treetops, Nightwalker and Sky released their grip on each other, opened their wings, banking sharply so they were flying parallel to the ground at incredible speeds. In seconds, they slowed their flight and landed gently on a bush. Caws, gurgles, squawks and screeches filled the air in appreciation of the daring show. Isabella released her breath and did not know whether to clap or scold the birds when they returned to the balloon.

"So, what did you think, Isabella?" asked Nightwalker, his star twinkling and his eyes bright with excitement.

"So daring and so frightening," said Isabella.

"It was wonderful, Teacher. Thank you so much," said Sky breathlessly. "We look forward to more such fun when you return from your travels." The coven of ravens flew several lazy circles about the balloon and then disappeared.

"So what did our Esteemed Advisor have to say?" inquired Nightwalker as he settled back into the basket with Isabella.

"I don't know. I was so taken with watching you and the other ravens, I didn't have a chance to finish his letter," said Isabella.

"Well, don't keep me in suspense, child, read! Read!"

Isabella unfolded the thick paper and read:

Dear Miss Isabella,

I hope you are well. I was delighted to hear you decided to do some exploring. There is much to see in the kingdom and Nightwalker is a worthy guide, though I would not tell him I said as much for fear it will go to his head.

On a more official note, the king has asked that I inquire as to any news of the book he discussed with you prior to his leaving the castle. He hopes you are making progress.

The Ladies Jillian and Joanna send their regards. You are missed and thought of often. When you are ready, we look forward to your return.

Sir Alfred

Nightwalker watched the girl fold the letter in half and slip it into her pocket.

$\star$

YOWLING IN THE NIGHT

The man was lying in bed reading a book. Suddenly he heard a child's blood curdling cry. The sound was too far away to be either of his children who were fast asleep in their rooms across the hall. The yowling began again ebbing and flowing like a police siren. He quickly got out of bed following the sound downstairs to his wife's office.

The shrieks stop instantly when he turned on the lights illuminating the family cats. The soft round Tabby was curled in a ball seated deep in his wife's reading chair. Her sister, a tiny black Bombay, sat Sphinx-like on his wife's laptop keyboard. Both stared at the man with unblinking eyes.

"I know," he sighed, "I'm scared too."

✦
THE ELITE GUARD

Several days after being visited by the young ravens, the wind stopped, and the balloon drifted towards the ground. It landed on a rocky outcrop jutting over the edge of a canyon. On one side the canyon was so wide and deep, Isabella could not see its floor or where it ended on the horizon. On the other a cacophony of rocks, gorges, towers and pinnacles stretched for miles.

"Oh my," breathed Isabella.

Nightwalker nodded in agreement and said, "We must be in the Northern Province of the kingdom. This canyon forms a natural boundary keeping all intruders from entering the Lower World."

Not taking her eyes off the sight before her, Isabella said, "I thought visitors were welcome in the Lower World."

"There are those who rightly belong here and others who do not," said Nightwalker solemnly. The raven hopped from one side of the balloon's basket to the other turning his beak first one way and then the other as he smelled the air. "Isabella, I don't think the wind will return for some time. I suggest we explore the area."

"If you think so, Nightwalker, but I would like you to lead," said Isabella as she climbed over the side of the basket. Once on the ground she looked around and said thoughtfully, "King Stefan was called to the Northern Province because there was trouble. I wonder if he is still here." Suddenly the idea of exploring made her feel uneasy. "Please stay close to me, Nightwalker," she said. "I feel funny. There is something in the air that is not right."

The terrain was rocky and sparse. Scraggly pine trees dotted the land, and mammoth boulders made walking difficult. After picking their way among the rocks and crevices, Nightwalker spotted wisps of smoke rising above distant stone pillars and suggested they make their way there. "Do you think the smoke might be coming from intruders?" asked Isabella nervously.

"We will proceed slowly and cautiously," answered the bird. "Let us make our way up this ridge and see what awaits us below."

What lay below was a military camp. Simple tents and small fires dotted the landscape. There appeared to be hundreds of soldiers in the camp, but very little activity. "This is odd," said Nightwalker. "By the looks of the uniforms and weapons I would say these men are part of King Stefan's Elite Guard, but it is too quiet. Even at rest these soldiers drill in constant preparation for battle. Something is amiss. Let us proceed with caution, Isabella." An hour later, the travelers came within shouting distance of the first tents. Nightwalker called out, "Hello, hello – I am Nightwalker and this is Isabella. We are friends of the king. May we come forward?"

One of the tent flaps was thrown back and a short burly man stood glaring at the girl and the raven. He motioned them forward. The man's close cropped beard and hair were streaked with white and his short muscular body bore scars of past battles. He wore the insignia of a commander. The air seemed to crackle around him. His piercing blue eyes rested on Isabella and so fierce was his stare that she blushed. He nodded slightly. "I am not surprised," he growled. "I am General Darius Acorant. I was about to eat. If you wish, you may join me and my staff. I believe you have come a long way," he said gruffly.

The commander turned sharply from the two travelers and made his way into the camp. Isabella and Nightwalker followed silently. When he reached a large cook fire, Darius motioned for a group of grim faced men seated around a crude wooden table to make room for the visitors. The men wore black hooded tunics, leggings and sturdy boots. Only their armbands bearing the insignia of the twin dragons identified them as officers of the Elite Guard. All were engaged in cleaning and repairing their weapons. Darius ordered the cook to set two more plates for the travelers

"What has happened here?" Nightwalker asked as they settled down. Stony silence and sullen stares were the only response. The tension in the air was so thick, Isabella could barely breathe. "Commander, what has happened here?" Nightwalker asked again, directing his attention to the old warrior seated at the head of the table.

"Evil has happened here, raven," the commander said tersely.

"What are you saying?" asked Nightwalker slowly, the feathers of his ruff bristling.

"I am not sure myself," the commander said with a short bitter laugh. The soldiers stared silently at their leader.

"I do not believe in evil," Nightwalker said.

"Is that so?" The soldier who spoke was large and intimidating. He held a sharp pointed dagger used in hand-to-hand combat. He spit on the dagger then wiped it against his leggings as he sneered, "Do you not believe in spirits, raven? Black magic? Are these not of your domain?"

"That is enough, Rufio," Darius said brusquely.

"Spirits!" said Isabella startled. "There are no such things as spirits!"

"So I thought," said the commander stiffly as he fixed his stare upon Isabella.

"If you stay here long enough, you will believe in both evil and spirits. It seeps into your bones without notice or defense," said Rufio scanning the faces of his peers. "One does not know when violence will strike or who will be the perpetrator. Friend becomes foe and one does not even notice how or when it happened." Several of the men nodded.

A menacing silence enveloped the group. Isabella felt the Curiosa's heat radiate through her shoulder and chest. She decided to take the pendant off so she would not feel the need to ask questions. Something was wrong here, terribly wrong, and she did not want to know of it. As she reached to unpin the broach, Sir Alfred's voice filled her head: 'The Curiosa will keep you safe, Miss Isabella. Do not be afraid to search.' Isabella slowly lowered her hand from the pin and asked in a trembling voice, "Can you tell us what happened?"

The commander pulled a bag of tobacco and a pipe from his vest. He filled the bowl, struck a match and inhaled deeply. Darius held the smoke in his lungs for several long seconds then slowly exhaled. The scent of clove, cocoa, and licorice filled the air. Crossing his arms and cradling the pipe against his chest, he said, "Months ago, King Stefan began receiving reports that the citizens of this province were uneasy.

They felt they were being watched, even followed, though they could not see who was doing either. We dismissed it as foolishness."

Darius stopped and drew on his pipe a second time exhaling slowly, the scent of cloves swirling through the air. He shook his head and said, "Then the alleged attacks began. People claimed to be assaulted in fields, in the market, even in their homes. I say alleged for the citizenry claimed they could not see their attackers to defend themselves. The king ordered us here to investigate."

"He is a good king," said Nightwalker approvingly.

The other soldiers looked at each other and quickly dropped their eyes back to the tasks of cleaning swords, axes, crossbows, and shields. Isabella glanced at Darius. If the commander noticed their frowns, he did not acknowledge them. "When we arrived, reports were now coming in that men, women, even children were being attacked daily, but as we patrolled the area we did not see anything out of the ordinary."

A second man who had been sharpening his pike paused momentarily and said, "Over and over we scoured the countryside but did not see anyone who did not live in the province. We decided the villagers were lying."

Darius nodded and said, "Finally, I ordered one of my spies to dress as a traveling worker and take a job as a farm laborer. I thought if there were attackers, they might show themselves at a home unguarded by troops, or if the villagers were lying, my spy would learn of their malice. Tell them what you observed, Christian."

A young clean shaven man sitting next to Isabella put down the bow he was stringing. A quiver of arrows tipped in black and white feathers rested against his leg. "I was staying with a family held in high regard throughout the province," Christian began. "Father, sons, daughters worked side by side in the fields – hard workers all of them. One night at dinner they were discussing crop prices and what they hoped to receive from the year's harvest. Sadly, it was a disappointing year. They talked through the evening of how difficult it would be to get through the winter, what sacrifices would have to be made, that perhaps the children would have to go and stay with relatives in another village that had not suffered such deep losses. Their hearts were heavy. Suddenly

175

the father jumped from the table and began wildly swinging his arms screaming, 'Get away! Get away from me!' But there was no one there. It was so unexpected; we were all shocked."

"What did you do?" asked Isabella. Her hands had begun to tremble as Christian spoke. So as to not draw attention to the tremors, she pushed her hands under the table twisting the cloth of her dress in agitation.

"At first, I did nothing," said Christian turning to look at Isabella. "His wife and children tried to calm him, but the man became more agitated. He was screaming that something was hitting him, scratching at his face, pounding on his back. The man grabbed a chair and started swinging it as though defending himself. I jumped up to take the chair away, but before I could reach him, the farmer hit his youngest boy, a child of two, and knocked the babe to the floor."

"Oh, no," said Isabella, putting her hands to her face.

"The blow knocked the child unconscious. Blood spilled onto the floor from a deep cut on his forehead," said Christian, shaking his head. "The younger children began to cry and the older boys lunged to restrain their father who had not even noticed the child on the floor. Father and sons struggled until the fire had gone out of the man."

While Christian paused, the cook placed a pot of stew and platters of hot bread on the table. The stew was thick with leeks, carrots and barley, along with chunks of rabbit and boar. The bread was dark rye and Isabella could smell the honey baked deep inside. No one moved to take the food or the tankards of dark ale the cooked served.

Christian continued, "The father looked a changed man. He had aged by ten years in barely minutes. He tried to explain that something had possessed him. Fearing for her family, the mother took the babe and young children out of the house and ran to the neighboring farm to seek safety. The older boys and I eventually tied the man to his bed for he grew increasingly agitated and seemed to have lost all reason," said Christian. "Later as I spoke with the sons, they could not explain the behavior. They had never seen their father in such a state before."

"That is terrible, just terrible. Commander, what did you make of this?" Isabella asked anxiously her arms now crossed tightly against her chest.

"Frankly, I thought the man a liar. The family had just been discussing the hardship of the coming winter; I think the man's pride and shame got the best of him, and he took it out on the family. He used this nonsense of attacks to cover his loss of control," Darius said coldly. "Still to be sure, I sent out other spies to see what they could discover. When they returned, all had similar reports: men, women, even children going about the daily business of their lives when they suddenly became enraged, erratic, often injuring others or themselves, sometimes seriously."

"Dangerous, very dangerous," said Nightwalker almost to himself, the shine beginning to fade from his feathers.

"Dangerous indeed," growled Darius. He paused, lifted his tankard and drank deeply until it was empty. He slammed it on the table, wiping his mouth with the back of one hand, and motioning for the cook to refill it. "I traveled back to the castle and requested King Stefan come and lead our efforts. By the time we returned the situation had greatly deteriorated." The men shifted uneasily in their seats. Darius said, "The citizens began to do terrible things to one another. This is a province of many faiths where all have been accepted for generations. Yet over the days slurs were spoken, places of worship broken into, random beatings of church leaders occurred.

"Then one night a holy service was held celebrating women and children. Others of a different belief came and barred the doors and windows from the outside, doused the building and torched it. By the time my troops arrived the building was in flames with the screams of the women and children filling the air. We could do nothing to save them. Their neighbors – neighbors of many years – stood there in grim satisfaction, not even trying to escape our wrath. Upon questioning they said those families deserved to be punished for past injustices."

The blood drained from Isabella's face and beads of sweat dotted her forehead. She wanted the conversation to stop but no one even noticed her distress. All eyes were fixed on Darius as his voice grew louder and louder. "Other atrocities occurred," he thundered, "neighbor brutally attacking neighbor. People who had lived side by side for years now fought over differing political views. Men of one clan dragged men of another out of their homes into the night ranting of lost

177

property and stolen lands, beating old friends to death and throwing them in common graves. Nights later, others scavenged in those graves trying to find loot." Darius stopped. "There were no foreign attackers. People who had known each other for generations were killing each other." He drank from the tankard again. When it was empty the cook reappeared to fill it again.

"What was the king's response to this?" asked Nightwalker solemnly, his eyes black, his beak sooty, all light gone from his star.

"He came, but he did not lead as I expected," Darius said tightly, his face flushed red; the pipe in his hand grown cold.

"That angered you, Commander?" asked Nightwalker quietly.

"Anger is not the word I would use." Darius pushed away from the table and threw down his pipe.

"The king has his own ways." said Nightwalker.

"Indeed, raven, he does and this time he has erred grievously," said Darius, his eyes blazing with rage.

"What did he do?" asked Isabella in a tiny voice. She could barely utter her next words. "He didn't run away did he?"

"Almost as bad," snarled Darius as he rose from his seat and began to pace back and forth. "When he arrived, he watched, listened and talked to the people of the area. After several days, he called me to his quarters and told me we were not dealing with an ordinary enemy. Well, that was obvious," he said bitterly. "Then he sent for the Oracle Sofia, from the Southern Province."

"I know of her," said the raven, nodding thoughtfully. "It is told she is a direct descendent of the Ancient Ones and is very powerful and wise sage."

"I don't care who or what she is. She is not a military leader," Darius said angrily as he smashed his fist to the table. "This past week, the king and the Oracle met privately for two days. Two days," he said shaking his head in disbelief, "and I was not consulted even once – not once. How dare they plan a course of action without involving the military?" Darius grabbed a piece of wood and threw it into the fire with such force sparks flew everywhere.

"The king has lost his courage. He is afraid to fight. He has been ineffective since the war with the Empress," Rufio muttered from his

178

seat next to Nightwalker. Immediately the air around the table crackled with anger.

"What did you say?" hissed Darius.

"You heard me," snarled Rufio, "and you know I speak the truth." Darius charged Rufio – grabbing him by the chest and yanking the man to his feet.

"You dare blaspheme the king? I should kill you for your insolence!" roared Darius.

Instead of backing away, Rufio stepped closer to Darius towering over the commander. "Truth, not insolence!" the soldier bellowed. "Stefan is a coward and a weakling. He is afraid to do what must be done. You said yourself the military should rule. Why do you not take command, declare martial law and deal severely with these people? They are murderers and monsters!"

"You have doomed yourself speaking treason, filthy traitor," hissed the commander as he drew his sword. Instantly the group exploded from the table. All had drawn their weapons, brother against brother. Half stood behind Darius, half behind Rufio. Before anyone could move, Darius thrust his sword forward. As blood burst from Rufio's body, Isabella screamed and fell to the ground.

✦
DARIUS

Darius threw the bloody sword onto the floor of his tent furious with himself for losing control, furious with Rufio for daring to challenge the authority of the king, furious for almost agreeing with the soldier. So deep in thought was the commander that he did not hear the rustle of silk in the far corner of his tent. When he felt someone move in the darkness, he pulled his dagger from his belt and turned to confront the intruder. He dropped to his knees when he saw the woman emerge from the shadows.

"Majesty, forgive me. I had no idea it was you," the commander said as he knelt before the Queen Mother.

"I would expect no less from a warrior, Darius," said the Queen Mother gently. "Rise, my friend, we have much to speak of."

"As you command," he said as he rose from the ground extending his arm to her.

The Queen Mother placed her hand gently on his arm and was led to a table covered with maps and troop communiqués. "Tensions run high," she said softly as they seated themselves.

"Yes," said Darius grimly. "We are at a dangerous impasse, Majesty. One I do not think I can control or want to control."

"I see," said the Queen Mother gently tilting her head, gazing intently at the soldier. "You oppose Stefan's strategy in dealing with the violence here?"

Darius stared at the maps, unwilling to express his true feelings to the Queen Mother.

"Darius, you have served us well. I have never doubted your commitment to protecting the inhabitants of this kingdom. I do not doubt your commitment now. Please, I ask you to speak freely," said the Queen Mother. Darius looked into the Queen's eyes and saw only compassion and acceptance.

"Majesty," he said, "all I know is battle. I do not understand the Oracle's way and that is what Stefan has committed himself to."

"What do you fear will happen, if Stefan proceeds with this course of action?" she asked calmly.

"I fear he will fail to eradicate the violence in this province."

"And then what would happen?" she asked.

The commander rose and began to pace the floor. "I fear the violence will overwhelm all who live here and then spread from this region of the kingdom to others."

"And then?" the Queen pressed gently.

Darius turned to face the Queen Mother and said, "Madame, if left unchecked, I fear what is happening here could overwhelm the entire kingdom. It would be disastrous. It could destroy us all."

"You care deeply."

"It is my job to protect the citizens of this world and to protect the young king as well," Darius answered gruffly.

"You love him, don't you?" she asked.

"Majesty, what can a soldier say of love? I have served Stefan from his birth; he is my king," said Darius greatly distressed as he returned to his seat before the Queen. "I owe him my loyalty, Majesty, I am loyal. I oppose him now for his own good."

"I see," said the Queen Mother, nodding. The wind picked up and rattled the canvas walls of the tent. The candles that gave them light flickered and then became steady as the wind dropped off. The scent of lavender and mint filled the tent. "I know you are committed to his wellbeing and to that of the kingdom, Darius. It is why I trust you."

Darius nodded, grateful for the Queen's understanding. Then she surprised him by asking, "Do you trust me?" The old warrior looked into the Queen's eyes. He tried to see her anew, to assess her strength and wisdom. With a sigh, he chose to trust her again as he had so many other times in his years of service.

He knelt before his Queen. "I do, Madame," Darius said solemnly, "More than anyone in this kingdom."

"Would you trust me still, if I asked something of you to which you disagreed?" she asked reaching out her hand and lifting the old warrior's face so she could gaze into his eyes.

"Though it might test me, I would like to say yes, I would trust you."

"Good," she said. The glow of the candles grew brighter. The Queen Mother took the scarred hands of the Commander of the Elite Guard into her own and said, "Then I will ask, if you believed I could work with Stefan so this violence would not spread to the wider kingdom, would you allow me that chance, even if we did not employ your troops in this endeavor?"

"Majesty," said Darius with a groan.

She squeezed his hands slightly and said, "Please, Darius, allow yourself a moment to think on my request."

Darius looked into the Queen Mother's eyes again. He stood slowly drawing himself to full military attention. He brought his arm to his breast plate and barked, "I am at your command, Madame."

The Queen Mother smiled. "Thank you. I appreciate all you have done and will continue to do for us all. I honor you, Darius. You have kept us safe for such a very long time," she said softly.

"What are your orders, Madame?" said Darius his eyes fixed straight ahead.

"I wish for you to break camp tomorrow and return all the troops to the castle garrison. Should I need you, Darius, I will not hesitate to call you back," said the Queen quietly.

"It will be as you wish, Madame."

With that the Queen Mother rose from her chair and took Darius's arm. The commander led her to the opening of the tent. "I will proceed from here alone, old friend," she said and disappeared into the night.

A STEP BACKWARDS

Isabella awoke in a strange tent. For an instant she wondered where she was. Then images of splattered blood exploded through her mind. She bolted upright gasping for air. "I am here, Isabella, I am here," whispered Nightwalker. He hopped onto the cot opening his great wings to embrace the girl.

"Rufio…?" She could barely say his name.

"He will survive. It was a wound to the arm – deep with a great loss of blood."

"Nightwalker, I was so frightened." Isabella started to tremble. "Please, take me away from here. This place is not safe. Everything happened so quickly: the yelling, the pushing, the weapons. I have never seen such things. Blood everywhere…"

"I know. I know," murmured Nightwalker as he preened Isabella's hair.

"Please don't leave me alone, not even for a second," she whimpered. The flap of the tent jerked open and Darius entered the tent. Isabella pushed herself deeper into Nightwalker's embrace. *Small, I must get small so he will not see me or hurt me* she thought.

The commander stood silently staring at the raven and child. Then he said, "I have come to tell you we are breaking camp and will return to the castle garrison today. You are welcome to travel with us if you so choose." Though his tone was curt the rage was gone.

"This is most unexpected. Why are you leaving?" asked Nightwalker, his wings tight around Isabella.

"It is at the request of our Queen," the commander said briskly. "If you will excuse me, I have much to do." He turned to leave the tent.

"Nightwalker, ask him where the king is," Isabella whispered.

Darius stopped, his back to the raven and the girl, and said without turning to face her, "I do not know where Stefan is. It is out of my hands. Let my men know if you will travel with us." He stepped out of the tent and made his way back into the camp.

Nightwalker peered down at the little girl hidden in his wings and said, "Isabella, what do you wish to do? We could travel back with them to Sir Alfred."

"The soldiers scare me," she whimpered, "but I do not wish to remain in this place of evil people. Let us get back into our balloon and sail back to Sir Alfred, Nightwalker. I want to go back to where I feel safe," she cried. "I do not want to search for the book or play any more silly games."

"That is what we shall do then, child, as soon as you are ready to leave," said Nightwalker rocking the girl back and forth.

"Thank you," said Isabella gratefully. "I am ready. Let us leave now."

✦
THIRTEEN SECONDS

The clock in the dark room marked midnight; the hour and minute hands neatly aligned one over the other. The machines in the room wheezed, whirred and beeped as the woman lay silent, a marble statue on the white bed. Where there had not been a flutter of her eyes for weeks, there was sudden eye movement back and forth, back and forth beneath her closed lids. Hands that had lain flat along her body suddenly clenched into fists. Her eyes opened and her pupils dilated as they adjusted to the darkness of the room. The woman's head turned slightly to the left and her eyes focused on the man asleep in a chair next to her bed. She stared at him for thirteen seconds. Then her eyes closed; her hands relaxed flat. The machines continued to whir, wheeze and beep.

✦
THE SWAMP OF DARKNESS

Later that morning, Isabella and Nightwalker made their way back to their hot air balloon. As soon as they climbed into the basket, the wind picked up and a gentle current pulled the balloon high into the air. Isabella huddled on the floor of the basket her legs pulled tight to her chest. She rocked herself back and forth, back and forth. "Nightwalker, did you see all the blood? How could Darius have attacked one of his own men? Could the story be true that citizens of the province burned women and children? How could that father have hurt his baby the way he did? Nightwalker, did you see all the blood?" She was shivering though the air was hot and muggy.

"So many questions for such a little girl," murmured the raven as once again he wrapped his great wings about her body.

"Your feathers are so soft and comforting," she sighed though her trembling did not abate. I am beginning to hate questions. In fact, I want to take the Curiosa off. What good does asking questions do, if there are never any answers? Not having answers makes everything worse."

"If that is what you wish to do, of course you can take her off, Isabella," said Nightwalker kindly. "I think though, the Curiosa has taken hold of you so whether you wear her or not, the questions will arise."

"Sir Alfred said the same thing."

"It is part of her gift. After we are safely away from here, I will tell you her story, but not now. You have been through quite a lot. Why don't you try to sleep a bit?" he said.

"Only if you hold me, will I try. At least if I sleep I need not think of all I have seen."

"I will gladly hold you," replied the bird.

"Thank you," said Isabella, "you are kind, so very kind." Before drifting off to sleep she sighed once more and said, "We were having such fun traveling and playing games, weren't we, Nightwalker? Why did it all have to be ruined?" She closed her eyes and entered the dreamtime.

Immediately she was standing in the village cemetery. *I have been here before* she thought. All around her, graves were covered with stones to keep the forest scavengers from digging for the dead. Isabella looked down and saw she stood at the lip of an open grave. "Mother!" she wailed.

Then, as before, she was sitting on the stoop of her cottage. Isabella could hear sobbing coming from inside the house. She stood and slowly entered the house her heart pounding wildly in her chest. The girl knew what she would see. From the doorway, Isabella saw her mother crying with her head on the edge of their table. Her father stood staring down into a coffin which was laid across benches in the middle of the floor. Candles surrounded the coffin, their flames flickering as Isabella entered the room. She knew neither parent would look up as she entered.

Fear churned in her stomach and her legs were so heavy Isabella could barely make her way to the coffin. When she looked down she once again looked into a face so like her own but not. Though covered with a sheer cloth, she could see the girl's bloated features and the black and green mottled skin. A terrible odor filled the room. *Who is she?*

Again, Isabella ran outside and vomited. Again, she turned and ran from her home. She knew where she was going. In minutes, she reached the edge of the forest and ran blindly into the woods. She tried to block the images but could not. The sight of the girl in the coffin – the stench of the room – her parents' pain – it all overwhelmed her. *I think I know her. It is not me. Why can I not remember who she is?* On and on she ran, hot tears of sorrow burning her cheeks. Finally she began to tire and slowed her pace. As she did so, Isabella noticed something wrong with her surroundings. She knew this was not her forest, and she knew the weather would change. Instantly, the wind picked up, tossing the tree branches back and forth. It began to rain.

Then, as before, the temperature began to plummet and snow began falling. Then as before, barefoot and in a thin cotton smock, Isabella stood perfectly still in the swirling snow, thick flakes sticking to her arms and face. *No one will be looking for me here* she thought. *Mother and Father are too sad to be looking for me.* Then as before, Isabella dropped to her knees. *I have done something terribly wrong and now I am going to die.*

"Isabella, Isabella, wake up. Wake up. You are having a bad dream," said Nightwalker as he gently shook the girl. The girl opened her eyes and stared at the raven blankly. It took her a second to recognize Nightwalker.

"It was only a dream. Thank goodness, it was only a dream," she cried hugging the bird close to her. Oh, Nightwalker, make all this dreadfulness go away." Before the great raven could respond, the wind blew its last breath and the balloon began its descent.

"Why is the balloon dropping?" Isabella asked alarmed. Nightwalker did not answer. In minutes, the balloon completed its drop and settled on a muddy scrap of land in the middle of a bog. "Where do you think we are?" Isabella asked, rising from the floor of the basket moving from one side to the other trying to see where they were.

"I fear we are in a swamp, child," the raven replied. "The Lower World has but one; I believe the wind has brought us to the Swamp of Darkness." True to its name, the fen was a place of shadow. Sulfur gases bubbled up from the dark water; skeleton trees, burned by some great fire, stood guard over a land where nothing lived. The air was clammy, cold and smelled of rotting mud. There was not a single sound of life. Isabella looked at the raven her eyes wide with fear. The sulfur was already burning her nose. She whispered, "What are we to do? Imagine us out of here, Nightwalker. Please."

"The power of shadow clouds my magic, Isabella. Now you must listen to me," Nightwalker said, his eyes piercing hers. "I am going for help. I do not want you to leave the balloon. Do you understand me? Do not leave this balloon for any reason." The girl nodded. Nightwalker spread his great wings and took flight to a blackened tree shrouded in gray moss. He turned to look at Isabella. "Do not leave the balloon," he ordered.

The moment the raven left her side, Isabella began to tremble uncontrollably. "Nightwalker, I've changed my mind," Isabella shouted. "Let's just stay here together. I am sure the wind will come back. Nightwalker, come back, please! I am afraid."

"I must fly ahead and look for help, Isabella. The wind will not return," the mighty raven cawed. He opened his powerful wings and in seconds was gone from sight. Isabella dropped to the floor of the basket, knees to chest, rocking back and forth.

Hours passed, and the sun began to drop in the sky. *Darkness is coming soon. Why has Nightwalker not returned?* Isabella strained to hear any sound of the raven's call or the beating of his wings. Then she heard a voice so faint she thought she might have imagined it. "Isabella, help me!" Then again she heard, "Isabella, please come and help me!" *Something has happened to Nightwalker. I must go help him.* Again she heard, "Isabella!"

His warning forgotten, the child climbed out of the basket. "I'm coming, Nightwalker," she shouted. "I'm coming." The trail was narrow and muddy – thick black water lapped at both sides of the path. As far as Isabella could see dead trees cluttered the swamp like submerged bodies; their branch-like fingers clawing through the water reaching for help that never came. Isabella called to Nightwalker as she moved quickly along the trail, stopping to listen for his reply. There was only silence and the sweet sickly stench of decay. *I know I heard him* she thought as she followed the twisting and turning path. But after repeated calls were met with silence, she began to doubt herself. *Perhaps I was wrong; perhaps I just imagined it. I should go back. Nightwalker was so insistent I not leave the balloon.*

When she turned about, Isabella was horrified to discover the trail behind her had disappeared. Her way was blocked by fallen trees; their rotting trunks covered with mottled mold and spores of fungus. She had no choice but to continue on. As night fell, the silence of the swamp was broken with the sounds of waking animals. An owl screeched; a cougar screamed in the distance; snarling hyenas fought over a kill; mice scurried in the underbrush. *I must find shelter* she thought anxiously.

Just then Isabella saw something through the trees. She stopped to see if she could hear anything ahead. Silence… She cautiously made her way forward and saw a dwelling set back from the trail. Staying in the shadows, she watched to see if there was movement in the hut. Nothing… Isabella crept to a narrow wooden window and peered inside. The fireplace was cold though there were a few large pieces of wood by the hearth. A filthy mattress and blanket were shoved into a corner. Dirty bowls and scraps of food littered the floor and table. Dust and dirt covered everything. A gaunt rat scurried across the floor. *This place is abandoned. I will stay here until light and then go on. Where is Nightwalker?*

Trembling she entered the hut leaving the door open. As she moved to the center of the room, the door behind her closed and the bolt dropped. "I have been waiting for you," growled a voice behind her. Isabella's knees buckled as fear drove her to the floor. "You fell for my trick, stupid girl; that was me calling you." The dark man from her long ago dreams stood behind her.

"You thought you escaped me, didn't you, Isabella? But you came to my home." His voice grew softer and colder as he moved closer to Isabella. Still she could not stand or face him. "I watched you in the Village World," he sneered. "I watched you come here to my world your head filled with stupid questions, fun, that pathetic book. Then the Northern Province – that was a treat for you wasn't it? You started to remember, didn't you? That's when I knew I had to finish you."

The predator moved one step closer and knelt quietly behind Isabella. She could feel the heat of his foul breath on her neck. She knew she should run but she could not move. "This was inevitable, you and me. I will now teach you what life is really about. It is all suffering and punishment. You know you deserve punishment, don't you for what you did?"

Isabella closed her eyes. She felt his hands around her neck. "Are you thinking about horses with red saddles now, Isabella? Are you thinking about those stars in the sky and your imaginary lives?" He began to squeeze her throat slowly then tighter and tighter. "How about the girl in the coffin; are you thinking of her? What you did?" he hissed. Isabella could no longer breathe and the room was growing dark.

Suddenly, there was the shattering of wood and the wild flapping of wings. Nightwalker burst through the window and flew straight towards the man's back – his talons extended like knives. The raven cleaved onto the man's shoulders and furiously stabbed the man's head and neck with his razor sharp beak. The man bellowed in rage releasing Isabella, swinging his arms wildly trying to throw Nightwalker off his back.

Isabella slumped to the floor drawing in great gasping breaths. Nightwalker screeched, "ISABELLA, GET UP! FIGHT! DO YOU HEAR ME, FIGHT!" Struggling to her knees, Isabella desperately looked around the room for anything she could use to defend herself. She crawled to the hearth and grabbed a piece of firewood. Staggering to her feet, Isabella stumbled towards the predator and Nightwalker who were locked in a frenzied dance of rage and blood. The girl swung the wood hitting the man in the groin.

The man had not expected the blow. His legs buckled, and he fell to the floor. As he struggled to right himself, Isabella raised the wood and hit the man again, this time on the side of the head. She saw blood spurt from a wound. A look of disbelief crossed the man's face. With a scream of fury, he reached behind his neck, grabbed the raven's leg and snapped the bones. The predator threw Nightwalker to the floor and kicked the raven into the hearth. Then he lunged toward the girl grabbing the front of her dress. Isabella jerked back and felt her gown tear and the Curiosa fall to the floor. As Isabella crouched to escape the blows from the man, the predator grabbed her by her hair and swung her across the room. Isabella slammed into the door of the hut and slumped to the floor.

Desperately Isabella reached to throw open the bolt, but the man grabbed her hair again pulling her to him. The girl screamed in pain and terror. "You cannot get away from me," he said breathing quickly. "I am going to finish this now," he said as he squeezed her tiny neck.

From across the room, the great raven saw Isabella's body go limp. With his last bit of strength Nightwalker flew towards the man driving his beak deep into the predator's ear. The man roared in pain as he dropped the girl and brought a hand to his bleeding head. "She is dead and now I will kill you, you filthy bird!" he screamed reaching for a knife in his boot.

As the predator stabbed Nightwalker, the raven's screams broke through Isabella's awareness. With a last bit of strength, she threw the bolt and crawled from the hut. The girl could hear curses from the man as she stumbled into the bog. Isabella knew she had to get far enough away to hide in the brush. If the man caught her, she would not escape again.

As Isabella lurched through the swamp, the wind picked up, the trees thrashing back and forth like demons in a mad dance. Branches whipped at her face and roots grabbed at her feet. Suddenly, Isabella heard the man crashing through the brush behind her. "I am coming to get you," he screamed. "You have no more protection. Can't hear the bird, can you?" The man started laughing wildly. "I broke his neck, right in half, yes I did."

The girl sobbed as she stumbled through the swamp. Rain started to fall and then sleet. In seconds it was freezing snow. *It is summer. How can it be snowing?* Her dress was wet and heavy on her body; each piece of ice hit Isabella like a fist.

"Selfish," the first ice sliver screeched as it tore at her face.

"You are going to get what you deserve," screamed an icy stiletto piercing her arm.

"You should have died, not her."

"Now is the time for your punishment," screeched an army of ice shards as they slashed her legs.

Isabella could no longer hear the man behind her but still she staggered forward. *I must find a place to hide* she thought desperately. In minutes Isabella's dress was frozen, and she knew she had two enemies, the man and the cold. She had to hide and warm herself to survive. She slipped and fell to her knees, crawling through the underbrush looking for anything that could give her shelter – a hollow log, a fallen tree – anything. But there was nothing. In desperation, Isabella huddled on the ground at the base of a two dead trees and tried to cover herself with moss and mud.

"Help me; someone help me," she whimpered curling herself into a tiny ball. "Nightwalker, don't be dead. Please don't be dead. The snow was falling furiously and covered Isabella's body in seconds. *They all lied. Nightwalker, the king, Setine, even Sir Alfred. They said there would always be help, but there is no one for me. I am alone. I am dying.* Seconds later, she lost consciousness.

✛ LOSING GROUND

Intensive Care was dark and the nurses' station subdued as the evening shift settled in. Suddenly, the monitor alarms for Room 2 went off; the patient's blood pressure and heart rate were dropping rapidly. The brain waves were fluctuating wildly.

The nursing supervisor moved quickly towards the woman's room. As she crossed the threshold, she turned back to the medical team and yelled, "She's stroking! Get in here stat!"

✧
THE WOMAN IN THE WOODS

Moving urgently through the frozen mud, the woman searched for the child. She knew she was there. When the woman found Isabella, she brushed the snow away from the girl's stiffened body. Removing her cape, the woman covered Isabella and lifted the child into her arms. Slowly, the woman made her way out of the icy swamp, cradling the girl close to her.

The woman was worried for Isabella was barely breathing. When they reached her cottage, she quickly covered the girl with heavy quilts and built a roaring fire in the hearth. She pulled her chair close to Isabella's bed and tried to coax a spoonful of warm broth into the girl's mouth, but the liquid froze when it touched the girl's lips. When Isabella began to shiver violently, the woman slipped under the quilts to warm the child with her own body.

Within hours, a raging fever enveloped the girl and Isabella entered the dark dreamtime. One moment she was sinking into quicksand and could not breathe as thick mud filled her mouth and nose; in the next moment a hooded figure wearing her lost Curiosa presented her with nesting dolls. As she opened each doll, a body part – finger, ear, foot – tumbled out. Then without warning she was being chased by headless dogs – worms and maggots spilling from their severed stumps. Always she came to a room where a dark man stood behind her. Isabella could smell his foul breath and feel his hands tighten around her throat.

The woman gave the child special herbs to break her fever, but they had no effect. She placed cold compresses on the girl's body to soothe her, but they began to simmer and cook in seconds. Two nights and two days passed before Isabella's fever broke in an ocean of sweat. The woman gently bathed Isabella in lavender water and clothed her in a

194

gown of the finest soft cotton. The girl slept peacefully. When she woke, Isabella saw a woman cooking over a blazing hearth. *Is this another dream?* she wondered. All she could remember was the predator and the cold snow.

The woman turned and saw Isabella was awake. She moved quickly to her bed and said, "Oh, Isabella, thank goodness." Her voice was as warm and kind as any Isabella had ever known. "Do not try to talk. You have been through quite an ordeal."

She knelt by the bed and took the child's hand. "You are safe," she said softly. "You are with me in the village of Agape. Nightwalker alerted the villagers you were stranded in the swamp. The men went to the hut and captured your attacker as he was in pursuit of you. There was a terrible fight, but the man was restrained and is now in jail. The constable will keep him there until you are well enough to decide what you would like to do with him."

Nightwalker...? Isabella's throat so damaged by the man's hands, she could not speak.

"He was very seriously injured but is alive. He is being taken care of by a wonderful healer, and she will send news as soon as she can about his condition." The woman gently brushed the hair away from Isabella's face. Tears rolled out of the corners of Isabella's eyes.

"I know. I know, child, it was terrible. But you are safe now. You are safe here."

Exhausted, Isabella closed her eyes and drifted back into kaleidoscope dreams. She was in a cemetery. Had the woman lied? Was Nightwalker dead? She was in Sir Alfred's courtroom on trial for murder. Whose? She could smell the stench of death and hear the cries of mourning. Everything went dark, and she was afraid.

Suddenly, waves of warmth and light flowed through her body. No longer was she in darkness but was sitting in front of the woman's fireplace on a pile of sumptuous furs. Setine sat beside her dressed in a gown of shimmering silver silk. Her arms and ankles were adorned with bracelets of white gold and platinum. Strands of braided pearls fastened by a huge diamond encircled her head. She illuminated the cottage glowing like the moon and stars against a black sky.

"Dear Isabella, I had to come to see you," she said as she took Isabella's hand. "I want you to know the woman who found you is wonderful, and she will help you get well."

Isabella – healed and restored in the dream – threw her arms around Setine's neck. "Setine, please make these terrible dreams stop. This is your kingdom, you can make them stop," she implored the queen. "I cannot bear them. Help me."

"It is your mind's way of trying to make sense of the attack in the swamp," Setine said softly as she put her arms gently around the girl. "The dreams are trying to help sort through the feelings of what happened to you. Do not fight them; as you release the feelings the darkness of the dreams will lessen."

"I was so afraid. I did not know anyone could ever be that afraid," Isabella wept. She laid her head in Setine's lap and cried for a very long time. *I will cry forever.*

"Your tears are good, Isabella. Each one washes away a tiny bit of the pain," the queen said as she stroked the little girl's hair. "I will stay with you until there are no more tears this night."

Indeed, the tears began to slow. In a moment of respite, the child confessed mournfully, "Nightwalker has been terribly hurt. I don't know where he is. I don't know if he will survive. He may already be dead, and it's my fault. He died trying to protect me."

"He is not dead, child," said Setine tenderly reaching out to stroke Isabella face. "He is with me. I am caring for him. He was seriously hurt, but he will survive."

Isabella sat up. Her eyes widened. "You are telling me the truth?"

"I am," the young queen nodded, the diamond on her forehead reflecting firelight throughout the room. "He told me to tell you he was proud of you." Setine smiled lovingly. "He said you gave that man a good-sized gash on the head when you hit him with the wood." Setine gave Isabella a reassuring hug and said, "Now, doesn't that sound like our Nightwalker? It will take time, but he will be fine and visiting you as soon as he can."

"Highness, thank you – thank you!" Isabella said squeezing Setine with all her might. "Please tell Nightwalker I love him. Tell him how grateful I am that he saved my life."

"He knows, dearest. Now lay your head back on my lap and let me brush your hair. I think you like that, yes?" The girl gave a slight nod and settled deep into the furs, with Setine's lap a pillow. As Isabella relaxed, the Queen of the Dreamtime sprinkled star dust through Isabella's hair: silver and gold, purple and red sparkled on every strand. There would be no more dreams that night.

The following morning, Isabella awoke to the smell of cinnamon bread. She had no appetite, but the blazing fire and the smell of warm bread and hot chocolate soothed her. The woman was sitting by her bed reading. When she felt Isabella stir, the woman smiled as she closed her book and knelt by Isabella's bedside. "Good morning," she said softly. "How are you?"

I cannot move whispered Isabella through her thoughts.

The woman nodded. "You are very weak, that is why you can't move," she said.

I cannot speak.

"I know. Your throat needs time to heal," the woman said, stroking Isabella's arm, her touch as light as a feather. "I have a special poultice wrapped around your neck. It will help with the healing."

How get here? Isabella was so tired she found it difficult to organize her thought words.

"I was sent word you were in trouble, so I went to the swamp to find you."

Sent word?

"You have many friends in the Lower World, child. I received pleas for help from them all," said the woman. "We can speak of that later. Right now, do you think you might try a tiny, tiny sip of broth? We need to start building up your strength."

Isabella shook her head no. *Too sore to swallow... Who are you?*

The woman smiled. "My name is Kriya. I want you to know I will take good care of you." She was true to her word. Over the next several weeks, Kriya lovingly attended the child. The ordeal in the swamp had taken a terrible toll on Isabella's body and spirit, and she could do little for herself. At first, Isabella slept much of the time, but as the days passed she became more alert to her surroundings though she could only speak through fragmented thoughts.

While she was awake, Kriya talked to Isabella as she went about her daily activities. Each day the woman explained something new to the girl. She showed her the plants and herbs she collected from the forest describing the healing qualities of each and how they were helping Isabella grow in strength. She discussed the habits of the animals that came into their clearing each day. After coming in with firewood, she would tell Isabella about the subtle changes in the trees and wind and what that told her about the coming weather.

Isabella could not take her eyes off her rescuer. Unlike other women, Kriya wore men's trousers and shirts though they were not ordinary men's clothes. Much of her clothing was bold red or vibrant purple. Her hair, which she wore loose and free, tumbled down her back. It was thick and curly black, streaked with silver. Her wide set eyes were emerald green, her mouth was full and red, and she had deep laugh lines around her eyes. Her skin was the color of golden honey. As Kriya moved about the cottage, Isabella smelled the scent of meadow flowers that seemed to follow her. She watched the woman cook, eat, laugh, sing, work and rest. Every action was filled with love and goodness, honesty and humor. The child was grateful this woman had found her in the swamp.

Slowly, slowly Isabella began to recover – sipping broth one day, sitting in bed a few minutes another, finally speaking one syllable at a time. Time stopped for the girl and place existed only within the walls of Kriya's cottage. There was nothing more, and Isabella was content. One evening Isabella sat in a chair next to Kriya as the woman stitched a beautiful quilt by the light of the fire. The girl could speak softly now and asked about the unusual pattern. The woman said, "This is a memory quilt. I have a number of them. Each square represents a person, place or event that holds meaning for me. Right now I am stitching you into my quilt."

"Me?" Isabella whispered.

"Yes, you," smiled Kriya. "See this piece of cloth? It is part of the cloak I wore the night I found you. I have embroidered it with your name: Isabella, Explorer."

"I am not an explorer," Isabella said softly, her eyes dropping to her lap. "There will be no more adventures for me and no more questions.

They just brought me bad things." The fire crackled and sparks shot through the chimney. Isabella looked up and sighed. She watched the woman work on her quilt, her face so calm and serene.

"Kriya?" she whispered again.

"Yes, child?" said the woman her green eyes shining as she stopped her stitching and looked into Isabella's eyes.

"You have been so kind to me. I do not know how to thank you."

Kriya said, "There is no need for thanks for I have so enjoyed being with you." She chuckled, "Actually, you remind me of myself as a child."

Isabella rose from her chair to give the older woman a heartfelt hug. "I would be proud to grow up like you," she murmured. The woman patted Isabella on the back and kissed her cheek. "When you are stronger, would you like me to show you how to stitch your own quilt?" she asked after Isabella was settled back in her chair. "No," replied the girl, "it is enough watching you."

Kriya nodded and resumed her work. After watching the woman for several minutes, Isabella thought *I know so little of her.* Kriya looked up and with her radiant smile said, "What do you wish to know, sweet one?" Isabella blushed. "No need to be shy, Isabella. Please, ask me whatever you wish. I know your throat is tender so perhaps you might speak through your thoughts." *Thank you.* Isabella sat gazing at the fire, questions tumbling through her mind. *She is so kind; one could not wish for a better mother. I wonder if she has children of her own.*

"Why, yes, I do," said the woman smiling broadly as she reached for a square embroidered with a pair of wolves. I have twins – a boy and a girl. They are grown and on their own now. I take great delight in them."

Twins! What are their names? Isabella asked curiously.

"Setine is my daughter and Stefan is my son."

Isabella gasped, her hands going to her throat. *Did I hear her correctly?!* She rasped, "Queen Setine and King Stefan? You are the Queen Mother?"

The Queen Mother laughed so hard the raccoon peering into the window fell off the sill. When she composed herself the Queen said,

"Darling Isabella, take care not to strain your voice; you are healing so beautifully. Perhaps you might continue with your thought voice."

Isabella could barely think the words. *Are you really the Queen Mother?*

"I am indeed," Kriya smiled nodding her head as she made the next stitch in the memory quilt. Outside, the raccoon was joined by a fox, deer and owl all peering through the window most curious what would happen next. Wide-eyed Isabella thought *The king said you enjoyed nature, but I thought he meant you held court at a country estate!*

"Not a cottage? Quite frankly, I tired of court life long ago, too much pomp and circumstance for me. I much prefer the company of animals and plants. Besides, Stefan is a wonderful king, and Setine is a wonderful queen. The kingdom is well served by them both, and I do visit them often."

Majesty, I do not know what to say – I am sorry to have been such a burden. Isabella moved off her chair and knelt before the Queen Mother. Kriya gently pushed aside the quilt and sat next to Isabella on the floor. "Dear Isabella," she said taking the child's face into her hands and tilting it up so that the girl could look into her eyes. "Look at me. You are not a burden; indeed I am joyful to be in service of you." The raccoon, fox, deer and owl all nodded in agreement.

Majesty, it should be the other way around. I am nothing and you are a Queen.

"You are everything, Isabella."

Isabella's face blazed red, and she pulled away from the Queen. *No, Majesty, I am not. You do not know me. There is so much darkness inside of me.* The Queen reached for the quilt that had dropped to the floor and wrapped it about Isabella's shoulders and placed her arm round the girl. "You are everything, Isabella, everything," the Queen Mother murmured. As woman and child gazed into the fire, the flames dancing and embers shimmering, the Queen began to hum a lullaby of the forest.

The guests outside smiled and settled down into sleep. Soothed by the fire and the song of the woods, Isabella, too, relaxed ever so slightly. As she felt Isabella soften, Kriya began to sing in a deep sweet voice the lullabies of Isabella's village birth. On and on and on the Queen Mother sang until the girl sighed and slowly, ever so slowly, began to let the Queen's words of care seep into her weary heart.

✦

TIME

Months passed as Isabella regained her strength and ability to speak. Kriya watched the girl closely never pressing her to do more than she could. Of more concern to Kryia was the heaviness of the child's spirit and Isabella's difficulty accepting the Queen Mother's genuine love and affection. The girl was often quiet, her shoulders stooped, and her face dull. Yet the Queen Mother was infinitely patient and knew time and love could heal all wounds.

One morning after a breakfast of hot bread, butter, honey and blackberry preserves, a rasher of bacon and a soft-boiled egg, a wedge of cheese and a pot of mint tea, Kriya said, "If you are feeling well enough today, I would like to show you something outside. It will not take long."

"If that is what you wish, Majesty," Isabella replied quietly as she dried the breakfast dishes and returned them to their home in the kitchen cupboard.

"Isabella, what do you wish?" asked the woman quizzically, one eyebrow arching upward.

I fear I have upset her. So not to displease the Queen Mother Isabella replied, "Perhaps a little air would be good for me. I have not been outside since I came to you."

Kriya nodded as she walked to the clothing wardrobe opening doors carved with butterflies and wildflowers. This day the Queen wore forest green leggings; her tunic was brilliant turquoise linen cinched at the waist with a braided cord of orange and yellow; sea shells dangled at the ends of the cord. Her feet were covered with soft boots of brown leather laced to mid-calf. After rummaging a bit in the closet, she pulled out a yellow flannel shirt, black wool trousers and a yellow leather belt. She walked across the cottage to the kitchen space and handed Isabella the clothes. "I want you to be warm, and I think these will fit you nicely. I hope you don't mind the pants; I don't have any dresses here."

"Oh, Queen Mother, I do not want to trouble you. I can make do with my clothes." Isabella had been taught to say no to gifts lest she give the impression of need, but she had been troubled of late for her own clothes had grown too small. The girl had been startled when she dressed the first time after leaving her sick bed. Her skirt was too short – not even hitting her knees – and her sleeves barely covered her elbows.

"Darling, you are no trouble at all. A growing girl needs comfortable things to wear. You certainly have grown taller and the weight suits you well. Now go and get dressed while I feed the birds breakfast. They should be here shortly; they are very punctual. Then out we go; I think you will enjoy what I have to show you."

Isabella stood looking at the clothes given to her by the Queen Mother trying to decide if she should voice her confusion to the woman. *I am going to trust my questions won't bother her. She invites me to ask anything I wish.* Kriya smiled to herself as she bent over fifteen small bowls filling them with birdseed and apple cake crumbs.

"Queen Mother, I am confused why my old clothes seem small. Each day I feel so much better and you are such a wonderful cook, but I have grown so much it does not seem natural."

"Perhaps the time difference is at work here," the Queen Mother said matter-of-factly turning to the girl as she brushed apple cake crumbs from her hands.

Isabella furrowed her brows and said, "Time difference? I don't understand what you mean."

"From the expression on your face, I gather neither Nightwalker nor Sir Alfred explained how time operates in the Lower World? Why don't you change quickly while I make some hot chocolate, and then I will explain."

Isabella quickly undressed and pulled on the trousers, buttoned up the shirt, and cinched her belt. Everything fit perfectly. When she returned to the kitchen table, Isabella found the Queen settled comfortably before the window waiting for her and the arrival of the

202

breakfast birds. On the table were two steaming mugs of hot chocolate spiced with cinnamon, nutmeg and vanilla. "The clothes suit you well, Isabella," the Queen smiled approvingly.

"They make me feel good and sturdy. Isn't that funny? Perhaps because I know they are your clothes, Majesty, and they smell like you – lavender and mint," Isabella said shyly. "Thank you."

"Darling, you are more than welcome. All that I have is yours. You may want to try on other things later, if that is to your liking. I did always enjoy going into my mother's wardrobe," the Queen smiled wistfully. After taking a sip from her mug, Kriya said, "Let us now speak of time." As if on cue, a coven of fifteen flaming red cardinals fluttered onto the window sill each taking a seat before their own bowl. As they began their breakfast they watched the woman and girl with keen interest.

Cradling the mug with her hands, Kriya said, "Time in the Lower World is very different than time in the Village World. It is much faster and far less precise than your time. What may be a day or so in your world could be a week here; a month in the Village World could be a year in the Lower World. It's often hard to tell. "

"Why is that?" Isabella asked, eyes widened for she had never heard of such a thing.

"Different worlds are ruled by different principles. What is important for you to know, though, is that because you are a visitor and not a resident of the Lower World, your body is affected by our time."

"Which means what?" asked Isabella, starting to feel uneasy.

"That you are growing up more quickly here than you would in your village. That's why your clothes are suddenly too small for you."

Isabella had visions of waking with white hair, wrinkled skin and few teeth. "Does that mean I am going to become an old woman soon?"

The Queen reached over and patted Isabella's hand reassuringly. "Oh my, no; the changes are not that drastic," she said kindly. "We would never allow visitors to our world if we knew our time would hurt them."

So comfortable had Isabella become living with Kriya, she had given no thought at all to her own village since the attack. Now a million questions flooded her mind. *Though I have lost her, the Curiosa is still at work* she mused. With the floodgates opened Isabella asked, "How long have I been gone? How much longer will I be here? How old will I be when I get home? Will I ever go home?" As she paused for a breath so as to begin the next set of questions, the Queen Mother raised her hand gently.

"I really don't know the answers to all those questions," the Queen Mother said softly. "They are quite complex. It is because of that complexity that we seek to focus primarily on one particular unit of time."

"Which is?"

"The present moment. It is where our lives are lived most fully, and sometimes it is all that we have," said the Queen, taking another sip of her hot chocolate. "And if we live in the moment totally present, we are often shown right action for the next moment and the next, on and on....moment by moment."

Isabella nodded, her fingertips tapping the side of her mug as she reflected on the Queen's words. "I think I understand a bit. It feels as though I have been living that way since I came to your cottage. Is there anything else I need to know?"

The Queen smiled. "Well, there are two other differences." Isabella's fingertips stopped mid beat and she sighed a sigh so deep the fifteen cardinals, who had been enjoying their breakfast and the human discussion, sighed in support of the girl.

Kriya patted Isabella's hand and said, "It is not so bad, dear. The first you already know. While we basically have night and day and the same seasons, they sometimes fall in a different order than you experience in the Village World, and they may also be shorter or longer than what you know to be normal. Haven't you noticed that, Isabella?"

The girl nodded sadly. "I have. The night you found me began as summer and ended in terrible ice and cold."

"Yes. The other is rather interesting actually. One member of the kingdom may have a cycle of time very different than another."

"Now that I don't understand that at all!" said Isabella thoroughly perplexed. The cardinals began to twitter and whistle wildly amongst themselves as they sought to explain the phenomena to the girl. The Queen gave them a glance, and they quickly settled down.

"Some survive frozen in the past while others breathe in the present, still others live in the future," the Queen Mother continued.

"How do you all live together then?"

Kriya's face broke into a radiant smile of such warmth, the cottage began to glow and shimmer. "That is a wonderful question, the answer to which is we meet in the present moment! That is why it is our most important unit of time."

"My head is swimming, Majesty," Isabella said shaking her head. Looking down at her clothes she asked with a weak smile, "I know I am growing, but is it safe to say I will not be fifteen tomorrow?"

The Queen Mother patted Isabella on the hand. "Actually this morning you look exactly fifteen."

"I was just trying to make a joke!" exclaimed Isabella. "I am eleven. Fifteen is almost a woman!" All fifteen cardinals began to jump up and down and applaud for Isabella for they loved the number fifteen.

"These are complex ideas and normally I would explore them with you until you felt clear, but I think I am going to offer a distraction, at least for this 'present moment'," the Queen said with a wink. "Do I have your permission to do so?"

"What might that distraction be?" asked the girl, thoughts of fifteen swirling in her head.

"Our outing! I have something I would love to show you."

✦
SEASONS

The man gazed out of the window onto the hospital courtyard. The snow was falling thick and silent blanketing trees, sidewalks, and the few brave souls out on a blizzard night. He reflected back to the first time he sat in this room, in this chair, staring out of this window. The trees had been shimmering green. Over the months those same trees blazed red, orange, and yellow. Then their leaves dropped lifeless to the ground leaving them barren and vulnerable. Now the trees were clothed by snow in the dead of winter. He wondered if he would see them come back to life in the spring.

✦
WOLVES

The woman and girl bundled themselves head to toe in woolen coats and fleece throws, head scarves, mittens, and boots and stepped through the door. Everything was white. The trees were covered with snow, and huge drifts surrounded the cottage. A cold wind blew sheets of ice dust through the air covering the woman and girl. As they trudged through the drifts, the girl asked, "So this is normal to go from the middle of summer to deep winter without any warning?"

"As you named this morning, winter came the night you were attacked and has remained," was the Queen's simple reply. After walking a mile, she pointed ahead to a sturdy lean-to fashioned from pine branches. "That's where we are going." After reaching the shelter, the Queen said, "Wait for just a second please. I wish to make us cozy and warm." The Queen crawled into the lean-to. When she reached the far corner, she began to dig deep into the snow with her hands until she uncovered a bundle of fleece. Isabella watched as Kriya untied a binding cord and unfolded several huge rugs spreading them over the lean-to floor. "Come in, come in," Kriya said beaming. "Isn't this a wonderful shelter? Now in a bit you will see something even more wonderful."

Within minutes, a family of wolves trotted into sight. The pack consisted of twelve wolves: five adults, two yearlings and five pups. They were beautiful hearty animals, each a different color of gray, brown, white or black. Though they sniffed the air and knew the woman and girl were there, they did not seem disturbed.

Isabella stiffened. Sensing this, the Queen Mother said, "You have no need to fear the wolves. My friends know me well and will pay us no mind. Let's see what happens." But Isabella could not relax. The men from her village often told stories of wolves. They hated the animals, accusing them of killing livestock and even snatching sleeping babies from their yards. The men were always organizing hunting parties to kill the animals.

Isabella was shocked when the wolves began to play. The adults romped and jumped in the snow as joyfully as their pups. They threw themselves against each other as they ran this way and that playing some game only they seemed to understand. The pups tried to keep up with the elders but often tumbled over themselves landing in little puppy piles. Some concerned adult would then stop their play to ensure the babies were fine. After the pack tired, they lay in small groups grooming each other. It was obvious the animals had great affection for one another.

"Why do people hate these animals?" Isabella asked.

"I don't know. Unlike those terrible tales we hear, wolves are friendly and highly intelligent. I have watched this pack adapt to many challenges and can tell you they have strength, endurance and a fierce loyalty to their family. I think we humans could learn much from my friends here."

"But they do kill, don't they?" Isabella was not able to take her eyes off the pack as they lay dozing on one another in the winter sun, their grooming complete.

"Of course they do but only to eat. The wolves usually hunt weak or old animals that live in the forest. They do not attack people, and they kill livestock only in famine."

"Interesting how different they are from what I was taught." Isabella was intrigued by the animals. "What do you like best about them, Queen Mother?"

"How they communicate with each other. Their facial expressions are almost human at times, and they have wonderful voices, especially when they howl." The Queen Mother turned to look into Isabella's eyes. "Have you ever heard a wolf howl?" she asked.

"Yes," said Isabella shivering and huddling deep into her winter wraps. "It frightens me."

"I was just a little girl when I heard a wolf howl," mused the Queen. "It is what drew me to the forest the first time. I had to find the animals that made such a sound for I had never heard anything so wild and free. Quite frankly, I knew then I was not made for court; my spirit belonged to the forest." Without warning, the Queen Mother rose to her knees. She took a deep breath, threw back her head and howled at the top of her lungs. The leader of the pack, a huge coal-black male, stood immediately, ears twitching, tail up. The Queen took another breath and howled a second time. The other wolves sat up on their haunches looking at the two humans. They became utterly still, all breathing together in perfect rhythm, watching Isabella and the Queen, deciding what to do next.

When the Queen howled a third time, the leader responded with a series of enthusiastic barks. The remaining pack members joined in the excitement with their own barks and grunts. When the black leader began howling, the whole family joined in a communal song. Isabella had never heard such sounds. The howls echoed through the trees bouncing back even louder. A wild longing tore at Isabella's heart.

"Isabella, what is wrong?" the Queen Mother asked when she noticed Isabella shaking.

"I want to join in, but I am afraid I will sound and look foolish."

The Queen took Isabella's gloved hands into hers and said, "Child, there is no one to judge you out here. This is about enthusiasm not performance. Simply let yourself go. Take a deep breath, throw your head back and howl!" Isabella looked at the Queen and then at the wolves. She sat up straight and tall as the Queen had done, took several deep breaths and closed her eyes. The girl opened her mouth and just as quickly closed it. She opened her eyes, took another deep breath, and then sat down on the fleece rug. She could not bring herself to make such a noise. Ashamed, she turned away from the Queen and the pack.

"It is alright, child," said the Queen Mother gently. "There will be many opportunities for you to sing with the wolves. I have no doubt you will find your voice. For now, see if you can allow yourself to feel their joy."

Isabella was silent, and continued to sit with her back to the pack in shame. The Queen placed her arms around the girl and held her as the wolves howled in total abandon. For miles around, the sound of their voices reverberated through the forest proclaiming their delight in being alive.

✦
WORDS FROM AFAR

The Queen Mother gazed out of the window lost in thought. Though dusk was deepening the trees stood in stark relief against the thickly falling snow. Not a hint of wind ruffled the branches nor sounds disturb the silent fall of white. All was still. All was calm. The Queen Mother turned back to stitching her quilt. After a few moments she said, "The constable came to visit again today while you were with the wolves."

Isabella did not look up from the page she was reading so engrossed was she in *The Emotional Lives of Animals,* one of the Queen's favorite volumes. Kriya had introduced Isabella to the wonder of books just as she had done for her son pulling volume after volume from a bottomless cedar chest. "My magic library," the Queen called it. It had not taken long for Isabella to understand why the king loved to read.

The woman continued stitching a few minutes more before saying, "He was curious to know what you wanted done with the man from the swamp." Isabella's stomach tightened, but she continued reading. After she read the same paragraph three times, she closed her book, walked over to the Queen Mother's chair and dropped to the floor amidst colorful swatches of fabric: silk, velvet, linen, gingham, cotton and sack cloth, of all size, color, texture and pattern.

"I have forgotten about the swamp; or rather I was forgetting about it. I would prefer to not to think about it anymore," Isabella said tightly as she singled out a piece of red velvet from the pile of fabric. "Can't I just let the magistrate take care of everything? I don't need to be involved. I trust he will do the right thing."

"No, Isabella. As I have explained to you before, in our kingdom you must decide what is to be done with the man," replied the Queen calmly as she put aside her work and gazed at the young woman sitting below her. "It is one of our laws. You were the victim in the attack, the one done violence to, and you alone can prescribe the consequence."

"Punishment seems like a grownup activity," Isabella said as folded and refolded the velvet square. "They certainly spend a lot of time talking about it. At least the men in my village did. It was a constant topic of discussion." Isabella tossed the red velvet square back to its friends. "I hated listening to them. They were always so angry."

The Queen nodded. "I understand, my dear, but in the Lower World only you can decide what happens to him." The snow fell silently. The fire in the hearth burned silently.

And though Isabella was silent, her body raged. "They hang very bad people in my village," she said through clenched teeth.

"Is that what you wish done to him?" the Queen asked quietly.

"A part of me says yes, so he can never hurt me or anyone ever again." Acid filled her throat as memories of the attack seeped back into her awareness. "A part of me says no. Perhaps the constable can lock him up forever," Isabella said turning her face toward Kriya, her eyes searching the woman's face for affirmation.

The Queen said, "That is a possibility, but I must tell you the jails here are not very strong. I suspect he would escape in time."

"Can he be banished from the kingdom forever?" asked Isabella hopefully as she remembered the endless canyons of the Northern Province. She was on her knees reaching for the Queen's hands.

"I suspect with his anger, he would find his way back," returned the Queen Mother.

"Well, what else can be done with him then? There are no other options," Isabella cried as she put her head into the Kriya's lap. "I am so frightened of him, Queen Mother. I will always be frightened of him."

The Queen stroked Isabella's hair as she said, "The constable can do any one of the things you have suggested. That is for you to decide, but I would like you to think about something. As I have watched the animals in the forest over the years, I have found those that are the most dangerous have usually been wounded themselves. They have been injured by a hunter or trap and are in great pain. They don't know what else to do with their pain but attack any who cross their path."

"What do you do with such an animal when you find it?" asked Isabella raising her head to look at the Queen. She imagined Kriya killed the creature to end its pain. She knew the woman would be compassionate, but the image of the Queen doing any violence frightened her deeply. Isabella's arms reached around the Queen Mother's waist seeking a reassurance she could not name.

"I help them heal," said the Queen.

Isabella pulled back sitting on her heels, startled. "But if they are wounded that deeply they are crazed and dangerous – beyond healing."

"Nothing is ever beyond healing in this kingdom, Isabella." The woman's calm presence radiated love throughout the room.

Stunned, Isabella armored her heart against the softness in the room. Brusquely she said, "What has any of this to do with the man in jail?"

"I think you know," the woman said staring at the girl intently.

"Help him? He is worse than a crazed animal," Isabella stammered as she stood and walked away from the Queen. Her voice grew louder and she shouted, "Help him? Never! He is a monster. I am the one who needs help to feel free and safe. What you suggest is unthinkable. I thought you cared about me. How can you suggest such a thing?"

Before the Queen could answer, Isabella jumped to her feet and stomped angrily to her sleeping quarters. *I thought she cared about me. I thought she might even love me. Now she says I should help him when he tried to kill me. How dare she! How dare she! How dare she?* Isabella burned with rage and did not speak the remainder of the evening.

The following morning she left the cottage without a word, traversing the woods and visiting the village. She did not return until the sun was low in the sky. After a silent dinner of salt cod, beans, pickled beets and black bread, the girl pulled her chair as far away from Kriya as possible, and opened her book staring at the same words over and over. The Queen was sorting her healing herbs on the kitchen table when there was a knock on the door. When the Queen opened it, there stood Critiques.

He bowed deeply to the woman. "Hello, Majesty; my apologies for disturbing you at this hour. I am on urgent business for King Stefan on my way to Kronos. I can only stay for a moment, but hoped I might be able to see Isabella and deliver a package the king has sent her."

"You are welcome any time, Critiques. Come in. Come in. How is that son of mine?" the Queen Mother asked, her eyes dancing with joy at the mention of her beloved boy.

"He is well, Majesty," Critiques said with a broad smile, "and he sends his love."

"How wonderful," she replied. "Since you are not in need of me, I hope you will not be offended that I leave you. I was just going to visit one of the villagers in need of my herbs. There is food in the cupboard and a warm chair by the fire. Please stay as long as you wish."

"Thank you for your hospitality, Highness," the little man replied as he helped his liege with her cloak and satchel of herbs. He bowed again as Kriya left the cottage both glancing at Isabella who had not murmured a word

During her stay in the Lower World, Isabella had grown accustomed to having a random thought and suddenly seeing it become reality before her eyes. It was no coincidence that Critiques was standing before her now. She had been thinking about him earlier in the day. As he moved towards her, Isabella rose to greet him.

"It is good to see you, Critiques," the words ringing true in her heart.

"And you, Isabella. You look well. Actually, you look wonderful! I think the Queen Mother's cooking agrees with you. You're actually taller than me now!"

He, too, looks so different than the day he taunted me in the castle mused Isabella. *I will never forget Sir Alfred picking him up and marching out of my rooms!* Gone was the wild hair. Gone was the terrible buzzing noise. Gone was the mad dancing. Critiques looked groomed, peaceful and happy. Isabella motioned for him to sit with her by the fire. As the flames shivered with anticipation, Critiques smiled gently and said, "This reminds me a bit of our time at the forest campfire. I have come, in part, to thank you for that night."

"That night seems so long ago, Critiques, doesn't it?" Isabella responded sadly, gazing deep into the fire. "So much has happened to us both since then, hasn't it? You seemed to have fared much better than I."

"I am sorry to hear that, Mistress. Would you like to speak of it?" he asked kindly.

Isabella looked up from the fire and smiled ruefully. "Now that is a change is it not? If I remember correctly, you shared at the last fire. I would like you to tell me the happier story you seem to be part of. You really do look very well, Critiques."

"Thank you; I am well. And the story began that night at the campfire," he said thoughtfully.

"How so?" asked the young woman.

"It was the first time I remember being shown kindness as an adult. It was the first time someone was not so repulsed by me that they did not try to run away from me. It was the first time anyone asked me a question about myself."

"You are too kind, Critiques. I cannot take credit for what the Curiosa did," said Isabella, saddened again by the loss of Sir Alfred's royal pendant.

"Yes, Sir Alfred told me he gave you the Curiosa when you came to the Lower World," nodded the little man. "I am glad you accepted his gift. I am glad you followed her promptings. That night, though difficult for me, gave me an opportunity to speak of painful things I had long buried and forgotten." Isabella nodded.

"After you left for Kronos, Sir Alfred came to see me and asked if I would like to be in service to the king as a courier. I agreed until he told me there was a training period. Well, I told him I could jump into any position immediately and do it better than anyone else had ever done it and without any training. Actually, I told him I wanted to be an overlord so I could tell others how to do their jobs!" Critiques laughed and slapped his knee in amusement. "My, my," he chuckled, "Sir Alfred has the patience of a saint! At any rate, he remained firm in the face of my protests. I thought it ridiculous, but I did long to be in service to the king and to be a better man, so I agreed to the training."

As she had done so long ago, Isabella rose once more and laid logs on the fire. The flames danced with joy tossing sparks of red, blue, yellow and white throughout the hearth and up through the chimney. The room hummed with a quiet pleasure as it filled with warmth scented with pine and birch.

When she seated herself, Critiques continued. "One day Sir Alfred invited me to his quarters. He handed me a leather pouch which contained five stones, each inscribed with a question. He said when I felt agitated in any way I was to go somewhere quiet. Once settled, I was to reach into the pouch for a stone and answer the question inscribed on that stone. Then I was to reach in for the next stone and the next until I had answered all five questions. Finally I was to come to him and talk about what I discovered."

Isabella laughed with delight. "That is so like Sir Alfred; he loves questions. I am still amazed by what I witnessed in his courtroom with the use of his 'enlightened questions'! So what happened?"

"Well I thought the whole thing was ridiculous and told him so!" the little man said, his eyes twinkling. "But my outburst did not ruffle Sir Alfred in the least. He simply smiled and suggested I think about his request."

By now, Isabella was intrigued. "And?" she asked. The flames leaned closer to hear the tale.

"I realized to take my place in service I had to at least try this process. So the first time Lady Jillian and Lady Joanna irritated me, I went off to the stables. I was actually surprised by the first question – intrigued enough to reach for the second stone. Without even realizing how it happened, I answered all five questions and left the stables feeling better. So I thought I would try it a few more times before I went to see Sir Alfred." He smiled as he said, "The funny thing was the stones and questions always came out of the pouch in the exact same order! No matter how hard I tried shaking the pouch! No matter how many times I used the pouch! Eventually I did speak with Sir Alfred about my insights and before I knew it, he said I was ready for my first mission. It went well and here I am a courier in King Stefan's service. I love it."

"I am happy for you," Isabella said. *Why has it not been so easy for me?* she thought peevishly. *If I was not so embarrassed I might ask him about the questions.* The young woman and little man watched the embers and sparks grow lazy as the fire died down.

"Ah, Isabella, the fire tells me it is late. I wish I could stay longer, but I must deliver royal correspondence to Kronos. You know how important punctuality is to the citizens," the little man said with a wink. Critiques stood and reached deep into a large leather satchel hanging across his chest and said, "I have a package for you from the king. He thought you might be interested in the turn of events in the Northern Province after you left. Critiques drew a brown wrapper from his bag and handed it to Isabella. As he turned to leave, he took Isabella's free hand, gently kissed it and took his leave. At the door he turned back, bowed and said, "Thank you, Isabella, for your curiosity and compassion. I am forever in your debt." Then he disappeared into the night.

After closing the door, Isabella walked to her chair by the fire and sat down. She rose and threw several more logs onto the embers watching the fire grow brighter and hotter. She returned to her seat and when the hearth was blazing removed the wrapping from Stefan's journal and began to read.

FIVE STONES FIVE QUESTIONS

As Critiques left the clearing, he was met by a pair of large wolves. The male was coal black; his mate pure white. "Might you please deliver this to the young mistress in the morning?" he respectfully asked the pair. The female nodded yes. Critiques hung a small leather pouch around her neck, bowed to the guardians of Kriya's home and headed to Kronos. Inside were five stones:

Amethyst: Where in your body do you feel the emotion that troubles you?

Rose Quartz: How do you feel towards it?

Red Garnet: What does it wish to tell or show you?

Jet: What fears does it hold?

Blue Lace Agate: How might you help ease its burdens?

STEFAN'S JOURNAL

DAY...

This place disturbs me. Today there were three reports of fighting among my soldiers – unheard of within the Elite Guard. I, myself, berated Darius in front of his men yesterday over a minor infraction. I have never done so before but could not seem to control myself. What is amiss in this place?

DAY...

Sofia summoned me to her tent this morning. Her assessment of the situation is bizarre to the point of disbelief. Have I erred calling for her help? Have I made a mistake heeding Mother's counsel to listen to this woman? My heart and mind long to be with my men.

DAY...

Sofia and I spoke again today. She remains certain there are invaders in the province though unseen to us. She believes them to be from a tribe known as the Legacy. Their realm, she claims, is our Lower World but of a different time and place. When I asked of their intention, she said they cannot rest.

"Are they a ghost people?" I asked. "Is that why we cannot see them?"

Her reply continues to puzzle me. "Yes and no," she said. "They are distant relations to us but so far removed to have been forgotten. They come to pass on burdens they could not release in their own time."

"Why would they do that?" I asked incredulous.

"They know no other way to be," she replied.

I do not understand. In fact, I dismiss her assessment. There are no such things as ghosts or spirits, and what is this nonsense of burdens? I will send her back to the Southern Province.

DAY...

Darius was waiting for me when I returned to my quarters. He was stunned I met with Sofia without his presence. He insisted I send her away. Though I had just decided to do so prior to his demand, I became enraged he should challenge me; that he make any demand of me; I am the king. I ordered him from my tent with instructions not to return unless I called for him.

DAY...

Terrible reports have found their way to me this day. The scouts found a mass grave. Men have come forward and confessed to slaughtering neighbors and friends having been caught up in a rage of madness. I am at a loss. I feel duty-bound to decree marshal law and initiate harsh punishment for anyone involved in these heinous crimes. But before I make that decision, I feel compelled to speak to Sofia one more time.

DAY...

"Why have these ghosts of yours come to this time and place?" I asked Sofia.

"They are not my ghosts. They invade us all. Do you not feel at odds with yourself in this place?" she asked.

"How can I battle them?" I demanded.

"Who will you battle here? Yourself? Your own subjects?" she asked me. "That would be a futile war, an unnecessary war. There is another way." All of me demands that I fight and yet her words 'unnecessary war' are daggers in my heart. Over and over in my mind's eye, I see the carnage of the trade wars with the Empress – so many dead littering the battle field of an 'unnecessary war'. She says there is another way. She irritates me beyond words.

DAY...

Mother joined Sofia today. My troops have broken camp to return to the castle. I am here alone.

DAY...

What I have seen today seems impossible. In the first hours after dawn, Sofia asked me to join her. We traveled by foot for several hours and ascended the highest mountain in the province. In an act I can only call a spell she called upon the Ancient Ones to cast a white light over the land. It was so. As far as I could see there was a light a hundred times brighter than the sun, but it did not blind or burn me. In fact, I have never felt such peace as I did standing in that light. I do not know how much time passed, but the light faded and she said it was time to return to the village: that all would be seen clearly.

When we returned to the settlement there was panic in the streets: people horrified, children screaming, chaos. We could now see the invaders. They were merged with the bodies of my subjects – like a second skin. At times I could see a villager; then they would blur and become something else, something hideous: skin hanging from bones; clothes rotting on bodies; walking skeletons. What haunts me are their eyes: dead black eyes covered with a terrible gray mold oozing phlegm. I walked the streets stunned by the sight of the living and the dead – one and the same.

DAY...

My aide finds me in the market as I walk among my people horrified by what I see, horrified by their distress. He comes with news that Mother and Sofia wish to see me. I am both relieved and angry. I both seek and resist their counsel. Who is the ruler in this land? Is it not me, the king? Do I need the help of women, no matter how well intentioned they are? When I return to my tent, they are waiting for me. They are bathed in the white light.

There is a peace here. I realize there are answers here.

DAY...

Today I met their leader – a filthy decayed corpse. Sofia, Mother and I made our way into a forest clearing. I asked for his presence and he appeared. I ask why they have come. His answer – they have been here for years. He is surprised we have not noticed before.

I ask his intentions. The monstrous ghoul says, "Release. We carry such heavy burdens and only know to rid ourselves of them by passing them on to those of our line – generation after generation. Still we have no peace." Mother tells him peace is available if he so chooses. He listens to her plan and agrees. He says their pain is too terrible to carry any longer; their shame in burdening their progeny too heavy to bear; they seek release for us all.

DAY...

We stood side by side at the lip of the canyon – King of the Lower World and King of the Legacy. Behind us stood Mother and Sofia: behind them, our blended subjects. Sofia once again called upon the Ancient Ones and instantly there appeared a bridge of brilliant light spanning the breath of the canyon; a bridge so long, I could not see its end.

As he was asked to do, the ghoul king stepped onto the bridge and turned to face me. When he did so, the light traveled from where he stood, up through his feet, up through his legs, his body, his head so that a young man of my age stood before me – not a filthy decaying corpse but a regal young king. He smiled. Then he called for his tribe to come forward and stand behind him. I watched not knowing what would happen. The first ghoul stepped out of a man standing behind Mother. Mother stepped aside to he could pass. The specter made his way to the bridge where he hesitated. His king smiled and said there was nothing to fear. As the ghoul walked onto the bridge, he too became a man. He turned to face us as he took his place behind his king. He face was calm and clear.

One by one the people of the Legacy left their hosts and took their place on the bridge: men, women, children, some old, and some young, now all whole. On and on they came until their numbers were so great, I could no longer see where their line ended. We stood in silence facing one another. Mother touched my arm and said gently, "It is time, Stefan." In that moment, proud king and warrior that I was, I was

222

frightened I could not do what was needed; what my subjects needed; what I needed. I am tired and will write more after I rest.

DAY...

I continue to reflect on the day at the bridge. The air became still, not a sound heard from the birds or the trees or the people behind me or before me. Suddenly, I was in another place and time. I was back on the trade route battlefield surrounded by my men, the Empress' men, innocent women and children. So many were dead, dying, screaming; blood saturated the land. Why had I fought? What had propelled me into such wrong action?

The Legacy King looked into my eyes and said, "We have passed on to you your ego and the unquestioned use of violence and war. You have carried the burden of force being the only way to rule from my time."

Though I be the king whose role it is to protect and lead, I said, "I no longer wish to carry the burden of force." I gathered up the bloody swords and arrows and knives and spears from the battlefield and placed them at the feet of the Legacy King. "I return this burden to you, not in malice or as punishment but because it is not mine to carry. Please take it, feel the weight of it and return it back through the generations – back and back and back through time until these burdens journey to the place where all is transformed and healed."

The king nodded, gathering up the bloody weapons, holding them in his arms, feeling their weight. Then he turned and passed them to the one who stood behind him, who passed it to the one who stood behind her and on and on until the burdens were seen no more. I bowed to the Legacy King. He bowed to me.

I stood aside and motioned for my subjects to come forward and do the same. What a sight it was. Each man, woman and child came and placed at the feet of the king boxes of bloodied bandages, barrels of whiskey and ale, bushels of whips and switches, vials of bitterness, satchels of fear, pots of shame, wells of tears, chains of slavery, broken mirrors, trunks overflowing with lies, swamps of self-hatred, and all else they carried not of their time and place. With each person, the king looked into the eyes of the giver. He received that which the individual

223

sought to release; that which was not their own. He held the weight of the burden, and then passed it back and back and back to that place where all was healed. This continued through the day and night and day and night and day and night.

DAY...

When the last burden was beyond sight, Sofia stepped onto the bridge of light and took the hand of the Legacy King. They bowed deeply to us. Then all on the bridge bowed, turned and made their way across the canyon. The white light of pure love I had experienced on the mountaintop with Sofia blazed for just a moment and all were gone.

Mother touched my arm and said, "Dearest son, when you are ready, invite into yourself all that was lost; all those qualities you wish to fill the space within you that has cleared." What did I wish for then and now? Peace, compassion, wisdom, right action, love.

DAY...

As I did, so too did each resident of the Northern Province, reflect on that which they had released and invited into themselves those qualities to take them into the day and the next. When they were through, a gentle rain fell, washing us all clean and there was softness in the land.

DAY...

When all had left, I gazed out onto the canyon. A child approached me and asked two questions. "Will they be back?" was the first.

"Will they return? One or two may try, but most will not. If they do come back, we now know how to release them and ourselves," I replied.

"Why were you crying at the bridge, Highness?" was the second.

Even now, as I write, I am not quite sure why I cried. I do know though that before he turned to leave, I gazed deeply into the eyes of the King of the Legacy and saw gratitude and love.

DAY...

As I leave for the castle today, my thoughts turn to Isabella and her quest for the book. There are perilous times ahead for us all. I hope she will be able to face her fears as I faced mine for then we all will truly be free.

HAPPY BIRTHDAY

"Ready?" their father asked.

"Yes, Daddy, we're all here. We're ready," said his son.

"Okay, on the count of three I'll put the phone by Mommy's ear," the man said. "One...two...three..."

"Mommy, I'm here," yelled the little girl.

"Me too!" said her brother. "Grandma and Grandpa are here with us. We're going to sing to you!"

The man heard them burst into song, "Happy birthday to you, happy birthday to you, happy birthday to Mommy, happy birthday to youuuuuuu!" There was clapping and shouting, "We love you. Come home, Mommy. We miss you."

Their father brought the phone to his ear and said, "That was beautiful guys. I know Mommy just loved it. I will see you all in a couple of hours."

✦
BLAME

The day was clear but bitter cold. Isabella pulled her cloak tightly around her body as she trudged to the jail. "Well, well, Isabella. Welcome! I was wondering when you would stop by," the constable said when Isabella came through the door. He was a short stout man with a jolly smile. He had a white beard, white hair that fell to his shoulders and the rosiest cheeks Isabella had ever seen. The jail's outer office was of a good size with a trestle table and benches arranged before a large hearth. A wool rug woven with scenes of the forest covered the pine wood floor. There were tall windows on each wall so the room was filled with light. The space was tidy and clean and smelled of beeswax and lemon.

As Isabella oriented herself to the room, the constable said, "That fellow in there is quite disagreeable," he said. "Frankly, I would like to be rid of him, so I am eager to know how you would like us to dispose of this matter. Here, let me get you some tea while you put those wet wraps by the fire. That was quite a long walk in this cold. I have never seen a winter like this one."

As Isabella spread her cloak by the fire, she said, "Sir, I am not sure what I want you to do. I thought you would have some ideas, being the constable and all."

The constable looked at her kindly as he handed her a steaming cup of chamomile tea. "I am sure the Queen Mother explained only you can make that decision."

Isabella sighed. She was hoping for a different answer. "Where is he?" she asked.

"He is in a cell under heavy lock. In this moment, you are quite safe here with me," the constable said as he poured himself a cup of tea adding a splash of milk and honey. He also laid out a plate of lemon cakes and cherry tarts as he seated himself across from Isabella.

"I think I want to see him," Isabella said hesitantly.

The constable, who had just swallowed a mouthful of lemon cake, started to cough. When he caught his breath, he said, "Why on earth would you want to see him after that scare he gave you?"

"I am not sure." Isabella's head started to pound. Sleep had eluded her since the visit with Critiques and her reading of the king's journal. Conflicting thoughts and feelings were pulling her heart apart. To complicate matters, she was still so angry with the Queen she had not spoken to her for days. Isabella felt she had lost the one person with whom she could speak of the confusion that filled her.

"Well, he cannot hurt you from his cell, but he has a nasty mouth and nasty appearance. I offered him a bath and clean clothes, but he refused both. Are you sure you want to do this?"

"I think so – I don't know – maybe," stammered Isabella.

"Why don't you take a few sips of your tea, and then let me know what you would like to do," said the constable. "I have some papers to attend to," he said motioning to his desk in the corner of the room, "so take your time."

Grateful for a few quiet moments to think, Isabella sat drinking her tea warming herself by the fire. Only the sound of the crackling wood disturbed the silence. After a while she said, "Sir, would you please show me the way to his cell?"

The constable rose from his desk and led Isabella out of his office to a long windowless corridor. At the end of the hall was a heavy door. The constable turned the key in three locks and swung the door open. Peering across the threshold, Isabella saw two small barred cells – neither had a window. A chair had been placed in front of each cell for visitors. One cell was empty. The man from the swamp was in the other. "Would you like me to come in with you?" the constable asked, his jolly smile now a serious frown.

When Isabella shook her head no, he said, "I will leave the door open. If you need me, call out, and I will be there in a second." When she nodded, he left, his footsteps fading away to silence.

Isabella stood rooted in the doorway for a long time. The scent of rusted metal and sickly sweet blood filled her nostrils. *It is his scent. I remember it.* Her heart was pounding and her breathing was shallow. *This was a mistake. I don't need to see this terrible man.* Just as she was about to turn away, she heard beloved Nightwalker whisper, "Isabella, you are not the girl you were before. You have come far. Listen to your heart for the right next step." She closed her eyes and stood very still. When she opened her eyes a minute later, she walked very slowly to the chair facing the man's cell and sat down.

The man lay on his cot, his face to the wall. When he turned his head and realized it was Isabella who sat outside the cell, his face darkened with hatred and rage. She drew in her breath: images from the night in the swamp flooded her. "You have come to name my punishment," the man snarled as he sat up. "I have been waiting for you."

Standing before her was a man tall and muscular with matted blond hair that fell loose to his shoulders. A coarse beard covered his face and neck. His frayed brown tunic and sagging leggings were crusted with dirt. He smelled of blood and decay. "I have come only to meet you," she whispered, dropping her eyes.

"So you can taunt me with what is to come?" he said coldly. "Be afraid of me, Isabella. I will escape this cell. This is not over between us."

A shudder passed through the girl's body. Unable to raise her eyes, she said, "I need to know why you wish me harm. I do not even know you. What could I have done that you wish me hurt or dead?" She laced her fingers tightly together to keep them from trembling.

"Well now, isn't that interesting," he laughed coldly, sitting on his bed staring at the young woman. "Isn't that interesting that you want something from me. Well, I choose not to answer you," he mocked. "You not having answers gives me power over you. I like that."

Isabella tightened her clenched hands and continued, "That night in the swamp you said you did not wish for me to take this journey. Why?"

"You are no good," he spat.

229

"How can you say that?" Isabella raised her eyes slightly, though she still could not look into the man's face. "You do not know me," she stammered, her stomach twisted in knots.

"I know you well." The man's voice was flat and dead. "I have watched you. You are like me."

Isabella felt herself growing smaller and smaller under his hateful gaze. "I am nothing like you. I would never hurt someone like you did," she whispered her entire body trembling.

The man's body instantly became rigid. "You think you are better than me?" he shouted, his words like blows to Isabella's body. The man jumped from the bed to the jail bars. "I can hear your thoughts, you wretch," he said, shaking the bars. "You think I'm crazy? Disgusting?" Sticky spittle hit Isabella in the face. "Well you think about Alexandra. Think about what you did to her. You still think you are nothing like me?"

Isabella's head jerked up and she looked into the man's contorted face. "What are you saying?" she cried. Even as she spoke, she felt a locked door swing open in her memory. Beyond the door she saw the paintings in King Stefan's castle; she heard the sound of tearing trees; she smelled the noxious fumes and felt the burning flames; she saw a dead woman. "Stop!" Isabella screamed, covering her ears. "Stop!" She jumped from her chair and ran into the hallway, followed by the man's hideous laughter.

✧
ALEXANDRA

"Isabella, what happened child?" asked the constable as she burst into his office white-faced and trembling. "Did he hurt you?" The white haired man moved quickly from his desk towards the girl. Without responding Isabella ran to the hearth, threw her cloak over her shoulders and ran from the jail. "Wait! Wait!" the constable shouted but Isabella had already been swallowed up by the forest.

"I must get home. I must get home," sobbed Isabella as she ran blindly through the woods. *That horrible man; what was he talking about? Who is Alexandra? Why did he say I did something to this person? I would never hurt anyone.* As Isabella ran she became younger and younger with each step. Soon she was the age of six and, instead of running on the path to the Queen Mother's house she was running through her village cemetery.

"Oh no," she moaned. "Please I do not want to be here again." Isabella stopped and stood once more at the lip of the open grave.

"Mother!" she wailed.

Then, as before, she was sitting on the stoop of her cottage. She stood and slowly entered the house; her legs so heavy she could barely walk. She knew what she would see. She moved slowly to the center of the room and looked down into the coffin. This time when she looked into the face so like her own, she saw not herself but her sister, Alexandra.

Instantly a kaleidoscope of images spun through Isabella's mind. Like a shattered mirror, each shard was a reflection of her sister. There was beautiful Alexandra, ten years older than Isabella, stroking Isabella's hair the night she lost her childhood doll, Maya, in the fire. Kind Alexandra had gone back to the village the following day and picked in

231

the fire finding bits and pieces of Maya. She brought them back to
Isabella. "Dear sister, we must bury Maya properly and mourn for her.
Until you grieve for your beloved friend, you will not be able to open
your heart to another." She and Alexandra had decorated a wonderful
box for Maya and buried her by the river amongst the water lilies.

Another shard sliced the darkness of Isabella's memory. Alexandra
had comforted Isabella when she had been mocked by the headmaster.
Unlike her mother who forced her to apologize, Alexandra had praised
her for her courage and conviction. "How proud I am of you, Isabella,
to be so young and to see the truth so clearly and to speak it. I pray you
never lose your clarity and courage. I pray you never lose your voice,"
her sister had said as they searched for eggs in the barn that night. "The
schoolmaster is just like our rooster," she laughed, "so puffed up and
self-important and no one likes to hear him in the morning!"

Yet another shard reflected Alexandra assisting in the birth of a
child. An apprentice midwife and medicine woman, Alexandra relished
ministering to the people in the village. No amount of pressure from
their parents to give up her work and marry deterred Alexandra.
Isabella adored her sister more than any person on earth.

More shards of glass slashed through the emptiness in Isabella's
mind. Her sister coming home exhausted after a difficult delivery.
Isabella begging Alexandra to take her back to the village to see the play
Isabella had so enjoyed with her sister the night before. Alexandra
laughing, saying she could never refuse her little sister. Later, the two of
them walking home in the darkness, hand in hand, reenacting the
wonderful story. More shards fell into place. Two men – strangers –
confronting them on the path – demanding their money. Alexandra
unafraid, telling them to be off. Terrible laughter – one man grabbed
Isabella by the hair causing her to cry out in pain. "Don't touch her,"
Alexandra screamed. Her sister lunged toward the man clawing at his
face and eyes. "Isabella, run, get help!" Alexandra commanded.
Isabella ran away into the darkness.

The shards were spinning and rearranging themselves faster and
faster and faster. A farmer and his sons found Alexandra in the woods,
badly beaten, strangled – her face and body in ruins. Their mother fell
howling to the floor like a wounded animal when they brought

Alexandra into the cottage; their father asked why his best daughter had been taken; Isabella standing guard over her sister but too late to save her. "My fault, my fault" moaned Isabella as she stared into the coffin. "You didn't want to go to the play. Why did I make you go? If we had not gone you would be alive."

Isabella, her arms wrapped tightly around her body, began to rock back and forth, back and forth before the coffin. "Why did I yell out? He would have let me go if I had just been quiet. If I had been braver you would not have tried to protect me." She started to sob as she reached into the coffin to stroke Alexandra's beautiful hair. "I should not have left you with them. We could have fought them off together. I know we could have. Forgive me, Alexandra, I was scared and I ran away. I was scared and left you alone. How could I have done that? How did I not stay and save you?"

The shards arranged and rearranged themselves like pieces in a puzzle until they came together in a ruined mirror. Three small pieces remained missing. One by one they appeared and fell into place. In the first, unable to face his pain, her father disappeared first into the gambling dens and then took leave from the village and their lives – his whereabouts unknown. In the second, her mother became forever silent. In the last, Isabella chose to forget her sister. The mirror was complete.

Time and space shifted abruptly, and Isabella was now back on the path to the Queen Mother's house, lying on the ground in the snow. The memories of that past experience seared into her mind never to be forgotten again. "My fault, my fault," she cried over and over again. "It is my fault you are dead. I killed you."

$\displaystyle \text{✦}$

SISTERS

Night had fallen when Isabella returned to the cottage. The room was dark save for the embers in the fireplace. Isabella felt her way to the Queen Mother's bed and stared into the Kriya's sleeping face. The woman opened her eyes and smiled at the girl. "I have a sister," whispered Isabella.

"I know," said the Queen softly, reaching to touch Isabella's face.

A tear fell from Isabella's eye. "I killed her."

The woman sat up and wrapped her arms tightly around the girl. "Tell me of it," she said.

"I cannot speak the words. I only wish to die."

"To die or stop the pain?" Kriya asked gently as she rocked the girl. "Perhaps telling me of your sister will ease your hurt?"

The girl shuddered and asked, "Do you hate me?"

"No, I love you," said the Queen Mother as she kissed Isabella's hair.

A second tear rolled down Isabella's cheek. "I wish to tell you of her, but I do not know where to begin," she said.

"I understand," replied the Queen Mother as she moved back into the bed making room for Isabella to lie next to her.

"Thank you," said the girl as she settled beside the woman. She was silent until her breath matched that of the Queen's and then Isabella whispered, "She was beautiful, tall and slender with the most beautiful dark hair. Her hands were like that of a musician – long fingers so delicate – and she was good and kind and her smile lit up the world." So Isabella began to speak of her sister, their life together and Alexandra's death. She spoke haltingly of it the next day and the next. For twelve cycles of the moon Isabella spoke of the one she loved so deeply and had betrayed. For twelve cycles of the moon she cried and cried, laughed and cried again. Through it all the Queen Mother listened and loved Isabella.

On the night the full moon rose for the thirteenth time, the girl dreamed of Alexandra. In her dream Isabella was walking through a hawthorn grove, the tree branches so heavy with blossoms the branches bowed under the weight of the flowers. A warm wind swept through the grove and the air was thick with the scent of white petals falling like snow. Walking towards Isabella through the shower of flowers was Alexandra – radiant and smiling, her arms reaching out for Isabella. "How is my darling sister?" Alexandra said as she hugged Isabella.

Isabella's heart filled with joy and then darkened with shame as she felt her sister's warmth. "I am so sorry," she stammered her eyes downcast, her body rigid.

"It was not your fault, Isabella," Alexandra said softly holding her sister in her arms. "The men committed murder not you." Alexandra pulled back from Isabella and cupped her sister's face in her hands. "Look at me, dear." Alexandra's brown eyes sparkled with joy. "I am happy you are safe," she said, "and even more so that you remember me again."

Isabella drank in the beauty of her sister's face. "I am sad, Alexandra. Now that I remember, I do not think I can live without you," cried Isabella.

"You can," Alexandra said taking Isabella's hands into her own, kissing the palm of each one tenderly. "You must. There is so much for you to explore in this life."

"I do not wish to explore. There is a darkness inside of me that overwhelms me – that makes me want to be dead," moaned Isabella turning her face away from her sister.

The gentle wind swept through the grove shaking more velvety petals from the trees. Alexandra gently brushed several blossoms from Isabella's hair and once again took her sister's face in her hands. She looked deep into Isabella's eyes and said, "I want you to give me the darkness."

Startled by the request, Isabella said, "That is not possible. Even if I could, I would not want you to carry this terrible burden."

"I am here to help you, Isabella. I want you to live again – to be happy again," smiled Alexandra. "Now, close your eyes. The darkness will show its form to you, if you wish it to."

"I am frightened, Alexandra," said Isabella her body trembling.

"I am here, and you are safe. I will not allow harm to come to you. Have I not always protected you?" She smiled a smile of radiant love.

"You have," Isabella said.

"Then trust me again. Close your eyes and find the darkness."

"My darkness keeps me tied to you. If I release it, I will lose you again," Isabella said mournfully.

Alexandra shook her head, flowers falling from her hair. "We are tied together in better ways, dear one." As she had so many times before, Isabella followed her sister's counsel and closed her eyes. After several deep breaths Isabella placed her hand on her throat. Slowly she moved it down to her chest; Isabella could feel her pounding heart. Little by little her heart steadied and her chest began to feel warm. Isabella sighed as she pushed her hand through her skin like a knife through softened butter. Isabella pushed deeper into her chest until her hand came to rest on what felt like an oily sac. "Give me the darkness, Isabella," Alexandra said firmly.

Isabella tugged at the sac. It would not give. She pulled harder and still it would not move. Then she felt Alexandra's hand next to hers; together they pulled a roiling boil out of Isabella's body. Isabella opened her eyes and gasped as she stared at the black slick growth in their hands. The stench of rot was so strong she gagged and dropped her end of the boil. It broke open, and maggots spilled out onto the ground.

"Not to worry, dear one," murmured Alexandra as she gracefully knelt to the ground and scooped up the broken sac and writhing maggots. As she gathered the bag and its contents to her body, all instantly turned into white blossoms. Alexandra laughed in delight as she threw them into the air. "Look inside again, Isabella," she said. "See if anything is left to release."

Isabella closed her eyes once more. "The darkness is gone. I am empty. So very empty," she murmured sadly.

"With what do you wish to fill that space, dear one?" Alexandra asked softly as wind and swirling petals encircled the sisters.

Isabella opened her eyes and reached for Alexandra's hand. "Your forgiveness," she whispered.

As soon as she spoke, Isabella was filled with the warmth of a thousand suns. Light flowed from the soles of her feet, up through her body and burst forth from her hands and head. She stood a brilliant beacon of light in the grove. "Oh Alexandra!" she gasped in delight, "Oh, Alexandra!"

"My forgiveness has always been yours, dear sister," Alexandra kissed Isabella's cheek. "It was inside of you patiently waiting for you to accept it. Slowly she stepped back from the girl. When the young woman took several more steps away from her, Isabella asked, "What are you doing?"

"It is time for me to leave," Alexandra said softly.

"No! You can't leave," said Isabella startled. "Stay with me, Alexandra – or let me come with you. Please don't leave me again," Isabella said anxiously, grabbing her sister's arm.

"No, this is as it should be," Alexandra replied gently as she pulled away from Isabella's grasp. "You are of this world; I am of the next."

"No, please don't go! I beg you, please don't leave me! I need you!" Isabella cried throwing her arms around her sister, tears flowing down her cheeks.

"Isabella, I have not left you, not even for a moment since that day. I am in the wind, in the smile of everyone you love, in the rain, everywhere. I love you, sweet sister, how could I ever leave you?" A gust of wind blew through the grove and Alexandra dissolved into a thousand swirling white petals. Isabella slumped to the ground, her face in her hands. All about her the flowers swirled and swirled and swirled singing, "I love you. I love you."

She felt a gentle brush against her cheek and looked up hoping to see the face of her sister. Instead she looked into the eyes of Nightwalker. "I thought I killed you too," cried the girl.

"You did not, Isabella. Look at me. I am healed," said the mighty raven, his feathers shining, and the star on his forehead blazing bright.

"I am so sad Alexandra has left me again," cried the Isabella. "I am so alone, Nightwalker. I do not think I will ever be happy again."

Nightwalker wrapped Isabella into his wings and said, "It will take a very long time, Isabella, but I know that light will come back into your world. Remember I hold the potential for all things. I will hold the possibilities of hope and happiness for you until you are able to hold them for yourself."

"You are kind but I am beyond hope and happiness, Nightwalker," the young woman sobbed.

The great bird stroked Isabella's hair and said, "I will stay with you this night if you will allow me to do so."

"I love you. I love you," the petals sang swirling about the girl and the bird.

Isabella nodded.

"I love you. I love you. I love you," whispered the petals.

✧
WITNESSING

The Queen Mother entered the jail and sat in the chair facing the prisoner's cell.

"Why are you here?" snarled the prisoner.

"I wish to know you," she said, the scent of lavender and mint enveloping the man.

"It is too late for that. You missed your chance long ago. Where were you when I needed you as a child?" he hissed. "Where were you when I needed you on the battlefield? Where were you when it became my job to carry the burden of hatred for the kingdom?"

"I was there but you turned your eyes away from me. You see me now," said the Queen Mother gently.

"It is too late. Go away and leave me. You sicken me." The man's face was red with rage.

The Queen did not go away. Each day, she trudged through the snow to the jail. Upon seeing her, the man hurled insults and threats through the bars of his cell. Other days, he turned away and ignored her. Sometimes he would stare at her in stony hate-filled silence. Day after day, the Queen Mother sat calmly looking at the man as though he were a boy. Each day she would say with calmness and sincerity, "I wish to know all of you."

One day he spoke of a memory – a handful of razor words. Several days later, he added a handful more. The next day a few more and so it went. He wove a story of horror and hurts so terrible the Queen Mother cried tears of compassion for the little boy locked in the angry man before her. One day the cell door stood open between them. The Queen walked into the cell and sat next to the little boy. He did not look at her. Finally, he said with such sadness in his voice that the

Queen put her arms around the child, "It was my job to keep her from remembering even if I had to kill her. The kingdom could not bear any more pain. You saw the paintings. I believed the kingdom could not bear any more pain if she remembered; that we would all die." The Queen Mother stroked the boy's head. The boy began to cry. "But then I made her remember. I didn't mean to but I could not stand how she looked at me – judged me. I wanted to make her hurt as much as I hurt. I am sorry I made her remember. What shall we do? Can the kingdom survive her memory?"

"I do not know," said the Queen Mother softly, as she held the weeping boy. "But it is not done. It is not done."

CROSSROADS

The woman's husband and parents stood at the right side and foot of her bed. They knew the ventilator, inserted at the time of the stroke, had to be removed. The longer she was dependent on the machine, the less likely she would ever be able to breathe on her own. At the same time, the physicians could not assure them the woman could survive without the ventilator.

Knowing her stance on heroic measures, they had made a decision. The doctor looked at the woman's husband. When the man nodded slightly, the doctor removed the breathing tube and turned off the machine.

✦
SPRINGTIME

Nightwalker continued to visit Isabella's dreams each night. At first they were simple dreams filled with his reassuring presence and calming words. Then Isabella began to dream she and Nightwalker were enveloped in swirling mists of pink, orange, and soft blues. Several nights later a layer of sound floated through the colors: running water, wind rustling through trees, the music of birds. Finally the scents of lavender, cut grass, and warm bread filled her sleep. Each day she woke more refreshed eager to share her dreams with the Queen. And each morning the Queen would smile and say, "How lovely! You and Nightwalker are having springtime dreams."

One morning sitting at the breakfast table nibbling hot cinnamon buns Isabella said, "Last night I dreamed warmth. Nightwalker was there in the beginning of the dream and then said he had to attend to royal business and might be gone for a while. I thought I would be upset but I felt fine. Odd isn't it?"

"I would say encouraging, actually," the Queen Mother replied pouring mint tea for them both, "I have noticed a softening in the air, haven't you?"

"Not really," replied Isabella.

"I don't believe I have ever been through such a long winter," Kriya said as she swallowed the last bite of a blueberry muffin. Reaching for a strawberry scone, she asked, "And what are your plans for today?"

"To walk again," the girl replied as she took her last bite of oatmeal. "I don't mind the cold anymore. It just feels wonderful to be outside." After breakfast, Isabella pulled on an extra pair of fleece trousers, two sweaters, her wool coat, a cloak, hat, scarf and mittens.

The Queen Mother laughed and said, "No wonder you are dreaming warmth!"

When Isabella opened the cottage door she was stunned. Not only was the snow gone, but the air was warm and moist, so much so that the trees swaying in the warm wind were covered with tiny leaves the color of baby peas. "Oh my!" the girl exclaimed.

The Queen Mother stood next to Isabella beaming and said, "Well, my sweet magician, you have dreamed spring into being! No need for your wraps today!"

"I did this?" Isabella asked in stunned disbelief.

"You and Nightwalker!" the Queen replied with a huge smile. "Well, we can fold away our cloaks and fleece and bring out springtime clothes." The Queen turned back into the cottage and knelt before her private chest searching through its contents. She pulled out pink leggings and matching tunic, leather slippers, and a broad brimmed straw hat banded with pink lace. "I used to love wearing this," the Queen Mother said wistfully looking at the hat. "My mother gave this to me long ago when I first discovered the woods. She called it my springtime crown because I would tuck wildflowers into the lace band. Would you like to wear it?"

"It would be an honor!" Isabella said as she placed the hat on her head. "I hope I will be able to find some flowers so I can decorate my own crown!"

Kriya gave the girl a hug and said, "No need to worry about that. There are many awaiting you. Now off with you. Enjoy spring in the Lower World; it is lovely."

Isabella had only experienced the Queen's forest covered in snow so when she left the clearing and stepped into the woods, she felt she entered a magical land. Stretched before her as far as her eyes could see was a carpet of fairy slippers. Each plant held a single rose-colored orchid. All stretched upward striving to catch drops of sunlight floating through the leafy canopy to the forest floor. Isabella did not move into the woods for fear of crushing the fragile blooms. The flowers, sensing her dilemma, sang, "Not to worry, young mistress, we will make a way for you. We wish for you to continue on and take greetings to our cousins deeper in the woods." Some fairy slippers leaned to the left and others to the right so that a path was made.

"Thank you, friends," Isabella said as she stepped into the sea of pink. In time the pink gave way to purple fairy bells and orange fairy lanterns which gave way to the white blossoms of the starflower. So deep was Isabella in the forest, that the starflowers sparkled like constellations in the night sky. Everywhere she looked there were clouds of butterflies and bumblebees pollinating flowers and creating more life.

Indeed as the days passed, Isabella experienced new life everywhere. Once during a walk deep in the woods, Isabella came upon two newborn fawns dozing with their mother. Hidden under a bower of branches, the light spilled onto the sleeping fawns through the spaces between the leaves. The fawns were almost invisible. The doe raised her head, looked at Isabella and went back to her nap. When the small family did not seem disturbed by her presence, Isabella laid in the grass watching the clouds and fell asleep alongside them.

It did not take many days until Isabella decided to untie her winter braid and let the wind blow through her long thick hair. She turned a cartwheel and then a somersault and then another cartwheel. *Why would anyone ever want to wear a dress?* she thought as she brushed the dirt from the seat of her trousers. *The Queen Mother is right. Dresses are so restrictive. In fact, I am never going to wear another dress again – ever!* The girl was content in a way she had not been since she arrived in the Lower World.

One morning Isabella woke to summer. The air was hot and a wild wind danced through the woods. The deep blue sky was filled with gigantic cotton ball clouds. Far off in the distance, Isabella noticed a slight darkening in the sky that meant rain later in the day. She hurried off for an early morning swim in the river. As she ran through the woods, Isabella had a strange feeling she was not alone. Then she saw the leader of the wolf pack trotting ahead of her. She was pleased to see him. Over the months, she and the pack had crossed paths many times.

Instead of going to the river, the wolf turned and headed deeper into the forest. Isabella decided to follow. Aware the girl was with him, the wolf slowed down. He snuffled along smelling the ground, sniffing the air and marking trees with his scent. Soon they were in an area of the forest unknown to Isabella. She wondered if the wolf was patrolling the boundaries of the pack's territory. Abruptly, the wolf stopped. His body tensed, and his coat bristled as his nose caught a scent that disturbed him. In seconds, Isabella saw a silver wolf slinking towards them. The wolf was a young male, slightly smaller than the black leader but healthy and strong. He was not from their family.

Isabella stood very still. The Queen Mother had explained young males often left their families in the spring to start new packs. Many tried to stake their own territories by challenging an older leader of an existing order. Isabella knew these battles could be violent, and she suddenly feared for her friend's safety.

The two wolves faced one another. The black wolf's ears were taut and bent forward. He bared his teeth and lifted his tail straight in the air. His growl made it clear it would be foolish for the young male to step closer.

The silver wolf was not intimidated. Without hesitation, the young wolf charged his opponent. Wise in the ways of battle, the black leader sprang forward slamming his body into the younger wolf, clamping his jaws on the throat of the young rival. The two wrestled fiercely for a several seconds, and the challenger broke away, unhurt. The silver male backed away to plan his next move. He let out a series of sharp barks and stepped forward as though to charge again. Then suddenly, he turned and trotted off in the direction from which he had come, deciding this was not a good day to fight. To make sure there was no question of his victory, the black wolf sprinted after the young male chasing him over a ridge. The alpha male returned to Isabella only when he was satisfied the intruder had left his territory.

Isabella had been shaken by the confrontation between the two wolves and was sitting on the forest floor when the black wolf returned. "I do not feel safe," she said. "I want to go home to the Queen Mother. Will you show me the way back?"

The wolf licked Isabella's face. "You had no need to fear. I would not allow harm to come to you; you are part of my pack," he said to her.

"You could have been terribly hurt," Isabella countered.

"Isabella, I simply let the young one know the boundaries of my territory. In my world this was a lesson in respect," the wolf replied calmly

"What if he had not accepted your warning? He is young and strong and foolish," she persisted.

"I have discovered that once someone knows a boundary is real, they respect it."

"Was it really so important?"

"It was very important," the leader said. "Come with me, please." Isabella followed him to a stream deep in the pack's territory. When the black wolf scampered to a cleft between rocks under an overhang, Isabella understood the significance of the encounter with the silver intruder. Lying in the sun was the black wolf's mate, a beautiful snow-white wolf with their five pups sound asleep around her. Judging by their size, Isabella thought the pups to be two months old. Any day they would be weaned, and the family would rejoin the pack but until then they were vulnerable to intruders. *What an honor to meet the newest members of the family* she thought.

"I am pleased you brought me to meet your children," Isabella said to both parents. "They are beautiful."

"How many pups do you have?" asked the white wolf.

"Oh, I am much too young to have pups," said Isabella blushing.

"I am surprised," the she-wolf replied. "You have the smell of a good mother. You are certain there are no pups?"

"I am certain," Isabella laughed though the question tugged at her heart in a way that surprised her. She sat watching the family and felt joy in her heart. "I wish I could gift you in some way," she murmured.

The mother and father glanced at one another and said, "We have not howled for our children yet. We did not want to announce their arrival until they were large enough to leave the den and join the rest of the family. Now it is safe to do so. Would you join us in welcoming them to the forest?"

"Oh yes, I would love to do that," smiled Isabella. "Thank you."

The mother and father sat upright on their haunches. The father threw his head back and howled with utter delight announcing the birth of his children. His mate followed with equal passion. The pups, startled out of their nap, looked about and upon discovering the howling was coming from their parents began to yip and yap and mew and chirp. They soon tired of the commotion and collapsed back into sleep. The wolf leaders paused and looked at Isabella tilting their heads to one side waiting to see what she would do next. Isabella took a deep breath and exhaled. She took another and then opened her mouth. Out came a gurgle. "Young mistress, you can do better than that," chuckled the mother wolf.

"Yes, I think I can," said Isabella breaking into a smile. She drew air deep into her lungs and stomach and throwing her head back shrieked, "aaaaAAAAAAAAAaaaa!!!"

The pups looked up sleepily. "Better," said the black wolf.

"I want to try again," said Isabella flushed. One breath, two breathes, and after the third she exhaled forcing the air from her lungs. A vibration started in her lungs and filled her body, "aaaaAAAAOOOOOOOOOOOOOWWWWWWWWWWWWWWLLLLLLLLLL!"

"Magnificent!" said the mother.

"A noble announcement," said the black wolf, his tail swishing back and forth in delight.

"Oh we're not done," said Isabella beaming. "We're just beginning." And so the trio howled and howled introducing the newest members of the pack to the forest. As expected their calls were soon answered by the celebratory howls of their own tribe. To Isabella's delight they also heard calls from distant relatives echoing through the woods welcoming the babies. When Isabella and the proud parents finally tired, the male led her home.

"Please, do not be a stranger to us," said the black wolf as they approach Kriya's cottage, "we sing well together." Isabella leaned down and hugged the wolf. She hummed as she crossed the clearing to the cottage door.

That night at dinner Isabella told the Queen Mother of the new pups. "They can barely walk, yet they were trying to jump on one another and wrestle. They were so funny. Please come with me tomorrow. I would love for you to meet them."

"I would be happy to do so," said the woman with a smile.

After taking a few bites of venison stew, Isabella said, "I want to ask you something." The Queen Mother put her spoon down and nodded for Isabella to continue. "Do you ever feel I am a burden to you?" Isabella asked timidly.

"Of course not; what makes you ask that?" asked Kriya curiously.

"I know you are used to living alone, and you like your freedom and privacy," Isabella said choosing her words carefully. "You were kind to say I could visit as long as I wanted."

"And I meant it," said the Queen.

"I know you did – the visit part anyway – but I want to stay with you not just for a while. I want to stay forever," Isabella said her words tumbling out in a rush. The woman had known of Isabella's desire for some time. Many a night she had felt Isabella's longings.

"Isabella, you can stay with me as long as you want, as long as you need to," replied the Queen Mother patting the girl's hand. "I think there will come a time when you will wish to spread your wings and fly. Even after that, you may return whenever you wish."

"You are wrong, Queen Mother, I will never leave you. Oh, thank you! Thank you! Thank you!" Isabella's smile lit the evening room.

"I am curious though. What will you do about the book Stefan asked you to find?" the Queen asked casually as she picked up her spoon.

"It was foolish for me to start the quest," Isabella said as she reached for the bread. "I have no ambition to find the book, Queen Mother. I only wish to stay here with you. Indeed there is nothing amiss with the kingdom. All is perfect here!" The Queen nodded thoughtfully and did not say a word.

⟡
COUNCIL IN THE OAKS

Dusk was falling in the dell protected by a circle of ancient oaks. In the center of the clearing, a massive table and five thrones awaited their guests. One by one they came and found their place at the royal table. "What ails our little girl?" Sir Alfred asked gravely.

The Queen Mother smiled kindly. "Alfred, she's not a little girl anymore. She's a young woman – as tall as I am and quite lovely I might add."

Sir Alfred blushed red, "Well, Madame, is that not a good sign? She's growing."

"Something is wrong," broke in Stefan. "The canvases in the castle are changing again."

"How so?" asked Setine, her panthers lounging behind their queen's chair, their tails swishing back and forth lazily.

"The fires and earthquakes have been replaced with fog. Painting after painting is filled with fog. Only it is not fog as I know it," said Stefan shaking his head.

Nightwalker flapped his wings and said, "I saw them this morning. It is not fog. The paintings are being erased; the land is being enveloped by nothingness."

"Nothingness," mused Setine. "That is interesting because her dreams ceased two days ago. Did something happen?"

"She asked to live with me two nights ago," replied the Queen Mother.

"Oh dear, that is not good," said Sir Alfred shaking his head. "Highness, has she said anything about seeking the book?"

The Queen Mother said, "She said the book is of no interest to her; that one only need look around to know all is well in the kingdom."

"Oh dear," said the Royal Advisor, "she does not want to continue."

The Queen Mother glanced around the table. "Are there suggestions as to how we might help her change her mind?" she asked.

"Madame, I defer to the council on this matter. I fear logic will not cure what ails Miss Isabella now."

"I believe you are correct, old friend," said Nightwalker. "I have given this some thought, and I think the fairies may be of assistance to her. I know my girl; it will be hard for her to resist their magic."

"Interesting," said the Queen Mother nodding thoughtfully. "That may be so, but I think one more step needs to be taken before we call upon our woodland friends."

"We must hurry, Mother," said Stefan. "We are running out of time."

SAUL

The day was hot and humid. Even the mosquitoes could not conjure enough energy to take nourishment from the Queen Mother and Isabella as they dug in the earth preparing the garden for late summer planting. Stopping to wipe the sweat from her brow, the Queen leaned on her hoe and looked at Isabella. "I was fishing with the constable the other day," Kriya said nonchalantly, tucking a red kerchief into the waistband of her yellow trousers.

The hair bristled on the back of Isabella's neck. She continued to break up chunks of dirt with her spade without speaking. "He was curious as to whether you had given any more thought to the prisoner. Quite some time has passed since you last visited him," the Queen said. Isabella concentrated on the dirt clods as though they were the most important things in the world. "Isabella?" the woman said as she dropped the hoe, and she walked over to the young woman.

Isabella stabbed the earth with her spade and said tersely, "Let him rot in jail. He is a horrible man."

The Queen Mother put her hand on Isabella's spade forcing the young woman to stop her work. "I have spent some time with him, Isabella," she said softly. "I think it might be a good idea for you to go back."

Isabella's head snapped up. "You what?" she sputtered. "You met with him? You have spoken with him?"

"Yes," the Queen nodded calmly.

"You did not think to tell me?" Isabella said angrily, jerking the spade away from the Queen's touch. "You did not think to *ask* me?" she demanded as she threw her spade to the ground. Isabella shouted,

"Did you not think it might disturb me that you would go to him behind my back?!"

"That was not my intention," the Queen replied calmly.

"Well that is exactly what it feels like!" raged Isabella. "This is the second time you have betrayed me. You wanted me to help him. That is why I went to the jail the first time, and he was horrible to me. Don't you remember that? Don't you care about me?"

"I do care about you – deeply," said the Queen Mother as she reached for Isabella's hand, "and I also care about him."

The woman's words hit Isabella like a blow to the face. The young woman jerked her hand away from the woman. "You care about him?" she shouted in disbelief. "You care about him? He tried to kill me. How can you care about him? You should hate him."

"I hate what he did to you," said the Queen solemnly. "I hate what he has done to others, but I do not hate him. He is a subject of this kingdom, and he has a right to be as every subject of this kingdom has a right to be."

Isabella could not believe her ears. An icy fist closed around her heart. "That is ridiculous," she replied coldly. "Your words tell me you care only for your subjects, only for your kingdom. You care nothing for me. I am simply a visitor here, an outsider. What a fool I have been to believe otherwise."

"Isabella, you must face him," the Queen Mother said earnestly. "If you do not, you will continue to be his prisoner – his victim." She reached again for Isabella's hand. "It is possible to do that now. I will go with you, if you so wish. I will help you both."

"Leave me alone," cried the girl as she broke away from the Queen and ran from the garden. In minutes she was in the forest. *How could she do this to me? How could she side with him? I cannot stay with her. I will not stay with her.* Suddenly, she saw the constable running towards her.

"Oh, Isabella, I am so glad I found you," he gasped trying to catch his breath. "The prisoner has escaped. I must not have locked the cell when I brought him food this morning." He shook his head in misery. "I went back to get his tray, and he was gone. I suggest you get back to the Queen Mother immediately. He would not dare harm you there. I must go back and organize a search party. Hurry, Isabella."

Oh my thought Isabella as she stood stunned, watching the constable disappear back down the trail. *Where can I go? I will not go back to the Queen Mother.* No sooner had those thoughts slipped through her mind, than a man stood before Isabella blocking her way. The traveler was tall and muscular; his blonde hair pulled back and neatly tied with cord, his face clean shaven. Though his clothes were worn they were clean and he carried a sack and sleeping mat. His blue eyes searched Isabella's face. Though he looked different Isabella had no doubt this was the man from the swamp.

The woods went perfectly still and silent as the man and girl stared at one another. From nowhere, the black wolf and his mate stepped from the trees. One moved to Isabella's right side, the other to her left – their hackles raised, their ears flattened, and their teeth bared. All stood in silence. Isabella looked at her protectors and then at the man. Slowly and fiercely she said, "I am tired of being afraid of you. I will not run from you ever again. Do you hear me? I will not run from you ever again."

Unexpectedly, the man dropped his gaze. "You no longer need to fear me," he replied gruffly. "I have no desire to hurt you."

Isabella's eyes widened and then narrowed into slits. "I do not believe you," she spat, the wolves pressing against her legs. "This is a trick."

"No trick," said the man as he took several steps back from Isabella and the wolves, his arms hanging limply at his sides. "The constable left the keys in the cell door. I walked out and was headed out of the province." The man stopped speaking standing silently for a few moments. He shifted the sack from one shoulder to the other and said haltingly, "I could have gotten away." Again he was silent for several moments and then said brusquely, "I have never apologized for anything I have ever said or ever done." The man cleared his throat and said roughly, "I had time to think of many things while in the jail. I am sorry for what I did to you. I came back to accept any punishment you decide for me."

Though filled with a rage that wished the man dead, Isabella stood silent unable to speak or move. The moment seemed to last forever. Then, though the forest was silent and absolutely still, a white hawthorn blossom drifted out of nowhere and landed on the man's shoulder. A second blossom fell to the ground between them and then a third brushed her face. Isabella felt a sob in her throat.

The wolves pressed even closer to her and the white wolf said, "You need not do this alone, young mistress. The Queen will help you."

Isabella nodded. Haltingly she said, "Your Queen wishes me to speak with you. I do not agree but because I am a visitor to her kingdom I will consider the request. If I do speak with you, it will only be in her presence. You are to stay here with the wolves. Once I reach her cottage, the wolves will bring you to her if she and I decide that is appropriate." As the young woman turned to walk away, she stopped and without looking back said in a voice as cold as ice, "If you do anything that threatens me or the Queen, I will tell the wolves to kill you." Without waiting for an answer she walked stiffly down the path.

The man called out, "Isabella, all this time you have never asked my name. My name is Saul. I am Saul." Isabella did not stop walking. *How odd* she thought coldly *my father's name.* The forest was suddenly filled with sound.

THE CURIOSA

When Isabella reached the cottage, the Queen was sitting under her favorite maple tree reading. After a terse conversation, Isabella strode into the house and slumped into a chair by the window. Isabella watched the Queen walk to the edge of the clearing and clap her hands. Within seconds a cloud of tiny white butterflies enveloped her. When the Queen Mother finished speaking with them, she clapped again and they were gone. She approached Isabella's window and said, "I have sent a message instructing the wolves to escort Saul to our cottage." The girl did not respond. In less than an hour, Saul and the wolves entered the cottage clearing and approached Kriya. After a nod from the Queen, the wolves broke away and trotted to Isabella's window.

"One of us will stay with you at all times to insure no harm comes to you while the man is here," growled the black wolf.

"Thank you," said Isabella gratefully.

"I must attend my children though I will return this evening," said the white wolf. She and her mate nuzzled one another, and the she-wolf disappeared into the woods. The black leader settled under Isabella's window and both turned their attention to Saul and the Queen. The man and woman were engaged in deep conversation. Finally, the Queen Mother motioned toward the lean-to at the farthest edge of the cottage clearing which served as a tool shed. Saul nodded, walked to the shelter and put down his sack and sleeping mat. Slowly, he began to drag the contents of the shed into the yard examining each item thoroughly. After his review was complete, he began to clean and repair tools that were worn and in need of mending.

The Queen, knowing the constable was putting together a search party, sent a fox to notify him that Saul was visiting and all was well.

255

Fearing the Queen Mother and Isabella had been taken hostage and the message was a trick, the constable arrived at the cottage mightily out of breath. He could scarcely believe his eyes. The Queen Mother was hanging linens out to dry, Isabella was staring sullenly from the cottage window while a black wolf surveyed the clearing, and Saul was cleaning a scythe.

"Highness, may I speak with you privately?" The constable's red cheeks were almost scarlet.

"Oh, no need for privacy; we are all friends here," said the Queen serenely as she shook out a coverlet. "Might you help me spread this over the line? It is quite cumbersome."

"Of course, Highness, let me help you," said the constable reaching for one end of the quilt. "Highness, is this course of action wise? The prisoner I mean, not the laundry," the constable stuttered. "I do not mean to be presumptuous but this man is very dangerous!"

"I am aware of his history," the Queen replied.

"My apologies, of course you know his history. It is only I feel I must do my job by keeping you safe!" said the man struggling to throw the coverlet over the line.

"I so appreciate your vigilance, Constable. You do keep us all very safe. In this instance though, Saul is my guest. I will insure safety for us all," the Queen said with a gentle smile. "Would you like to join us for a cup of tea and honey fingers before you return to town?" Knowing he could not change her mind, the constable bowed to his Queen and bid her a good day.

Over the next several weeks, the Queen turned the maintenance of the cottage over to Saul. He chopped wood, repaired the thatch roof of the cottage and tool shed, finished turning the soil for the garden, planted seedlings, whitewashed the walls of the cottage and fixed anything he could find that needed repair. Isabella stood apart from Saul, faithfully guarded by the wolves watching his every move. She was not ready yet to discuss his presence with the Queen

One morning while she and the white wolf were sitting on the cottage stoop, Isabella observed Saul fashioning a scarecrow for the garden. "Come with me, please," she said tersely to the she-wolf.

"You are sure of this, mistress?"

"I am."

Isabella walked to the garden and watched Saul stuff a bundle of straw into the arm of one of the Queen's old turquoise and pink shirts. "Were you ever in Kronos?" she asked stiffly.

Saul paused for only a second as he stuffed a second bundle of straw into the other arm. "I was," he answered without looking at the young woman.

"So, you *were* trying to sell the book that the king was interested in," Isabella said accusingly.

Not taking his eyes off his work, Saul said, "I knew of the task Stefan had set before you and the path you were taking through Kronos." Saul bent to pick up a broomstick lying on the ground and ran it through the arms of the scarecrow's patchwork shirt. He laid the half-finished scarecrow on the ground and turned to look at Isabella. "I had a book I stole from a monastery and passed it off as royal. I wanted you to hear of the terrible man who had it in his possession so you would be frightened into giving up the search and go back to your village." Saul bent to pick up a shovel lying by the edge of the garden. The white wolf stepped forward and bared her teeth. "I will not harm her," Saul said gruffly as he started digging the hole for the scarecrow post.

"Let us leave, mistress," said the wolf, her coat bristling with tension. "This is enough for the moment."

Isabella stared at the man. "I hate you," she spat out. "You think you can make up for all the terrible things you did by being friends with the Queen, but you never can."

"Mistress," said the she-wolf, her ears and tail straight up, "this is not wise." Saul continued to dig the post hole.

"Did you hear me?" Isabella hissed.

Saul drove the shovel into the ground and said brusquely, "I have something for you." The she-wolf jumped between the man and young woman, hackles raised, her tail straight in the air. "I said I would not harm her. Allow me to give her what is hers," the man said dropping both arms limply to his sides. The wolf sniffed the man then nodded warily.

257

Isabella's body stiffened as Saul slowly put his hand into his tunic and pulled out a scrap of blue cloth. When he unfolded the fabric, there in his hand lay the Curiosa. Isabella inhaled sharply. He had torn the Curiosa from her dress the night of his attack on her. Saul cleared his throat and said, "I thought you might want this back."

Isabella stared at the pendant in disbelief: the violet silk covering the crossbar was torn, and the clasp was broken; the diamonds and ruby were covered with dirt but all remained intact. Her eyes hardened seeing Sir Alfred's beloved Curiosa so damaged. She snatched the ornament from Saul's hand. "You ruin everything you touch," she said flatly as she closed her fist around the Curiosa. She and the wolf turned back to the cottage. Isabella took only a few steps when she stopped. Twisting around to face the man, her face blotched with anger, she hissed, "Why did you return the Curiosa to me? Did you think that doing so would buy you forgiveness?" When Saul did not answer she spat out, "If you did, you will be sorely disappointed. I will not forgive you, ever. Do you hear me, ever! I despise you."

Saul's faced reddened. "What I seek is more difficult."

"And what is that?" she asked sarcastically.

"To forgive myself for what I have done to you and others."

"How noble," she sneered. "You think that is the harder?"

Saul dropped his head. "How would you answer that?" he asked softly.

"What did you say?" Isabella's head snapped back. "What did you say?" she hissed taking a step towards the man.

"Careful, mistress," said the white wolf tugging on the young woman's trouser leg. "This has gone far enough for now. I urge you to involve the Queen Mother in this dialogue before it moves beyond our control."

Isabella struggled to compose herself. Drawing herself up to her full height, she said, "As you said to me in the jail, 'this is not finished between us'. To appease the Queen, I have agreed to have her mediate a discussion between us. Once it is done, I will decide your punishment." Saul nodded and went back to his digging. Isabella stood staring at him the Curiosa clenched in her fist. "I hate you. I will always hate you for what you did to me – for what you took from me," she said, her voice cold with fury. She turned and walked into the woods.

VISITATION

The man was setting out bowls and cereal for breakfast when his son came running into the kitchen. "Daddy, Daddy, Mommy came to see me last night!" the boy said his smile lighting up the room.

"You mean you dreamed about Mommy," the man said, gently tousling the boy's curls. "That's really nice."

"No, no! She was sitting on the edge of my bed touching my face. She had on a pretty pink outfit with a hat that had flowers sticking out all over the place. She said to remind you to get my library card because she couldn't do it. Then she kissed me and hugged me and said to tell everyone she loved us all so much and that she was sorry. I told her it was okay about the library card and she started crying. Daddy what's wrong, what's wrong?" he asked as his father frantically dialed the ICU.

RESTORATION

Isabella spent the next several days in the woods with the wolves and their family. When the Queen Mother felt Isabella's blood rage had cooled, she suggested a discussion between Saul and Isabella begin two days hence. On the appointed day, Saul, the Queen, and Isabella were seated around a trestle table under the maple. Both wolves lay at Isabella's feet. The tension in the air was heavy and thick, and no one reached for the tea or food the Queen had prepared. Finally, the Queen Mother said, "What has passed between the two of you must be spoken of. Though it will be difficult, we are in a place of safety, and I will keep it such." Neither Saul nor Isabella spoke. The woman continued, "Isabella, you carry much pain from the attack."

Isabella twisted her hands nervously in her lap. She was not able to move her eyes away from the tea cup placed before her. Finally, she said, her voice trembling, "I don't care about the attack. I don't care about pain. All I want to know is he one of the men who killed Alexandra."

The man sighed heavily and said, "No, I was not part of that."

Isabella raised her eyes to him and said sharply, "If you weren't part of that, how did you know about it? Then why did you try to kill me, if not to keep me from identifying you?" Saul dropped his eyes. "Don't look away from me," Isabella snapped. "Do you know what you did to me? Do you know how afraid I always am? Do you know what you took from me?" Still the man did not respond.

"Tell him so he will know, Isabella," said the Queen Mother gently.

"Why?" asked Isabella bitterly, "it will not change anything."

"I disagree," said the Queen. "It is in telling him that you will be free."

261

Isabella sighed and dropped her eyes to the tea cup once again. "Even if that were true, I cannot speak the words," she said thickly. "It is too difficult; it is too confusing."

"Will you allow me to help you then?" pressed Kriya.

"How?" the young woman asked suspiciously.

The Queen Mother opened her hand to Saul and he placed his calloused hand in hers. "Now give me your hand, Isabella."

Isabella shifted uneasily in her seat. "For what purpose?" she asked.

"Once you do so, your memories and feelings will flow through me to him. He will know it all. More importantly, he will feel it all." Isabella's stomach lurched at the thought of sharing herself with him in such an intimate way. Immediately the wolves inched closer to Isabella and rubbed their heads against her legs. She smiled weakly at her protectors.

"Isabella, can you trust me?" the Queen Mother asked, her hand outstretched.

Can I trust her? I cannot, she betrayed me twice. Can I trust her? She saved me over and over and over again. Can I trust her? Isabella sat still as a statue. Then slowly, slowly, slowly, she drew her hand from her lap and placed it on the table close to the Queen. She could go no further. Kriya gently laid her hand over Isabella's. With the connection complete, all three were enveloped in a golden light so bright Isabella was forced to close her eyes.

Yet within the light, she felt safe to remember and feel. *Stefan felt this in the Northern Province.* As the moments passed, tears began to stream down her face and soon from Saul's eyes. The man from the swamp began to weep and then sob as memory after memory of his pursuit, his vicious attack and its horrendous emotional impact on the child flooded him. Only after Isabella's face dried, did the Queen Mother gently release their hands. The three sat silently.

"I did not know this is how it felt," Saul said hoarsely. "I did not know this is what I did to you." His shoulders slumped as he seemed to collapse inward.

Isabella sat stunned by the realization that he truly felt the toll of his actions upon her. "Why did you pursue me?" she asked simply.

A thin sheen of sweat broke out over Saul's face as he struggled to speak. After several moments he said, "In the beginning I only wanted to frighten you away." He could not look at the young woman.

"Why?"

Saul shifted back and forth in his chair; his hands running up and down his thighs. "I believed you were a danger to the Lower World. I knew the paintings in the castle were tied to you and I believed your coming here would only make the situation worse – that the pain of you remembering Alexandra would be more pain than the kingdom could bear and we all would perish." Saul began to tap his fingers on the table. "I thought I was saving the kingdom by getting rid of you. I told myself I was protecting us all, doing my duty, redeeming myself." His entire body seemed to be moving, jumping – legs, arms, hands.

"You meant to kill me in the swamp."

"The terrible truth is in the swamp, I wanted someone else to hurt as much as I did. I did want to hurt you – kill you."

"What could possibly have wounded you so much that you would want to commit murder?" Isabella asked incredulously.

His eyes began to twitch and his mouth to tremble. When it seemed as though his body would fly apart, he lowered his head to the table. A sob racked his body then another and another. No one moved to comfort the man. Finally the Queen placed her hand upon his head. The Queen then turned and looked deep into Isabella's eyes. "There are things you need to know, Isabella," she said softly.

Isabella reached for the Queen's outstretched hand. Instantly, Isabella's mind was flooded with scenes of war: soldiers, old men, women, children on holiday; all dead. So many dead children caught in the crossfire; bodies burned, bloodied, broken; the land was filled with silence, stench, sorrow, and overwhelming pain.

Isabella gasped and drew her hand away from the Queen and the man. "The trade route war, the war with the Empress, you were there. You did things…" she said to Saul.

"I did terrible things," the man moaned, his head cradled in his arms on the table. "All I wanted was to be a good soldier to do my duty to the king, to protect the kingdom. My job was to protect the kingdom, but I only killed those weaker and innocent. I almost did the same to you."

"You have not seen all he has to show you," the Queen said softly.

"I do not think I can bear more."

"I will not allow you to be overwhelmed," the Queen reassured the young woman. Isabella closed her eyes and drew a deep breath. She took the woman's hand once again and did not take it away until she had witnessed and felt all of Saul: a childhood of abandonment, poverty and abuse; a youth in search of purpose in the king's service; an unjust war that created a monster. A world that had no place for monsters and yet a monster who sought redemption in the most twisted of ways. When there was no more, she drew her hand back. All were silent and exhausted. Evening shadows filled the clearing. "I think it wise to stop," said the Queen Mother. "A walk, food, rest are in order. We shall continue tomorrow

As Isabella slowly rose from the table she thought *I do not think I can continue this tomorrow.* Isabella trudged into the cottage and collapsed onto her bed. Spent, her head pounding, she pulled her coverlet over her body. As she tucked the comforter under her chin she thought *What is this? This does not feel right.*

She sat up, pulled the candle closer, and saw her quilt had been replaced by another. Running her fingers over the coverlet's squares she recognized herself in the boat on the river; Nightwalker was stitched in another as was Sir Alfred and the king; there was a square for Stefan's journal; many more for the Legacy, Saul, Alexandra, and swirling hawthorn petals. Everyone and everything she had encountered in this strange world had found its way into a memory quilt. *So this is what she stitches each night. She has been embroidering my quilt all this time.* The young woman felt strangely comforted as she drew the blanket tightly around her body and laid her head on her pillow.

When she fell asleep Setine was waiting for her in the most secret corner of the Lower World. Isabella stepped over a bridge of moss covered stones and stood before the Queen of the Dreamtime. The young queen was wearing a gown of pure white silk covered with thousands of seedling pearls, thousands of undreamed dreams. "I have something to show you. Setine led Isabella to a waterfall which flowed into a series of cascading pools. "The water is very hot," said Setine motioning to the pools. "Perhaps you would like to bathe."

Isabella looked down to see she was wearing a funeral shroud. With Setine's help, Isabella pulled the gray shroud over her head revealing her hair and body smeared with mud, excrement, vomit, filth and blood. She moved toward the steaming pools and slowly lowered herself into the water. The young woman sighed as the water covered her. "Let me wash your hair, Isabella. It is so beautiful," Setine said as she poured oil of jasmine onto Isabella's head.

Isabella leaned back on the pool edge as the young queen's fingers massaged the oil into her scalp and locks. Then Setine rinsed Isabella's hair with rain water from a sapphire pitcher. Finally, the queen took at diamond comb and pulled it through Isabella's tresses over and over again. Moonlight, steam, fragrance, and touch soothed Isabella to her core. Only then could she ask, "What am I to do, Setine? I am so confused. There is so much violence and pain between Saul and myself – so much loss in each of us. How can there be even one next step between us?"

"There is an ancient law in the Lower Kingdom, Isabella. Hatred never ceases by hatred but by love alone is healed," replied the young queen. Isabella turned to look at Setine. The queen smiled and continued, "Have you not observed that? Critiques, Sir Alfred, Stefan, the Legacy; only love healed all that ailed their hearts.

Isabella began to weep. "I do not have their strength. I do not have their faith," she mourned.

"Of course you do, beloved," Setine said as she leaned forward and kissed Isabella's hair. "There is restoration for you, for Saul, for all who sincerely seek it." The queen waved her hand to the falls and pools and said, "I have brought you here for a purpose. These are healing waters, Isabella. Let them wash away your pain and wounds. Let them wash away all that blocks your heart from loving." Just as Isabella was about to ask a question, the young queen smiled and faded away. All that was left were thousands of seedling pearls that shimmered in the pools.

"Wait!" exclaimed Isabella, but she was alone in the forest. Isabella rose from the hot water, cleansed. She rested at the side of the pool eating berries that grew along the edge of the water and cooled her body. She bathed again, rested and ate. After bathing for the third time she fell asleep on a bed of violets and did not wake until dawn in her own bed in Kriya's cottage.

THE RIGHT NEXT STEP

At dawn Isabella arose and went outside the cottage. The white wolf stood and asked if she was needed. Isabella stroked the wolf and gently shook her head. The wolf nodded and trotted into the woods. The sky was pink with the rising sun; the air was warm and moist. There would be rain that day. She found Saul kneeling over the seedlings he had planted in the garden. He stood and awkwardly brushed the dirt from his hands when he saw Isabella approach. "I will go back to the lean-to," he said roughly.

"You need not go," said Isabella haltingly. After an awkward silence she said, "It feels like there will be rain today."

Saul shifted from one leg to the other. "Yes," he grunted.

"It will be a nice garden, don't you think?" the young woman said.

Saul looked at her with surprise. "I think it will be a fine garden," he answered.

The two stared at the neat rows of plantings: neither wanting to leave, neither knowing what to say. Her heart pounding Isabella began. "Alexandra forgave me for her death, but it did not help." Saul did not reply. The young woman sighed. "There was a part of me that believed you were right to kill me; that I deserved to be killed because I failed her. There are still times I want to be punished for the many wrongs I have done."

Saul stood silently. Finally he cleared his throat and said brusquely, "I am the same."

Isabella stared at the rows of the garden. She shook her head slightly. Not able to look at Saul she said, "I want peace."

"I, too," he said gruffly.

"I believe the Queen Mother was wise in urging us to speak with one another." Isabella stopped not sure she could continue. "As important as that was, I think it is the next step that will free me from you. She stopped and turned to look at the man. "I must choose to forgive you – not the terrible things you did to me. I must choose to forgive *you* – the actor, the being that you are. I have to do that to free myself."

"You can do that?" he asked incredulously.

"I will have to choose it," she said simply. "I have wounds to heal that will take much time but I chose not to be chained to you through vengeance." She paused and turned back to gaze upon the garden. "You are free to go, Saul," she said. "There is no punishment I wish upon you. It is done."

"I do not know what to say," said the man from the swamp.

"I do not require that you say anything," said Isabella.

"And Alexandra?"

Isabella sighed. "My beloved, Alexandra…" She stood silently lost in the memories of swirling white petals filling the air. "I must forgive myself for her death. I have invited the intention into my heart and will tend to it. I think the seed will bloom in its own season."

After a long pause Saul said, "I am so very sorry for all the harm I have done to you. I thank you for your willingness to forgive. I do not know how I will forgive myself." Isabella nodded sadly. "I will leave tonight," Saul said staring at the tender seedlings stretching towards the morning sun.

Isabella nodded once more and turned toward the cottage. As she entered she found the Queen folding linens. Kriya looked up and murmured, "This is such a simple task yet it soothes me so. And you dear one, how are you doing?"

"You heard us?"

The Queen Mother nodded gently.

"I am not sure what I am feeling quite honestly," replied the young woman. "I think I will walk by the river; it is what soothes me," she said with a sad smile. The Queen hugged the young woman as Isabella reached for Stefan's journal and walked out the door.

That afternoon as the sun dropped low in the sky Saul packed his few belongings. The lean-to was once again a tool shed, all trace of Saul removed. Kriya stood by him silently watching. "Where will you go?" she asked.

"I am not sure. Back to the trade routes maybe; perhaps to my birth village. There are answers for me in both places." He glanced around one last time and turned towards the cottage. "I would like to say goodbye to Isabella." Just then Isabella and the wolves entered the clearing. Seeing Saul and the Queen Mother standing together, the young woman made her way to the lean-to. As she reached them Saul said, "I am leaving." The girl nodded. Saul looked down at his feet and said, "I am not good with words, Isabella, so I made something for you." He pulled a second scrap of cloth from his pocket. Isabella took the cloth from his hand. When she unfolded it there lay a miniature book, intricately carved and polished. It was a work of beauty.

"Thank you," she said.

Saul nodded. He lifted his pack, bowed and walked down the trail into the evening dusk. He paused, turned and raised his hand one last time. "Good-bye," he called to them.

"Peace be with you," the Queen Mother murmured.

When they could no longer see him, Isabella asked, "Will he find what he seeks?"

"In time," the Queen Mother said softly. "And you?"

"In time...."

PNEUMONIA

"Has something happened?" the man demanded when the charge-nurse came to the phone.

"I was just going to call you. Your wife was breathing just fine yesterday, but when the internist checked her lungs last night about 2:00 AM, he noticed a rattling. We brought in the x-ray machine and the x-rays confirm pneumonia. It frequently happens when a patient has been on a vent for as long as she was. We are infusing her with massive doses of vancomycin and will watch very closely, but pneumonia is tricky."

"This can't kill her, can it?"

The nurse sighed. "Her body is so fragile, anything can happen."

THE LIBRARY OF THE ANCIENTS

In early fall Isabella was picking the last of the tomatoes and peppers from the garden. Kriya had promised to teach Isabella how to preserve vegetables for the winter and the young woman was eager to harvest the last of the garden's bounty. As she broke off a beautiful green pepper and gently placed it in her basket, she heard the faintest whisper of her name. Thinking the Queen Mother called her from the river, she smiled. *I wonder what mischief the Queen is about.* Then she heard again, "Isabella!" This time Isabella looked around, but she was alone. "Here, please," called the tiny voice again. It was only then that Isabella saw a small fairy perched on the shoulder of the garden's scarecrow. "I hope I am not interrupting," the fairy said sweetly.

"Not in the least," said Isabella as she bent to better see her visitor. "I have never met a fairy before. You are beautiful."

"I am. Thank you," the fairy said with a curtsy. The creature was only six inches tall and as slender as a reed. She was clothed in a wisp of gold silk fastened at her shoulder with an emerald set in white gold. Her wings were purple gossamer and shimmered in the sunlight. A tiny silver pouch hung from her waist. "I have something for you from King Stefan. He asked me to place this in your hands." She flew off the scarecrow and hovered in front of Isabella. Two delicate hands held out a tiny letter.

"This is much too tiny for me to read," said Isabella smiling. "Perhaps you can read it to me."

"Oh, it is magic parchment," trilled the fairy. "Once I drop it into your hands, it will grow larger." And so it did. Isabella opened the royal letter and read:

Dearest Isabella,

I hope this letter finds you and my mother doing well. I told you she was an interesting woman. I have recently received news about the book we spoke of during your visit to the castle. I understand it has been secured by the Library of the Ancients. If you are still interested in locating it, the fairies will take you there. Sir Alfred sends his regards. You are missed by us all.

Cordially,
King Stefan

Isabella reread the letter twice. Then she said, "Can you return tomorrow at this same time? I will have my reply for you."

"I will be back," said the fairy. "Goodbye." Off she flew on a puff of wind.

Moments later the Queen Mother came strolling into the cottage clearing, her arms filled with white flowers. "Look what I found," she said happily, "dream flowers!" Perfume filled the air as she held the bouquet to Isabella's nose.

"Hmmm, they smell wonderful," Isabella said as she drew in their fragrance. "I have never seen a dream flower."

The Queen Mother chuckled, "They are hard to find unless you know where to look. Actually they are snow trilliums but I prefer to call them dream flowers. Let's get them inside into some water." After the flowers were arranged throughout the cottage, Isabella handed Stefan's letter to the woman. A tender smile crossed the Queen Mother's face as she read it. "Persistent isn't he?" she said. "I like that. I also heard from Setine. She invited me to a party." Motioning for Isabella to sit next to her in front of the fire, she asked, "What will you do?"

Isabella had long ago given up any desire to pursue the book. In fact, after Saul's departure all thoughts of the past receded, replaced with a spaciousness previously unknown to her. No longer filled with fear or anger, Isabella smiled more, played with the animals in the forest, delighted in Kriya's company, cooked, cleaned, read and felt safe in the routine of their small life.

Yet in recent days she had begun feeling restless and, though she would never tell the Queen, a bit bored. It was then that the first thoughts of Stefan and the book crept into her mind. Isabella tried pushing them away thinking she was foolish to consider taking up the search and facing an unknown path, but now Stefan's letter was in her hands. Isabella had to face her change of heart. She wanted more than a safe life with the Queen Mother; she wanted to seek the book.

"I want to go to the Library of the Ancients," the young woman announced.

The Queen Mother beamed. "Good for you!" she said. "It sounds quite mysterious to me, and I always did love a good mystery," she whispered playfully. "When will you leave?"

"Tomorrow morning," said Isabella grateful for Kriya's approval.

"Well, let us have a lovely dinner tonight. Latisha sent me a new recipe for stuffed grape leaves I would love to try," she said with a wink.

"You are not angry with me?" Isabella asked looking into the woman's eyes.

"Whatever for?" exclaimed the Queen.

"For leaving you?"

"Nonsense – I do not see this as you leaving me. I see you pursuing something your heart desires and that delights me."

The next morning, Isabella and the Queen went into the yard. The fairy was sitting on the scarecrow's head waiting patiently. This time she wore a gown of ruby clasped with a sapphire broach. Her tiny pouch was platinum. "Good morning, Majesty. Good morning, Isabella." Her voice was so light it danced on a sunbeam.

"I am ready for you to take me to the Library of the Ancients," Isabella announced. "Can we leave now?"

"Of course," sang the fairy, "I am at your disposal."

Isabella and the Queen Mother hugged and kissed one another goodbye. "I will be back," cried Isabella as she and the fairy headed down the path. Kriya smiled as Isabella disappeared from sight. Humming she went into the cottage and began sorting through her fabric basket. When she found the perfect materials she settled by the window and began stitching the next row of swatches into Isabella's quilt.

Once Isabella and the fairy were deep into the woods, the young woman asked her guide, "Do we have a long way to go?"

"If we walk it is a very long trip," the fairy said hovering close to Isabella's face, "but I know a quicker way." With that she reached into her pouch and pulled out a tiny sliver flute. As she played a tune, a cardinal joined into her song, and then another and another until she and Isabella were caroled by a flock of brilliant red birds perched in the branches above.

"How beautiful," said Isabella looking up, "but how can this help us get to the Library of the Ancients?" The fairy reached into her pouch again and pulled out a handful of elfin dust. "Shut your eyes," she instructed and blew the dust into Isabella's face before Isabella could say a word. Immediately Isabella began to shrink until she was tinier than the fairy. Isabella looked up at the fairy in stunned surprise. "I am tall for my people," the fairy said smiling sweetly. When she saw her words did not amuse Isabella, she said, "Do not be concerned. You will return to your size when we reach our destination."

The cardinals flew from their perch in the trees and settled onto the ground close to Isabella and the sprite. "You shall ride with me," instructed the fairy. "Get on and hold tight to my waist." In seconds the two were soaring through the air on the back of a magnificent red bird, his crest blazing orange and black, its beak gold. Isabella looked about and marveled at the waves of red birds in front of them, behind them, to the left and to the right as far as she could see. "Isn't this wonderful?" the fairy laughed.

This time I am truly flying. A laugh started deep in her stomach and worked its way up her throat and out of her mouth. Isabella threw her arms out wide and laughed, "Yes it is wonderful. It is more than wonderful – it is stupendous!" Startled by her laugh, their cardinal dipped. Caught off balance, Isabella tumbled from his back but before she could utter a sound, she was swooped up by another red bird.

"Now you have your own steed," the fairy giggled as both cardinals caught a wind current and soared through the air. The wave of red rolled through the sky for hours finally washing upon the rocks of a hot spring. Isabella immediately recognized her surroundings. She was back at the falls and cascading pools where she had bathed with Setine.

"We're here," trilled the fairy as the birds touched ground. Their task complete, the flock bowed to their riders and returned to the skies.

Isabella looked about and said, "I do not see a library."

The fairy smiled, "Actually, you can see the library quite well from here."

"Where?" asked Isabella, turning this way and that.

"Up there," pointed the fairy with a delicate sweep of her hand. Looking straight up, Isabella saw a building floating on a billowy cloud. "Oh my!" Isabella exclaimed. "How do I get up there?"

"Do not worry. My friends and I will help you," smiled the fairy as she clapped her tiny hands. The air filled with the sound of wind chimes. Then a shimmering mist curled through the trees blending with the steam of the pools until the clearing was filled with a mist that shimmered blue then green then yellow then red. As Isabella stared at the mist, she realized it was not a mist at all but thousands of fairies – each a different color, each carrying a tiny basket filled with bells. The fairies flew in a spiral up to the cloud. As they reached the cloud's outermost edge they emptied the contents of their baskets. The bells dissolved into sparkling dust that drifted downward through the sky. In minutes the fairy dust became a spectacular rainbow stretching from the Library of the Ancients to Isabella's feet. Isabella's fairy trilled, "The rainbow is a magic stairway. We have pleased you?"

"Oh, yes!" said Isabella, her eyes sparkling like the fairies' jewels.

"Safe journey, Isabella," the fairies called out in joyful unison, as they disappeared into the forest like mist burning off in the morning sun. Only Isabella's guide remained. "I have a gift for you, Isabella," she said. She knelt before the young woman and reached into her pouch one last time. Out came two golden bracelets which she clasped onto Isabella's ankles. When the fairy stood, she said, "Fear not for your steps are always guided." The fairy bowed and flew off to join her friends.

Isabella looked down at her feet and then stepped onto the rainbow stairway. Immediately, she felt herself begin to grow; she smiled. So it was with each step until she reached the top of the rainbow and was her former size. As she stepped off the stairway she stood before the Library of the Ancients. The building was circular in design, made of white marble; there were no windows. The roof of hand cut crystal sparkled so brilliantly it almost blinded Isabella. A black gravel path led to a single entrance, a massive red door. Isabella walked to the door and pushed against it. It was locked. As she turned to search for a second entrance, the lock clicked and the door slowly swung open. It groaned with such force, Isabella wondered when someone had last entered. She stepped inside.

The building was dark and cool and smelled of sage. It took several seconds for Isabella's eyes to adjust to the light coming in through the prism roof. When she could see, she found herself at the head of a wide center aisle carpeted in deep red. The aisle appeared to run the diameter of the building though Isabella could barely see the distant side of the library, the building was so large. On either side of the center aisle, as far as she could see were rows and rows of mahogany bookcases from ceiling to floor filled with books: millions of books. Indeed, there were even stacks of manuscripts piled in front of those already shelved.

"Hello. Hello. Is anyone here?" No answer. "Hello?" she called. There was only deep still silence. Isabella turned into one of the stacks and looked at the volume titles. The language was unfamiliar to her. Farther down the aisle, the titles were in a script she did not recognize. Up and down the rows she went. In time, she found books in her language, but the content was beyond her understanding. *Everything from the beginning of time must be in this building. Each of these books is priceless* she thought awed by all that surrounded her. *How will I know or ever find the book Stefan is looking for?* "I must think about this. I know I will be shown a way," she said out loud.

Isabella continued walking through the stacks, running her fingers over the titles. *When the king spoke of his love of reading, he said something I thought odd at the time. Something about asking a question and knowing the right book would call to him with the answer. I wonder if I can do that. I wonder if the book he seeks will call to me.* As she relaxed, she thought *there is no need for me to hurry. There is so much to explore here. I think I could be happy here for a very long time* Isabella realized with wonder.

Then an intricate binding caught the young woman's attention. *What is this?* she thought. *It seems familiar. Why this looks exactly like the carving of Saul's little book!* Isabella pulled the book from the shelf. Indeed it was identical to the little carving she had in her pocket. She opened the first page and read: **Isabella and the Tale of the Unanswered Question**. She turned to the next page and continued reading:

LONGING

Long ago in a forgotten land and forgotten time lived a little girl in a forgotten village. She was smaller and more slender than most children her age. In fact, few people would have guessed she had just celebrated her eleventh birthday. Her black hair was pulled back into a thick braid that hung to the middle of her back. Much to her dismay strands of hair often escaped and fluttered about her face giving her an untidy look.

"How is this possible?" she muttered. "I am reading about myself!" She turned to the last page of the book and found it was blank. As she rifled back through the pages, she came upon the last printed words which were…

"How is this possible?" she muttered. "I am reading about myself!" She turned to the last page and found it was blank. As she rifled back through the pages, she came upon the last printed words which were…

Isabella dropped the book.

GRANDMOTHER SPIDER

As the book hit the floor, the crash echoed through the library like a cannon. *What trick is this?* Isabella thought staring at the intricately carved manuscript. Then she saw one of the splayed pages move. *More trickery!* "This is not amusing," Isabella shouted to the stacks of books. "I know someone is here. Stop this and show yourself." The silence was deafening. Isabella turned back to the volume on the floor and saw a tiny spider scurry from within its pages. The creature skittered up the shelves and into the books far above her head.

As Isabella scanned the shelves, she noticed what appeared to be a strand of dust fluttering from a shelf halfway down the aisle. As she approached it, she discovered it was the spider suspended from a shelf by a single strand of web. Spider and strand swayed back and forth hypnotically. As she moved closer, she was not surprised to hear it speak. "The Ancient Ones call me Grandmother," said the spider. "I am the Guardian of the Books."

Isabella stared at the little brown spider, a tiny red spiral etched on its back, and said, "I thought I was alone in the library."

"You are, except for me," said the spider as she continued to sway back and forth on her thread of silk. "You were quite surprised when you found your book, weren't you?" she said with a chuckle.

"What trick is this?" asked Isabella hands on her hips.

"No trick, young woman."

"Are you saying this book is about me?"

"Yes, as a matter-of-fact, it is," replied Grandmother. "I am too old to be playing tricks. I think it would be a good thing if you went back and closed the manuscript properly. I would not want it to be damaged lying on the floor like that. It's a one-of-a-kind." Isabella walked down the aisle, picked up the book, closed the cover and brushed it off. "Where would you like me to put it?" called Isabella.

"Just lay it down gently on the floor. I will take care of it later. You can come back to me now."

When Isabella returned to the spider, she found her furiously spinning a web of the alphabet – the letters forming the angles of her silken tapestry. "I don't understand any of this," said Isabella. "Why do I have a book in this library?"

"Every being – past, present and future – has a book in this library," the Guardian replied as she continued her frenzied weaving.

"Why?" Isabella asked as she ran her eyes over the countless shelves and volumes surrounding them.

"Because we all have a story to tell; because we are all so interesting, because we all have much to teach," laughed Grandmother Spider delighted with her own words.

Isabella watched with interest as the web grew and grew. Then she said, "Mine isn't done."

"No, it is not. You are a work in progress just like my web," said the spider as she continued her weaving.

"Who is writing my book?" Isabella asked.

The Guardian of the Books did not answer until the web was complete. "Come closer to me, Isabella," she said. When she did, Isabella was amazed by the hundreds of intricate patterns the spider had spun. "*You* are writing your own book," said Grandmother as she scampered to the edge of the web to better see the young woman. "You are the keeper and author of your own story. Everything you say, do or think is recorded in your book."

Isabella watched as Grandmother began to spin a second web, this one of numbers – even more complex than the first. When it was complete, Isabella asked, "Why am I to know this, Grandmother?"

"What do you think of this one?" the spider asked as she rested.

"It is beautiful," said Isabella.

"Did you know that each web I spin is unique?" said the spider proudly. "No two are ever the same. Life is like that, you know. It has infinite possibilities. Your life, Isabella, has infinite possibilities." Grandmother dropped from her web onto the floor and scurried down the aisle, turned the corner and disappeared. Isabella hurried up and down the aisles looking for the spider. "Why are you to know this, you ask?" piped Grandmother as she suddenly dropped right in front of Isabella, bobbing up and down on her silken thread. She swung her tiny body unto a shelf, eye level with the young woman. "It is rather important information to have, wouldn't you say. Would you rather not know?"

Isabella stopped short and said, "I am not sure. It seems a bit frightening and certainly a great responsibility to know I am responsible for my life story."

"It is," said the Guardian as she settled on the shelf. "But wouldn't you rather have that responsibility than allow another to dictate or control your story?" she asked earnestly.

Isabella looked at her and then at all the books that surrounded them. Turning in a circle she said, "Perhaps I would want to write my own book, but Grandmother, there are so many possibilities, infinite as you said. What is right for me? What if I choose poorly?"

The spider smiled, one slender leg crossed in front of another. "Your heart knows what it desires – what it is meant to do," she said nodding her head. "Claim that and yours will be a joyful story, even if there is hardship, for it is your heart's story, your soul's story." The Guardian of the Books dropped from the shelf and began to weave a third web. This was a spiral and though vastly different from the other two was equally beautiful.

"Why do you weave so many webs?" asked Isabella.

The spider laughed, "It is my purpose to create, create, create. I cannot help but create. I must create, Isabella, or I will die."

Isabella slipped to the floor, her back against the books and watched as the Guardian worked. Finally she said, "If this is my book, why does the king want me to bring it to him? And why did he say it was priceless? And how is this connected to the paintings I saw?"

Grandmother chuckled. "Good questions, Isabella. A talented author asks good questions."

"I wish to have the answers to those questions, Grandmother," Isabella insisted.

The spider stopped spinning and rolled into a little ball at the center of her web. She flipped unto her back and flexed one tiny leg at a time resting from her work. As she did so, she mused, "Stefan actually has a very interesting book himself; one he is still writing. Too bad you don't have time to read it." When she finished her exercise, she rolled close to the edge of the web and smiled at Isabella. "With respect to your question, he knew only that you had to *find* the book; he did not ask you to *bring* him the book. He was also correct in saying the book is priceless; he did not know why, he just knew. He was right though, because you are priceless. Your life is priceless."

"How is this connected to the paintings in the castle?" The spider was silent for so long Isabella thought she had gone to sleep. "Grandmother...?" Isabella called softly.

"I hear you, child," said the spider as her web bobbed gently. "You have so many questions; the Curiosa has settled deep into your heart, hasn't she? Well, child, I have a question to put to you." The web continued to bob gently. "Isabella, do you wish to remain in the Lower World or return home?" Without hesitation Isabella answered, "I wish to stay here of course. There is nothing for me in my village. This is my home."

Grandmother Spider returned, "You answer so quickly, child. You might wish to ponder a bit before you decide for your answer and the paintings are one and the same." The Guardian smiled kindly. "Now you are expected elsewhere," she said. "There is a carriage at the foot of the rainbow. It is waiting to take you to the castle. Why don't you go on? I will put your book back on the shelf."

✦
LAST CALL

"Life signs are weakening," said the nurse. "Her husband just went down to the cafeteria for coffee. Send someone to get him. Tell him it is time to call the family to come as quickly as possible – all of them."

THE PHOENIX INN

The carriage driver informed Isabella their ride to the castle would take several days; they would stop each night at an inn and proceed early the following morning. On the second evening, the driver pulled into a lovely courtyard. The sign above the door read *The Phoenix Inn.* "Mistress, I think you will enjoy your stay here. King Stefan recommends this establishment to all his court. I will secure our rooms," he said as he helped Isabella step out of the carriage.

As Isabella tucked in her ruby red shirt and smoothed her gray trousers, the driver added, "You might enjoy sitting in the garden around the back. I will come and get you when all is made ready." Isabella nodded and followed a gravel path lined with yellow and orange tiger lilies. It wound to a back garden and an entrance to the inn's dining room. Small cloth covered tables and silver and black cushioned chairs were scattered under leafy trees and a quartet of musicians serenaded the birds and the sky. A short muscular gentleman with close cropped hair was placing pitchers of lemonade and plates of cherry tarts on the tables. When he heard Isabella's footsteps on the gravel, he turned to greet her.

"Welcome to *The Phoenix Inn.* I am Darius and here to make sure your stay is comfortable," said the man with a huge smile.

Isabella gasped in amazement. "Commander...?" she asked stunned. "What in the world are you doing here?" The man stared at Isabella, but could not seem to place her. "Commander, we met some time ago in the Northern Province," Isabella stammered. "Don't you remember? I was with the raven, Nightwalker. My name is Isabella."

The commander's eyes widened. He clapped his big hands together and said with an even bigger smile, "Isabella, of course! My goodness, you've grown; I didn't even recognize you. What a bonnie young lass you are! How are you?"

"I'm fine, but what are *you* doing *here?*" Isabella sputtered. "How did you come to be an *innkeeper?*"

The commander took Isabella's arm and said, "Well, some things remain the same, don't they? You still ask a lot of questions." Both of them laughed. "Well, if you have the time for a tale, I will be happy to tell you how I got here."

"I wouldn't miss this story for the world," said Isabella shaking her head as Darius led her to a table under a magnolia tree heavy with fragrant white flowers.

"Please sit down. Would you like a glass of lemonade? It is freshly squeezed and quite delicious and I have some cherry tarts as well."

"Yes, thank you," Isabella stuttered. She couldn't believe her ears. *Is this the same man I met so long ago – pouring lemonade and serving cherry tarts?* After Darius attended them both Isabella asked, "What happened after we parted? You and your men were returning to the castle garrison. Everyone was so unhappy."

The commander snorted. "Well, you are right about that. Quite honestly, we were furious." He shook his head. "We knew the king was right that we were not effective in that situation. We were all exhausted, and we needed to rest, but it was a hard, hard order to follow. I was so bitter I left the king's service."

"Really?" said Isabella surprised.

He smiled a sad smile. "The first few months were terrible for me," he said sighing. "I didn't know how to be anything but a soldier. I started more fights than I can remember with anyone who looked at me wrong or said something I didn't like, and I woke up in many a strange place after having too many tankards of ale." The commander stopped and listened to the quartet of musicians playing a sweet waltz. "Pretty good, aren't they? I have come to appreciate music in my old age." Isabella and the commander sat listening to the music. When they finished, the musicians nodded to them, picked up their instruments and went inside leaving Isabella and the commander alone in the garden.

"What happened to you then?" asked Isabella softly.

"What happened to me?" asked the commander. He took a sip of his lemonade and said, "I inherited this inn from an uncle, a man I hadn't seen in thirty years. I took possession of the place so that I would have somewhere dry to sleep and drink. No more waking up in ditches for me, I thought. But the strangest thing happened; I discovered I had a knack for business." He shook his head as though he was still surprised. "I knew how to run an army," he continued, "and it did not take long to see I could use those skills to run a business. Who would have thought, eh? Want to hear something even stranger?" he said with a mischievous smile.

"Oh, yes. Please continue," said Isabella. *How can this get any stranger? I wish Nightwalker could hear this!*

"Not long after I took over the inn, my old army cook came through. He left the service shortly after I did and was doing odd jobs wherever he could find them. He told me he missed cooking for big groups; that at night he still thought of new ways to spice up the rations. Well, I needed a cook and hired him on the spot. Now he is *Chef* Lucia and has quite a reputation in the kingdom for his fine meals. People come from all over to taste his dishes. He even received a positive review by Latisha! Can you imagine that?" Darius chuckled in delight.

"Actually, I can." Isabella had come to expect the unexpected in the Lower World.

"Then more of my men started coming through. Do you remember young Christian, the young man who stayed with the farm family in the Northern Province; the one who witnessed the attack on the babe?"

"Yes, that was terrible," Isabella said grimacing.

"Well, Christian was the best spy I had in the squadron. He had so many disguises and ways of pretending to be someone else, I had a hard time knowing when the real Christian was around," the commander said slapping his knee. *Is this really Darius? How can anyone change so much?* The commander continued, "Well, one night a traveling theater group came looking for rooms. They were going to be performing in the village for several weeks. Do you know who the star of the production turned out to be?"

"Christian!"

"That's right," the commander nodded. "He told me he had a rough time leaving the service – same as me. He said he was sitting in a pub one night, drinking more wine than was good for him. Turns out he was watching this same theater group perform. Well, he thought he could do a better job than the star. After all, he had fooled enemy generals, right? He said he climbed right up on stage and took over. The cast didn't appreciate it, but the manager saw something in him. The next day when the boy was sober, the manager offered him a small part. Christian said something in him told him to say yes and the rest is history. Now he not only stars in the productions, he also writes the plays!"

"Amazing," said Isabella.

"I thought so, too, and it continued to happen over and over again. Do you remember Rufio?" Isabella gasped. "We parted badly," Darius said with a sigh, "but even he found his way to my inn. He used to be my lead scout. That man loved going on scouting missions, finding out where the enemy was camped and drawing their locations for me. Now he's working for a master mapmaker. He travels all over the Lower World and has mapped every square inch of it. His maps are in demand all over the kingdom." Darius took a sip of lemonade. "Isabella, I could give you a dozen more examples, and everyone is happy. *That* is the most amazing thing of all." Darius was shaking his head and grinning at the same time.

"How did that happen?" asked Isabella curiously.

"Well, I have given that a lot of thought, and I certainly don't have all the answers, but I figured out a couple things I think," the commander said thoughtfully. "Here we were a group of soldiers all young when we joined the army having no idea what we were good at. Our sole purpose was to fight and protect the kingdom. Yet even in the military we each somehow found a unique place for ourselves." A man came out and placed a beautifully arranged plate of fruit and cheese on their table. Isabella recognized the Elite Guard Cook. With a nod and a smile from Darius, he returned to the dining room.

"Then in the Northern Province, we discovered we were ineffective and unwanted. Well, it was a bitter realization, very bitter. A lot of us lost our way because we lost our purpose." The commander's face sobered at the memory. He took a sip of lemonade and his face relaxed. "It took a while, but we discovered if we were willing to try things differently we could use our skills in a peace time setting."

Darius laughed ruefully. "In some ways that was harder than fighting; to experiment and possibly look foolish now that takes real courage. He paused for a moment and looked toward the inn. With great seriousness he said, "If King Stefan needed us, we would go back in a second to defend the Lower World. I just hope he never needs to call us back."

Isabella smiled. "Darius, I am happy for you," she said as she reached for his gnarled hand and gave it a squeeze. He got up and broke a flower off the magnolia tree and handed it to Isabella. Looking around the garden he said, "You know why I named this place *The Phoenix Inn?*"

"Why?" Isabella asked as she tucked the flower behind her ear and breathed in its fragrance.

"A phoenix is a legendary fire-breathing bird that lives for hundreds of years. When it's time for its life to end, the bird builds a nest and is burned to death in its own flames. Only the ashes remain. Then the miracle happens. The phoenix rises from the ashes transformed and goes on to live a different and good life." The commander looked deeply into Isabella's eyes and for a long moment was silent. "I think that pretty much says it all, don't you?" he said softly.

"It certainly does, Darius. It certainly does."

"Well, girl, that's the story. I must say, not only do you ask good questions, you listen well too. I like that."

"Thank you," said Isabella as she raised her lemonade glass to toast the commander.

✦
FIELD OF DREAMS

That night a fierce storm swept through the area. Lightning crisscrossed the skies; thunder shook the earth; and rain slammed into the ground. The kingdom had not experienced such a tempest in decades. "Not to worry, folks. The Phoenix Inn is solid and tight as a drum," Darius said calmly as he addressed his dinner guests. As he drew several puffs from his pipe, the scent of clove, licorice and cinnamon wafted through the dining room mixing in with the aroma of mint rack of lamb and aurochs roasted with leeks – the evening entrees. "You will all sleep a babe's sleep tonight with your stomachs full and the rain on the roof as your lullaby."

The storm still raged in the morning forcing many travelers to take refuge at the inn because bridges had been washed away. When Isabella came down for breakfast, the dining room was abuzz with stories of near misses and dangers on the road. Isabella's driver went to investigate the status of the roads since they had planned to brave the storm and continue on to the castle. He returned with news that indeed, all the bridges were out. "Well, mistress, we are stranded here until the storm blows over and those bridges are repaired. The only good news in this situation is that all the bridge engineers are from Kronos, so you can be sure, those bridges will be repaired as soon as possible."

Isabella spent the day chatting with the other voyagers and discovered each had a tale to tell. A young woman was writing a book identifying all the plants and flowers native to the Lower World. She had traveled to every region and collected thousands of specimens she was now cataloguing. She was quite thrilled to have discovered a number of previously unknown flora and fauna.

A father, mother and their ten children were festival clowns on their way to a fair in Kronos. The father proudly proclaimed clowning had been in his family and his wife's family for six generations. They delighted Isabella with their antics and tricks. Isabella particularly enjoyed a man and woman who designed clothing. They were quite well known in royal circles and designed for many of the wealthy families in the Lower World. Both were utterly smitten with Isabella's shirt and trousers. "My dear, what a daring sense of style you have," gushed Georgiou. "We have never seen a woman wearing trousers before. Dona Ella, what do you think? Have we just discovered the next fashion trend?"

"We just might have," said his partner, eyeing Isabella's ensemble. "I do think, though, we will need to experiment with fabric and color." She reached out and tugged at Isabella's pants. "Can you just imagine these in black silk? Perhaps the shirt could be blue satin with crystal beading, and the belt – hammered silver might be interesting. Oh, the possibilities are endless!" she said with great enthusiasm. "Isabella, how exciting to meet someone willing to try something new!" they exclaimed together.

That is how the next several days went. Isabella delighted in meeting new people and hearing of their travels and adventures. Late at night, alone in her chambers, she mused *They all seem to have a purpose. They know what they love and their lives reflect it. Why is it not so for me?*

At the end of the week, the rain stopped, the sun came out and the sky was brilliant blue. Late that afternoon, Isabella's driver came to her. "Mistress, I told you those Kronos engineers are fast. They have already repaired the bridges. You and I will be leaving in the morning for the castle. We should arrive the day after tomorrow"

That night as moonlight bathed Isabella's room, she prepared for bed. She knew the Queen Mother would be playing with the wolves howling under the full moon. *Why was I so afraid to howl at first; because I didn't want to look foolish or stupid? How grateful I am I tried; all I would have missed if I had not risked looking foolish.* Lying in bed, Isabella watched the branches sway back and forth outside her window.

"You know where your answers are," the branches called to her.

"I do not." she sighed.

"Yes, you do," they crooned. "What do our dreams tell us?" The young woman smiled then burrowed deep under her covers and, as she drifted to sleep, murmured, "Setine, my friend, please take me back to the Cave of Mirrors." Instantly she was in the rose grotto.

"Hello, Isabella, I am happy you called me," said Setine. Clothed in a gown of crystals and sapphires, the young queen sparkled in the moonlight. She and Isabella were sitting on the ground outside the Cave of Mirrors.

"It is time for me to go back into the cavern," Isabella said as she warmly embraced the young queen. "I didn't understand what I saw before. I want to see it with new eyes."

"I am delighted," replied Setine as she pulled away from the young woman, "but what you search for now is deeper in the cavern."

"And what would that be, Highness?" said Isabella in surprise.

"Do you not wish to find what will truly give you joy and fill your heart? Is that not your unanswered question?"

"It is," Isabella nodded.

A shower of shooting stars drew their eyes upward. When the last was but a trace in the sky, Setine instructed, "You will walk deeper through the Cave of Mirrors than you did before until you reach a waterfall. It will appear you can go no further, but in fact, there is a path that winds under the falls. It will lead you to what you seek."

"Thank you for everything, Setine," said Isabella smiling. She hugged the Queen of the Dreamtime and rose to make her way into the cave. Once inside Isabella felt she was home. As she walked past the mirrored reflections, she recognized many of her dream parts as the people and animals she had met during her journey through the Lower World. In time the mirrors ended though the trail did not. As she followed the rocky path it began to ascend, twisting and turning through a series of empty chambers. Then she heard the waterfall. Excited, she began to climb faster. She turned a corner on the trail and stopped – stunned.

A thousand feet below her were the falls. They looked to be more than a mile wide; their cascading waters crashing thousands of feet below into a churning lake. The force of the falling water was so great, powerful winds and spray whipped through the cavern. Isabella's eyes scanned the trail which seemed to end several hundred feet below her, far above the falls. *Setine said there is a path and that it would take me under the waterfall.* The young woman took a deep breath and, with her back flattened against the cavern walls, cautiously began her descent. Inch by inch she maneuvered down the trail. It narrowed to a sliver, and was soon running parallel to the thundering fall.

Just before reaching the bottom of the cascade, the trail turned into a series of tiny steps. The steps were slippery and wet, so the young woman sat and slid down one step at a time. When she reached the bottom Isabella saw an overhanging ledge protecting a new trailhead that turned under the falls. She smiled. Crawling under the ledge, the young woman inched forward until she was behind the cascading water. A wall of solid granite stretched endlessly behind her and a glistening wall of water before her. Thunder filled her ears as light danced through the sheet of water. She crawled until she emerged on the far side of the falls then lay down on the trail to rest. As she did so her face was only inches from a break in the path. She sat up. Four feet beyond the break, a torch anchored in the wall cast light on where the path resumed. Isabella dropped back to the ground and reached over the edge of the break feeling into nothingness. In the dark, the young woman could not tell if the break was a hole or a bottomless pit. *Now what? I have come too far. I will not turn back.*

Isabella laid down to rest. When she felt stronger she stood and walked back toward the falls. She stopped and turned, drew in a deep breath, took three running steps and jumped. When the young woman hit the ground on the other side of the break, she rolled and stopped. With a smile, Isabella got up, brushed herself off, and made her way to the torch. She pulled it out of the wall and proceeded forward for several minutes. When she turned a sharp corner, the trail led into a field of moonlit flowers. The cave walls towered above her but the roof of the cave was gone and the field – acres of snow white trilliums – glowed in the moon's soft light. *I am in an old volcano filled with the Queen Mother's dream flowers!*

Isabella was about to step into the field when she heard a growl. The trilliums began to rustle and shake. A mound of earth seemed to be rising from the flowers. Bigger and bigger it grew until Isabella saw a mighty dragon standing before her filling the cave. Isabella was frozen by the sight of the huge beast, smoke coming from its snout and mouth. For just an instant, she felt her old fears taking hold. *No* she thought *I have come too far. I have come too far.* With a single breath, she focused her attention on the present moment. *I will know the right next step* she thought *I will know the right next step.* She faced the dragon directly.

The creature was magnificent. Its hide was rough and dark forest green; golden scales ran from the crest on its head, down its spine, to the tip of its spiked tail. Great golden wings folded back against its body. The dragon's eyes were deeply hooded, but Isabella could see they were golden as well. "Who dares to wake me from my sleep?" the dragon growled as puffs of smoke filled the air. He moved his head to within inches of Isabella's face. She saw curiosity, not danger, in his eyes.

"I am Isabella, Explorer, and I have come to claim my field of dreams," she said with a respectful nod of her head, "I am sorry to have disturbed your sleep. I did not know you rested here."

"I am protecting this field until my mistress arrives. You claim to be her?" asked the dragon suddenly quite interested in this possibility, his spiked tail swishing this way and that.

Isabella stood tall and straight before the dragon. "I do," she said calmly.

"Others have come before you. How will I know you are the true mistress of this field?" the dragon growled as more smoke escaped his mouth.

"Please look into my heart to see if what I say is true."

"Isabella," said the dragon with a hint of a smile, "your confidence pleases me. I shall indeed look inside of you." The dragon dipped its great head and looked deeply into Isabella's heart. As his gaze intensified, her body was filled with the warmth of a dozen suns. After several long moments, he nodded and said, "You have come a long way, mistress. Welcome to your field." *Is it that simple?* The dragon smiled. "Isabella, the most difficult part of your journey has passed. Now begins a time of ease and wonder." He settled back pulling his golden wings close to his body. A gentle puff of smoke escaped its mouth as he said, "Speaking of ease, if you do not mind, I will return to my rest while you enjoy your walk." Without waiting for her answer, the great dragon became smaller and smaller and smaller until he was the size of a kitten. With a final puff of smoke and a nod of his crested head, he closed his eyes and went to sleep among the snowy flora.

"Thank you," Isabella murmured as she stepped into the flowers. She heard a tinkling sound. *They sound like chimes.* Holding her torch high, she reached to examine the trilliums. Within the petals of each flower was a tiny mirror. As she peered into the first, she was surprised to see her own face. A soft breeze floated through the air, rustling the snow flowers and filling the dormant volcano with the tinkling of little bells. Setine whispered, "Well done, Isabella. This field is slightly different than the Cave of Mirrors. It shows you your heart's desire for things to come. Enjoy your walk!"

With great excitement, Isabella strolled through the flowers searching the tiny mirrors. She saw herself on a great sailing ship traveling to distant lands; in another flower she was swimming with whales; in another she was eating exotic new foods. She saw herself riding the back of an elephant, leading a caravan of camels, listening to great symphonies. In other flowers, she danced the night away at a great masked ball; designed a grand garden, in the next created rooms of beauty. Many times, she saw herself reading and studying in the Library of the Ancients – writing in her book. In others she was teaching what she had learned.

As she moved deeper into the field, the reflections changed slightly. In one, she held her newborn child; in another, the hand of a dying friend; in another she kissed her beloved; in yet another, she was rocked by the betrayal of a trusted ally. Many flowers reflected joy and laughter – others tears of despair and loss. "My goodness," she murmured as she walked and walked through the flowers. "I will be having great adventures be they of the mind, heart, or soul." When she peered into the last flower she saw herself standing in the field of dreams. Joy filled her body. "Here I am in this strange and wonderful kingdom having the grandest adventure of all," she said to the swaying flowers. "I am doing my heart's desire! I am free to explore, learn and grow. I am loved by many in this world, and I love many. Everything I longed for when I came upon the gypsies so long ago has come to pass. How fortunate I am! I have found my home. I am home."

Outside the cave, the night sky was filled with shooting stars. The Dreamtime was celebrating Isabella's discovery with its own fireworks display. As dawn approached, a blazing firebird soared into the heavens spreading its magnificent wings until it filled the entire evening sky. It hung suspended for just a moment then flew towards the heavens disappearing from sight.

✦
NO MORE

Parents, husband, children stood mournful vigil over their daughter, wife and mother. The woman's breathing had grown more and more shallow. She drew a final breath and then no more. Her two young children wailed, "Mommy!"

✦

REUNION

Sir Alfred took Isabella's hand as she stepped from the carriage. "Miss Isabella! I hardly recognize you. How you have grown! How lovely you are!" he said beaming. "It is so good to have you back."

When her feet touched the ground, the Royal Advisor started to bow, but Isabella threw her arms around the old gentleman's neck. "Oh, Sir Alfred," she said hugging him fiercely, "It is wonderful to see you. There has not been a day I have not thought of you. Every time I asked a question or learned something new, you were with me. I do believe I may have asked over a million questions by now," she said in a rush.

"I have no doubt of that," the statesman said smiling as he smoothed his jacket and straightened his tie. "We can talk while we walk to your rooms. We have kept them neat and tidy for your return. Lady Jillian and Lady Joanna inspect them regularly," he said with a wink.

Taking Sir Alfred's arm, Isabella said playfully, "I am looking forward to the afternoon sun in the garden. Perhaps Critiques can come and visit me: only this time you need not rescue me."

As they walked through the castle, Sir Alfred said, "Do you remember how frightened you were by the first questions you posed to me?"

"I do," said Isabella ruefully. "That seems so long ago. Now I cannot imagine *not* asking questions."

"And why is that?" Sir Alfred asked turning his head to look at her.

"It was as you said: questions open all doors," she said thoughtfully. "There is so much you can learn and discover about people, places, things, yourself." Isabella paused and gently squeezed his arm. Sir

Alfred smiled at her kindly and patted her hand. "You have learned well."

Isabella stopped and turned to face the Esteemed Advisor. "Sir Alfred, I have brought the Curiosa home to you." She reached into her pocket and brought out a small red pouch. As she loosened the drawstring she said, "I loved her as best I could, but she sustained damage during my time away. I am sorry."

Sir Alfred took the Curiosa and examined her briefly. Then he said, "It pleases me that you have kept the pendant, Miss Isabella. As for the damage, I have found that one comes to love things that are a bit dog-eared, eh?" Isabella laughed and kissed the Esteemed Advisor gently on the cheek. "She is yours, dear," said Sir Alfred as he handed the Curiosa back to Isabella. "Remember she belongs to the line of queens."

"Thank you," she said hugging the old man.

When they arrived at Isabella's rooms, Sir Alfred said, "You have some time to rest before dinner. The doves will call for you when all is ready. I know Stefan is most eager to see you." He bowed to Isabella as he opened her door and said, "It is good to have you back, my dear."

As she crossed the threshold she saw her rooms were exactly as she had left them. She wandered through the sitting room stopping to smile at the portraits of Ladies Joanna and Jillian. Then she made her way to the little garden. Sunlight splashed the walls dancing with delight at the sight of Isabella. The fountain gurgled with happiness as she settled into a cushioned chair only inches away. *It is truly wonderful to be back* Isabella realized as she listened to the wind and the murmuring of the fountain. *I wish I could nap, but Sir Alfred said the king is waiting for me. What I need is a nice hot bath so I can organize my thoughts. Stefan and I have much to discuss.*

After bathing, she went to dress. Lying on the bed were six gowns: each a different fabric, color and style, and all very beautiful. Isabella clapped her hands in delight. *Sir Alfred thinks of everything though I was looking forward to seeing the king's face when I walked in wearing his mother's trousers.* After trying each one, Isabella selected a ball gown of star satin. The strapless bodice was stitched with metallic gold thread and embroidered with wildflowers covered with pearls and crystals. Fitted at the waist, the gown's full skirt billowed out like a cloud. Beaded wildflowers embroidered the hem of the gown as well as her slippers.

On the dresser were thirteen diamond hairpins. She walked to the mirror and placed them all through her long black hair. They twinkled like stars in the night sky. Isabella surveyed herself in the mirror. Reflected back was a tall young woman, healthy and strong. *I'm beautiful* she thought happily. Warmth flowed through her body. *How grateful I am to be here. How grateful I am for all I have learned. How grateful I am for each experience I have had.* Just then Isabella heard the cooing of the doves from the hallway. "Are you ready, mistress?" they called.

"I am," she replied happily.

This time her escorts led her to a different part of the castle. As she followed them down a white marbled corridor, the doors at the end of the hall swung open. Isabella's eyes opened wide in wonder as she entered the Grand Ballroom. Guardsmen in dress white uniforms stood at attention around the perimeter of the hall. White banners adorned with shooting stars fluttered from poles mounted in the walls. A hundred tables were dressed with white linen, flickering white candles and white roses. Crystal goblets and sterling silver tableware sparkled in the candlelight. White satin chairs were festooned with enormous white bows. When Isabella stepped into the banquet hall, hundreds of guests stood and broke into wild applause. Clapping and cheers filled the air. Sir Alfred stepped forward and offered his arm to the young woman.

As they moved into the hall, Isabella saw Nightwalker, Critiques, Mayor Roget and the citizens of Kronos, the fairies, the wolves, Saul, the constable, the Commander, his troops, the family of clowns, the dragon, even the gypsies. On and on she walked waving, hugging and petting all her friends from the Lower World. Finally, Isabella reached the royal table. There stood King Stefan, Queen Setine and the Queen Mother. "I don't know what to say," she said overcome with emotion. She hugged all three.

"We do know how to throw a party," smiled the Queen Mother, who tonight looked very much a Queen in a red sequin gown and ruby crown. "Come; sit at the center of the table, Isabella."

"Oh, no, that is your seat, or Setine's, or Stefan's," protested Isabella.

"Nonsense, it is your seat. It has been waiting for you to claim it," Setine said in her velvety voice.

"Yes, Isabella, I have been waiting for you!" piped the chair. Isabella laughed as Stefan pulled the chair out for her.

"What are we celebrating?" asked Isabella bewildered by the gala festivities.

"Why you, of course," Stefan said warmly.

"Why me?" asked Isabella dazed by all that surrounded her.

"Because you are priceless," said a tiny voice. Isabella looked about and saw Grandmother Spider swaying joyfully on a silk thread attached to Isabella's chair.

A night of merriment began. The evening was filled with great fun and festivities. Food, music, dancing, juggling and magic tricks entertained one and all. During dessert, the king leaned over to Isabella and said, "So, you found the book?"

"Indeed I did," said Isabella smiling. "I am truly curious why you sent me to find my own book."

The king shook his head slightly and said, "Isabella, I did not know that was the case. This journey has been as much of a mystery for me as for you. I only knew from the paintings *you* had to find it and that the book bound all our fates together. The rest I learned as you did: one step at a time."

"And the paintings?" asked Isabella.

"I will take you to them after dinner," replied the king softly. "I have something very important to do first." The young king reached to take Isabella's hand and kissed it. Then he stood and raised his glass of fairy ambrosia to her. He called out to the audience, "Friends, please join me in making a toast to our guest of honor, Isabella, Explorer!"

"Hear! Hear!" Sir Alfred cried as he stood. "To Miss Isabella, who questioned everything and discovered her own truth." He bowed deeply to Isabella.

"To Isabella, who displayed great courage by walking into the unknown," cawed Nightwalker, flapping his wings in delight, the star on his forehead blazing.

"To Isabella," said Setine raising a graceful arm, "who found meaning and purpose in the darkness."

"To Isabella, who discovered her own needs and wants," purred the Ladies Jillian and Joanna as they curled themselves around the table candelabras.

"Hear! Hear! You persevered through hardship and confusion with grace and dignity," toasted the constable.

"You choose to forgive when you could have punished," called out Saul from the back of the ballroom, wiping a tear from his eye.

"You took risks and trusted all would be well," chimed a hundred fairies.

"To Isabella, who took the time to play when she was tired," said Mayor Roget with a wink.

"Who offered compassion instead of judgment," said Critiques bowing deeply.

"To a woman with a fabulous sense of style!" proclaimed Georgiou and Dona Ella.

"To Isabella, a gifted writer and author," pronounced Grandmother Spider.

On and on the toasts went. Each and every guest in the great hall offered Isabella a blessing. Finally, only the Queen Mother remained. The Queen stood and raised her glass to Isabella. The room became silent. "To my darling Isabella, who learned to accept and give love," smiled the Queen Mother tenderly. "We are joyful you have taken your rightful place at the royal table." Isabella graciously nodded to her beloved Queen.

After dinner, Isabella took time with each guest, reminiscing and thanking them for coming. There was much laughter and joy and a few tears of grace. Isabella's heart overflowed with gratitude as she accepted the love of these precious friends. Late in the evening, Isabella stepped out into the garden and gazed at the full moon. She felt someone behind her.

Stefan said, "I would like to show you something, if you have a moment."

Isabella smiled and took his arm. He guided her through the hallways of the castle until they came to the room which held the paintings of so long ago.

"I will leave you here," he said. She nodded.

When Isabella entered the room, she saw several of the canvases had barely changed. Others were filled with a strange fog. Puzzled she walked to a chair in the middle of the room and sat down. As she began to focus on the paintings, she heard crying and looked about. *Are there children in the next room? Why are they so sad? It sounds as though their hearts are breaking.* The sobbing of the children grew louder and louder and the pain in their cries tore at Isabella's heart. *Where are the parents of these babes? Why doesn't someone help them?* With that question, time stopped in the room filled with broken canvases. In a moment without end, Isabella became aware of the choice before her. A flood of emotions swirled through her. Some screaming do this, others urging do that, some so quiet she could barely hear their counsel. In that endless moment, she listened to them all and then there was calm.

I understand. I understand what must be done. She took a deep breath and another and another. The crying stopped. Isabella saw a shoot of grass push through the burnt rubble in the first canvas. The sky began to brighten in the next painting. A bird flew into the third. A woodsman and two small children walked into another. Isabella watched the paintings fill with life. Finally she rose and left the room.

When she returned to the ballroom, dawn was breaking and only the royal family, Sir Alfred and Nightwalker remained. "What did you discover?" Stefan asked, rising as she approached the royal table.

"I must go back to my village," Isabella said quietly.

"We know, beloved," nodded the Queen Mother as she, too, stood and went to Isabella.

As the Queen put her arms around Isabella, the young woman said, "I must and yet, I am so very sad to leave you. I am also sad to leave the future I saw for myself in the Field of Dreams." Tears filled her eyes, spilling onto her face.

The Queen touched Isabella's face gently. "Do not be troubled, Isabella. In a sense you are not going far from us for in truth, we are only a thought or feeling away. Your dreams? You will manifest them in the Village World, child, just as Nightwalker taught you to do so here." Kriya took both of Isabella's hands in hers and looked deep into her eyes. "We, in the Lower World, are here to serve many, Isabella. You are now a bridge to help others find their way to our world so they too may learn our ways; so they may heal; so they may grow. That, dearest, has always been your destiny."

"I know," Isabella replied wiping her face dry. "I am resolute in my decision and I am sad. You will come to the river with me?"

"Of course, dearest, we will all join you," the Queen Mother replied.

"Thank you. I must go and change for travel."

Within the hour, Stefan, Setine, Sir Alfred, Nightwalker and the Queen Mother walked to the river with Isabella. The woman hugged each of her beloved friends and stepped into the boat that brought her to the Lower World so long ago. As it left shore, Nightwalker flew to her side. "We started this journey together, Isabella, and I would be honored to accompany you home."

"Oh, yes, my dear, dear Nightwalker." In the blink of an eye, Nightwalker and Isabella were sitting in the very spot on the riverbank outside her village, where the raven first called her.

"Do you remember when I asked if you were ready to leave?"

"I do," said Isabella wistfully.

"You have grown so," the great raven reflected.

"Will I be able to live here? I am afraid it will be too hard if I must live as I did before."

"Everything is different, Isabella, because you made this journey. It will take courage to live in your old world, but I have no doubt you will succeed in ways that serve your highest good." The mighty bird brushed his wing against Isabella's face and said, "As the Queen said there are many who need to know about your adventures with us. There are others who seek joy and happiness just as you did and you can show them the way. We are very excited for you. Remember, we are all just a feeling, thought, or question away!"

Before Isabella could answer, Nightwalker and the boat were gone. Isabella stood up and for a second was unsure of what next to do. Then as she turned to walk in the direction of her cottage, two huge dogs, a black male and a snow-white female, came bounding out of the woods. Two children followed. "Lady! Hawke! Stop!" the children shouted.

The dogs ignored the children's command and continued their mad dash towards Isabella. The woman almost lost her balance as they jumped on her in enthusiastic greeting, licking her arms and legs as though she were a long lost friend. When the children saw Isabella, they stopped in stunned disbelief.

"My loves, I've come home," smiled their mother.

✦
EPILOGUE

The elevator door closed.

"Nice family."

"They are," the neurologist said nodding thoughtfully. As they turned away from the elevator he said, "You know – I still can't get over what happened after we called TOD. I know I'm repeating myself here but her vitals were flat; she was dead for five minutes – five. When her eyes opened and she started gasping for breath, I almost had a heart attack. I don't see how it is possible she came back."

"Like I said before, we've been doing this a long time; enough to know there is a lot we don't know and can't explain," replied the surgeon. "I'm just glad she took those breaths. What I am struggling with is losing Alex."

"I know," the neurologist sighed, "same here. Well, let's go; they're waiting for us." As the two doctors strode toward a group of residents clustered around the nurses' station, they passed a room where a patient was watching the evening news.

The woman anchor announced, "Antonio, we are closing with an update on a story we brought to you six months ago – a story very close to the hearts of all of us in this newsroom involving one of our own family. Isabella Michaels is being released today from Mount Sinai Hospital. Six months ago, Ms. Michaels and her sister, Dr. Alexandra Collins, were the victims of a vicious assault. The two women were robbed and viciously beaten in Central Park on their way home from the theater.

"Despite massive injuries, Ms. Michaels was able to crawl to a runner's path where a late night jogger discovered the two women.

Dr. Collins did not survive the attack and Ms. Michael's injuries were so severe, she was not expected to live.

"Michaels was in a coma for five months. Her husband and two children were with her when she regained consciousness. Doctors say there will be months of intense rehabilitation, but Ms. Michaels is expected to make a full recovery. The case is still under investigation.

"For our viewers, Ms. Michaels headed our Bosnian News Bureau during the UN conflict. She is also the author of the bestselling book, *Cry for the Children: The Yugoslav Chronicles* which came out of her experience in the region. Her sister was Director of Women's Health at Mount Sinai."

As the woman finished, she turned to her partner and said, "Antonio, I have had the good fortune of working with Isabella for years; she is an amazing woman and journalist. I think what I most appreciate about her is her uncanny ability to tap into the emotions of her subjects."

The man nodded and said, "I agree. I have never known anyone with a more curious mind and endless reservoir of questions." The woman smiled and nodded in agreement. Turning to the camera she said, "To Isabella – from your many friends and colleagues at this station – we look forward to your return. To all our viewers, thank you all for being with us this evening. For Antonio and myself, good night."

ABOUT THE AUTHOR

Like Isabella we each have a unique life story. Mine begins in 1953, born to Serbian parents, growing up in a small town in northern Illinois. Looking back I realize as a child I often reflected on "what makes someone happy?" Though the question remained unanswered for years, I continued searching for a secret map that would show me the way to happiness.

Professionally I followed a trail marked by change and growth through such diverse jobs as a correctional supervisor, a community organizer, a Fortune 500 business consultant, an advocate for survivors of gun violence and trauma, a creativity coach and most recently a psychotherapist in private practice.

Personally, I explored that question through education, spirituality, meditation, therapy, creativity, nature, family, friends, and animals (I have two cats – Jillian and JoAnn, 40 fish, countless outdoor feathered friends, deer and creatures that snuffle in the night). Somewhere around my fortieth year clarity began. As I turned sixty, I found *my* answer to happiness: kindness in all its infinite expressions.

For those readers who wish to join Isabella on her journey, she can be found on www.Amazon.com.

Cordially,
Linda Whittaker
June 2014

QUESTIONS FOR REFLECTION AND DISCUSSION

1. The author uses a parallel story line to track the consequences of an assault on a woman. Why do you think the hospitalized woman remains unnamed until the epilogue?

2. When the woman slips into a coma as a result of her injuries, her spirit begins a life review. What do you think happens to a person's consciousness when they are in a coma?

3. The author chose to use a fairy tale to explore the woman's life history. If you were to write your own story, what genre would you use? Why?

4. There was much magic afoot in the Lower World. Which scenes captured your imagination? Which characters? Why?

5. Were there any surprises in the novel as the story unfolded? What were they? What value did they add to the story?

6. In what ways do you see the challenges confronting 11 year old Isabella in your own life as a child growing up? Now as an adult?

7. Isabella was afraid of so many things in her life. What role did fear play in your childhood? How do you address fear now?

8. When Sir Alfred presents Isabella with the Curiosa, he tells her she has the right and protection of the king to ask one

million questions. If you had such safety and protection, what questions would you ask?

9. A number of requests are put to Isabella in her travels through the Lower World. Repeatedly she is told the choice to carry out the request or not is hers. What is her response to personal choice and personal responsibility over the course of the novel? What role does personal choice and responsibility play in your life?

10. Setine shares with Isabella that our dreams wake us up – teach us about ourselves. What do you dream of most frequently? What message might such dreams hold for you? Have you ever had a dream as a child or adult that just stays with you? What do you think is its message?

11. Stefan came face to face with the legacy burdens of generations of his people. Modern therapy points to such burdens as alcoholism, drug addiction, sexual abuse, rage and many others as being passed down family lines. From this perspective, what legacy burdens run in your own family line?

12. Isabella struggled with forgiveness of self and others throughout the book. What did she learn about forgiveness from those she met in the Lower World? How do you define forgiveness? What role does forgiveness play in your own life?

13. Grandmother Spider counsels Isabella on the value of writing her own story. To what degree are you writing the story of your life, or are others controlling and writing your story?

14. So often fairytales end with "and they lived happily ever after". What do you think happened to Isabella Michaels after she left the hospital?

15. What is the "unanswered question" in the book's title? What "unanswered question" runs through your own life story?

CPSIA information can be obtained
at www.ICGtesting.com
Printed in the USA
LVOW11s1527180117

521394LV00003B/629/P